FitzDuncan's Peril

John J. Spearman

ISBN: 979-8-9911755-1-7

DEDICATION

This book is dedicated to all the people who have believed
in me, even when it was difficult to do so.

ACKNOWLEDGMENTS

Many thanks to my editor, Martin Roy Hill, who has been of enormous help
from the standpoints of both technical expertise and moral support.

Deepest gratitude for Thea Magerand, the marvelous artist whose artwork
has brought Caz (and now Fenwick) alive. Every piece she has done
for my books amazes me further.

The FitzDuncan books owe a great deal to the inspiration provided by
Alexandre Dumas. Not only did I love his books, the 1973 film version
of *The Three Musketeers* remains one of my favorite all-time movies.

If you would like to stay abreast of my latest activity,
please visit my website: johnjspearmanauthor.com

1

Fenwick and I were aboard a carrack heading for Iradiem in the country of Hier on the southern continent. The winter wind was howling from the north, which actually helped push us on our way. We could have done without the accompanying sleet, however.

An emissary from Mooresa had arrived in Aquileia a few days before. About six months earlier, Fenwick and I traveled to the southern continent on a diplomatic mission. When we reached Iradiem, the capital and main port of Hier, we found the city under the control of a mage skilled in the Dark Arts.

Fenwick and I managed to escape. News of the problem in Hier spread to the other rulers on the southern continent. The grand vizier of Scaramouche, the emir of Garo, the bashaw of Mooresa, and the king of Vanda all contributed forces to restore order. We attacked the city and I slew the mage.

The Mooresan emissary arrived in Aquileia on the winter solstice, bearing awful news. After spending a couple of months restoring things in Iradiem and Hier, the rulers decided to take their forces south to Combrial, the place from whence the mage came. The emissary reported that, after coming into contact with the enemy, all of the leaders and almost half of the army were now enthralled by a different practitioner of the Dark Arts.

Fenwick and I, along with all two thousand members of the Castle Shield, filling fifty carracks, were sailing south at the most dangerous time of year to be on the open ocean. Today marked four weeks since the southern rulers set off for Combrial. The Mooresan said the remnant of the army was conducting a fighting retreat when he left them, but we had no idea whether they still survived as freemen.

On the home front, both Lucy and Julienne were pregnant, making it even more emotionally difficult for Fenwick and me to leave. And we were carrying with us a magical artifact, the Lance of Bellona, which Fenwick and I found in Rhetia. In addition to the soldiers and the Lance, we were also bringing nine priests of the Three Major Gods. In between bouts of seasickness, they were poring through weighty tomes, trying to find the incantation that would protect our soldiers from being enthralled by the dark mage.

Lucy provided us with ginger oil and licorice before we departed. In the past, those were successful in easing my seasickness. We carried only enough to be able to provide it to the priests. I reckoned they needed some clarity of mind that would have been impossible if they were overwhelmed by nausea.

Finding that incantation was one thing that was absolutely essential to our mission. They had been digging for several days but so far were unable to locate it. That, dear readers, should remind you where we left off at the end of my last batch of scribblings.

The weather on deck was miserable—rain and sleet mixed together. At night, when the temperature dropped, the rigging of the ship froze, making it difficult and dangerous for the sailors to do their jobs when the sails needed to be adjusted. The seas were heavy, and most of the soldiers were seasick. In their stalls in the hold, the horses were unhappy as well.

At the moment, I was relaxing in the canvas sling known as a serpentin, which we also used for sleeping. Fenwick was translating for the priests and the Mooresan. The Mooresan had heard priests utter the protective incantation in his own tongue. Fenwick was trying to help the priests find the proper wording in the Aquileian tongue. What made it so difficult to translate is that these spells were written in archaic versions of the different languages. The Mooresan could not remember the exact words his priests used and could only tell Fenwick what they contained in the current version of the language.

The weather was so wretched that for two days the captain was unable to take a sighting of either sun or stars, so we had no firm idea where we were. He did measure our speed through the water every hour. According to him, we were wallowing along as fast as these carracks could travel and, from that, he guessed approximately where we might be.

I hoped we would not need to fight immediately upon landing. It would take at least a day, and more likely two, before the men and horses recovered from this voyage. Also, all of the priests were aboard my ship. It would be impossible for them to address the entire group of soldiers until we disembarked. If the enemy held Iradiem already, our expedition might be doomed.

Not for the first time, I wished my familiar, a sparrowhawk who identified herself by the sound of her wingbeats—Shasha was the closest spoken equivalent—were able to come with us. She would have been able to fly ahead when we neared our destination. Through her eyes, I would have been able to see whether danger awaited us.

The distance over water was too great, and the weather too foul for such a small bird. She and I discussed it, though our "conversation" was in thoughts, not words. The bird knew my feelings intuitively and understood the danger we would face. She also understood that the journey was simply too long for her to make, especially in this awful weather.

Fenwick opened the door of our tiny cabin. In just the short distance between the hatch leading below deck and our door—no more than four or five steps—his cloak was soaked and he was dripping on the deck. His face bore a broad grin which I could see even in the dim light of the lantern swinging from the ceiling.

"Found it," he announced triumphantly.

"I'll bet it was hiding in the last place you looked," I said.

"It was," he said in a surprised tone. "How did you know?"

"Because only a simpleton would continue to look after he found what he was seeking," I remarked.

Fenwick growled in response to my jest. He took off his cloak. In punishment for my attempt at humor, he shook the cold water from it all over me.

"That was weak, even for you," he remarked.

"Not so weak that you avoided falling for it," I replied.

"In my defense, working with the priests and their learned books has attuned my mind to operating on a higher plane than your base fumbling attempts at witticisms," Fenwick said loftily.

"Or turned your brain to mush," I said.

"That, too," he admitted with a sigh as he slumped into his own serpentin. "I'm not enjoying this."

"Nor am I," I admitted. "It has much the same feeling as last year, when you took me to Rhetia."

"That *was* awful," Fenwick agreed.

"What made it so much worse was Lucy's reaction to your arrival when you came to collect me when we set off," I said. "She let her emotions leak out, and I realized there was a possibility I might not return."

"And this time?"

"Not more than her usual level of concern," I replied. "Though come to think of it, she did give me a reason to hope for the best. She said, 'When I see you next, there will be no disguising the fact that I'm pregnant.' That indicates I will see her again."

"She and Julienne are due at the same time," Fenwick said. "From the little I know about pregnancy, that means we will away at least a month, and possibly four months or even longer."

"I think it will be on the longer side," I suggested. "There is someone or something in Combrial that is the cause of this mess. From the difficulty we faced putting down the mage in Iradiem, we won't be able to dance our way into Combrial and simply dispatch this one."

"I'm afraid you are correct," Fenwick said. "Looking on the brighter side, there is a possibility we can free some of those who are enthralled from the enemy's grasp."

"Don't count on them being able to swell our ranks, Fenwick," I said. "It will be difficult to trust that they will stay free. We have wards we can give to the rulers if we manage to release them, but not their soldiers."

"You are determined to make this sound like we won't have fun, Your Highness," Fenwick complained.

"That is because we won't."

"Oh, come now. Don't we always have a wonderful time when we go on our adventures?"

"No." I laughed. "It's only much later that I am able to find any humor in the near-death experiences we share."

It was another three days before we saw the sun. We also saw the coast of the southern continent. The captain reckoned we were off the coast of Vanda and needed to head west to reach Iradiem. A few hours later, after consulting his charts, he confirmed this.

Unfortunately, the wind had changed direction. It was now blowing from the west. This meant we needed to tack back and forth—endlessly, it seemed.

After two days of this, I almost cheered to see storm clouds approaching from the north. The wind changed direction in advance of their arrival, and we were able to make more direct progress. The rain, sleet, and rough seas seemed a fair exchange for the resumption of progress. This storm lasted only half a day, and when it blew itself out, we then felt the kiss of a warm wind from the south and east.

"I hate to waste this wind," the captain commented, "but we'd best heave to during the night. We're close enough to Iradiem that we don't want to overshoot. And we have the shore to worry about."

That night our fleet reduced sail to almost nothing—just enough to provide steerageway. The lanterns hanging from a yard on every ship glowed in the night. For the first time since we left Aquileia, I heard music coming from several ships nearby. I must admit, it bolstered my spirits.

When the sun rose behind us the next morning, the captain consulted his charts. Signals passed through our fleet, and every ship made sail. The wind was still warm and fair.

"Only an hour or so, Yer Highness," he said, "and we'll see Iradiem."

With his announcement, my worry over what we might find returned. Fenwick caught sight of my expression and joined me. We stood on the quarterdeck in silence.

No sooner than he joined me, when my vision was taken over. Suddenly, I saw our fleet from above, our fifty-six ships scattered over the sea. It could only be Shasha. I reached within myself to find the reddish-brown mote that was our link and touched it with my mind.

Hello, Caz, she communicated to me in a way that I can only describe as mischievous. *I sense we are close. Is our destination ahead?*

"Yes," I replied, but not in words, only in thought.

You are confused. I cannot tell whether you are angry or happy.

"Shasha, I thought we agreed that it was too dangerous for you to come on this journey," I thought.

You said it was dangerous. I did not disagree. That did not mean I felt the same as you. It meant that I did not wish to argue with you.

"I thought this would be too far for you to fly."

It is.

Then Shasha sent me views of recent memories. In some, she was belowdecks, with men tossing bits of fish or salt pork to her which she caught out of the air to their great amusement. In others, she was perched on one of the yards while the weather was fair.

For Shasha, time was different. She seemed to collect memories of things that happened in the past without much attention to sequence. From experience, I figured out that she classified them in three broad categories—recent, as in the last few hours, lately, which could be a few hours old up to a couple of weeks, and before, which was anything that happened more than two or three weeks earlier.

"I am glad you are here, Shasha, but I wish you would have shared with me what you were doing."

I am sharing now.

"Yes, you are."

I was thinking how Shasha sidestepped my desire to keep her home and safe. The logic she used was very similar to how Lucy handled me. I shook my head, understanding that I would never get the better of either of the two women in my life—my human mate, Lucy, and my familiar, Shasha.

Shasha read my thoughts. She found it very amusing. Sparrowhawks don't laugh, but if they could, that's what she would have been doing.

"If you fly ahead, you will reach a city. When you reach it, share with me what you see."

I will. I am glad to feel you are not angry now. That is good. Joining you was no hardship. You should know better.

"When you return from viewing the city, will you travel with me?"

Of course.

Shasha broke the connection, and my normal sight returned. Fenwick was looking at me strangely. I realized I had been standing motionless next to him for a few minutes.

"Shasha," I explained. "She stowed away on one of the ships."

"I thought you both agreed it was too dangerous?"

"No, Fenwick. I stated that. Shasha did not disagree. That does not mean she would heed my wishes."

"Julienne does the same thing to me," Fenwick groaned.

"As Lucy does to me," I said. "It's a good thing she's smarter than I am, I suppose."

It was only a few minutes later when I saw the city of Iradiem from above. Connecting with Shasha, I watched as she flew over the harbor. I cannot say things were bustling, but there were people moving about, unlike the last time we arrived.

"Shasha, find the road," I communicated, sending her my memory of the road east toward Vanda that I used when I rode out of the city.

It took less than a minute. The road east was clogged with people and carts, fleeing the city. I took that to mean that the city was still safe, but the enemy was not far.

"Thank you, Shasha. Now I need you to head south until you see men fighting."

Of course, I didn't use words to communicate my wishes. Shasha would never have understood "south." Nor would she have grasped what I meant using the word "fighting." Instead, I pictured her flying in that direction—inland. Our link remained open, and I saw the same things she did.

"Well, the city is still free from thrall," I told Fenwick. "But the enemy must not be far away. People are leaving. The road to Vanda is packed."

"Did you have her fly further south?" Fenwick asked.

"Yes. She is on her way."

From the sparrowhawk's altitude, and given her remarkable eyesight, I could see for at least ten leagues. There were no signs of conflict. That was good news.

"Shasha, thank you. Please come to me."

You saw what you wished to see?

"I did not see what I hoped not to see," I thought back to her.

The thought I communicated was less confusing than the words I just used to describe it. If the fighting reached the outskirts of the city, that would have been dangerous. As it was, we would have some time to deploy our forces after we landed. The bird terminated our connection and I no longer saw through her eyes.

"We will be able to land safely," I told Fenwick. "Any fighting is more than a day's ride south."

"It will be awfully handy to have someone who can provide us a view of the enemy the way she can," Fenwick commented.

"I've often wished for that sort of advantage," I concurred. "I don't know why I didn't ask her to accompany us west we went to fight the Rhetians."

"Perhaps you didn't want her to take any risks," Fenwick remarked.

Once again, I marveled at Fenwick's perceptiveness. When he said that, I knew instantly he was right—even though it had not been a conscious thought of mine. Sparrowhawks are not large, fearsome birds. The idea of having Shasha anywhere near arrows or crossbow bolts made me shudder—even though it would have taken an uncanny marksman to hit her and one who realized the advantage she provided me to want to try.

A short time later, something approached me from behind. I caught it in my peripheral vision, and it made me jump. With a controlled flurry of wings, a sparrowhawk settled on the rail of the quarterdeck facing me.

I quickly accessed the node I used to connect with Shasha. Sure enough, it was her. She was amused that me startled me. This was the closest we had ever been to one another, and the first good look I got of her.

"My, aren't you handsome," I thought.

Your vision is so dull, she replied. *I have seen you many times and did not need to approach so closely, but I knew you would like to see me better with your weak eyes.*

"You do see further," I admitted. "And you see more color than I do. How would you appear if I could see you with your eyes?"

Shasha extended her wings. To me, the upper side appeared brown with a brindle pattern. Through her eyes, there were reds and yellows I could not discern. The underside was much lighter in color, and the pattern of colors was almost hypnotic.

"You are beautiful," I thought.

Shasha tucked her wings back to her body. I felt satisfaction from her that I had appreciated her appearance. She looked past me at Fenwick. Through our connection, I knew she was looking at him and he at her.

"This is my friend, Fenwick," I thought.

"Fenwick, meet Shasha," I said aloud.

"I am pleased to meet you, miss," Fenwick said, bowing as he did.

Shasha interpreted his greeting through my thoughts. She fluffed herself with a small hop and indicated she was pleased Fenwick was so respectful. Then she called out with a high-pitched, "klee, klee, klee, klee."

"Is she laughing at me?" Fenwick asked.

No. I like him, she thought. I passed that message along to Fenwick. He beamed with a satisfied smile.

2

The people of Iradiem met our arrival with relief mixed with concern. It took us until early evening to get everyone and all the mounts and baggage unloaded from the ships. As quickly as we could, we headed south through the city to where Fenwick was told we could set up camp for the night. Shasha flew off to who knows where.

I carried the Lance of Bellona in a rest the saddler of the Castle Shield made for me. The weapon was too long to tuck under the fender of my saddle as I did with our usual smaller lances. The rest allowed me to set the butt of the lance in it, and hold the spear upright as I rode. It was far less awkward than it would have been to try to carry it in my arms.

It was dark by the time we reached the spot to which our guides directed us. The men of the Castle Shield worked by torchlight to establish our bivouac. I was a bit embarrassed that they set up my tent before their own. When I tried to pitch in, Sergeant Hewko hissed at me.

"Yer Highness," he said, pulling me aside quickly, "you don't understand. The men almost came to blows for the honor of putting up your tent."

"Yes, Sar'nt," was all I could muster up in reply.

In less than an hour, a small city sprang up in an empty field just past the south gate of Iradiem. Cookfires were already burning, and I could smell salt pork stew. Fenwick, carrying a pair of folding canvas camp stools, found me. He snapped them open in front of our tent.

"As of the last report, the enemy was about thirty leagues from here," he said as he eased himself onto the stool. "They gain a league or two each day. The forces are evenly matched in terms of numbers."

"Then why do we lose ground?" I asked.

"Fear," Fenwick responded.

"That makes sense," I said with a nod of my head. "It was a stupid question."

"From what the Hierans tell me, the enemy is not trying anything fancy," Fenwick said. "They line up the same way every time—pikes in the middle, cavalry on the wings. The problem is that enemy fights without emotion—like automatons."

"Just as we saw when we battled the group at the palace," I commented.

"Exactly," Fenwick agreed. "They keep pressing forward, regardless of their losses. Our side eventually despairs and breaks into retreat. It also bothers the men that many of these mindless foes are their former comrades and that they can see their rulers on the other side of the lines. None of the rulers take any sort of active role in the fighting, according to what the men told me. Regarding the enthralled soldiers, they say there is no glimmer of recognition on any of the faces of the enemy."

"It's easy to understand why morale is an issue," I remarked with a sigh. "Perhaps we should think about building some earthworks? Having a fortified position might help our spirits."

"I've asked for maps, and they promised we would have them soon."

"Excellent," I said. "When they arrive, let's meet with Colonel Yankton and try to pick some spots where we can dig in and hold a line."

"Having a fortified position should help us stop the advance," Fenwick said. "From what they tell me, whoever is in charge over there is no military strategist. They use the same formation day after day. The enemy has not attempted any flanking maneuvers—just straight-on attacks. They succeed because they are simply relentless."

Some men came and delivered two bowls of salt pork stew to us, along with chunks of bread. We thanked them and began to eat. Shortly after, a man arrived with maps. Fenwick thanked him. I went to find Colonel Yankton.

"As far as we know, this is the terrain between us and the enemy," Fenwick said after he spread the maps out.

As I looked at them, I accessed my connection with Bellona and withdrew a tiny tendril. Immediately, two places jumped off the pages in my mind. I quickly pointed to them.

"Here, and here," I said.

The nearer of the two locations was just over eight leagues from where we were. The further was almost twenty. We would need to hurry to reach the more distant spot in order to construct fortifications before the enemy reached them.

The site closer to the enemy was a narrow gap between two hills. According to the map, the hills were covered with forest. What we did not know was the angle of the slope. For our purposes, the steeper, the better.

"I'll find a local and ask," Fenwick said, as though he read my mind.

The nearer location was where the road cut through a set of woods for nearly a league. With time available to fell as many trees as we wished, we could make this a nearly impassable obstacle. I looked over at Colonel Yankton and saw the trace of a smile on his face.

"Aye," he said when I caught his eye. "These will suit our needs quite nicely."

Fenwick returned with a Hieran soldier—an officer, I guessed, from the decorations on his tunic. They went over to the maps, and Fenwick showed him the place we picked which was close to the enemy's line. The Hieran explained what he knew to Fenwick and departed. From his hand gestures, I gathered that both hills presented steep faces.

"Good news, I think," Fenwick said. "The slopes of both sides are sharp. Though the map shows them covered in trees, the soil is only a thin layer over solid rock. As a result, the trees aren't much more than stubby saplings. From what he was telling me, I think we can anchor both sides of a rampart to the rock. We should be able to clear the trees on the far side of both wings and provide our archers with a clear field of fire."

"That would make it nearly impossible to flank us," Yankton said. "And with time to prepare, I think I have a way to prevent them from filling the ditch as quickly as the Rhetians did against us."

"How?"

"By burning the bodies, of course," Yankton said casually. "We'll have oil brought forward, pour it over the front and into the ditch, then light it. It will force the enemy to break off their attack while the fire is raging, and—"

"That's awful," I said.

"More awful than the ditch near Musser Pass, or the carnage at Lake Mago, Hamill Creek, or Farsall, Your Highness?" Yankton asked.

He was referring to our bloody battles against the Rhetians, not even a year before. In all four, we slaughtered our enemies. The Rhetians lost more than ten men for every one of ours who was killed. In the first battle, where we constructed a ditch and rampart, Rhetian bodies filled the ditch and enabled their men to reach the top of our fortification without difficulty after the fourth assault. As a result, we needed to abandon the position.

"The smell, the sound, the inky black smoke—yes, Colonel, this will be even more awful," I said. "I don't doubt that *our* men will be able to withstand it. It's our allies. These southern armies are—"

"I think after a month of fighting, they are much more hardened than you realize, Your Highness," Yankton said in a kindly tone. "Still, I understand your point. If it proves to be too gruesome, we won't repeat the endeavor."

While we were talking, Colonel Driscoll walked up. Driscoll's authority within the Castle Shield was second only to the king's and my own. He was an amiable man. While his knowledge of military strategy and tactics was superb, he stayed in the background. He had been a tremendous support in the war with the Rhetian Empire, but he was happy to remain behind the scenes. I'm sure if any of my plans were foolish, he would have stepped forth and gently pointed that out, but so far, there had been no need.

"As a strictly practical matter," Driscoll said, "burning the bodies allows us to make use of the ramparts for a few days more. Otherwise, they will climb on the mass of bodies to reach us as they did near Biscayville. We will, of course, keep an eye on the men. If it demoralizes them in any way, we will stop."

"Thank you, Colonel Driscoll and Colonel Yankton," I said. "You understand my concerns. From what I can see, the men seem in good spirits. In a few days, we will encounter the enemy. Going up against enthralled soldiers is eerie. Do you think they are prepared?"

"They're in a good mood now because we're on dry land," Driscoll said. "As far as the supernatural aspect of what's coming, they are counting on the two of you. Knowing that we have our own heroes blessed by Bellona gives them confidence."

"I hope it's enough," I said. "Lord Easton and I want to stop the enemy from advancing further while we search for a way to neutralize the supernatural aspect. Eventually, we will need to take the fighting south in order to resolve things. From what Lord Easton has learned, we are not going up against a great military mind. He does, however, have total and utter control over his soldiers."

The two colonels departed. Fenwick and I adjourned to our tent. After sleeping in swaying serpentins for the previous two weeks, an unmoving cot might feel strange.

The stationary nature of it did not keep either of us awake long. I fell into a deep sleep. In the midst of that repose, the Goddess Bellona appeared to me.

She seemed larger than a human, but there was nothing else I saw that I could use to compare. Her dark eyes, atop dramatic cheekbones, bored into my awareness. Her long black hair billowed behind her as though she was facing into a steady wind. She was dressed for battle, wearing a breastplate, arm guards, a leather kilt, greaves, and high boots. Bellona was breathtakingly beautiful and awe-inspiring.

She did not speak, and her expression did not change, but somehow, she made me know that there was something we needed to find. It was similar to the feelings she transmitted before Fenwick and I were washed overboard and ended up finding her lance near where we landed on the shore of Rhetia. There was a slight difference in what I felt.

Whatever the object was, we would find it useful in our current circumstances. It is impossible for me to put into words why I felt that way. I also knew I needed to look through my belongings for something.

When I understood her wishes, she disappeared. I woke instantly, sitting up on my cot. In the darkness, I sensed Fenwick was awake as well.

"Get me some light," I asked him.

Fenwick used his finger on the wick of a lantern, and the glow filled our tent. I rolled off my cot and went to my trunk. Fenwick followed, holding the lantern over my shoulder.

Flipping open the chest, I immediately started searching in the area where I stored several items Lucy prepared for us. Again, I had no idea why I began there, but it seemed correct. In with the vials and small glass bottles of different medicines and potions was a piece of paper.

That puzzled me. I did not remember packing it. Pulling it out, I unfolded the paper. On it was Miss Katherine's drawing of the Sword of Bellona that she had copied from one of Lucy's or Queen Liliana's books. As soon as I saw it, I knew that was what Bellona wanted us to find.

"I saw that sword in my dream," Fenwick said in an awed tone. "What is it?"

"When we returned with the lance, Lucy and Lily looked for more information about relics associated with the Minor Gods," I said. "Apparently, there are a variety associated with different divinities. This is Bellona's sword. From what Lucy told me, it was last seen in her Temple in Nagah. Like the lance, it also provides the user and his mount with unlimited strength. According to the legends, it will cut through anything—even solid rock."

"The Temple of Bellona in Nagah is fairly close to the borders of Combrial and Hier," Fenwick said. "At least, that's what I remember. I wonder if whoever is in control of Combrial is also attacking Nagah. If they are, the Temple is probably surrounded. I wonder if the forces of darkness have overrun it?"

"I don't think Bellona would have appeared to us both if that were the case," I said. "My guess is that the priests and acolytes have held them off somehow."

"Perhaps it is the sword that has made it possible," Fenwick mused.

"Why would Bellona send us on this errand and want us to leave our forces? That troubles me more than just a little," I said. "Not to mention what would happen to her Temple if we took the sword to aid ourselves. That might be the only way the priests have fended off the enemy."

"I'm afraid, Your Highness, that we won't find any of the answers until we are much closer to her Temple," Fenwick said. "As far as our soldiers, do you have confidence in Colonel Driscoll and Colonel Yankton?"

"That is not the issue, Fenwick," I said. "What is more important is how will our men react to our leaving on the eve of battle. How will our allies feel?"

"Hmm. I see your point," Fenwick admitted. "It will depend on how we phrase it."

"Beyond that, how far away is the Temple? How long would we be gone? We must reckon that the enemy holds the territory through which we must ride. Both of those problems are considerable."

"We'll need to look at the maps before we make a decision," Fenwick said. "And we must discuss it with our colonels and the leaders of the allied forces. All I know is that Bellona would not send us on this task for a frivolous reason."

Fenwick's remark sparked an awful thought in my head. Suddenly, I worried that the dark mage commanding the enemy might have sent us a false dream. I dropped to my knees beside my cot and opened my connection to the Goddess.

"Pray with me, Fenwick," I urged. "Pray with me for guidance. If that was a true vision, and we pray with our connections to her open, she will assure us of her will."

Fenwick looked at me with an odd expression. Neither of us was particularly religious, despite the strong ties we had to Bellona. I suppose it is easier to describe the two of us as having a rich and full spiritual life, while not paying much attention to the customary forms and rituals. Fenwick did join me on his knees.

It is difficult to describe what happened while I prayed. The Goddess did not reappear to me and provide explicit directions. I was infused with a sense that we interpreted the dream correctly. She wanted us to travel to her Temple, even though it would be through enemy territory, and we would leave our soldiers behind. I was also left with the feeling that it was necessary for us to do this—to the point that our success in the war depended on it.

"Well?" Fenwick asked as he rose from his knees.

"I'm convinced," I said as closed my connection to the Goddess, pulled myself up and sat on my cot. "She definitely wants us to do this."

"The outcome of the war depends on it," Fenwick added.

"You got that feeling as well, I see," I commented.

"Very much so."

"Did you see her?" I asked.

"No," he said quietly. "It's hard to describe, but the closest I can come is that she directed my thoughts. She did not put ideas in my head. Instead, she nudged my mind to follow a path."

"Well said," I agreed. "She did the same to me but I would have had difficulty explaining it as clearly as you just did. When morning comes, we need to meet with Colonel Driscoll."

Fenwick extinguished the lantern and we both returned to our cots. Sleep did not return quickly. My mind was busy gnawing at the new problem Bellona gave us.

I must have fallen asleep at some point because the bugler woke me. Fenwick and I dressed. He went in search of Colonel Driscoll as the men busied themselves in preparing breakfast and breaking camp.

"Come," Fenwick said a few minutes later. "Colonel Driscoll is waiting for us."

Men were already breaking down the colonel's tent, but a table still stood in front. The surface was covered by maps. Colonel Driscoll was examining them.

"Have you told him?" I asked Fenwick as we approached.

"No. I only said we needed to discuss something," Fenwick replied softly, "and that we needed maps."

"So, you're leaving it up to me?" I whined.

Fenwick's response was a grin.

"Your Highness, Lord Easton," Colonel Driscoll greeted us. "Someone will bring us food in a moment or two. Lord Easton said you had something of importance to discuss."

"We do, Colonel," I said. "What I will share with you may sound fantastical, but I ask you to suspend your disbelief until you hear me out."

"I'll do my best," Driscoll replied.

"It's no secret that Lord Easton and I have been blessed by the Goddess Bellona," I began.

"I was there at Hamil Creek where I saw the two of you manifest her presence when you defended the king," Driscoll said.

"A couple of months ago, the Goddess started to appear in our dreams," Fenwick said. "It's a convoluted story, but those dreams led us to recover the lance of Bellona that His Highness now carries."

"I've heard something of that," Driscoll admitted. "It has magical properties, does it not?"

"It does. She appeared to us again last night," I said. "She wishes for us to ride to her Temple in Nagah and retrieve another of her artifacts—a sword. Lord Easton and I are both positive that we will need this weapon in order to win the war. I wish I could explain more clearly, in more concrete terms, how she made that clear to us, but both of us are convinced."

"If it were anyone else than the two of you," Driscoll said after considering the matter carefully for a minute or two, "I would think they were hoping to escape the fighting. I know the steel that lies within you both, however, and I realize you would not come to me if you were not convinced this was necessary. Let me prepare a detachment to—"

"Colonel Driscoll, we will travel alone," I said. "That was also made clear to us."

"Are you sure that is wise?"

"Ordinarily, I would agree with you, sir," Fenwick said. "But it is the Goddess who directs us, and she would not lead us astray."

"We are concerned about how our departure will affect the men and our allies," I said. "We would like to explain why we are leaving. If possible, we would prefer to bolster their spirits instead of diminishing them."

3

"Men of the Castle Shield and our southern allies," I began. "The Goddess Bellona summoned Lord Easton and me, demanding that we travel to her Temple in Nagah. She wishes for us to retrieve a sacred artifact—her sword. Her message to us made it clear that this weapon will help us win the war. Lord Easton and I are not abandoning you. The Temple is roughly a hundred leagues away. We believe that our enemy controls most of that territory. Our mission will be dangerous, but the Goddess requires it."

"I'll go with you, Yer Highness," a voice shouted from the crowd.

"I wish you could," I replied with a smile. "The Goddess wishes for Lord Easton and me to make this trip by ourselves. You will have your own assignment. Colonel Driscoll and Colonel Yankton have identified places where you will hold the enemy at bay until our return. Lord Easton and I will return bearing a powerful weapon that will bring us victory. We do not enjoy leaving you, but we must heed the wishes of the Goddess. We will return as quickly as possible. Our biggest fear is that you will win the war without our help."

That remark drew some laughter from the men. I climbed down from the wagon where I stood to address the crowd. Fenwick was standing, holding the lance in one hand, and Andy and Davy's reins in the other.

Sergeant Hewko had packed supplies for our journey. Behind my saddle were my saddlebags, a bedroll, a bow sheath, and a quiver of arrows. The bags held two changes of clothes and a variety of food. Fenwick added a separate pouch for each of us filled with materials Lucy prepared.

There were vials of liquid for cleaning wounds in order to prevent infection. Others carried a paste that would numb the pain in the area where it was applied. Most of the small glass bottles contained a restorative elixir.

The lance of Bellona seemed to provide a limitless source of asomatous energy. With that, I could use my ability with Eir, the Goddess of health, to restore our physical well-being. To do so, however, required time and the ability to concentrate. Those conditions might be lacking when we most need to recover our strength. The elixir could put us to rights immediately. One interesting quality of the elixir is its smell. The aroma varies for each individual. To me, it smells like Lucy's hair when my nose is buried in it upon waking. To Fenwick, it smells like Julienne after a bath.

We set off, riding south for just over a league before turning onto a road to the west. The maps we had included a great deal of information about Hier. Beyond the border only important landmarks were included. For instance, we knew the approximate location of the Temple of Bellona, in a triangle of Nagah bordered by Hier and Combrial, but not what roads or tracks might get us to it.

Thankfully, Shasha agreed to accompany us. She would be able to scout the terrain for us where the maps were of no use. We also hoped she could provide us warning of enemy soldiers before we encountered them. Fenwick and I discussed earlier that we preferred to slip around them whenever possible. Armed confrontation would be a last resort, when we had no other options.

Almost immediately upon leaving the men behind, the weather turned against us. A hard, cold rain came from the north. The wind blew with such force that the rain stung our right cheeks.

Worried, I opened my connection with Shasha. I need not have been concerned. She was in the crotch of a tree somewhere, mostly protected from the rain and wind. As she could see through my eyes, she observed how the weather was lashing Fenwick and me. It amused her, though I did sense some sympathy for Andy and Davy.

The foul conditions continued until Fenwick and I sensed evening was drawing near. We left the road and entered the woods, looking for a spot to erect our little tent. Not far away, we found a small glade and dismounted. Fenwick hobbled and tethered the horses while I began setting up our shelter.

It took only a couple of minutes. Then I went in search of firewood. It was not difficult to gather plenty. While I was doing that, Fenwick took our water skins and collapsible canvas buckets in search of water. He found a stream nearby and filled them, setting a bucket out for each horse.

"At least with the rain we might not need to refill them," he cracked.

Fenwick pointed out a ring of stones that previous travelers left, marking a fire pit. They were buried by grass now, but that presented no obstacle. I began heaping up the wood I brought next to it, then went in search of more.

By the time I returned with another armful, Fenwick had a small blaze going. The parlor trick we learned to light candles, where we concentrated a small amount of our numinous energy in the tip of our finger, proved to be a tremendous advantage when it came to lighting a campfire in the rain. Given the unrelenting nature of the weather, we might not have had a fire otherwise.

The next day brought more of the same weather. When we returned to the road, I checked with Shasha. She was in a different tree from before but just as sheltered from the elements. Through her eyes, I saw her leave her comfy spot. She waited for a break in the wind, then began to fly.

"You didn't need to leave where you were," I thought.

You need me to look for soldiers, she returned. *It's no hardship. The weather at home is colder.*

Roughly a league from where we were was a small village. I could see smoke curling from the chimneys. That seemed to be a good sign. Shasha flew over the settlement and continued another three leagues.

"That's far enough for now," I thought to her.

There is another village. I will continue, then rest, she answered.

Sure enough, another league along the road and there was another group of houses. Not only did I see smoke from the chimneys, there were also animals— some goats at one place, a cow at another, pigs at a third. None of the animals looked like they suffered neglect—another positive indication. Shasha dropped our connection.

"Fenwick, there's a village about a league ahead," I said, "then another about four leagues past it. No sign of any soldiers."

"The second will be a good place to stop and eat," Fenwick said. "Did you see these towns?"

"Town would be an over-generous appellation, my friend," I replied. "They barely qualify as villages—hamlets might be a better description."

"So, no inn," Fenwick said glumly.

"No, but if you plaster your most winsome smile on your face, maybe someone will take pity on us and share some hot food by a warm fire."

They didn't. In the first village, we saw no one. When we reached the second, we allowed the horses to drink from the trough placed next to the road. We could see someone inside the nearest building. Fenwick called out to them in Hier, but they did not come out.

"Do you think they're scared?" I asked Fenwick.

"I have no idea," he replied. "I would need to speak with one of them to learn more, and no one seems to be in the mood for a chat."

We passed two more small villages that afternoon. There were definite signs of life, but no one stuck his head out of the door to say anything. The only thing I could figure was that they had news of ill tidings and did not wish to interact with anyone. Fenwick grudgingly agreed.

We encountered no other travelers. It was difficult to tell with the rain, but the road seemed as though it usually had regular traffic in the past. When we rode up upon a tinker with his mule near the end of the day, I was shocked to see another person.

"Majors and Minors!" I gasped.

Fenwick greeted the man in Hieran. They had a discussion of some length. Eventually, Fenwick dismounted and gestured for me to do the same. The tinker evidently knew a place to spend the night, which required us to backtrack a couple of furlongs.

We followed him off the road and found a clearing not too much different from the night before. Fenwick and I divided up our responsibilities in the same way. When Fenwick used his finger to ignite the fire, the tinker burst forth into frightened speech. I could tell Fenwick was trying to calm him down from the tone of his voice.

I took the waterskins and canvas buckets while Fenwick was busy with the man. He interrupted whatever he was saying to ask the tinker a question. The tinker replied and pointed.

"There's a small spring where he indicated," Fenwick said.

By the time I returned, the tinker was calm. He finished setting up his own tent, then took a bucket and a couple of skins in the direction of the spring. I waited for him to draw out of earshot.

"So?" I asked.

"They have heard there is trouble coming from Combrial," Fenwick said. "Most of the rumors say a dark lord has risen and taken control of the country. The tinker was worried we were associated when he saw me light the fire. I convinced him otherwise."

"A dark lord, or *The* Dark Lord?" I asked.

"Not *The*," Fenwick said, "at least, I don't think so. I will need to learn more, but I believe he is talking about an extremely powerful dark mage. It will be difficult to separate fact from fiction. As you can imagine, these tales grow more fantastical with every retelling."

The tinker returned. Together, orchestrated by Fenwick, we shared some of the food each of us brought and made a rather tasty stew. After we ate it, Fenwick gave the man some of our dried fruit.

The man began to talk. Fenwick translated for me. It seemed as though Packy—that was his name—never needed to pause to breathe.

Packy confirmed that people were scared, which is why they would not leave their homes. They knew him, as this was part of his regular route. He traveled a large loop along this road, the road we took after leaving the Castle Shield, an east-west road we would encounter in less than twenty leagues, and a north-south road quite a distance to the west. It generally took him half a year to make it all the way around, and he would just begin the circuit again.

When Packy began speaking about the "troubles" (as he called them), Fenwick stopped translating. I sensed that Fenwick was trying to sift through what Packy said to find grains of truth. There was quite a bit of material with which to work, as Packy only quit talking when Fenwick made excuses, telling him it was time for sleep.

In the morning, we broke camp in the rain and said our farewells. With a wave, Packy and his mule went clanking down the road. Fenwick and I headed in the opposite direction.

"Packy's route only takes him through Hier," Fenwick said, "so he knows nothing about Nagah or the near part of Combrial. The western part of his territory is less worried about the 'troubles' than the people we've seen."

"Or haven't seen, as the case might be," I added.

"Ha, ha," Fenwick said humorlessly. "As I expected, trying to glean the facts from what Packy had to say is not easy. I'll tell you the things that I believe are closest to the truth."

"I'm listening."

"A dark mage came from the mountains in the east of Combrial about two years ago," Fenwick said. "He established himself in the capital, Beata, and took control of the government by enthralling the king and queen. While there, this mage found two others with affinity for the Dark Arts. He woke their abilities and trained them. One he sent to Hier, the other to Nagah. Both of these subordinates failed—and died."

"Well, we knew about the one," I said (having killed her myself).

"The one who went to Nagah did not have as much success," Fenwick said. "Packy told a story about five spirit giants who caught the mage's army in the open near the border and sliced through it to kill the mage."

"Spirit giants? I think I know where they came from," I remarked.

"Priests or acolytes from Bellona's Temple, no doubt," Fenwick said. "I asked why the spirit giants did not continue to Beata, but Packy said they could not travel further east."

"I suppose we will learn more about why when we reach the Temple," I said.

"Agreed. Back to Packy's tale… When the dark mage in Beata learned his underlings were dead, he became furious. He decided to march north and conquer Hier first. When he finishes, he will return to deal with Nagah."

"What sort of danger will we face on our journey?" I asked.

"Packy could only tell me that we will be fine until we reach the east-west road about twenty leagues south of here," Fenwick said. "Once we pass that, we will reach a bridge ten leagues further on—then we will be in Combrial. We will need to stay on the road for thirty more leagues until we meet another east-west road that will take us to Nagah. He thinks we will travel twenty leagues west and then will need to ask the locals for directions to Bellona's Temple."

"So, the thirty leagues in Combrial is probably the most dangerous part of the journey," I commented. "Is there another way we could take?"

"I asked if we could take the east-west road which we will see in roughly twenty leagues," Fenwick said. "We could, but it would be much longer—by a couple of months. He explained that between the two east-west roads is a massive, impassable swamp. I know he's not lying because I've heard of this swamp on previous visits to Nagah. If we take the next east-west road, we will travel far to the west, then need to head south, then come back east. We have to take the road through Combrial. There is good news, though."

"Which is?"

"We don't need to hack our way cross-country at any point," Fenwick said. "Until we get quite near the Temple, we will be on roads like this."

"I reckon we've covered twenty leagues so far," I said, "with another eighty remaining. Does that agree with what you think?"

"Sounds about right," Fenwick said. "Eight more days in the saddle."

"Unless we run into trouble in Combrial," I warned.

The rain diminished, then stopped. Low, gray overcast continued. This weather stayed with us for the three days it took to reach the bridge Packy told us about. Combrial was on the other side.

We stopped short of the bridge and set up camp. Neither of us was very talkative that night. Though Shasha had flown ahead late in the afternoon and saw nothing to alarm me, I still worried.

In the morning, we broke camp and headed to the bridge. Shasha was overhead, but I severed our connection while I crossed the river. The hollow sound of the horses' hooves on the wooden bridge felt ominous to me.

Once back on the road, I connected with my familiar again. She was perched in a tree overlooking a village. Unlike those we passed through in Hier, I saw no smoke rising from the chimneys. Neither did I see any animals near any of the houses. It seemed to be deserted.

"Village ahead," I told Fenwick. "I don't know how far, but it looks empty."

"Huh," he grunted.

We rode on, reaching the houses about an hour later. Not only was no one there, but from the state of disarray, it looked as though it had been abandoned at least a year before. Only crops of weeds grew in what were people's garden plots. No preparations had been made before abandoning the place. None of the shutters were closed. In two houses, the front doors sagged open.

"Should we look?" Fenwick asked.

I knew what he meant. He was asking if we should go into some of the buildings to see if there were bodies. Though I did not want to, I nodded my head.

We dismounted. For some reason, I drew my sword and opened my connection to Bellona. I tried to extend my senses but felt nothing.

I went into one house, while Fenwick entered the one next door. Thank all the heavenly beings there were no bodies. Even so, I felt uncomfortable and did not linger. Fenwick exited at nearly the same time.

"Seen one, Fenwick, seen 'em all," I tried to joke.

I sheathed my blade and swung back up on Andy's back. We left the village without another word. I did not look back.

We passed through two more deserted communities that day. Neither of us felt the need to stop and investigate. Shasha communicated sporadically throughout the day. She saw nothing that worried her.

The next morning, after we'd traveled not quite three leagues, Shasha demanded my attention. When I opened our connection, I saw a group of five horsemen headed toward us. Their uniforms were dirty, and their horses did not look to be in good health.

"We'll have company in about a half-hour, Fenwick," I said. "Five cavalry."

"Five is nothing to worry about," Fenwick replied.

"Perhaps," I said, "but where there are five, there are probably plenty more. This is likely a patrol, split off from a larger unit."

"Mm. You're right," Fenwick agreed. "Have Sha keep an eye open for us."

4

The wind was coming from the south, and the reek of the horses reached us before we saw them. The nasty odor of saddle sores assaulted our nostrils. Upon smelling this, it is difficult to say whether I was angrier at the Combrians for mistreating the animals, or sad for their mounts who suffered this neglect. I sensed that my horse Andy knew what the stench meant and was troubled by it.

When we saw them, I opened my connection with Bellona completely. Andy and I seemed to nearly double in size while the Goddess's energy sang in my veins. I knew it was only an illusion, but it thrilled me nonetheless.

Fenwick and Davy also appeared larger than life as he threw his connection to the Goddess open. I lifted her lance from its rest and grasped it with the butt tucked under my right arm. Fenwick drew his blade. I unsheathed mine with my left hand, and then our mounts surged forward toward the Combrians.

As we drew closer, I noted the absence of expression on the riders' faces. They showed no fear but rode straight toward us. Bellona's lance made the first contact. It pierced the man's breastplate and lifted him from the saddle. As he fell, I allowed the butt of the lance to rotate up. I changed my grip so the lance would not be ripped from my hand by being stuck in his corpse. It was an awkward maneuver and would ordinarily have required great strength, but Bellona provided strength in great abundance, and it seemed as though the lance did not want to leave my hand.

By now I reached the group. While still twisting and lifting the lance with my right hand to recover it, I slashed with my sword at a rider on my left. I was able to accomplish both moves with an ease that slightly astounded me.

Past the men, Andy and I wheeled as I tucked the lance back under my arm. The horse carrying the man I had slashed with my blade was now stopped. His rider's head, nearly severed, lolled on the man's back, still connected by a strip of flesh.

While I watched, Fenwick dispatched a second of the riders. The third was turning to rejoin the scrap. With the slight nudge of my knee, Andy surged toward him. The lance struck him squarely over his heart. Again, I rotated my arm up and over to maintain my grip on the lance as the man tumbled to the road.

The five horses stood in the road dumbly. I closed my connection to Bellona, stepped the lance in its rest and slid from the saddle. Reaching the horse with the nearly headless man, I shoved him out of the saddle. I quickly loosened the girth and began to unsaddle the horse. Fenwick looked at me with a puzzled expression, then understood. He dismounted and helped me.

All five horses had open sores. The sight infuriated me. Animals should never be mistreated. I knew what I would do.

"Fenwick, find the numbing salve," I said. "Follow me and apply it when I finish with each horse."

As I mentioned earlier in these scribbles, one of my two lesser abilities was with Eir. I was far less knowledgeable about how to use her gift compared to my dominant ability with Bellona, but I was going to do my best. I opened my link with Eir completely and put my hands on the biggest sore on the nearest horse.

As I did, I envisioned the sore closing and the skin healing. While I watched, I saw a miracle take place, as the wound reacted in just the way I imagined. I moved my hands to the next spot, and did the same.

Before I finished the first horse, I needed to restore my asomatous energy twice from the diamond in the pommel of my sword. I realized I would drain it long before I healed the second animal, but then I remembered that Bellona's lance was an inexhaustible source of numinous energy. I went to it and felt the divine essence flow into me. It took only a moment more, and the diamond in my sword was filled as well.

Andy seemed to sense that I needed him close. When I went to the second horse, Andy stood by my side. I would not need my ring—I would simply touch the lance when I emptied my reserves.

While I healed the second animal, Fenwick was rubbing the numbing agent on the now covered sores on the first. I looked over, and could see the animal's bearing and posture change as the pain receded. Seeing that made my heart swell.

When we finished, Fenwick and I climbed onto our saddles. As we headed south along the road, the five horses seemed to have an unspoken conversation. They began to follow us. The sight made me smile.

Shasha broke into my vision. I opened my link to her. She sent a feeling of gratitude to me.

That is what they feel for you and your friend, she thought, *though it is much stronger than I can share.*

"You can sense the emotions of other animals?"

Only sometimes. When they are very strong, I can feel them. Too often, it is fear. I do not like that. This feeling, I like very much.

"I could not leave them, suffering like they were."

I know. You are Caz.

When she thought "Caz," she made the call that was her closest approximation of the sound. She closed the connection. Fenwick noticed the sound of her call.

"Sha sounds happy," he commented.

"So are our new friends," I said, jerking my head back toward our followers.

Fenwick had not noticed them before. As he did, his face broke into a broad grin. Then he started to laugh. His good humor was infectious, and I began to chuckle as well.

We continued on our way. Shasha was flying above, maintaining watch. The men we killed were thralls, and I suspected their master knew their fate. They were also part of a larger unit, which was surely in the vicinity. It was only a matter of time before they found us.

In the early afternoon, Shasha seized my attention. I linked to her and saw the larger group of horsemen approaching, roughly a league ahead of us. That gave us only half an hour before we would meet them.

"Fenwick, the rest of the cavalry troop is headed toward us, a league distant," I said. "Fight or flight?"

"How many?"

"Thirty-five."

"Flight, I think," he said. "These thralls aren't terribly bright. If we can find a game trail, we should be able to slip past them."

"What about our companions?" I asked, jerking my head back toward the horses behind us. "If they follow us into the woods, they'll leave a trail even an idiot could spot."

"Tell them not to."

"Fenwick, in my vast storehouse of magical ability, communicating with animals other than Shasha is not a talent I possess."

I can try.

"What?" I thought in response to Shasha.

I can try. Fear is powerful and unpleasant. Most animals can sense the fear of others. I can try.

"But I don't want the horses to suffer at the hands of those people," I thought.

I can try.

"Please do."

"Shasha thinks she might be able to scare the horses and keep them from following us," I said. "Find us a game trail."

"Thank you, Shasha. I hope it works."

I will try.

With that, I broke my connection with the sparrowhawk. I looked for the signs of a path created by the passage of untamed animals in the woods.

"Here," Fenwick said five minutes later as he pointed to the right.

Andy and I followed Fenwick and Davy off the road. As we did, I noticed Shasha alighting on a branch above where we turned from the road. Andy and Davy both suddenly balked.

Fenwick leaned forward and began speaking softly to Davy. I did the same to Andy, reassuring him that there was nothing to worry about, that Shasha was trying to convince the other horses not to follow us. Andy took an unenthusiastic step forward, then another, and another. His gait continued to be reluctant but the further we progressed from the road, the less nervous he seemed.

I needed to unstep Bellona's lance from its rest before it started to snag on low-hanging branches. As I did, I looked behind us. None of the horses had followed us along the game trail.

About a quarter-hour after we entered the forest, Shasha reached out to me. There was a different game trail on the other side of the road. The sparrowhawk was flying at the heads of the horses, trying to herd them into the woods. It was exciting to see it through her eyes. At many points, I worried that she would crash right into the skull of one of the beasts, but she managed to veer off at the last moment. She finally convinced one of the horses to step off the road and onto the trail. The others followed. Through Shasha's eyes, I watched their progress.

We proceeded into the woods for almost an hour in a generally westerly direction before we reached another trail that headed more or less north-south. Meanwhile, Shasha flew out of the woods and back down the road toward the cavalry troop she saw earlier. She found them quickly.

When they reached the trail where Shasha had herded the other horses, evidence of the animals' passing was obvious. The men turned into the forest. We watched them for a time.

It is done, Shasha sent to me. There was a feeling of triumph that accompanied the thought.

"You are the most clever and beautiful animal in the world," I responded.

I sensed her smug satisfaction. The view changed as she took flight. I saw the woods from above as she headed in our direction.

"Good news, Fenwick," I said. "Shasha directed the horses who were following us down a trail on the other side of the road. The cavalry followed them into the forest."

"Tell Sha that I think she is the most incredible bird who ever flew," Fenwick said.

I passed that thought to Shasha. From above us, we heard, "Klee, klee, klee." Fenwick and I both laughed at the sound.

As day was fading, we came across a grassy clearing—the first we encountered after leaving the road. When I saw Fenwick rein in and begin to slide from his saddle, I knew exactly what he was thinking. I did the same.

With the easy familiarity we'd developed, we did not need to say a single word as we set up camp. When the horses were watered, I plunked myself onto the ground next to where Fenwick was tending our pot of salt pork stew. He smiled.

"The Gods surely work their wonders in mysterious ways," he said. "It now seems preposterous that I tried to kill you."

"Multiple times," I said.

"Only twice when I was in control of my thoughts and actions," Fenwick qualified.

"Only twice," I smirked.

"I thought you'd forgiven me."

"Forgiven? Absolutely, my friend. Forgotten? Not likely to happen."

"I suppose that's my burden to bear," he replied with a shrug. "It could be worse."

"You might have succeeded. You almost did. By all rights, I should have died the first time."

"Stop," he pleaded. "I'm trying to make a point and say something nice while doing it."

"I know," I said. "You don't need to say anything, Fenwick. I feel the same way sometimes."

"We should probably go watch and watch," he said. "Knowing that there are a bunch of enthralled horsemen looking for us, I don't think both of us should sleep at the same time."

"I agree. Do you want first or second?"

"Whichever Your High-and-Mightiness prefers me to take," he quipped.

"Well, then, you jumped-up orphan," I replied, "I shall claim the first watch."

Fenwick shook my shoulder gently. I woke in an instant. My time in the Rangers years before taught me to sleep when I could, and also how to wake quickly.

I crawled out of the tent and took a seat near the embers of the fire. Without a word, Fenwick disappeared into our little shelter. I reached within myself and accessed my connection with Shasha. She was sleeping but woke when she felt me touch her mind.

"Will you please go to see where the horsemen are?" I communicated.

Before I even completed my thought, she had already launched herself into the air. It took longer than I would have thought for her to locate them. The game trail they followed had taken them far from us—probably five leagues away, as near as I could tell. When she did find them, it was the smell of the saddle sores that led her to where they were. I knew that from Shasha's disgust.

I did not even need to ask her to look for the horses that we did our best to heal. Shasha kept flying. She found them in open country further to the west, having left the forest behind. They were still on the move.

"Thank you," I thought, glad the horses were free.

It makes me happy, too, she replied.

When day broke, I fetched more water for Andy and Davy. By the time I returned to our little camp, Fenwick was stirring. We began to break camp, again in a practiced routine that did not require speaking.

"They're at least five leagues away," I told him as we saddled our mounts, "and heading in the wrong direction."

Fenwick asked about the other horses. I shared with him what I saw. He nodded with a smile on his face.

We found the game trail on the other side of the glade and entered the forest. Connecting with my familiar, I sent her to find out how far from the road we were. To my surprise, the distance was only roughly eight furlongs. I shared the information with Fenwick.

We encountered another game trial intersecting our current path and turned toward the road. In less than an hour, we reached it and resumed heading south. Shasha continued to scout ahead of us. I let her know how glad I was that she disregarded me and accompanied us over the Surrounded Sea. Her reply was nothing I could put into words, just a strong sense of smugness.

We passed three villages that day. All of them were devoid of people, though in the third, we had quite a scare. We heard sounds of movement coming from one of the houses.

Fenwick and I dismounted and drew our swords. We crept inside as silently as we could, following the sound. I must admit it did not sound quite human, but I did not know what noises an enthralled person might make, having never heard them utter anything.

We reached the kitchen. Fenwick kicked open the door. I don't know who was more startled—Fenwick and me, or the large black bear we caught rooting through the pantry.

Fenwick quickly grabbed the door and shut it behind us as we scampered outside. We mounted quickly and moved away from the house. I could not help myself. I started to laugh and could not stop. Fenwick joined in, and in a short time, we were clutching our aching sides as tears rolled down our cheeks.

"Whoo," he said shakily as he regained his composure. "I nearly crapped my pants."

"Me, too," I choked out as I started laughing all over again.

The rain returned. Another day of riding saw us reach the crossroads that would take us west. Shasha surveyed the road ahead of us. There were no other people on the way to where the north-south road we were on intersected with the east-west road. Once we turned west, we had a ride of two more days, according to what the tinker thought.

We camped well away from the crossroads. The two of us shared watches, and I allowed Fenwick to claim the first one. We spent an uneventful night.

The next day was just as free of human interaction and just as rainy. Before we encamped, Shasha flew ahead. What she saw was what Fenwick and I both anticipated.

A river served as the border between Nagah and Combrial. There were soldiers on both sides. The bridge between had been cut down. The winter rains had swollen the river. It rushed in a torrent between its banks. Even if we managed to find a ford, it would be a risky crossing.

5

It was another dreary, wet day. Before breaking camp, I asked Shasha to fly to the river. I hoped to find a ford. My experience in the Rangers told me that there would be one near where the bridge was built.

Fords predated bridges, and the road would have led to the shallow spot in the river. I hoped Shasha, with her uncanny eyesight, might be able to discern the course the original road followed. It had probably been hundreds of years since the bridge was built, however, so the forest probably erased any traces of a previous path.

It did not take long before she flew over what I was sure was the ford. The white-tipped turbulence of the river changed into a foaming effervescence as it passed over the shallow area heading north. That was bad enough, but then we would need to ride past dozens of soldiers to reach the spot. Even if we approached through the forest, we would still need to run a gauntlet of a dozen men armed with crossbows.

I explained the situation to Fenwick. My primary concern was for our horses. Even a stupefied thrall would be able to hit our mounts. If they were wounded before we attempted the river, we would not make it across.

"Ask Sha to look for willow trees," he said.

"What good will that do?"

"Just have her find us some willow trees."

About two-thirds of the way to the river, Shasha found a stand of eight willows. They were in the forest, on the same side of the road as the ford. I shared the information with Fenwick.

"Have her guide us there," he said. "Not on the road. We will follow a game trail as much as we can."

We broke camp. Once everything was loaded on the horses' backs, we looked for a game trail from the clearing where we spent the night that headed in the general direction of where we wanted to go. It took only a couple of minutes.

"You take the lead," Fenwick said. "Sha can guide you. She can't tell me where to go."

We could not find a game trail that took us directly to the stand of willows, so we needed to forge our own path. That slowed us down considerably. Daylight was fading when we reached our destination.

"Why willows?" I asked after I finished watering the horses.

"We're going to make armor for the horses," Fenwick said.

"What?" I exclaimed.

"These thin, whip-like branches," he said, holding one out to me. "We will weave them together and make shields for Davy and Andy's sides. The enemy has crossbows, you said?"

"They do."

"Then we will need to craft two layers," Fenwick explained. "A crossbow bolt will still penetrate through them and into their hide but won't have enough force to cause serious injury. I'm sure they won't be very happy, but they will survive. We will start in the morning. It will take at least a day. When do you want to attempt the crossing?"

"If the river was not raging, at night," I said. "But I don't want to try picking our way through the woods in the dark. Neither do I wish to endeavor to cross the river in darkness—it will be difficult enough. That means either dusk or dawn."

"I agree. I suggest dawn, the day after tomorrow," Fenwick said. "If we finish our weaving in good time, we can use the last light of day to make our way close to the river. We will spend a sleepless night waiting for sunrise, then make our attempt."

"What made you think of wicker?" I asked later.

"They use it fairly often here on the southern continent," Fenwick said. "Do you remember the protective shell that we used to approach the gate in Iradiem? The sides were wicker."

"I also remember arrows and bolts punching right into it," I said.

"Yes, but not completely," Fenwick countered. "Yes, they pierced the sidewalls, but the wicker caught them and arrested their progress. With two layers, Andy and Davy will be as safe as we can make them."

In the morning, we began weaving the thin willow branches together. Fenwick showed me how to get started, and I figured it out fairly quickly. By late afternoon, we had fashioned two layers of wicker armor for both sides of both horses.

The shields covered Andy and Davy from chest to rump. As Fenwick and I fastened them onto the horses, I sensed they were puzzled and slightly irritated. I hoped they would be happier tomorrow after we crossed the river.

There was no trail of any sort to follow. Rather than trying to ride, Fenwick and I led our horses through the woods. Shasha tracked our progress and guided us.

When twilight gave way to the dark of night, we stopped. We were about four furlongs from the bank of the river. Already, we could hear the roar of the water. We did not, however, hear the sounds of soldiers. I could not decide if that was good or bad.

We were both awake to see the gray of false dawn. Using that minimal illumination, we started picking our way to the river, trying to avoid making noise at first. As we drew closer, the sound of the rushing water became louder and louder.

"I don't think we need to worry about stepping on twigs," I told Fenwick.

He nodded, and we picked up the pace. We reached the edge of the forest not long after. Shasha had guided us right to the ford. Between the trees and the water was a space of only twenty yards. I reckoned that it was usually double that distance but the swollen river covered much of it.

Day was breaking, and I could see soldiers taking their positions as the watch changed. It did not seem as though a word was spoken. When a soldier reached his post, he stood stock still. A shiver ran up my spine. I wondered how our men were faring. Fenwick and I had fought blank-faced automatons outside the palace in Iradiem, and it was unnerving.

Fenwick climbed into the saddle. I followed suit. Both of us opened our connections to Bellona fully. We seemed to double in size, and her power fizzed through my arteries. After picking our way through the last of the brush, we urged our mounts to a gallop.

I heard a whistle sound out over the rush of the water. The soldiers turned and saw us. Before we reached the water's edge, some had already loosed their crossbow bolts. One knocked my helmet flying. Another pierced my armor, burying itself under my right shoulder blade.

Though the ford was shallower than the rest of the river, we immediately learned it was not shallow. Andy had to swim, and I needed to get off him so he could. Another bolt hit my upper left arm from behind. I seized Bellona's lance. The Goddess would be sorely disappointed if I allowed the river to snatch it from me.

That was the last thing I remembered before waking with an incredible headache in a large tent. It was far more spacious than the one Fenwick and I shared on our journey. I could hear voices outside. That was a relief. I reckoned it meant we had not been captured.

Trying to sit up caused a terrific coughing spell, which made my head hurt worse. My back was also sore, as though I had been beaten. I laid down again, thinking I should use Eir's power to heal myself. Before I could, Fenwick flipped open the flap of the tent, accompanied by a dark-skinned, short-haired Nagahny.

"Good. You're not dead," Fenwick said. "At least, not as much as when we fished you from the river."

Seeing Fenwick was in good spirits, I decided to play along. "How dead was I?" I asked, using the formula we'd employed dozens of times.

"You were sooo dead," he began to respond, but then stopped uncharacteristically. "You drowned, Your Highness. You *were* dead. This man," he pointed at his companion, "brought you back to life. He forced the water from your lungs and kept pounding on you until you started to breathe."

"Please tell him I am grateful."

Fenwick turned and said something in Nagahny to the man. The man smiled, bowed deeply, and left. I waited until he was gone before speaking.

"What happened?"

"A crossbow creased the left side of your head," Fenwick explained. "Fortunately, your thick skull did not allow it entrance to your brain cavity. It did render you unconscious, though. You sailed down the river, clutching Bellona's lance, for half a league before you got hung up on some rocks. It was the lance that stopped your progress. They had a difficult time prying it from your cold, dead fingers."

"Did Davy and Andy—?"

"Yes. They are both fine. They each had a couple of holes poked in their hides but no serious wounds."

"And you?"

"They got me three times—left shoulder, right buttock, left thigh. Walking is an unpleasant adventure. Now, as far as what happened to you, I was not there. It was all I could do to haul myself out of the water. The Nagahny took off after you and pulled you out. I heard about Sabu bringing you back from the dead later."

"Sabu?" I asked, remembering our espionage mission into the Rhetian Empire. Fenwick portrayed himself as a Nagahny trader, Ako something-or-other. I was Sabu, his speechless servant. The proper term is "dumb," but I refuse to use it to describe myself.

"Yes. Ironic, isn't it? Anyway, the reason you were coughing just now is that you still have water in your lungs. Sabu says it will take a couple of days to clear."

"You said the lance is safe?"

"Is it ever!" Fenwick exclaimed. "Three acolytes from the Temple of Bellona are guarding it."

"They aren't going—?"

"Majors and Minors, no!" Fenwick said. "They can't even touch it."

"You mean they're not allowed?"

"That's right. The head priestess would disown them if they tried. That, by the way, is why the dark mage did not succeed in entering Nagah. As we suspected, the priests and acolytes from the Temple spearheaded the resistance. They did great things on the battlefield and inspired the regular Nagahny soldiers to stand fast. The head priestess slew the dark mage in command of the initial attack herself. When we entered the river, manifesting Bellona, they recognized us as kindred souls. They raised the alarm that led to your being pulled from the water."

"Will they allow us to take the sword?" I asked.

"That depends," Fenwick said. "They will if the sword 'chooses' me."

"What does that mean?"

"With the lance, when you or I touch it, we can draw unlimited asomatous energy from it. They don't feel a thing."

"What?"

"They can tell it is a divine artifact and sense its power, but they cannot access that energy," Fenwick explained.

"The priestess was astounded that both of us are 'chosen' by the lance, or chosen by the Goddess to wield it—their grammar is a little murky sometimes, and you could interpret what she said either way. Regardless, two people chosen at the same time is something never encountered in their lore. Because of that, and the shared dreams I told her about, she believes it is almost a certainty that the sword will 'choose' me. Her name is Leora, by the way."

"And they will allow you to take it?"

"Yes. From what he explained, the lance and the sword have chosen different—let's call them champions—at critical points in history. The champions emerge in the midst of a crisis. She says we are certainly in a critical situation now with Combrial."

"The champion keeps it for life," Fenwick continued. "Then, somehow, the artifacts make their way back to the Temples. She wasn't terribly clear on that. I also shared with him that Lucy and Julienne are pregnant, and both babies have Bellona as their dominant affinity. She said that often happens with the champions Bellona chooses, that the affinity passes down."

"I wish Lucy or Lily could speak with this woman," I said. "This is much more than I learned when I visited the Temple in Aquileia."

"For me as well, but each of us had far less experience with the supernatural when we visited the Temple than we do now. If they explained this to us then, we would not have been able to understand any of it."

"True," I said. "What else?"

"That's pretty much all I know," Fenwick said. "Once you can travel, we go to the Temple."

"I was about to try to heal myself when you and Sabu came in," I said. "To do it properly and as completely as possible, I need the lance. Can you help me to it?"

"Can you fix me, too?" Fenwick inquired. "I hate to ask, but—I think we have a lot more work to do and no time to do it."

"Of course."

Fenwick helped me up, which triggered a coughing fit. I noticed I was bringing up thin sputum. When I stopped hacking, we headed outside.

A number of Nagahny were watching when we exited the tent. They looked somewhat awed at the two of us. Fenwick didn't seem to notice. Perhaps he was accustomed to it by now.

Limping slowly, he took us to another tent and pulled back the flap. The lance was there, lying on a rug. Next to it was an acolyte wearing the same garment I remembered from my visit to Bellona's Temple in Aquileia. She was on her knees, sitting on her haunches. She spoke to Fenwick, then rose and departed.

"She asked how she could help us. I told her why we were here, and that Eir is one of your lessers. She asked if we would wait while she fetched the head priestess. I agreed."

"You should have asked for a mirror," I said. "It will make it easier for me to see."

A minute later, an extremely dark-skinned woman wearing the kaftan of a priestess of Bellona entered. She spoke with Fenwick. He answered, telling her what we planned to do, and asked for a mirror. Leora, the priestess, barked an order at the acolyte, then sat back on her haunches to observe.

The acolyte returned with a brass mirror a minute later. I knelt down and touched the lance. The unlimited energy flowed into me, restoring what I used before being struck in the head while crossing the river. When I felt "full," I began.

"Please ask her to hold the mirror so I can see the wound on my head," I requested.

Fenwick relayed my wish, and the acolyte stepped forward. It took a moment for her to position the mirror properly. When I saw the wound, I hissed in surprise. It was no wonder my head ached so much. A deep furrow ran from the back of my head to my temple. Fenwick's comment about my thick skull made even more sense. From where the bolt struck me, it should have punched a hole into my brain.

I opened my connection with Eir completely and placed my hand above the wound. It was really as simple as seeing in my mind's eye the healing of the gash. In the past, Eir's assistance in healing was something I could only use sparingly and in small increments. The amount of asomatous energy required to do even a small amount of healing would drain my reservoir quickly. With the power flowing from the lance, there was no such limitation.

Leora watched as the side of my head healed. In the mirror, I could see the scab disappear, replaced by new pink skin. My headache disappeared. I moved my hand over the length of the furrow the bolt left and tried to sense if there was other damage that I could not see. From what I could tell, there was none.

Leora asked Fenwick something. He answered but stopped abruptly. When I finished, he asked me a question.

"She wants to know if you can always heal yourself so quickly," he said. "I started to tell her but thought you needed to answer."

I explained to Fenwick about how draining Eir's help was. He knew that already, as we discussed it in the past. When I finished, he provided Leora with a lengthy discourse. She asked another question when he finished and he provided a one-word answer.

"For these next two, I'll need your help, Fenwick," I said. "Even with a mirror, I won't be able to see the punctures. You need to remove the bandage and then tell me when to stop."

With difficulty, I pulled off my shirt. I noticed it was clean and lacking holes or bloodstains. It was clearly not the shirt I was wearing when we crossed the river. Fenwick gently removed the bandages from my shoulder and upper arm. As before, I pictured the wounds healing. I needed to do it by feel since I could not see them.

Fenwick told me when he thought I was finished in each case. I flexed my upper back and moved my left arm. There seemed to be no lingering effects of the injuries.

"Now you, friend," I said to Fenwick.

Fenwick blushed furiously. The location of his injuries was such that he needed to strip completely. He began to do so slowly.

"C'mon, Fenwick. We don't have all day," I quipped, twitting him for his embarrassment.

When he stood naked, he turned his back to Leora to preserve what little modesty remained. I started with his left shoulder, then moved to his right buttock, and finished with the left thigh. Before I let him dress, I moved my hand over the different places, trying to sense if there was any hidden injury.

"Move around a bit. Tell me how you feel," I requested.

"Right as rain," he said after experimenting. "That's an amazing ability you have."

Though my description of this healing does not take long to read, it took most of the day before we left the tent with the lance. Two steps into the open air, I smelled food. My stomach noticed also and responded with a loud gurgle.

You are not dead, Shasha communicated. *You were for a time, but your spark returned.*

"I almost drowned in the river," I sent back, though what I sent wasn't words but how I imagined I must have looked being swept downstream and then Sabu pounding on me to force me to breathe again.

No, it looked like this, and she sent me her memory of watching me tumble helter-skelter down the river.

"Worse than I thought."

I'm glad you are not dead. I would miss you.

6

Fenwick and I set out with Leora the following day near midday, after I healed the puncture wounds on Andy and Davy. As Fenwick promised, the wicker armor had prevented them from receiving more serious injuries. Nevertheless, both our mounts seemed happier after I tended to them.

The ride to the Temple was not long, but it was difficult. The track was narrow and rocky. We climbed uphill most of the way.

Leora was curious about our tan-zyan rings and how we obtained them. The tan-zyan gem was particular to the Goddess Bellona. Wearing it enabled us to siphon off some of our asomatous energy and store it in a diamond.

She had seen rings like ours before, belonging to two men—one from Nagah and the other a Combrian. Both of them had made a pilgrimage to the Temple to learn more about their abilities as young men but obtained the rings later. Leora disapproved of both of them, as they had used their abilities to become assassins for hire. Fenwick had the decency to blush at her comment.

We shared that we had encountered these two and defeated them, though almost at the cost of our lives. You may recall the story from an earlier batch of my scribblings. She was pleased to know they were both dead.

"The gifts of the Goddess should not be used for such a low purpose," she said.

I agreed heartily. Fenwick remained silent. He changed the subject and told her of how we obtained our jewels by trading with the Grand Vizier of Scaramouche. Leora laughed and even clapped her hands in delight at one point. That story is another detailed in my earlier writing. Amusing as it is (and it is one of the more amusing tales I think I will ever tell), I have no wish to take you, dear reader, over previously plowed fields.

We reached the Temple late in the afternoon. Acolytes came out to take our horses. When they saw the lance, however, they stopped and stared until Leora called them back to their tasks.

"The lance is similar to Bellona's sword," Leora explained. "It seems to radiate with the essence of the Goddess. We knew the lance existed from our books but never dreamed we would see it. As far as we knew, it resided in the Temple on the northern continent. Now, come. Let me take you to Her sword."

We entered the Temple. In size and architecture, it was quite similar to the Temple in Aquileia. Mounted on the wall behind the altar, we saw the sword. It was nearly identical to the drawing Miss Katherine made, though it was even larger than I expected. We crossed to it.

"May I touch it?" Fenwick asked.

"Please. Take it down," Leora said.

When Fenwick's hands grasped the sword, his expression changed to one of astonished wonderment. Without thinking, his hands caressed the blade. Suddenly, he broke from his reverie.

"It feels different from the lance," he said. "Here—touch it."

I put my hand on the pommel and immediately understood what Fenwick was trying to communicate. The sword was just as full of divine energy as the lance, but there was a subtle yet telling difference. It was as though the sword would allow me to use it, but it was not meant for me. I mentioned that to Fenwick.

"That is what I feel when I touch the lance. It seems as though the sword wants me to wield it, and I don't get that feeling from the lance. It's also bigger than I thought—not quite a two-hander, but more than one."

"It's a cavalry sword," I reminded him.

"That's true."

Fenwick realized Leora was eagerly waiting to hear from him. He began speaking to her in Nagahny, obviously trying to explain how the sword and lance felt different. She nodded sagely, then spoke at length.

"You were both chosen by the Goddess," Fenwick reported she said. "Prince Casimir is most accustomed to cavalry-type action. That is not to say you don't ride well, Lord Easton, but there is probably a difference in training. Bellona gave each of you the weapon you would wield most effectively. Remember, she is in us and of us. When you manifest her, as you did at the river, she is present. It is by no means her full strength. Our human bodies are frail compared to any of the Gods or Goddesses. If Bellona tried to channel her true might through you, you would not survive."

"Has that ever happened?" Fenwick asked.

"Twice in human history that I know of," she said. "In both cases, her complete power was needed to defeat the Dark Arts. The only witnesses who survived to tell the tale were far from where it happened. All of them describe a sound like a thunderclap and an intense flash of light. Afterward, every person and animal within a certain distance was killed, and her servant disappeared, never to be seen again."

Hearing this concerned both of us greatly. I cannot say why it did, when we both freely undertook what we knew would be an extremely dangerous mission. Leora saw the change in our expressions.

"We are not sure, but we believe you must pray to the Goddess for this to happen," she said. "There are stories of those who did pray for her intervention, and their prayers were not answered in this way. Victory was achieved by other means. Bellona clearly cherishes you both. She has saved your life, Prince, twice in the last year."

"Twice?" I asked after Fenwick told me what Leora said.

"In Iradiem, when you slew the mage, and just now in the river," she replied. "You do not think the lance caught on those rocks by mere chance, do you?"

"How do you know about Iradiem? Did you hear what happened?"

"I did. It is obvious to me that, without Bellona's assistance, you would now be trapped in the Seven Hells."

"That is what my wife and the queen told me," I replied.

When Fenwick shared this with her, Leora asked to know more about Lucy and Lily. He told her about both of them. She then asked if he was married and if his wife possessed supernatural abilities.

"No, but she is the daughter of Herbert Traval and a trader in her own right," he said.

"The name Traval is known even in Nagah," Leora said. "I believe she has visited our country in the past. They say she is beautiful and exceedingly clever."

"Thank you," Fenwick told her. "I agree."

"It is a pity we have no one like your queen. I have heard of the spirit of the white witch. It is rare to find someone who has woken the ability. I have read that most of the few who possess the affinity never know of it and live their whole lives ignorant of their potential."

"My wife and the queen have found a young woman who can see auras," I said. "They are training her so she can scour our country to try to find someone with the affinity for Ceridwen Sospita."

"What a wise idea!" Leora said. "We should do the same. When this crisis passes, and Combrial is no longer under shadow, I will speak with the priest of the Temple of Freyja if he survives."

"Is the Temple of Freyja in Combrial?" Fenwick asked.

"It is."

"Should we be worried about them?" I inquired.

"Yes and no," Leora answered. "You should not worry because they might be dead already, most likely. The Dark Lord suffers no rivals—even the Minor Gods. Their souls will be at peace, however, as Freyja will keep them from the Seven Hells."

"How many Temples are there in Combrial?" Fenwick asked.

"Combrial has four: Freyja, Andvar, Mielvanir, and Sadu. Nagah has three: Mentula, Njörun, and Bellona. Scaramouche has Saga's Temple, and Etelään, the furthest country south on the continent, is where Eir's Temple is located," she said.

"Is it difficult to reach Eir's Temple?" I asked.

"Extremely," she said.

"Huh," I grunted when Fenwick translated. "It's the same for us. Eir's Temple is far to the north, in a land of perpetual snow."

"As it is in Etelään," she said.

"I wonder why?" Fenwick mused.

"Ah! It is time for supper," she said, hearing a bell chime outside the Temple. "Come. It will be a lively meal. We have heard of the two of you before this, you know. Your great deed in Iradiem is the most well-known story, but I know of other of your adventures. I will try to let you eat before they demand to hear your exploits."

Dinner was indeed an animated affair. Leora did her best to delay questions from the other priests and acolytes until we finished eating. The food was delicious—spicy, but in a different way than the countries on the Surrounded Sea. The Nagahny ate with their fingers, however, just like their northern neighbors.

As I did not speak Nagahny, it was up to Fenwick to do the talking. He asked me questions occasionally to refresh his memory of certain events. His audience was enthralled, hanging on his every word. They would have kept him up all night, but when Leora saw Fenwick yawn for the third time, she called an end to the evening.

The three of us stayed to talk just between ourselves. Leora told us how she and the others from the Temple crossed the river to meet the dark mage who was approaching. They received word of the danger from people fleeing the mage's advance.

"We waited in the woods for the mage to approach on the road. He was no military mind, and most of his force was made up of thralls. The mage in Iradiem was probably similar to this one in skill and power. We flew out from the trees and attacked, catching him and his people by surprise. I had the honor of slaying the mage with my own blade," Leora said proudly.

"How did you protect yourself against the mage?" Fenwick asked.

"Priests of the Three Major Gods prayed over us," Leora said. "The mage had no sway over us."

"Did you free the thralls?" I asked.

"To do that, we needed priests of the Three Major Gods," Leora said. "We rode back to fetch them. By the time we collected them and returned to the river, the thralls were already under the control of the mage in Beata. That is enough for tonight. I can see you both are weary."

An acolyte took us to our beds for the night, and I think I was asleep before my head reached the pillow. Once again, my dreams were disturbing. Bellona did not appear. What I saw I recognized as a Temple of the Three Major Gods, horribly desecrated. The statues of the Three Major Gods were lying on the floor, broken into pieces. The faces of each were smeared with human feces.

There was a man sitting on a throne. Amid the overturned stone benches, people prostrated themselves on the filthy floor. One of them writhed in agony as the man on the throne grinned at his pain.

My attention was drawn to the altar. It, too, was covered with a grime of congealed blood and who knows what else. Sitting in the center was an oddly shaped object. I'd never seen anything like it.

It appeared to have twelve pentagonal sides. Each of the corners on all the faces was adorned with a small, solid sphere. There were circles cut out of the middle of each pentagonal face. It seemed as though something was inside the object, but when I tried to look more closely, it hurt my eyes and made my head ache. The thing was pure evil, and I wanted to destroy it.

I woke in a cold sweat. My skin was clammy, and I was panting in fear. I heard Fenwick panting in the cell across the hall from me. Sitting up, I used my finger to provide light. He looked the same as I felt—frightened.

"What was that thing?" I asked in a whisper.

"I don't know, but I think we're supposed to destroy it," he replied.

I extinguished the light and tried to sleep. The image of the thing I saw prevented me from doing so. When I heard the sound of others stirring, I got out of bed. Fenwick did the same.

One of the acolytes saw us in the corridor and took us to the dining room. Leora was already there. She looked at us strangely.

"Did you dream of an object—?" she began to say.

"You saw it, too?" Fenwick interrupted.

"Yes. It was … disturbing," she replied. "I need to ask our loremaster about it."

Not long afterward, an older man wearing priest's robes entered. Leora pulled him aside and started talking to him. Fenwick later told me she was explaining the object we saw in our dreams. When she finished, the man seemed to understand what she described. He nodded and left the room.

"He has seen something like the object before," she said to us. "He is searching for the book in which he saw it. While we wait, tell me what you think the reason for the dream is?"

"We must destroy it," Fenwick said. "It's evil."

"Of its evil nature, I have no doubt," she replied. "You feel compelled to destroy it?"

"Yes."

"Does the prince agree?"

"Yes," I stated when Fenwick asked me.

The man returned, carrying a tome four inches thick. He set it on the table. After he found the page he marked, he beckoned us to look. There, on the page, was a drawing of what we saw in the dream.

"What is it?" Fenwick told me Leora asked.

"It is a dodecahedron," the man said, "which only describes its shape—a twelve-sided object. According to what is written, it is an amplifier of the power of the Dark Arts. A dark mage can increase the power of his spells, the distance at which they are effective, and hugely augments his span of control."

"Span of control?" Fenwick asked.

"The number of thralls he is able to control at any given time."

"We have the urge to destroy it," Leora said.

"That will be difficult. They are thought to be a direct link between the mage and the Dark Lord himself," the man said. "Ordinary weapons or tools would be—"

"Would the sword of Bellona?" Fenwick blurted before the man finished.

"Yes, but—"

"He has been chosen by the Goddess to wield Her blade," Leora said. "And the other carries Her lance."

"Oh, my," the man said. "When did this happen?"

"Last evening. Come to think of it, you were not at supper," she said.

"I was with my books," he sighed. "I have lived with them since the darkness came from Combrial, spending the hours searching for anything that can help us. Yes. Yes, the sword of the Goddess should be able to destroy the object. The lance cannot. The only divine artifact, other than the sword that I think would be able to eliminate the thing would be the hammer of Andvar."

"What can you tell us about the sword and the lance?" I asked.

"May I see them?" he asked. "I need to know what their current configuration is."

"What do you mean, their current configuration?" Fenwick asked, while Leora issued orders to some acolytes to bring the sacred weapons.

"When not in the hands of the chosen, the sword and the lance are cavalry weapons. One reason for that is Bellona loves both warriors *and* their mounts. Both artifacts bring some benefit to the horse of the chosen."

"We had heard that," I said.

"Not only are they cavalry weapons, but in their normal state, they are ideally suited for use by cataphracts," he explained. "To the best of my knowledge, no one has fielded a force of cataphracts since the days of the old empire."

"What is a cataphract?" Fenwick asked.

"A cavalry unit where both rider and horse are heavily armored," the man explained. "A small group of cataphracts could scatter even the most staunch infantry formation."

The acolytes returned carrying the sword and the lance reverently. At Leora's gesture, they carefully placed them on the table. The old man looked at them and hmphed.

"As I said, cataphracts."

"You hinted that they are not always this size," Fenwick said.

"Yes. The chosen can ask the Goddess to alter them to his or her own use," the man said.

"How?"

"Open your link to the Goddess, grasp the sword, and pray to her, asking for the sword to be the perfect weapon for you. It's that simple."

Fenwick blinked after a moment. I knew he just connected with Bellona. He grasped the sword and lifted it from the table. Before our eyes, the weapon changed shape.

"Majors and Minors!" Fenwick gasped.

His hands now held a swept-hilt rapier. I could see the blade was slightly longer than his current weapon. Fenwick moved the sword gently through the air.

"It's … perfect," he murmured in amazement. "Does it stay this way?"

"As long as it is in your possession," the man said. "Which is to say, the rest of your life. Or, unless you ask to change it again."

"Praise all the heavenly beings," Fenwick breathed. "Thank you, O Goddess."

"Now you," the man said, looking at me.

As Fenwick did a minute before, I accessed my bond with Bellona, throwing it fully open. I placed my hand on the butt of the lance. Silently, I prayed to the Goddess to make the lance the perfect weapon to match my skill.

As we watched, the lance flowed into a new shape. As it did, it seemed to tremble in my hand. When it stopped changing, it was no longer the long, heavy, and unwieldy weapon we retrieved from Rhetia and that I had carried since. Now, it resembled the shorter spears I trained to use since my boyhood and that I employed while in the Rangers in the Eastern March against the horsemen from the east and, most recently, against the Rhetians. It, too, was slightly longer than what I used most recently, but not enough to seem strange or awkward. On either end it sported a wickedly sharp leaf-shaped blade at the tip. I lifted it from the table, and the heft and balance were ideal.

"Majors and Minors!" I breathed in astonishment, just as Fenwick had a moment before. I could not help myself. "Thank you, O Goddess!" I remembered to say.

7

Acolytes took the weapons away. As they left, others brought food for breakfast. After we finished, Leora asked us to come with her.

We followed her to her quarters. There was a desk near the door, covered by a huge map. She asked us to access our connection with Bellona and look at the map. It was beautifully detailed and included all of Nagah, Combrial, and Hier. The cities, roads, and rivers were all clearly marked.

"We are here," she said, pointing to a place on the map. "Beata is here. The dark mage is in Beata. Where is your army?"

I studied the map carefully with my link to Bellona, allowing only a small trickle of her essence to flow into me. Examining the road from Beata to Iradiem, I saw where we planned to erect the first fortification. I hoped they had been able to hold the line until now.

Unbidden, the image of the dodecahedron flashed in my mind. At the same time, my eyes sought Beata. I tried to envision rejoining the army and marching from the north. Again, the mysterious device demanded my attention, and I found myself looking at Beata on the map.

Clearly, Bellona did not want us to return to the army. She wanted us to head straight to the Combrian capital. I traced that route with my eyes and knew immediately that was what Bellona desired.

"She wants—excuse me, demands—that we go directly to Beata," I said. "Do you agree, Fenwick?"

"Yes," he confirmed. "When I tried to think of alternatives, she would not allow me."

"I agree," Leora said. "After dinner last night, I studied the map. I prayed for guidance. The Goddess wants the two of you to move swiftly to Beata, destroy the device, and slay the mage."

"Just the two of us?" Fenwick asked.

"I queried the Goddess, imagining that I would join you with some of my people," she said. "The Goddess did not approve. When I thought of only the two of you making the journey, she made it clear that was what she wanted. It must be that she believes the two of you will evade detection more easily than a larger group."

"We will be detected as we try to cross the river," Fenwick protested. "In case you don't remember—"

"There are other places you can cross that will be much safer and not draw any attention," Leora explained. "Four miles south of here is an old road, no longer used. There was no bridge, only a ferry. It is at least ten years since the ferry was last used, but the boat remains. When I asked Bellona if you should cross there, she let me know I was correct. This is where the ferry was," as she pointed to a spot on the map.

My connection to the Goddess was still active, and I looked where Leora indicated. When I imagined a ferry taking Fenwick and me across, the Goddess let me know I was correct, the same way she did when I studied the maps before our battles with the Rhetians not quite a year before. I nodded my acceptance to the priestess.

"From her concurrence," Leora said, "I believe the boat is still usable. We will need to stretch new guide ropes across, but that is the work of only a few hours. From the river to Beata is a ride of seven days. The first five of those days take you through a forest. When I last traveled that way, a dozen years ago, the villages on the way were already nearly abandoned because most of the traffic followed the new road."

"Why? What is the difference between the two?" Fenwick asked.

"The old road dates back to the height of the old empire," she said. "Their builders prided themselves on creating roads that were completely straight. If they encountered a hill, they did not attempt to find an easier route. They simply continued in a direct line, without deviation, as though proving their dominance over nature. The new road bends around nature's obstacles, making it much easier, especially for wagons. The old road has some stretches that are very steep. It should not present a problem for two men traveling light."

"After we leave the forest?" I inquired.

"Enormous agricultural estates, belonging to the wealthiest and most powerful Combrian nobles—at least, they did. Who knows what state they are in now. The poorest peasants did the work. Given that we are in the middle of our winter season, all the fields lie fallow. You might not see a single person until you reach Beata."

"Do you have a map of the city?" Fenwick asked. "We would like to take it with us and study it. From the dream we shared, the mage is in the Temple of the Three Major Gods—probably the one which was the largest and most well-appointed one in the city. We will not be able to ask the locals for directions."

The priestess went to a set of shelves on the wall. She foraged through what I guessed were maps rolled into cylinders. When she found what she sought, she brought it to her desk and unfurled it.

"If you stay on the old road, you will enter the city here." She pointed. "The largest and grandest Temple of the Three Major Gods is here." She pointed to a spot near the center of the city. "This," she said, tracing her finger along streets drawn on the map, "will be the most direct path to reach it."

"Will you mark those locations for us?" I requested.

Leora found a sliver of graphite and did as I asked. She then rolled the map back up and handed it to Fenwick. He sighed heavily.

"Remember when I said, 'We won't be able to dance our way into Combrial and simply dispatch this one?' Don't blame me," Fenwick complained, "it's Bellona's idea, not mine."

"Spoilsport," I said. "I was definitely planning on teasing you about that. If things turn sticky, I might still."

We departed not long after and made our way to the main Nagahny camp near the ruined bridge. I communicated with Shasha to let her know what we planned to do. Fenwick needed to fashion a way of carrying his blade. After trying to wear it in different places on his body, one of the acolytes suggested Fenwick hang it down his back, with the weight of it on his shoulders. That seemed to be the best solution, and with the help of a few men from the camp, they made a sling of sorts. Fenwick practiced reaching behind his head to draw the blade, then pronounced himself satisfied.

I needed to replace my helmet. Nagahny armor was different from Aquileian. Their helmets had a pronounced cone shape. Though I thought it made me look foolish, I certainly would never comment.

They brought us food, which we ate with relish. For the next few days, Fenwick and I would be stuck with salt pork stew. After dinner, we waited until darkness fell, and then Leora collected us. With a group of a dozen soldiers, we made our way south to where the ferry was.

It was not difficult to find the ferryboat. The last people to use it pulled it from the water and left it on a stand of logs. The boat was not large. It would hold Fenwick and me, as well as our horses, with not much room left over. Resembling a larger flat-bottomed rowboat, the distinguishing feature was the two tall posts, one on either end, with a large hole for the guide rope. With a dozen men, it was not much of a challenge to lift it from where it was and bring it to the edge of the river.

The bigger challenge would be stretching the rope across the swollen river. They tied one end of the rope securely around a tree and fed the other end through the guideholes on the posts in the boat. Then, they attached a sturdy twine to that end.

"What is the twine for?" I asked.

"Trying to swim the width of the river dragging the rope would be nearly impossible," Leora answered after Fenwick relayed my question. "It will be dangerous enough as it is. They will take the twine across, and then use it to pull the rope. They will then pull the rope as taut as they can, and then anchor it around a tree. Once that is done, we will put the boat in the water, and the two of you will pull yourselves across. The men on the far shore will cut the rope after securing it around one of the guideposts. Then we will pull it back."

I watched as four men stripped and prepared to swim across the river. That was not something I had any desire to do. Once they were ready, they walked quite a distance upstream. I reckoned the current would push them at least even with us, if not past.

Then, the only sign that anything was happening was the twine spooling out. There was no sound, and in the darkness, we could not see them in the water. The twine uncoiled slowly, at an uneven pace. Then it stopped.

Just as I was beginning to worry that the men failed to make it across, the twine was tugged across swiftly and powerfully. The rope began to follow it, with the strength of the current pulling it downstream. At last, there was no more rope. A few minutes later, it started to grow taut. First, the downstream angle started to disappear, then, the rope lifted from the water.

I could tell the men were straining to draw the rope as tight as possible. It moved with small jerks as they cinched it more and more. At last, the rope was as close to horizontal as they could make it. There was a slight bow in the middle due to its weight, but I doubt that could be helped. Suddenly, the rope bounced twice.

"That's the signal," Leora said.

"Fenwick," I whispered, "I think the only way we make it across is if we make use of the strength of the Goddess."

"I was thinking the same thing," he said. "Let's get the horses on first."

Andy was no fool. He did not want to step foot on that small boat. The roar of the river let him know how violent it was, which he remembered from our crossing a few days before. I spoke to him quietly, telling him it was necessary, and that I would not subject him to this otherwise. I promised that Fenwick and I would do our best to make sure the trip was as short as possible.

When I finished, he allowed me, with great reluctance on his part, to lead him onto the boat. Fenwick and Davy joined us a moment later. I looked at Fenwick and nodded. We both opened our connection to the Goddess completely.

As soon as we did, the men shoved the boat from the bank. Fenwick and I immediately began pulling the boat across the river with all of our Goddess-enhanced strength. As we pulled away from the bank, the current tried to sweep the boat out from under us. I stopped pulling the rope and instead braced my feet against the upstream gunwale while pushing against the rope as it fed through the guideholes. Even with the help of Bellona, I could feel the strain on my body. It was all I could do to keep the boat from swamping.

Fenwick pulled us along as quickly as he could. In the darkness, we could not tell how far we'd come or what distance remained. Just as I was beginning to despair, I felt the bow of the boat nudge the far bank. Andy and Davy scampered off, almost knocking over two of the men waiting for us.

"Let's get away from the river," I suggested. "Who knows if thralls can conduct patrols, but if they can, I'd have them watching the riverbank."

We rode for what I reckoned was an hour, then dismounted and moved to the side. The forest was already beginning to encroach upon the road bed, so we could not move far in the dark. I took the first watch while Fenwick slept.

In the morning, the sky we saw past the barren branches of the trees was gray. The weather smelled like rain. Sure enough, in midmorning, just after we allowed the horses to graze in a clearing, it began coming down in buckets. In the late afternoon, we reached an abandoned group of houses, all with sagging roofs and showing signs of neglect. We chose the building which seemed the sturdiest and made that our bivouac for the night.

It was more than a hut, but I wouldn't say it quite qualified as a house. The inside smelled musty, but it was mostly dry. The roof leaked, but only in spots. Fenwick lit a small branch and held it up the chimney. This served two purposes. It was the quickest way to learn if the chimney was blocked. We were pleased that it was not. The burning stick also helped to warm the chimney, which would help it draw.

When we were confident we would not smoke ourselves out, we collected the horses from their grazing and brought them inside. It made for rather cramped quarters, but neither of us wanted to leave them out in the weather. The two of them were content to stand placidly. I imagined they were happy to avoid the rain.

The bad weather continued the next day. We learned as we rode what Leora told us about the empire's engineers' disdain for yielding to terrain. The road went straight up hills and straight down, only deviating from its course if it ran into a sheer wall. This only happened once, and the road returned to its previous bearing immediately past the obstacle. Again, we stopped for the night in an empty hamlet. The chimney was blocked in the first building we tried but clear in the second.

The third day dawned crisp and clear. We sat and waited for the horses to finish eating. Suddenly, I had an idea.

"Fenwick, I have a feeling this first part of the journey is relatively safe. It's when we come out of the forest that troubles me. Yes, I know it's winter, and there is no reason for anyone to be in the fields, but where will we spend the night? If we ride through the night, we can reach the city in a day. We have Lucy's elixir to restore our strength, and when Donald Farquahr kidnapped my father, we both saw how Lucy used her ability from Eir to allow the horses to recover enough to continue."

"Let's both mull it over with the Goddess," Fenwick suggested.

I tugged out a tiny tendril of Bellona's essence. Then, I reviewed what I just mentioned to Fenwick. In the most vague sort of way, I felt I hit upon the right idea.

"It seems like that's the right idea," Fenwick said with a shrug a moment later. "I just wonder if we will be spotted as we approach the city. When we pass through the gates, I'm sure the alarm will be sounded, but—"

"I have a feeling there will be no one keeping watch," I said. "As far as the mage knows, he faces a threat in the north from our men and our allies and another at the border of Nagah. We have to suppose that the thralls did not pick up any sign of our crossing the river. The mage has no reason to man the walls of the city—if there are any—or to mount a watch."

"You think we will reach the city unseen, then," Fenwick said.

"I do. Of course, once we enter, we will be spotted, but the mage will not have time to prepare the elaborate barricades that we faced in Iradiem," I said. "I will be surprised if we need to fight our way past fifty heavily armored soldiers as we did outside the palace. He will undoubtedly use the helpless thralls he had groveling before him to slow us down."

"You really do think we will just dance right in, don't you?" Fenwick commented.

"There will be one important difference," I warned. "This mage will be stronger and more skilled than the one we faced in Iradiem, and he has that device to increase his power."

"We should probably try to eliminate that immediately," Fenwick said idly.

"*You* should, you mean," I corrected him. "I will do everything I can to enable you to get to it."

"You're making this sound too easy," Fenwick said.

"It depends on whether we do, indeed, catch him by surprise. If we are successful in that, then, yes, the physical challenge will not be as great as Iradiem," I said. "The mental and emotional aspects, however…"

"Ah," Fenwick sighed.

"This mage has had no connection with either of us," I said, "so I don't expect to see him conjure up images of those we love. But it will be difficult to reach him. What I experienced in Iradiem was that the closer I came to the mage, the more physically difficult it was to advance. Even with all the power of Bellona aiding me, I barely made it to her."

"Can you fight with the lance on foot now that it's shorter and lighter?" Fenwick asked.

"I've never tried," I confessed. "I imagine I could. Come to think of it, there were some practice forms my grandfather taught me when I was a boy, but I thought that they were only to build up my strength. In that, they were effective. They also were humiliating, in a way. I was only nine or ten years old, swinging a six-foot cavalry lance around. It brought out every bit of clumsiness in me. 'Control! Control!' I can remember him saying, as the weight of the damned thing would make me lurch and stagger."

"Perhaps you should ask the Goddess for help," Fenwick suggested.

As soon as he said that, I knew he was right. We still had three nights before we would make our final push into the city. I would pray to Bellona for her assistance and spar with Fenwick whenever we stopped to allow the horses to graze, and in the evenings until the light faded.

8

When we stopped later that morning to let the horses munch grass in a clearing, I slid the lance from where I had it tucked under the fender of my saddle. I closed my eyes and concentrated, trying to remember the practice forms I was taught as a boy. The beginning of the drill came back to me, but I quickly faltered. I was embarrassed, and felt as clumsy now as I did then.

Fenwick caught my eye, frowned, and mouthed, "Bellona."

I wanted to smack myself in the head for being an idiot. Instead, I opened my link to the power of the Goddess. In addition, I decided to pray for her instruction. As soon as I finished my plea, the steps and movements of the drills were now firmly in my mind.

I began to work through them, slowly at first. My muscles were unaccustomed to how I was using them. As I progressed through them, I realized some of the steps, lunges, and strikes I was making were not among those I remembered from the exercises of my youth. The new moves fit naturally and seamlessly into the drills. It amused me in a wry way that my grandfather had not known *all* of the forms. When I finished the complete set of exercises, I was sweating despite the cool temperature and the slow pace I used.

"We have time for one more set," Fenwick said. "Try to move a little faster, but maintain the control you held at the slower speed."

"Are you my teacher now?" I asked.

"No. The Goddess is, but she is watching through my eyes," he replied.

I understood what he meant. He, too, opened his connection with Bellona while he observed me. With Fenwick scrutinizing my movements and my internal evaluation of how things felt, I would learn more quickly—I hoped.

At one point, I misstepped. My hiss of frustration came at the same time as Fenwick clicked his tongue. It was the same sound my grandfather used to note when I made a mistake.

"Why did you make that sound?" I asked when I finished.

"After Madam Andrés took me in, she told me that she knew I could fight like a ruffian," Fenwick replied. "But she also wanted me to be able to fight like a gentleman. She hired a fencing master to train me. He used to make that sound when I moved improperly."

"My grandfather made the same noise," I said.

"Huh!" Fenwick grunted. "Perhaps my fencing master and your grandfather knew one another or trained together. After all that's happened with the two of us, it would hardly surprise me to learn it was true."

"Our styles are very similar," I commented. "In fact, if we engaged on the piste with formal rules, it would be difficult to tell us apart. It's the other things that make us slightly different."

"I learned some things on the docks," Fenwick said with a grin.

"And I in the Rangers," I added.

We stopped again in the afternoon. I unlimbered the lance and withdrew a tendril of Bellona's energy. My first pass through the forms I did at a slightly quicker pace. This time, I did not make a mistake. Without Fenwick prompting me, I started over, increasing the speed of my movements slightly.

I faltered at the same point as in the morning. When I finished, I went back to the part in the drill just before I misstepped. I went through it again slowly.

"Ah!" Fenwick said. "Too far. On the lunge two moves before, you extend your right foot an inch or two further than you should. It leaves you off balance. When you move slowly, you can compensate, but not when you use a quicker pace. Go back several moves and try again."

Fenwick instructing me generated feelings of irritation and amusement at the same time. It amused me because it made me feel young again—my grandfather's pupil. The irritation came because I did not consider Fenwick to be my better in any respect. Then I remembered that his insight did not come from his own knowledge. Fenwick had never, to my knowledge, trained in how to use a spear of this type.

I started the drill five movements ahead of where I was making the mistake, moving as fast as I did previously. When I came to the lunge Fenwick mentioned, I did not extend my right foot as far. The problem was gone. I went through that section of the drill three more times before we needed to resume riding, in order to help myself remember for the next time.

When we stopped for the night in another abandoned village, Fenwick told me not to worry about helping him with the chores. He demanded that I practice until the light was gone. I went through the entire drill four more times, increasing my speed with each pass.

"Well?" he asked when I came inside where he was waiting for me with a bowl of salt pork stew.

"No mistakes," I said with a smile. "And my last attempt was almost as fast as I could move. Tomorrow, I think I would like to move away from drill and begin to spar."

"Not with me," Fenwick said defensively. "I don't mind fighting against pikes and halberds. They're heavy and move slowly. I can offset their greater reach with how fast I can move. The lance, as it is now, will be too quick for me to beat it with speed alone. If we sparred, one or both of us might get badly hurt."

"The point of the drills is to teach how to move properly," I said, stating the obvious. "An actual fight does not unfold like a drill. I need to spar."

"I understand," Fenwick said. "I'm also not going to spar with you."

"Then how am I—?"

"Use your imagination," Fenwick said.

That was a very unsatisfying answer. I needed to spar with someone. There was no one else with whom I could practice other than Fenwick. *Use my imagination—*

"Oh!" I breathed when I finally understood what Fenwick meant.

When we stopped to graze the horses the next morning, I unlimbered the lance and moved away from Fenwick. I accessed my connection to the Goddess. Then, I imagined a soldier in heavy armor carrying a pike was attacking me.

It was the oddest sensation. I knew there was no one in front of me, but in my mind's eye, that enemy existed. While I was still trying to process what was happening, the soldier advanced, and I needed to back away very quickly. I discovered it was easier if I closed my eyes.

Dear reader, you probably think I have lost my mind, but I swear to you I have not. When I struck or parried the enemy my imagination conjured up, I could feel it. The shock of the lance striking my opponent was as real as anything I ever felt. When I drove the lance through his chest, it was as though I actually did it. But when I opened my eyes, there was no one there.

"That, Your Highness, was interesting," Fenwick said. "Do it again."

I shut my eyes and imagined another opponent, armed with a short spear similar to mine. This was a more difficult fight. The man and his weapon moved much more quickly. There were times when I was forced on the defensive, and I thought of a move or counter too slowly. Eventually, I triumphed over this spectral foe as well.

I closed my connection with the Goddess and opened my eyes. I was panting and covered in sweat. Fenwick was holding the horses but looking at me strangely.

"What?" I asked.

"That was… You moved so much more gracefully than when you were doing the forms," Fenwick said. "I can now see how the forms teach the movements. It was odd watching you. I could tell when you blocked your opponent's strike or he blocked yours. The absence of sound made it eerie."

"I made plenty of mistakes," I said. "My mind moved too slowly. I needed to *think*. With a sword in my hand and connected with the Goddess, I don't. My blade moves without conscious effort—more quickly than any thought."

"Then don't think," Fenwick said.

"I'll need to think about that," was my reply, somewhat facetiously.

In the afternoon we stopped for the horses. While we rode, I considered what Fenwick said. Understanding came to me when I quit wrestling with the idea. Because I was so comfortable with a blade in my hand, I did not need to think, but that was not the reason my movements were so quick and fluid under Bellona's influence. My level of confidence allowed me to surrender control to the Goddess. Fenwick clearly did the same, hence his remark. I resolved to try this.

I took the lance and opened my connection with the Goddess. Before I tried to conjure up the mental image of an opponent, I prayed silently to Bellona for the confidence and courage to surrender my will to hers with her lance in my hands. Taking a deep breath, I then imagined I was pitted against Fenwick and tried to clear my thoughts.

Majors and Minors, he was fast! I struggled to deflect his blade, but he came on relentlessly. He was too quick. His image disappeared when he struck a fatal blow.

"Seven Hells!" I cursed, knowing my mistake.

Don't think. Don't think. Surrender to Her. Surrender, I repeated in my mind.

I failed again, just as quickly. Then I set the lance down and tried again, only imagining myself with my own blade in my hand. This was much better until—

"You're not using the lance!" Fenwick scolded me.

"I wanted to see what it felt like—here," I said, tapping my head, "when I used a weapon that I know better."

"And?"

"Let me try again," I sighed.

I picked up the lance. Before I tried again, I suddenly remembered the techniques they taught me when I visited the Temple of Bellona in Aquileia. My biggest challenge at that time was learning how to clear my mind. Until I mastered that, I could not find the mote within myself that was my link to the Goddess. That tiny spark within myself, in a place that did not have a physical location as we think of it, was essential in connecting to and accessing the power of the Goddess.

By now, I knew how to find it, even in moments of great stress. In those days, however, I could not. They taught me how to empty my mind of conscious thought. When I did, I was able to locate that tiny mote.

Before I made another attempt, I employed those exercises and emptied my mind of everything except imagining that I would spar against Fenwick. When I saw him in my mind's eye, I let go of the thought.

The phantom Fenwick attacked. This time, my body and the lance moved without my specific direction. Fenwick was still wickedly fast, but I blocked his first strikes and gained the space I needed to employ the greater reach the lance provided over a sword. We traded blows for a time, and then I was able to go on the offensive. That made me happy—happy enough that I broke my concentration and suddenly Fenwick slipped under my guard and—I returned to the here and now.

"You were much faster and more graceful," Fenwick commented from the saddle. "What happened at the end?"

"I was finally able to try to launch an attack. It made me so happy, that I started to think again," I told him as he handed Andy's reins to me.

I put the lance away under the fender of my saddle. Putting my left foot in the stirrup, I swung onto Andy's back. My mind was dissecting how I failed this time.

"I need more practice," I said glumly.

"Well, it looked like a good fight until the end," Fenwick said. "What sort of opponent did you imagine?"

"You," I replied.

"Me—what?"

"I was fighting you," I said.

"Why me?"

"Is there anyone more dangerous I could match myself against that comes to mind?" I inquired.

"Your Highness—I'm flattered," Fenwick said.

"You may take it as a compliment," I said, "though I am not trying to inflate your sense of self-worth. I am just being truthful."

"You could have chosen yourself," Fenwick said.

"That would be too strange," I said.

"Actually, that's not a bad idea," I said much later.

"What's not a bad idea?"

"Imagining fighting myself as well as fighting you," I replied. "This mage won't have access to our memories, so he won't be able to conjure up the appearance of Julienne or Lucy."

"But he could make us think we were fighting each other," Fenwick said, completing my thought.

"Or ourselves," I added. "It would certainly confuse me to no end if I were unprepared to see it."

"Good point."

When we stopped for the day, Fenwick again shooed me away from helping with the task of gathering wood, fetching water, and making dinner. I took the lance and worked to clear my mind. When I tried to imagine fighting myself, it was too ridiculous and I could not keep my mind as empty as it needed to be. I used Fenwick for my opponent instead.

This time, when I was able to press my phantom foe, I maintained a state of mental surrender. Merely making an attack, however, did not end the bout. The imaginary Fenwick fought cleverly, and it took much more effort before I finally defeated him.

"Well done," Fenwick said. "That lasted quite a long time. You're dripping with sweat. Was it you, or was it me?"

"You," I said. "It was too difficult to pretend I was fighting myself. I couldn't do it without thinking it was silly."

"I was thinking about it," Fenwick said. "When the mage in Iradiem put on Julienne's appearance, even her voice matched. If the one we will face does try to make the people who attack us look like each other, he will probably do everything he can to fool us. He won't be able to read our minds, however, so we should have a simple signal that allows us to know which is the real Caz and which is the true Fenwick."

"That's easy," I said. "Just say something that we know that a stranger would not."

"For instance?" Fenwick asked.

"Theo."

"Toby," Fenwick said.

"Freddy."

"Compote."

"Good one," I laughed. "You get the idea. Don't repeat any of the ones that we used before. That will tell us it's an imposter."

"Ah—good idea," Fenwick agreed.

In the morning, we started our last day of riding through the forest in a light rain. When we woke the next day, we planned to ride straight through to the city, compressing two days of riding into one. We stopped for the horses to graze and Fenwick turned to me as I prepared to practice fighting an imaginary foe.

"You and I have both forgotten something so simple, you will want to kick yourself when I tell you," he said.

"What?"

"When we enter the city, we would be complete simpletons if we did not manifest the Goddess," he stated.

As soon as he said that, I did indeed feel foolish. In training myself how to use the lance, I had been only accessing the merest trickle of Bellona's essence. Before we went through the gates of Beata, Fenwick and I would both want every bit of her divine power at our disposal.

"You're less of an idiot than I am," I said. "You remembered it first."

This time, I did not even try to clear my mind. Instead, I found the mote that was my link to the Goddess and opened it without any restriction, to allow her strength to fill me. I seemed to be twice my normal size, and felt as though my blood was fizzing through my veins. I then imagined Fenwick as my foe.

The phantom stood no chance. In less than a minute, I dispatched him. Then I imagined Fenwick in his Goddess-enhanced state. This was a battle! I lost track of time. It was only Fenwick clapping his hands that brought me out of the living daydream I was in.

"That, my friend, was the answer," Fenwick said. "I've only seen you move that swiftly out of the corner of my eye, when we fought against the Rhetians, and then when we faced the thralls outside the palace in Iradiem. Were you fighting me again?"

I nodded since I was short of breath.

"But?" he said, gesturing with his hands to show "bigger."

"Yes. It was … magnificent," I said after I thought of the right word. "I wish you could have seen it."

"I saw half of it," he reminded me. "Enough to be impressed."

9

As we started to ride again, I connected with Shasha. Through her eyes, I could see Fenwick and me from her perch in a tree ahead of us. I shared with her that Fenwick and I planned to ride straight to the capital after leaving the wooded section of the road.

Why? There is no one, she replied.

Shasha shared with me her memories of what she saw flying over the fields. As I mentioned, her concept of time in the past is different, and her memories are not necessarily sequential. These were recent, though, and a bit eerie.

Leora told us the area was covered by massive estates owned by the nobility and worked by peasants. The fields were covered with the stubble of harvested crops, but Shasha saw no people. She flew over peasant huts and the huge manors of the nobles, and nowhere was there a telltale wisp of smoke from a chimney.

Given the cold and often rainy weather we'd been experiencing, the lack of fires in the hearths was a clear indicator that there were no people anywhere nearby. Shasha had flown until she could see the city of Beata, and it was the same everywhere she went.

"Thank you. This is very interesting. When we do reach the city, we will need you again."

I know, she replied, then broke our connection.

"Fenwick, Shasha just showed me that the area between the end of the forest and the city is deserted," I said. "We don't need to ride overnight."

"Does the Goddess agree?" he asked.

"Why do you ask?"

"While you were fighting the illusory me, I began to feel uneasy," he said. "Consider the question of whether to press on and allow the Goddess to look over your shoulder."

I did as Fenwick asked, with my link to the Goddess open a tiny bit. Immediately, I understood what he was feeling. I then considered not stopping for the night at the end of the day. There was a faint sense of wrongness.

"She does want us to ride straight through, beginning tomorrow morning," I told him. "But I don't think she wants us to ride through the night."

"Timing, Your Highness," Fenwick said. "If we rode through the night, we would arrive at Beata in darkness. That is not in our best interests. Leaving in the morning means we arrive in the morning the next day. That seems preferable. I would much rather face this challenge in the full light of day."

"I wonder why we feel this sudden urgency," I asked. "We could have cut days from our journey if the Goddess wanted."

"Urgency?" Fenwick queried. "I think that is too strong a word. There is no sense of imminent disaster we will face or we will cause if we travel at our current pace. Riding through, beginning in the morning, is Her preference, though."

"It makes me wonder how the Castle Shield is faring," I said.

"Hard telling, not knowing," Fenwick said.

His quip made me laugh despite the serious nature of our discussion. We both grew up in the Eastern March. The dry, laconic phrase he used was one commonly heard in that area.

"They haven't broken yet, is my guess," Fenwick continued. "Are they getting near the limit of what a sane person can withstand? We have been gone for over two weeks. They have been fighting an army of thralls every day. We fought thralls outside the palace in Iradiem that one day, and I found it a disturbing experience—one I don't relish repeating. The men are probably tired and sick at heart. I know I would be. I believe Bellona wants us to end this before they reach the maximum of what they can stomach."

When we made camp that night near the edge of the woods, I helped in the usual fashion. Fenwick did not insist that I work with the lance. Earlier, when we paused in the afternoon for the horses, my practice session went just as well as it did in the morning. This time, I imagined fighting the heavily armored thralls we encountered outside the palace in Iradiem.

After we finished eating, Fenwick and I both sat in silence for a time. I was thinking about what we might face when we reached Beata. It turned out that Fenwick was, too.

"You know, when we rode into Iradiem," he said, breaking the quiet, "I was excited. Part of the reason was I had no idea what to expect and did not anticipate it being as awful as it was. I also wanted a measure of revenge against the mage who enthralled me. As far as Beata, though, I have no illusions. I anticipate it will be just as difficult and disturbing, but in ways I probably haven't imagined."

"My feelings are similar," I responded in a soft voice. "My sense of duty compels me to go forward, though I wish we did not have to."

"Duty to the Goddess? Yes, I feel the weight of the debt I owe her for the gifts she has given me," Fenwick said.

"To the Goddess, but also to the people," I replied. "The Grand Vizier, the Bashaw of Mooresa, the king of Vanda—I like all of them. They are not quite friends but they could be, given time. And I remember seeing the people of Dunland recover their wits after being enthralled, and how disturbed they were. This mage has done the same on a much larger scale. I cannot turn my back on the people he has enslaved."

"True," Fenwick agreed.

"Finally, the Goddess would not have given us this task if it were beyond our abilities. I find that I need to remind myself of that fairly often."

"Sometimes I wonder if her judgment of what we can accomplish is over-optimistic," Fenwick said.

"Me, too. "

There did not seem to be much more to say. We passed the next hour or so quietly, studying the map of the city in the flickering light of the fire. I fell asleep quickly.

Bellona appeared in my dreams again, in all her fierce beauty. It was unlike my other visions of her. Instead, I began to feel a calm confidence that grew and grew. It was as though she were saying that, yes, our mission was difficult and dangerous, but she chose us as her champions—out of all the other people in the world whom she blessed.

When I woke, the gray light of false dawn was in the sky. I looked over and saw Fenwick starting to sit up. Our eyes met.

"We have a job to do," he said. "I am ready to get on with it."

I merely nodded. We broke camp and set off down the road. For the first time since leaving the river, we were no longer surrounded by forest.

Soon, we reached the first of the stubble-covered fields I had seen through Shasha's eyes. The sky was covered by a low, gray overcast, but it did not feel as though the clouds held rain. Fenwick and I proceeded in silence.

We stopped twice to let Andy and Davy crop the stubble by the road. When twilight started to fade, we halted again. Holding the lance to access its seemingly limitless power, I opened my link with Eir. Placing my hand on the chest of each animal in turn, I envisioned restoring their energy as I had seen Lucy do once before.

We dismounted in the middle of the night to allow the horses to graze for a bit before continuing. It was Fenwick's suggestion. He remarked that it might be a while before they had another chance to eat.

As darkness faded to the gray before the dawn, we could see the city of Beata roughly a league away. Once again, I restored the horses' energy but also did the same to Fenwick and myself. In addition, I fished two of the vials of elixir Lucy prepared for us and gave one to Fenwick.

"This is as good a reminder as any as to why we are doing this," he said after pulling the stopper from the neck of the bottle.

"What does it smell like to you?" I asked.

"Julienne," he responded, with a blush I could barely see in the dim light.

"Mine smells like Lucy's hair when I wake in the morning," I said. "Lucy told me the smell is different for everyone. It is who you love most."

"Aye. What a curious effect it has, though. You just restored my energy, but now I feel mentally sharp—as though we did not ride all night."

I suddenly saw us from above. Shasha was overhead. I accessed my link to her. She continued on, flying over the wall of the city.

No one was stirring yet. There were no people in the streets. She proceeded all the way to within sight of the Temple of the Three Major Gods, and there was no activity.

"Thank you, Shasha," I thought.

It is good. I will watch, she replied, then severed our communication.

Fenwick and I mounted and began to approach the city. By the time we neared the open gate, day was breaking. It would be another gray day.

Fenwick caught my eye and nodded. Instantly, he and Davy transformed in size as Fenwick opened his connection to the Goddess fully. He reached behind his head and withdrew Bellona's sword.

I followed suit, sliding the lance from under the fender of my saddle. This time, in addition to what I usually felt when I invited the Goddess to manifest herself through me, I also felt an unaccustomed exhilaration. The only factor to which I could attribute this was the elixir I just drank.

We made our way along the city streets. The only sound was that of Davy and Andy's shoes striking the cobbles. We saw the first person two furlongs past the gate. From his frightened reaction when he caught sight of us, I reckoned that he was not a thrall. I remembered the six horsemen who pursued Fenwick and me after we escaped Iradiem. They were not under his direct control, but they served the mage, coerced either by threats of punishment or promises of rewards.

We began to see other people in the streets. Some were thralls who did not react to our presence. Others bolted from fear.

My vision was taken over by a sight from above. I opened my link to Shasha. She showed me a group of men assembling on a side street roughly two blocks ahead of us.

"Thank you," I sent and dropped our connection.

"The second side street ahead, on the right," I warned Fenwick. "Men, armed with whatever they could lay hands on—sticks, mostly—no weapons."

"That's where we would turn to approach the Temple," Fenwick said. "But we can use the next street almost as easily. I would rather avoid them so that Davy and Andy don't need to change directions at speed on these cobbles."

We turned right at the next intersection, then left two streets further. When we reached the street where the men had been gathering, they were moving to intercept us but were too late. We turned to the right, leaving them behind.

Shasha broke into my vision again. When I connected with her, I could see another group forming in front of the steps of the Temple. Already, there were about twenty.

They were wearing light armor—breastplates and helmets—similar to ours in weight, but the helmets had a conical shape similar to the ones the Nagahny wore. Their chest armor was constructed of overlapping rows of iron scales instead of the solid pieces we were wearing. They were carrying swords. I saw no pikes and no archers, which was a relief. After I dropped communication with Shasha, I shared what I saw with Fenwick.

"As we hoped, the mage was not anticipating our arrival," Fenwick said. "Perhaps we will simply dance right in and eliminate him."

"Much as I would like that to be the case, dear friend, I am not getting my hopes up."

"Neither am I," Fenwick said with a grin.

We turned to the left. Ahead of us, we could see the Temple. In front of it, we saw the men. Others were joining them as we watched, moving with the placid pace of thralls.

"Before we reach them, we dismount and let the horses go," I suggested. "They will have a better chance on their own than if they stay with us."

"Agreed. I only hope they do, and don't try to accompany us regardless," Fenwick said.

"Andy is the smartest horse I've ever known," I replied, "and Davy is no dummy either. They'll get enough distance to protect themselves, though I'm willing to bet that they will be close enough to whistle for them when we are finished."

"I won't take that wager," Fenwick said.

We stopped about twenty yards short of the assembled soldiers. Fenwick and I dismounted with practiced ease. I slapped Andy on the rump to encourage him to scamper away. Fenwick did the same to Davy. Both horses trotted off— Andy to the right, Davy to the left. From the corner of my eye, I saw that they stopped when they felt they were out of danger.

Fenwick and I shared a look before we started for our foes. We both smiled. Turning to face the soldiers, I saw the dull red gleam deep in their eyes that was a telltale sign of their enthrallment. Their lack of reaction as Fenwick and I drew nearer was another. Both of us, with the Goddess manifest in us, appeared to be at least ten feet tall.

Though these soldiers were guilty of nothing more than being enslaved by the mage—a power they could not fight—I did not allow that thought to cloud my conscience. Later, when the fight was over, I could allow my compassion free rein. At the moment, they were only obstacles standing in the way of our objective.

By now, their numbers had increased to more than forty men. When Fenwick and I were five feet away, they moved forward toward us. With the Goddess fully present in me, I felt strangely relaxed mentally, though poised for physical action.

What followed was a bloody frenzy. The thralls had no fear. They advanced unflinchingly. As they did, Fenwick and I cut them down.

At one point, I saw Fenwick in the corner of my eye. His movements were swift, uncannily graceful, and lethal. Our earlier comments about dancing right up to the mage came back to me.

Fenwick and I are leading a dance with death, I thought with savage humor.

Bellona's lance moved almost of its own accord. My concerns over whether I would be able to wield it properly proved baseless. That is not to say I escaped injury.

With as many blades against me as there were, some slipped through. None of the wounds they delivered were serious. They hurt, of course, but they did not impair me. Fenwick did not escape unscathed either. I heard him grunt several times as a sword slipped through.

As we dispatched the soldiers in front of us, I became aware of others assembling at the top of the steps. This neither surprised me nor was it the cause of much concern. I knew the real challenge Fenwick and I would face was behind the massive entrance of the Temple.

Suddenly, there were no more foes immediately before us. Those at the top of the steps did not advance toward us. I looked at Fenwick. His face was blood-splattered, and his sleeves and breeches were both torn in spots and entirely blood-stained.

"Any important injuries?" I asked.

He nodded. "Here," he pointed to his upper left arm, "and here," he indicated his right thigh.

"Keep an eye on our friends," I said. "I'll stop the bleeding, at least."

I closed my connection with Bellona and opened the one to Eir. Fenwick held his left arm toward me. I could see the deep gash on his bicep. Holding my hand over it, I closed my eyes and pictured the wound healing. When I opened my eyes again, the wound was closed, leaving only a scar. I then did the same for his thigh.

When I finished with Fenwick, I attended to myself. I had been stabbed in my left side, just under my ribcage. It didn't seem like anything vital was damaged, but I did not want to take any chances. I also had a nasty slash on my right forearm and felt it beginning to hamper my movements. When I sensed the pain and weakness disappear, I closed my connection with the Goddess of healing and reopened that to the Goddess of War.

Those were not our only wounds. We sported a variety of cuts and gouges from calves to shoulders. None of mine hindered my ability to fight, and I suspected Fenwick's were of a similar lack of importance.

"Ready?" Fenwick asked.

We climbed the steps together. There were fewer men waiting than we faced earlier. As we approached the last riser, we attacked together.

10

There were twenty-eight more soldiers waiting for us. Fenwick and I waded into their midst. They enjoyed less success than their counterparts below.

When we dispatched them, Fenwick asked me to mend a deep gash on his right side. I received no wound worthy of attention. When I reopened my connection with Bellona and restored my larger-than-life appearance, Fenwick and I entered the Temple.

A throng of children was there, pleading with us in Combrian. I was fortunate that I did not understand the language. Immediately, I asked Bellona if that was truly what they were. For a brief glimpse, I saw the downtrodden thralls who had been abasing themselves on the floor before the mage. Now, they all held knives and were trying to surround us. Fenwick was slightly befuddled since he spoke Combrian and knew what they were saying. I noticed he lowered his blade.

"Fenwick, they're all adults with knives! It's an illusion!" I shouted as I began to swing my lance at those who approached the nearest.

Fenwick gave his head a shake and followed my lead. The children transformed into pitiful old women. I ignored their appearance. In the press of bodies, Fenwick and I were separated.

As I feared, suddenly, I was facing a horde of Fenwicks. I imagined he was seeing all of them as me. They all looked exactly like Fenwick, with the same ripped and bloodstained clothes.

"Duncan!" I called.

"Ariana!" he answered, and I knew which of the Fenwicks was true.

Immediately, the thralls called "Duncan" or "Ariana."

The thralls kept coming. I lost track of which one was truly Fenwick. He must have had the same problem.

"Mark!" he shouted.

"Lily!" I answered, and we knew which was the other.

We worked our way through Lucy & Julienne, Theo & Toby, and Freddy & Greta before the last of the thralls were slain. It was only then that we were able to turn our attention to the man sitting on the throne next to the altar. He was clad in robes of luxurious fabric, deep scarlet in color. His appearance was benignly magisterial, with flowing white hair and a trimmed white beard.

On the bloodstained and defiled altar, not far from him, was the dodecahedron. It radiated an unholy energy. It hurt my eyes and my head to gaze upon it.

Fenwick and I started to advance toward him. He held up his hand, and further movement became unbelievably difficult—far more arresting than what I had experienced in Iradiem. The mage smiled in a kindly and non-threatening way.

"Come now, friends," he said, his voice magnificently deep and mellow in timbre, "for we could be friends, the greatest friends possible. Why do you wish me ill when together we could rule the world? Both of you are touched by Bellona herself, bearing her ancient weapons. There is no doubt that you are the mightiest warriors in the entire world. I have no quarrel with your Goddess, yet you seek to kill me. What have I done to you?"

Neither of us could answer the question. We stood, silent. His words made sense. My mind was beginning to feel confused.

"Why, even with only one of you by my side, together, no one could oppose us," he said in a sly manner.

The words slid into my ears like the sweetest honey. I began to question why I wanted to kill him. Serving him did not seem evil, and I was prepared for evil. This sounded logical and sensible. If it had not been for Fenwick, I might have severed my connection to the Goddess.

But Fenwick chose to attack me.

He caught me by surprise, and it was all I could do to fend off his first blows. Fenwick's assault turned me so my back was to the mage. The fury of his onslaught pushed me toward the altar and the throne step by step.

Fenwick seemed to have lost his mind, and I was convinced that, somehow, he was under the mage's control. I worried that the time he was enthralled by the dark mage in Iradiem left him vulnerable to this one. From my rear, I could sense the mage's great pleasure at Fenwick's action.

It was then that I realized our freedom of movement was restored. The mage had stopped us from approaching, but now, as Fenwick forced me back, we drew nearer and nearer. I understood what Fenwick was trying to do.

By now, I recovered from my initial surprise and could have held Fenwick at bay. Instead, I gave ground slowly, inches at a time. I could not relax, though. Fenwick mixed thrusts with feints. He attempted a prise de fer, snarling angrily in my face when we were close. If I relaxed my guard, he would, at the very least, wound me severely.

For my part, I was shouting at him, "Fenwick! What are you doing? Have you gone mad? Fenwick, stop this at once! I am your prince, and I command you to drop your weapon! We must slay the mage, not serve him!"

Every one of my futile utterances seemed to please the mage behind me. I felt the first of the steps to the altar with my right foot. I climbed one step at a time, while Fenwick's sword and my lance whirled with inhuman speed.

When there were no more steps behind me, I knew we were only a few feet away from the altar. Fenwick's attacks grew more violent and vicious. I began to wonder if he really had fallen under the mage's sway.

Backward two steps more, and I felt the altar at my back. The mage began to laugh with delight, thinking I was about to die at Fenwick's hand. Suddenly, Fenwick's eyes dipped down as he raised his sword and swung as though to cleave my skull down the middle.

As the blade zipped toward my head, I dropped to my knees. Fenwick's almost indetectable sign to me told me he had a different target and I correctly guessed what it was. The sword of Bellona struck the dodecahedron and split it in two pieces.

There was the most incredible *crack*, as though a bolt of lightning struck the altar where the device was. Though I could not see from where I was, I sensed the bolt was not one of light, but one of the most intense darkness. I did see Fenwick flying backward, blasted away by the force of the paroxysm caused by the destruction of the device.

Fenwick sailed through the air until he hit one of the large columns. His body slid to the floor. From the way his head lolled, I knew he was knocked senseless.

"Nooooooo!" I heard the mage scream faintly through my ears, which were deafened by the thunderous crack a moment before.

Slowly, I began to draw myself up. First one leg, then the other, and I stood with wobbly knees. I turned to the mage.

His appearance was no longer human. He looked like a drawing I once saw that depicted one of the demons of the Seven Hells. Twelve feet tall—even taller than my Goddess-enhanced appearance—his body seemed to be made of red-hot coals from a fire. Flames licked along the edges of him. There were two fiery horns atop his head and a long, whip-like tail. Where his eyes should have been were two black pits. His hands and feet were huge, tipped with sharp black claws.

Everything about him radiated evil and menace. I lifted the lance to attack. The demon struck me with a backhand blow that knocked me off my feet and down the altar steps to the side. Where his hand hit me burned painfully.

I struggled to my feet as he came after me. Just as I stood, he swatted me again, with a forehand, toward the middle of the Temple floor. I tumbled over chunks of broken granite benches. Despite Bellona's power, again, I felt the searing burn where the demon stuck me. I sensed a couple of my ribs were broken from landing on the remains of the benches.

Again, I pulled myself to my feet just as he neared. He drew back his right hand to smite me, but I leaped out of the way, escaping his blow by the smallest amount. Any reprieve was short-lived. His tail whipped out and wrapped around my left ankle. He yanked me off my feet, dragging me over the broken benches.

He smacked me once more, sending me skidding across an open area of the filthy floor. I struck one of the columns with my shoulder, and Bellona's lance slipped from my grasp. Stunned by my impact with the column, I was slow to scramble after the lance. Crawling on all fours, I barely reached it and rolled onto my back as the demon prepared to strike me yet again.

From the ceiling of the enormous Temple, I saw a streak of reddish-brown darting directly for the monster's eye. At the last possible moment, the streak veered away, revealing it to be Shasha. The fiend swiped at the sparrowhawk, missing her only narrowly.

The distraction Shasha provided me allowed me to reach my feet. Turning his attention back to me, the demon aimed another blow. I ducked under at the last moment but sliced his right arm deeply as it whizzed over my head.

There was a gash of yellow fire where the bladed tip of Bellona's lance struck. The monster howled in rage and frustration. He struck me again, and I was late in moving. I slid across the floor.

The damned thing was on me before I could rise. I braced myself for the impact. The tiny reddish-brown tormentor flew at his eye again. While the demon swatted at Shasha, I stabbed him in the left leg.

I earned a backhanded wallop for that. My back slammed into one of the columns not far from where Fenwick lay. I could not breathe—my wind was knocked out of me.

As the monster's fist came flying at my head, I rolled away in the nick of time. The demon's left hand sank nearly a foot into the solid marble column. Even the floor trembled with the force of the blow.

The fiend cursed in a language I could not understand, then howled in pain and frustration. As I came to my feet, I saw his left leg dripping fiery yellow ichor from where I pierced his hide. As he stalked after me, I noticed a slight limp. His left hand was hanging by his side and not held at the ready the way his right was.

"I might bring the demon down eventually," I thought to myself, "but I'll be reduced to a sack of pomegranate seeds by then."

I was still gasping for air. My back hurt. My head was throbbing. Several ribs were cracked. Yet, I was on my feet, the lance in my hands.

It occurred to me that I was not afraid. I was slightly puzzled as to why I wasn't. This creature was the most fearsome thing I could ever imagine, but I was not scared. What I felt was anger. With the anger came a determination that I would not yield to this thing as long as I drew breath.

And it was a thing, no longer a man, I realized. Whatever humanity had once existed had departed from this unholy flesh. This was a creature of the Seven Hells.

I realized that even with all of Bellona's power, this thing was stronger. What I needed to be was quicker. When it approached again, I danced away from the blow he aimed at me and stabbed it in the right foot for his trouble.

He howled again with his head tilted back. By all the heavenly beings, I laughed. I was not trying to taunt the beast, but somehow, laughter was what my body generated at that moment.

As you might imagine, the creature did not appreciate my reaction to its pain and displeasure. It stormed after me. This time, my reaction was a trifle too slow. He grazed my head, sending me cartwheeling, but earned another gash on his arm in repayment.

The thing reached me before I could get off the floor. He lifted his foot to stomp on my head, but my tiny avian ally distracted the beast, flying directly at its eye again. I was able to roll out from under and clamber to my feet.

I managed to put a column between me and the thing. That bought me almost a minute of time to clear my head as we feinted and dodged around it. The monster grew annoyed with the game and ended it. He smashed the column in the middle, knocking it down with a thunderous crash.

I ran to the clear space in front of the altar steps. The beast came after me. I thought it moved more slowly, with the wound in its left leg and another in the right foot, but it might have been wishful thinking on my part.

The damned thing swiped at me with his right hand. I ducked and danced underneath and planted the razor-sharp, leaf-shaped blade of Bellona's lance in its right thigh. The blistering-hot yellow ichor bubbled from the wound.

I sank the tip of the lance more deeply than I intended and needed to tug it free. That gave the foul thing enough time to swing around and clout me as it screamed in anguish. The blow sent me in a somersault to the steps, with the lance flying out of my hand.

As I scrabbled to grab my weapon, I saw the creature's foot raise. Before he crushed me, he screeched in frustration again. Looking up as I regained the lance, I saw that he tried to swat something from his face.

I'd lost count of the number of times Shasha saved my life in this fight. My heart swelled with admiration for her bravery. Something so tiny, attacking something so huge and menacing, was courage like I never had seen.

I dashed behind another column. With a double-feint, I caught the demon off-balance. Darting forward, I slashed the back of its left leg where a hamstring would be in an earthly creature, thinking I might knock it to its knees.

No such luck. While I did open another deep gash, the monster stayed on its feet. He rewarded me for my effort with another swipe that sent me careening forward.

I fell on my face after several stumbling steps. As I fell, the lance flew from my hand. I crawled forward using the momentum of my staggering run. When I reached the lance, I grabbed it and turned to face the demon approaching.

He was closer than I expected. I held the lance up as if it could protect me from the blow I saw him preparing to unleash. The reddish-brown sparrowhawk came darting in. This time, to my great horror, the creature's hand connected with the bird, swatting it to the side with great force.

Something within me snapped. I became filled with righteous fury. Already appearing to be twice my normal size since the Goddess was manifest in me, suddenly I sensed that it was not merely an illusion—that my corporeal being was now just as large.

I attacked the monster, no longer feeling as though it was bigger or more powerful than I was. It lashed out with its hands and its tail, but I was too quick. Every attempt it made to strike me earned it another stab or slash.

The fiery yellow ichor oozed from a dozen places on its body and limbs. The thing's swipes at me became more clumsy. It was backing away from my savagery. I grinned with the smile of death, furious to avenge the death of my brave familiar.

The demon started suddenly. Its mouth gaped open in surprise. An instant later, I saw the point of a sword pop out of its chest. I seized the opportunity and slashed the throat of the foul thing with the bladed tip of the lance as the sword point withdrew.

Its head lolled back. The creature's hands scrabbled toward the ceiling. A moment later, almost too fast for the eye to capture it, Bellona's blade severed the demon's head from its neck. As the head tottered and fell, I heard the clatter of the sword hitting the stone floor.

The two pieces of the creature returned to human form. It was a man—a decidedly average man in appearance. He was not the majestic figure we saw earlier, nor the demon we fought.

A whirlpool of the deepest black opened up. It took the man's body first, then the head. I thought I saw a look of abject horror on the man's face as it swirled deeper into the abyss.

Then Fenwick's body seemed to be caught in the suction of the vortex of utter darkness. He started to slide within. I saw Bellona's sword lying on the floor—no longer in his hand. I leaped across.

"My hand, Fenwick! Take my hand, and don't let go, for the love of all!" I screamed.

We clasped wrists, his right in my left. My right hand was wrapped around the lance. The pull of the whirlpool was intense. Slick with blood and sweat, our hands began to slip. I was losing my grip on the shaft of the lance.

I begged Bellona for the strength to save us both. Fenwick's hand and mine no longer clasped the other's wrist. We were palm to palm and slipping more quickly. Only the ends of my fingers clung to the lance.

"Please, Goddess!" I moaned in despair.

11

With a snap, the vortex disappeared. Fenwick and I were lying on the grimy floor of the Temple. The Goddess had given us just enough strength to survive being pulled down to the Seven Hells.

Tears rolled down my cheeks, and I thanked the Goddess again and again. Despite our victory, I was filled with the deepest sadness. I began to crawl painfully in the direction where I thought I would find Shasha's body.

She was behind the altar. One wing lay awkwardly on the ground. To my amazement, she was still alive. As I scrambled to her, I opened my link to her. I started to open my connection to Eir, but Shasha quieted me.

It is fated, she communicated to me. *My body is beyond repair. The Gods allowed my heart to beat only so we could say farewell. Do not be sad, my mate, for I am not. I have no regrets. What is fated, must be.*

Our connection ended. The reddish-brown mote within me was there no more. I picked up her broken body and held it tenderly in my hands as I sat, keening in anguish. Even in the most difficult periods of my life, I had never felt such loss.

Fenwick found me. He sat next to me and put his arm around my shoulders without saying a word. I leaned my head on his shoulder and cried like I never cried before.

It was later that I noticed we were no longer manifesting the Goddess. I checked within myself and the link was present but not open. I wondered when or how that happened. With a deep sigh, I opened it a small amount.

"What should I do to honor my friend?" I asked the Goddess in a silent prayer.

Instantly, the face of the priestess Leora came to mind. I wondered if that meant I needed to return to the Temple in Nagah. Leora again captured my thoughts, but not the Temple.

"Help me find something to wrap her in until we see the priestess," I asked Fenwick.

He nodded. He stood and helped me up, as my hands still held Shasha. Both of us moved stiffly and slowly. Even when Nils Pedersen had one of his men beat me for hours I did not feel as bad as I did now.

As we passed the altar, I saw the dodecahedron split in half. I made a mental note that we should have the pieces smelted down so no one could ever restore it. We retrieved the sword and the lance.

"Hold a moment, Fenwick," I said.

With my hand on the lance, I felt Bellona's numina fill me. I opened my connection to Eir. Before I started on myself, I turned to Fenwick.

"Where are you hurt the worst?" I asked.

"My head."

"Can the rest wait?"

"Yes."

"Hold her, please."

Fenwick gently took Shasha's body from me. I placed my hands over the back of his head, where I saw it strike the column after he destroyed the dodecahedron. There was a sense of serious damage—his skull was cracked, and blood was clotting underneath.

Using the ability Eir granted me, I healed both problems. It took several minutes. I realized that without the power in the lance, I would not have been able to save him from dying as a result of this injury. The thought made me weep anew.

"What's wrong?" he asked.

"The blow to your head would have killed you in a short time," I said wearily. "Without the lance and Bellona's strength, I could not have prevented it. I could not lose you, too."

"Thank you," he replied, his voice suddenly husky.

"Lucy would have been mad at me for hours, if I let that happen," I tried to joke, with my voice cracking.

"Sit down and take care of yourself," he said, the ghost of a smile on his lips.

I did just that, feeling for the most burned and battered areas of my body, and using Eir's ability to heal them. Fenwick sat next to me, cradling Shasha's body. We were there nearly an hour before I felt I'd done enough for the time being. Both Fenwick and I would need further attention, but there would be plenty of time for that later.

He handed Shasha back to me once I stood. We turned toward the entrance. The sight before our eyes was horrific. There were nearly a hundred bodies on the floor—the miserable thralls who were prostrating themselves before the mage for his sick amusement. He'd put knives in their hands and used them to attack us, forcing us to slaughter them all. I felt even more sick at heart.

"I'm glad you figured out my attacking you was a ruse," Fenwick said. "Otherwise, you would have chopped me into ribbons. That lance is a frightening weapon the way you wield it."

"It did take me a moment, but I will concede that it was a brilliant idea. There was no other way we could have regained freedom to move," I said as we exited the Temple.

Returning to the outside did not improve the view. Here were the soldiers we'd killed, with even more at the foot of the steps. We picked our way through the bodies and began climbing down to the street. Fenwick whistled loudly three times.

By the time we reached the street, Davy came walking up. Andy followed not far behind. Fenwick went to his saddlebag and pulled out one of his shirts. He held it out for me, to place Shasha's body in it. When I did, he wrapped her up carefully and stowed the bundle in his bag.

"Now what?" I asked.

"Now, you pull two vials of that elixir out, and we drink them," he said. "Eir is marvelous for the physical, but Lucy's elixir is what we need for our minds and spirits."

I went to Andy and rummaged in my saddlebag to find two more of the small vials. Handing one to Fenwick, I unstopped the other. I took a deep whiff of the contents, smelling Lucy's hair. Just the scent helped dispel some of the gloom I was feeling. I drank it and felt even better.

"I'm going to look for thralls who were priests of the Three Majors," Fenwick said. "If Beata is anything like what I saw in Iradiem, or we both observed in Dunland, most people are frozen in place right now. We can bring them back with our wards, but it will go much faster if we can free some priests."

"Where will you find them?" I asked, genuinely curious.

"From what we saw of this mage, I think they will be close by," Fenwick said. "He made sure to desecrate the Temple. It's reasonable to guess he would make the priests his personal slaves for humiliation, torment, or torture—though if he tortured them, probably none would still survive. Let's hope that's not the case. If they are not here, then they might be at the palace if the mage took it over for himself."

We did not find any priests near the Temple. The residential building where the priests would live was a disgusting mess but devoid of people. We rode to the palace, not far away.

Along the way, we saw dozens of people frozen in place. We also spotted a few capable of movement, but they skittered away when they saw us. These were people who pledged their allegiance to the mage without needing to be enthralled. I imagined most did it from fear, but there were always some people who would ally themselves with evil if they thought they would benefit.

We saw several more of this type when we arrived at the palace. As before, they ran when they saw us. Of course, Fenwick and I did present a rather scary appearance, covered in blood as we were, clothes torn, and, in my case, singed.

"You!" Fenwick shouted at the next one we encountered. "Stop, or I'll be forced to kill you!"

The man stopped. Then, he seemed to think again. He was leaning forward, and I could tell he was preparing to bolt.

"If I have to chase you, I will kill you slowly and painfully!" Fenwick yelled.

The man stayed where he was. Fenwick walked up to him. After looking him up and down, Fenwick leaned in close to the man's face.

"You, my friend, have much to answer for," Fenwick sneered. "You know that once they are free of the mage's spell, your countrymen will remember that you betrayed them. What was your price, eh?"

The man did not answer. He stood silently, his lip quivering in fear. Fenwick gave him a look of pure disgust.

"Where are the priests?" Fenwick demanded.

"I don't know what you are talking about," the man stammered.

Crack! Fenwick slapped him across the face. "Try again to remember."

"They're below," the man blubbered. "In the cells. The master—"

"Your 'master' is no more," Fenwick whispered in a nasty tone. "I cut his head off. A black whirlpool sucked him down to the Seven Hells, where he will endure an eternity of torment for failing the Dark Lord. Where are the keys to release the priests?"

"I—I can get them."

"We will all go," Fenwick said menacingly, eliminating the man's feeble hope of trying to escape.

Our captive did not need to go fetch the keys. He had them on a ring attached to his belt. Fenwick slapped him again when we learned that.

We found eleven priests of the Three Major Gods in the dungeon of the palace. All of them were pale and thin, with bruises everywhere. None of them had been enthralled.

"He wanted us to feel every punishment," one said.

His name was Lukas, and he had been second to the head priest of the Temple that the mage desecrated. He told us that the head priest was dead. The dark mage had flayed the priest on the altar. Hearing that made me wince.

Fenwick quickly explained that the dark mage was dead, but the people he enthralled were still in the hold of the spell he cast. Lukas nodded in understanding. Fenwick requested the help of the priests in freeing the people.

"I don't know the spell—I mean, I don't have it memorized—but I do know where to find it," Lukas said. "Of course we will help. We must."

"Thank you," Fenwick said.

"No, it is we who should thank the two of you."

"Be that as it may," I said after Fenwick translated, "the Goddess Eir has blessed me with her ability. If any of you are injured in such a way that it will—"

"We are bruised and battered," Lukas said, "but the two of you look like you require Eir's assistance more than we. Most of what we suffered was in the form of degradation at the hands of the mage and his minions. Providing us the opportunity to serve the Three Major Gods again will be ample salve for those types of wounds. How can we help you, our redeemers?"

"We both need a hot bath," Fenwick said, "but it can wait. We have our own food and should have no problem finding a bed for the night. You need to help us begin freeing the people."

Lukas called the other priests together and explained. I noticed the man who brought us here and unlocked the cells had disappeared while we spoke with Lukas. There was nothing we could do about him. Others would serve him his just desserts in time.

Together, we all left the palace. We returned to the Temple with the priests on foot while Fenwick and I rode. Lukas and the other priests gasped when they saw the dead heaped at the foot of the steps.

"How did you—?"

"We are blessed by the Goddess Bellona," Fenwick explained. "We carry her sacred weapons."

He gestured to the sword on his back and the lance.

"Praise all the heavenly beings!" Lukas and the other priests said.

They left us and scurried back to the residential part of the temple complex. Fenwick and I dismounted. He took a seat on the stone wall that paralleled the street and connected to the steps. He patted the space next to him. We sat together, keeping the dead out of our line of sight.

"Um, thank you for saving my life at least twice today," Fenwick murmured.

"You're welcome," I replied equally quietly.

"I missed most of it—from when I struck the thing until just before I stabbed the demon in the back, actually. How bad was it?"

"I wish I could make a joke about it," I said. "That would be normal for us. I can't. Shasha saved my life five times, each time attacking the creature just as it was about to crush me. The last time…"

Fenwick patted my shoulder.

"I wish you could have seen it, Fenwick," I said with my voice choking from emotion. "Such unflinching bravery deserves to be remembered by more than just one person. People should sing songs about her, instead of about me. Five times, she launched herself at the thing, streaking right for its eyes. The last time, the demon finally hit her."

"So much courage in such a small body," Fenwick commented after a pause.

"She fought to stay alive so that we could say our farewells."

"Perhaps one day, I will gain a familiar," he said. "When I do, I know I will understand your grief more fully. For now, I can only guess, but seeing your anguish tells me it is a terrible, terrible loss."

"I would not begrudge you a familiar," I said. "It is a wonderful thing to have such a bond. But I will hope that you never experience pain like this."

"Tell me what happened when I struck the object," Fenwick requested a few minutes later.

I shared what I saw and felt. Fenwick did not experience the cataclysm that followed when he split the device with Bellona's sword. He did not remember being launched into the air, only to smash into a column.

I then described my battle with the beast. Fenwick could see where the thing struck me, as my clothing was singed—in some places, there were burned holes. He also told me some of my hair was burned away.

"You'll need a proper haircut before you see Lucy," he teased.

"She was mad at you when you made me cut my hair for our visit to Rhetia," I remarked.

"I am well aware," Fenwick said. "After she and Julienne rescued us, she threatened to turn me into a newt if I did it again."

"She must have been quite upset, then," I said. "You're in good company, though. Sir Oliver West is the only other person she has threatened with that particular consequence."

"The Principal of the City Watch? But he's only a baronet, where I am the Earl of the Eastern March."

"Said the jumped-up orphan of no particular parentage," I joked.

"That crack would have wounded me deeply if it had not come from the Bastard Prince," Fenwick teased.

"Is that what people call me?"

"Eh, some do," Fenwick said. "You know the type."

Indeed, I did know the type. These same people had shunned me for my whole life. It used to bother me… I suppose it still did, but I tried not to let it.

"Sorry," Fenwick said.

"Unnecessary. I consider the source."

That night, we erected our tent in a small park near the Temple of the Three Major Gods. After we finished our evening meal of salt pork stew (by now, we heartily wished for a change of menu, but it was all we had), it started to rain more heavily than we had experienced on our journey to this point.

The sound of the raindrops pelting the oiled canvas of the tent lulled me to sleep despite all the many things on my mind. The Goddess appeared in my dreams.

I felt a mix of emotions from her. She was satisfied that Fenwick and I accomplished our task. More than that, I felt she was proud of us and pleased that she had chosen us as her champions. Mixed in with those feelings, I sensed a degree of sorrow for Shasha.

The Goddess faded away, and I woke to a crisp, clear morning. Fenwick stirred at nearly the same time. From looking at him, I knew the Goddess visited his dreams as well. When we spoke about it, what we felt from her was similar. He, of course, did not feel any sorrow emanating from Bellona, but he had no reason to.

12

The next few days were strange. The priests fanned out immediately a few hours after returning to the Temple once Lukas found the proper incantation to revive those who were enthralled. He asked for our help in only one thing. There were three other Temples of the Three Major Gods in the city. Lukas was sure the other priests were imprisoned somewhere.

He showed us on our map where the gaols were where the priests would likely be found. Fenwick and I freed another eighteen priests. None of them had been enthralled. The dark mage allowed them to retain their wits so their humiliation and despair would be undiminished. Those we found in the gaols were forced to serve some of the people in the city who followed the dark mage of their own free will.

Together with Lukas and his men, the priests we freed worked tirelessly for two days. They hurried to bring the people of the city out of the nightmarish state of enthrallment. After we found and released the priests, we learned that the mage killed the king and queen of Combrial, along with their children, when he took power. There was hope that one of the king's cousins survived, but that was unknown at the moment.

"Our work here is done," Fenwick said. "Why are we staying? We should return to our soldiers."

"I am waiting for the head priestess, Leora, to come," I said.

"Why?"

"I asked Bellona what I should do to honor Shasha. The Goddess indicated Leora would know. I considered riding to meet her or riding north to meet our people, but I believe they are all coming here. All of them know we were successful. If you wish to leave, you won't upset me."

"I think we have both spent a sufficient time in the cold and wet, and slept on the ground enough nights, that I am content to stay," Fenwick said. "I was only curious, not afflicted by wanderlust."

We watched as the city returned to life, day by day. Fenwick and I found an inn where the owner took us in—eagerly—after one of the priests informed him that we were the two who killed the mage. We finally had the chance to bathe and change into clean clothing. Using Eir's ability, I healed our other wounds. The most difficult were the burns the demon inflicted upon me when he hit me.

Exactly a week after we slew the mage, Leora arrived with three acolytes. Lukas told her where Fenwick and I might be found. We were preparing to sit for dinner when she strode in.

"Congratulations and well done!" she said. "We knew the instant when you slew the mage. All of the thralls froze. Priests of the Three Major Gods have been fanning out from the border, freeing people as quickly as they can. The weather is not our friend, though. Some of the enthralled will probably die of the cold before the priests reach them."

"Leora," I asked, using Fenwick to translate, "I have an unusual request I must make."

I then explained about Shasha. Leora herself once had a familiar, so she understood the bond I'd shared with the sparrowhawk. I told her of Shasha's courage and daring, saving me from imminent death, and how she died.

"The Goddess indicated you would know how I could—"

"Such a brave, brave bird!" Leora said quietly. "I would like our loremaster to hear the tale. He did not come, and I know you must leave soon, so will you promise to write it down and send it to us? Someone will be able to translate it when we receive it."

"I'm touched that you think it is worthy of remembrance," I said.

"We have a compendium of such tales," she explained. "The courage and loyalty of our familiars in the worst of times is sometimes as heroic as anything people have done. Do you still have her body?"

"Yes," Fenwick responded.

"We have a ceremony that we perform, calling upon our Goddess and all the other heavenly beings to guide her passage to whatever awaits her. Would you like us to conduct one for Shasha?"

"Yes, please," I said as tears rolled down my cheeks anew.

Leora and her acolytes joined us for dinner after we received permission from the innkeeper. He had told us earlier that his supplies were limited to what he had stored since none of the markets were yet open. Dinner turned out to be a thick pea soup with chunks of salt pork and root vegetables. It was hearty, served in satisfying quantity, and tasty. Then again, I am fondest of simple dishes prepared well.

When we finished eating, she sent the acolytes away on errands while she stayed to chat. We were able to share the more comprehensive version of what took place in the Temple. She interrupted us several times to ask questions. When we finished, she asked us again to describe what happened when Fenwick smote the dodecahedron.

"As our loremaster told you, we believe that the device provided a direct link to the Dark Lord. As such, we believe it might have allowed him access to our plane of existence," Leora explained.

"What does that mean?" I asked.

"When you access the numina of Bellona, her power is confined by your body—limited by the boundaries of your physical form," Leora explained. "Imagine if it were not—that the power which you accessed could leave your body, floating free. It could then find a new host who possessed the proper affinity."

"You think that some of the Dark Lord's numina is loose?" Fenwick asked in order to understand what Leora said better.

"We do," Leora said, "and it is now unable to return to the Seven Hells. After identifying the dodecahedron, our loremaster delved further into the records. The last time we know that anyone encountered such an object was several hundred years ago. A mage blessed by Andvar smashed it with the relic known as Andvar's Hammer. For a generation afterward, dark mages appeared with much greater frequency than usual. They were stronger, too, according to the records."

"What about the mage who attacked your borders and the other who took Iradiem? Would they be part of this greater proliferation?" I asked.

"I do not believe so," Leora said. "In the case of these two, I believe the dodecahedron acted as a beacon for those with an affinity for the Dark Arts. They were drawn to it, and it awakened their abilities. The dark mage here provided training to some degree. Chances are, if the device did not exist, they would have lived their lives never knowing of their affinity."

"Would you expect this outbreak to be limited to the southern continent?" Fenwick inquired.

"No. The reports make mention of the same thing happening in the northern continent and also far to the east, beyond the realms of the horse nomads," Leora said. "We have no information from the lands far across the ocean to the west, but it would be no surprise to learn they struggled with the same problem."

"May I ask if it is known how long the dodecahedron was in existence before Andvar's Hammer destroyed it?" I asked.

"I do not know the answer so will ask the loremaster," she said. "But while I am not certain, I think it was a span of years. The loremaster said the darkness came from far to the east. It probably took years for the mage's power to spread far enough to reach us on the southern continent. We know the one who destroyed it was from somewhere in the east, not from the southern continent or Aquileia. Why do you ask?"

"My next question will tell you why," I said. "How long do you think this dodecahedron was in existence?"

"Ah!" she said, understanding my line of reasoning. "Not quite a year, I believe. You think that the shorter amount of time it was used would lessen the amount of dark numina that escaped?"

"I do—at least, I hope so," I said. "Fenwick and I have now battled two mages of the Dark Arts in the last few months, and another less than two years before that. Even though that one was the least skilled of the three, both of us nearly succumbed to his power. I have no desire to fight another in my lifetime."

"That is greatly to be desired, Prince Casimir," she said, "but I am not so optimistic."

"When you say that the device resulted in more frequent appearances of dark mages, what does that mean?" Fenwick asked.

"Here on the southern continent, a dark mage generally appears once a generation—every thirty or forty years. It is probably the same in Aquileia," Leora said. "In the thirty years after the last dodecahedron was encountered and destroyed, a dark mage would appear every three or four years."

"So, it's not dozens popping up everywhere all at once," Fenwick summarized.

"One every three years is ten times more frequent than one every thirty," Leora said.

"This adds new urgency to Lucy and Lily's desire to find another person who has affinity with Ceridwen Sospita," I remarked to Fenwick.

"One blessed by the white witch would be an invaluable ally," Leora said after Fenwick translated my comment. "The strategy of actively searching for those with the affinity instead of waiting for them to reveal themselves is something we should pursue, but an important question remains: who will train them, if they are found?"

"Our queen has spent her life learning more about her abilities and has searched for information throughout Aquileia," I said. "The need to keep the forces of the Dark Lord at bay transcends national boundaries. I am certain she would be willing to train anyone from the southern continent along with anyone we find."

"I will share that idea with the head priests of the other Temples of the Minor Gods on the southern continent," Leora said. "Freyja's people will be the most important, as only those blessed by Freyja have the ability to perceive the auras of others. That you found the priests of the Three Major Gods here in the city alive and their minds free gives me reason to hope the priests at the other Temples here in Combrial were dealt with in a similar fashion. If they do not survive, we will need to ask the priests of Freyja's Temple in Aquileia for assistance."

"What about Rhetia?" Fenwick asked. "They do not believe in the Gods. They only acknowledge their one. What would happen if a mage of the Dark Arts arose in Rhetia?"

"It has happened several times in the past," Leora said. "In fact, we believe that their false religion was begun by a dark mage in order to control Rhetia more easily, and to turn the people against the true Gods."

"Really?" Fenwick asked incredulously.

"Think how simple it would be for a single dark mage to gain control of their church," Leora said. "He or she would then have the whole country under his sway without needing to enthrall a single person."

"That's—diabolical," I murmured when Fenwick translated. "It also makes perfect sense." To Fenwick, I asked, "How do we not know this?"

"The old empire controlled most of the northern half of this continent," Leora explained, "even Nagah for a few hundred years, when the strength of the empire was its greatest. Across the Surrounded Sea, well, Aquileia was the home of—and I mean no offense—illiterate barbarians wearing animal skins. The empire possessed the knowledge of centuries. And though much was lost when it fell, some still remains. Even though we live under different rulers now, the caretakers of the Temples of the Minor Gods have always remained in communication with one another, maintaining and sharing our knowledge. Aquileia has grown and matured since the fall of the empire and now eclipses the nations to its south in power."

"But not in knowledge," I suggested.

"No. Your Temples of the Minor Gods were established by disciples from the southern continent. I do not mean by this that Aquileians were ignorant of the Gods—they were not. Long, long before the fall of the empire, there were already Temples of the Three Major Gods in Aquileia. Even when your people were crude and unsophisticated, they understood the true nature of the cosmos. There were shrines for the Minor Gods. The disciples from the south helped convert them into the Temples that exist today. It is unsurprising that there is not the same depth of knowledge in the north."

"Ceridwen Sospita was an Aquileian," I offered.

"She was indeed," Leora agreed. "Here is an area where Aquileia may exceed the south in knowledge. In the years to come, I believe we would all benefit from that knowledge."

"Should we consider establishing a Temple for Ceridwen Sospita?" I asked.

"She is not a member of the Pantheon," Leora said, "so a Temple would not be proper. A school, however, would be of use to all humanity. There is a saying that the more knowledge is shared, the more it increases."

"How long do you think it will be before we see another dark mage appear?" Fenwick asked.

"Who can say?" Leora replied. "Certainly, within three or four years, if history is any guide. It could be that the person arises somewhere other than in Aquileia or on the southern continent. There are the nations of the horse nomads and a small kingdom on their eastern border. Further to the east is a much larger realm on the other side of a vast desert. Then there are the lands across the western ocean."

"Wouldn't the mage appear closer to here since the dodecahedron was here?" I asked.

"Perhaps, but perhaps not," Leora said. "Remember, geographic distance is no impediment to the supernatural. On the other hand, the Dark Lord is spiteful and vicious. He might greatly desire vengeance against those who thwarted his latest attempt."

"Are Fenwick and I cursed, then?" I asked, after having the opportunity to consider what she said.

From the look of Fenwick's face when I said this, I could tell he was thinking the same thing. I thought of Lucy, pregnant with our first child. How could I avoid exposing them to the danger that seemed sure to pursue me?

"No, you are blessed," Leora countered with a puzzled expression. "Bellona has chosen the two of you to be her champions. It is an honor very few mortals have ever been granted."

"Does it mean that we will spend the rest of our lives pursued by the agents of the Dark Lord and responsible for protecting humanity from them?" Fenwick asked, taking the words out of my mouth.

"Ah! Now I understand your concern," Leora said. "Dark mages will arise where they will, as I explained before. None of them will know of you. And though the Dark Lord may desire revenge, he does not know where you are because you severed his conduit to our plane of existence. As far as protecting all of humanity, you have been chosen as Bellona's champions. If your assistance is required, you will give it freely."

"What if—?" Fenwick started to say.

"You will wish to help," Leora said. "Bellona would not have chosen you otherwise. And you will not be alone. Bellona is not the only Minor God. In times of crisis, the other members of the Pantheon will choose champions as well. Remember, the last dodecahedron before this was destroyed by the Hammer of Andvar, not by Bellona's champion."

"What other Gods will—?" Fenwick began.

"All of them," Leora said. "Some, like Freyja, Andvar, Mielvanir, and Mentula, choose champions with martial skills. Freyja's spear, Andvar's hammer, Mielvanir's sword, and Mentula's scythe are formidable weapons."

"Will we meet these other champions?" I asked.

"That is unlikely," Leora said. "There is no record of the champions of the different Gods working in concert with one another. In fact, the two of you are unique in history in that respect."

"Oh," Fenwick said, his face showing slight disappointment.

"You would like to meet them?" Leora asked with a broad smile on her lips.

"Of course," Fenwick answered. "Think of what a team we would make!"

"It is probably for that very reason that it will not happen," Leora advised. "Together, you would be too powerful, and you are only human."

"What do you mean?" I asked.

"If the champions of the Minor Gods assembled, who could oppose them?" Leora asked. "All of you would be tempted to use that power."

"I would hope I could resist that temptation," I said, "but I have no desire to test myself."

"A wise answer," Leora said. "It is growing late. We will conduct the ceremony for your familiar at first light. One of the acolytes will wake you. Sleep well, champions. The Goddess is well-pleased with you both."

13

We walked to the small park near the Temple of the Three Major Gods. Leora's acolytes supplied a small wooden box in which we placed Shasha's broken body. The acolytes had also prepared a small pyre, suitable in size for a sparrowhawk.

Leora prayed aloud to Bellona, asking her to guide Shasha to a blessed existence in the afterlife. She then called upon me to tell Bellona of the bird's courage. Fenwick translated what I said into Nagahny.

By the time I finished, my tears were flowing freely. Looking around our small group, everyone had wet cheeks. Leora collected tears from all of us with her fingertip, wiping them on the lid of the box after each person. Leora then called upon Bellona to see our tears as testimony to a brave animal's courage and sacrifice. She then asked me to say my farewell.

"Farewell, Shasha. Thank you for saving my life so many times and for bringing me such happiness from being bonded with you. May the hunting always provide you with a worthy challenge. Farewell."

Leora placed the box on top of the pyre. She prayed again to Bellona, then asked me to kindle a flame. I used the tip of my finger and applied it to one of the bottom corners of the small pyre. It caught flame quickly, and spread.

In minutes, the box was consumed by the fire. Shortly afterward, I felt as though a weight lifted from my heart. I would never forget Shasha, but I no longer felt sad.

The next day saw the arrival of the Castle Shield and the allied soldiers from Scaramouche, Garo, Mooresa, Vanda, and Hier. A scout arrived at the main Temple of the Three Major Gods ahead of the group. One of the acolytes ran and warned Fenwick and me.

The rulers of the different countries, freed from the control of the mage, were riding in the van with Colonels Driscoll and Yankton. The Castle Shield followed immediately behind the rulers. The allied soldiers were behind them. When the Castle Shield saw the two of us, they broke into song.

Though we found it hard to believe,
Easton and the Prince had to leave,
"Stand fast, you men," is what they said
"We must cut off a mage's head."
Ditches filled with foes relentless
We prayed our prince would find success.
Then Easton swung his magic sword,
Sent the mage to the Dark Lord.

Under the colonel's firm commands,
They died by thousands at our hands,
With arrows, swords, and mural lance,
If they had wits, they'd shit their pants.
Still on they came in rank and file
Bodies heaped up in a huge pile.
We burned the bodies, soaked in oil
To clear some space for next day's toil.

"A new verse!" I nudged Fenwick in the ribs. "And it's about you!"

"It's about time," Fenwick sniffed haughtily, then ruined the effect by laughing. "How did they find out it was me, though?"

"What do you want to bet they have two versions—one for you and one for me, in case I did it?"

"I won't take that wager," Fenwick said. "The second verse is the new chorus, I think. I'm glad they kept the 'shit the pants' line, though. It's my favorite."

"Mine, too," I agreed. "I'm also happy I'm not the focus anymore."

"Until they learn that I spent most of the fight senselessly slumped against a column," Fenwick said.

"I'm certainly not going to tell them," I said.

Colonel Driscoll and Colonel Yankton saluted us. The rulers were not content with only a gesture. All of them dismounted and rushed over to Fenwick and me. Each, in turn, embraced and kissed me, doing the same to Fenwick. All were speaking at once. My ears were assaulted by the cacophony of five different languages.

All of them, including the emir of Garo, were effusive in their gratitude. It took Fenwick some time to get them to calm down and speak one at a time. All five of them, along with large numbers of their soldiers, were enthralled by the dark mage when they met the force from Combrial in the initial encounter.

They all described it as being in a horrible dreamlike state—powerless to wake and end the nightmare. Fenwick and I knew this from our own experience. The mage forced them to observe every battle. They had to watch as their enthralled soldiers attacked those still free of the mage's control, with many of both dying each day.

Fenwick and I left the inn to join the Castle Shield in their bivouac outside the city. We said our farewells to Leora and Lukas, wishing them well. I especially thanked Leora for the ceremony for Shasha.

Before we left the city, I asked the innkeeper if he knew where we might find enough ale for two thousand men. It turned out he did. He took us to a brewery that was just reopening.

The owner had been enthralled by the mage. He had only vague recollections of what he did during that time. He thought he had been sent to work in the fields for the harvest and then brought back to work as someone's servant, but he couldn't say for certain.

In any event, he was happy to sell us fifty kegs of ale. Fenwick haggled with the man regarding the difference in value between Aquileian coin and Combrian, but eventually they agreed on a price of ten ducats.

Fenwick and I rode into camp. We left the train of seven wagons carrying kegs of ale out of sight of the men. I went to find Colonel Driscoll immediately.

"Colonel, I took the liberty of purchasing fifty kegs of ale for the men," I said. "I am sure they deserve a reward after this ordeal. The wagons are down the road. When would you like me to bring them in?"

"Let's arrange a guard detail," Driscoll said. "The men will enjoy this, but we should wait until they've eaten dinner before we begin the drinking. I'll admit, I won't mind having some myself."

Driscoll found Sergeant Hewko and quickly and quietly informed him of our impending delivery. Hewko understood the need for guards and went off to arrange it. I rode back with Fenwick to where the wagons waited.

When we returned, word had already spread of what we were bringing. The men saw us leading the procession of wagons and broke into cheers. They began singing the song again.

A few hours later, I never saw so many people eat so quickly. No one, as a rule, eats more quickly than soldiers, but this was like nothing else I'd ever seen. Colonel Driscoll, Colonel Yankton, Fenwick, and I had barely begun eating when men came, hoping to clear our dishes away. Sergeant Hewko had informed everyone that the kegs would not be tapped until everything from the evening meal was properly tidied up. Not wanting to torture the soldiers, we tried to hurry. As soon as Fenwick, the last of us to finish, laid his fork down, the men whisked everything away.

Less than five minutes later, a cheer rose from where the kegs were. The men started singing the song again, adding, "Huzzah! Huzzah! Huzzah! Huzzah!" to the end of each stanza. Two men came to the table where we sat, holding mugs of ale for us.

"Sar'nt's compliments," they said.

We raised our ales in a silent toast and drank. Colonel Driscoll and Fenwick both began to speak at once. Realizing that, they both stopped, waiting for the other to resume. After a pause, they both spoke in unison again. We all laughed.

"I'll claim rank," I said. "Tell us what you endured after we left?"

"We reached the defile we chose for the first set of fortifications," Driscoll said. "There was enough time to do a proper job of it, and to establish redoubts on the hills on either side. When we finished, we sent messengers to the front lines, ordering them to fall back. We left two ramps in place over the ditch for that purpose. Once the men were across, we excavated those sections overnight."

"The thralls arrived midmorning the next day," Yankton said. "They stopped just out of bowshot and just stood dumbly for a couple of hours. Then they began to move. Into the woods they went, coming out with bundles of sticks in their arms. They started forward."

"As soon as they came within range, our archers began firing arrows at them. We killed nearly a hundred of them before they stopped. They just stood as the rain began to fall, and stayed there until sometime in the night. Under the cover of the darkness and rain, they began throwing the bundles of sticks into the ditch. They tossed the dead bodies of their comrades in as well. We had torches, so we could see what they were doing, but not well enough to shoot accurately."

"I didn't want to waste the arrows," Driscoll said. "We knew we would receive more from Iradiem but didn't know when or how many. I reckoned when they filled the ditch with sticks, they would attack. We waited until they were almost done, then tossed some of our torches over. It would have been a merry bonfire under other circumstances. That stopped them the first night. They did the same thing the next two days and nights. The fourth day is when things started to become uglier."

"What did they do?" I asked.

"Groups of their soldiers marched within bowshot. We fired and killed them all. Then they sent more. They kept this up for half the day, then they stopped. That night—another dark and rainy night—we could hear them approaching the ditch in front of our ramparts. They were dragging the bodies up and rolling them into the ditch in certain places, trying to build causeways with the corpses to reach the ramparts. Again, we waited until they were nearly level with the top of the ditch. Then we dropped pots of oil on the mounds they made and cracked them open by throwing bricks. When each pile was soaked with oil, we lit it."

"That was what we feared we would need to do," I said. "How did our people react?"

"Thank all the heavenly beings it was the middle of the night," Driscoll said. "Even so, it was disturbing. The sound, the smell… Only those on duty atop the ramparts that night really saw it. The rest of the soldiers knew what was happening, but they didn't see it with their own eyes."

"Did it work?" Fenwick asked. "Did it clear the ditch?"

"It did," Colonel Yankton said. "When morning came, only the bones were left. The enemy did not know that. They began an advance. Our archers fired as fast as they could, but some of the thralls reached the ditch. As soon as they did and saw that their effort to fill it failed, the assault stopped."

"Did they come back that night?" I asked.

"Yes, they did. They hauled the bodies of the dead from the field and heaped them in the same spots as the night before. We lit them on fire again. In the morning, the places where they piled the bodies the previous two nights were half-filled with the bones," Yankton explained. "I issued one of the most unpleasant orders I can imagine I will ever give. We ordered the men to quickly weave some large nets out of rope. Then, we sent men into the ditch to remove the skeletons. Some of the bodies were not completely consumed by the fires."

"While our men were clearing the trenches, the enemy tried to advance again. Our archers kept them away from the ditches but we were running out of arrows," Driscoll said. "If they pressed the attack the next day, they would reach the ditch. That night, they rolled their corpses into the ditch, and we burned them as we did before."

"This sounds horrible," Fenwick commented.

"It was," Yankton agreed.

"The following morning, they advanced again. We ran out of arrows by midmorning," Driscoll said. "The enemy began to drag the bodies to the ditch and pile them in the same spots where the bones from the night before were. As before, we allowed them to get near to filling the ditch, then dropped jars of oil and ignited them. This was the first time we needed to do this in daylight, and it made it more difficult to stomach. The thralls backed away only slightly and stood and stared. That they displayed no emotion, being so close to that horrific sight, made it all the more unnerving."

"How many do you think you killed by this point?" I asked.

"Perhaps a thousand," Driscoll said. "We expended roughly five thousand arrows, but it took four or more to kill most of them. Even with three or four arrows in them, they would keep crawling to the ditch."

"The worst part was that some of the bodies they rolled into the ditch were not dead," Yankton said. "Before we torched them, we could see some of them still squirming. "

"Majors and Minors!" I gasped.

"The next day was the worst yet," Driscoll said. "They came to the same places which were now half-filled with the bones. The thralls stepped right onto the skeletons and moved toward the rampart. We could hear the bones cracking under their feet. Others followed them, and began climbing on the backs of those in front. Gradually they formed a sort of ramp and were close to reaching the top of the rampart. Our men began using mural lances against them."

"What's a mural lance?" Fenwick asked.

"Remember how long Bellona's lance was? Add another five or six feet," I said. "From the top of a rampart to the bottom of the ditch is usually around sixteen feet. Mural lances are eighteen feet, designed so someone atop the fortification can attack someone at the bottom."

"We were unable to prevent the enemy from nearing the top. When we took some casualties, I gave the order for oil and flame," Yankton said. "This time, we all knew we were burning men alive. It affected our allies most of all. Some of them recognized comrades among the thralls."

"Fortunately, that night, we received arrows from Iradiem, along with a new supply of oil," Driscoll said.

"We repeated the same cycle for the next five days, running out of arrows on the third day. More arrows and oil came, and the next five days were more of the same."

"On the sixteenth day, however," Driscoll said, "we were out of arrows, and nearly out of oil. That night we made the decision to fall back to the next set of fortifications we constructed, closer to Iradiem. We left under cover of darkness."

"It took the enemy two days to reach us, then the same progression of attacks resumed. We did not exhaust our supply of arrows again, but oil supplies were thin. In order to keep the ditches clear, we needed to order the men to distribute the enemy corpses throughout the ditch. That was the most horrible thing I will ever order soldiers to do," Yankton said. "The thralls arrived before we pulled the men from the ditch and we lost some."

"Then, we saw the most glorious sight," Driscoll said. "Midday, on the eighteenth day of fighting, the enemy froze in place. It took a few minutes for us to realize what must have happened. Word spread quickly. Our men and our allies crowded to the top of the rampart. Suddenly, they began to cheer. We sent the priests of the Three Major Gods over with soldiers to protect them, just in case. They began freeing the enemy soldiers."

"Where are they now?" I asked.

"With their countrymen," Driscoll said. "Most of the enemy force that remained was from the allies. Very few were from Combrial. Most of the Combrians simply drifted away."

"Where are our allies?" Fenwick asked.

"Encamped elsewhere just outside the city, I believe," Driscoll replied. "Their rulers feel an obligation to try to restore things in the city. The king of Combrial's nephew is married to the king of Vanda's daughter. The nephew came with us. He was not allowed to take part in the fighting, much to his frustration. Vanda's advisors feared that the king of Combrial and his family was dead—I learned this morning that is indeed is the case—and the nephew is closest in the line of succession. Now, tell us of your adventure."

14

Before we began, we all agreed a refill was in order. When we neared the kegs, the men broke out into song once more. They gave us some drunken huzzahs for bringing them the ale.

"Your Highness," Driscoll said, "while I wouldn't recommend it on a regular basis, the men needed this."

"What you described just now was as gruesome as I thought it would be," I said. "I thought the men could use a chance to forget. How many men did we lose?"

"Nineteen," Driscoll replied. "Most when we didn't get the men out from the ditch in time."

We returned to the table where we'd been sitting. Fenwick and I told them of our experience. We omitted Shasha's role, as I did not think the colonels would quite understand. They accepted that Fenwick and I were connected to Bellona but seemed the type of men who did not want to know anything more than that.

Our march back to Iradiem began in the morning. Most of the men looked worse for the wear after the ale the night before. Colonel Driscoll took pity on them and kept the pace slow, and we stopped for water frequently.

The night before we reached Iradiem, I composed a report for the king. I kept it short, and glossed over most of the supernatural aspects since I knew it would make Mark uncomfortable. The primary purpose of the letter was to let him (and Lucy and Julienne) know that we were successful and safe. I would have one of the caravels hurry back to Aquileia with the news.

The carracks were waiting when we reached the port. We wasted no time in boarding them. Before we hauled anchor, I met with Captain Hardy from *Freyja.* He and the other caravel captains had stayed in Iradiem while we were down south. They were eager to get back to being pirates.

"The month o' Porri starts tomorrow, Yer Highness," he said. "Ships that ha' been at anchor the last three months'll be loaded to the gunwales."

"I want one of you to sail immediately for Aquileia and deliver this dispatch," I asked. "They are not to stop to take prizes on the way. Draw lots to determine who it is. I suggest you and the other captains agree beforehand that you'll share a portion of the prize money you win while they are away with the crew of the ship chosen. That will ease the sting and prevent any hard feelings."

"Aye, Yer Highness," he said. "We prolly woulda struck the same bargain, but only after raised voices and a bit o' temper. 'By the Prince's command' gets us there quicker."

The next day, we set sail for home. We enjoyed "fair winds and following seas" as the sailors say, and made good time. While still three days away from Aquileia, we saw *Farsall* heading south, eager to rejoin her sister ships off the Rhetian coast.

When we arrived at the port of Aquileia, we needed to heave to for a few hours, waiting for the tide to change. The delay was frustrating—seeing our destination so close but forced to wait. It did mean that Fenwick and I were greeted at the pier by Julienne and Lucy.

My heart soared at the sight of my lovely wife. Both of the women looked radiant. I could see Lucy was now showing a slight swelling, though not the bulge she would develop soon.

As Fenwick and I embraced our wives, the men of the Castle Shield decided to favor us with the new verses of the song. It caused Lucy and Julienne to begin laughing while Fenwick and I were kissing them. The women then waved to the men who were lining the rails of the carrack.

The horses were lifted from the hold. Thankfully, Andy and Davy were the first two to appear, already saddled, with our saddle bags fastened behind.

Bellona's lance was tucked under the fender of Andy's saddle. Fenwick and I left the ladies briefly to collect them. We could tell that both our mounts were happy to be off the ship.

"We came in separate carriages," Lucy said. "Do you think Andy will mind…?"

We said our goodbyes with hugs and kisses on the cheek. Fenwick and Julienne went to one carriage. Lucy took me by the hand to the royal carriage that waited just ahead. She sniffed once we were inside.

"You do not smell as bad as I expected," she said.

"While we were waiting, I had the crew man the pump and hose me down," I replied. "It amused them greatly to see me dancing a caper as the cold water blasted me."

"Thank you. We received your report but I sense there is a lot you left out. For instance, the blade on Fenwick's back does not look as I expected, if it is the sword of Bellona."

I started telling the whole tale from the beginning. By the time we reached the castle, I was nowhere near finished. Lucy paused me until we reached our quarters. She asked our maid, Wilma, to prepare a bath for me immediately.

While we waited in our bedroom for it to be prepared, I resumed my narrative. When the bath was prepared, I stripped and slid into the blissfully hot and clean water. Lucy followed me into the room but did not move to join me in the tub. I raised my eyebrows in a silent entreaty.

"Hot baths are not permitted for me," she said. "The midwife explained that we don't want to cook the baby. Tepid water only. Now, continue."

I washed myself as I related the story. I had just reached the part where Fenwick and I entered the Temple of the Three Major Gods. From her expression, I could tell Lucy thought Fenwick's ruse of attacking me was very clever. Then, I reached the point where Shasha intervened to save me for the first time. I noticed Lucy's cheeks were wet with tears already.

"You know?" I asked.

She nodded silently. Kneeling next to me, she clasped my hand. Choked with emotion, I could say nothing for a while.

"We conducted a ceremony for her," I said. "I am still sad and will always miss her, but the feelings no longer threaten to overwhelm me completely."

"I'm sorry," Lucy said.

I resumed telling her the rest of the story. Finishing my ablutions, I rose and dried myself. Lucy enfolded me in a hug that restored my soul.

"Fenwick and I need to share the conversations we had with the head priestess of the Temple of Bellona with you and Lily," I said.

"Tomorrow," Lucy said, as she pulled me willingly into our bedroom before I had the chance to begin dressing.

"Make yourself at home, Fenwick," I said the following morning, when I saw him comfortably settled at our dining table when I came down for breakfast. "Oh! You already did."

"I thought you would appreciate things returning to normal right away, Your High-and-Mightiness," he retorted.

"Jenny! Please tell me you have some qava prepared," I called out to our cook.

"It will be ready momentarily, Your Highness!" she replied.

"What rousted you so early from connubial bliss?" I asked Fenwick.

"Julienne had an early meeting," he said with a shrug. "I thought it would be best if you and I shared what we learned from Leora with Lucy and the queen as soon as possible."

"I agree. You actually saved me from sending a page to summon you. Lucy sent a note to Lily last night. She will see us at nine."

"Fenwick! What a nice surprise!" Lucy said when she appeared. "I did not think Julienne would set you free so quickly."

"She has business to attend," he replied. "Caz and I learned some things down south that we find troubling and want to discuss them with you and the queen."

"Caz hinted at that but has kept his thoughts to himself this far."

Jenny came bustling in carrying a large tray. The qava service was on it but also hearty breakfasts for all three of us. We thanked her as she served us.

"To tell the truth, Your Highness, I've missed cooking for you and Lord Easton," Jenny said. "The two of you make me smile when you're together, cracking on each other the way you do."

"We have a meeting at nine?" Fenwick asked Lucy after Jenny left.

"We do. Can you give me a hint as to what it will be concerning?" Lucy asked.

"Leora, the head priestess I mentioned to you, is extremely knowledgeable about much more than just Bellona," I said. "I did not see it, but she indicated that her Temple has a vast library. They also have a dedicated loremaster, whose only duty is to know what is in the books. Both Fenwick and I felt you and Lily would benefit greatly by meeting her."

"Now, it may be the case that the head priest at our Temple of Bellona is just as well-acquainted with everything we discussed as Leora was," Fenwick said. "Caz and I possessed only the most rudimentary understanding of the supernatural when we visited. If there was more that they could have shared, they probably knew we would not comprehend it. But Leora's knowledge is incredibly broad—surprisingly so."

"I'm intrigued," Lucy said. "Tell me more."

"Alas, fair princess," Fenwick said, "I would then need to repeat myself for the queen."

"For once, Fenwick is not trying to be coy," I said. "Leora told us a great deal, and it is better to start at the beginning."

Lucy was not happy that we were putting her off. Fortunately, we were saved by the appearance of Katie—I mean, Miss Katherine. Fenwick and I both stood to greet her. She curtsied gracefully in response.

"Good morning, Miss Katherine," I said.

"Good morning, Your Highness. Good morning, Lord Easton," she replied.

There seemed to be little trace of the farm girl who was awed by her surroundings. She now seemed perfectly at home. Jenny brought her some breakfast. Katie checked to determine if we were already dining. After a subtle nod from Lucy, she began to eat.

"How is Miss Sera?" I asked, inquiring about her horse.

"She's wonderful," Katie gushed as soon as she finished her mouthful. "She is so clever! Jerry says that Miss Sera is every bit as smart as Bella, and Andy, and Davy. Did Davy and Andy make it back with you safely?"

"They did," I said.

"Though they did take some wounds," Fenwick said. "Nothing serious, and His Highness healed them immediately. Our journey would not have been successful without them."

"I'm glad they are safe," Katie said. "Jerry has been worried about them."

"And how is Jerry?" I asked after giving Katie a chance to eat some more.

"He's marvelous with the horses," Katie said. "Miss Sera and Thunder seem to know exactly what he is saying and what he wants them to do. He's not as good with me, though."

"What do you mean?" Fenwick asked.

"Well, anything to do with the horses he is confident and clear-spoken," Katie said. "Other than that, he gets tongue-tied and awkward."

Fenwick and I laughed out loud. Lucy's expression told me she'd heard this before. I calmed myself quickly, not wanting Katie to feel embarrassed.

"Miss Katherine, perhaps you don't realize it, but you are developing into quite a lovely young lady," Fenwick said. "Poor Jerry is only a boy. I think he is probably awestruck in your presence."

"But I don't want him to be," Katie protested. "I just want a friend. Yes, he's younger, but he and I are not so different, are we?"

I sensed this was dangerous ground on which to tread so I kept my mouth shut. The expression on Lucy's face told me I chose wisely. Fenwick, however, waded right in. Fortunately, he took the best approach.

"Miss Katherine, boys are slower to grow up than girls," Fenwick began. "Even though Jerry, for his age, is uncommonly mature and responsible in certain ways, in terms of being with people, he is at a disadvantage. Please be patient with him."

"I'm trying," she said.

"She is growing up quickly," Fenwick commented after Katie left.

"We need to find some friends for her," Lucy said.

"I thought you had some ideas in that regard," I said.

"I did, and we introduced Katie to some young ladies her own age. They are perfectly nice girls, but there is one problem."

"Which is?"

"Katie cannot talk to them about what she is learning from Lily and me," Lucy said. "Lily and I have not forbidden her to say anything, but Katie knows that these girls would not have the slightest idea of what she was talking about."

"I see," I replied.

"We need to find another candidate to be a lady-in-waiting with Katie," Lucy said. "With luck it will happen soon."

"Are you actively searching?" Fenwick asked.

"No, but another opportunity is about to present itself."

"What do you mean?" I asked.

"I suppose you'll just have to wait until someone tells you," Lucy said with a smirk, playing the same card against me that we used a few minutes earlier to put her off.

"I have seen that device in one of my books," Lily said.

We started our meeting with Lily shortly before. Fenwick and I just explained about seeing the dodecahedron in our shared dream. He had even made a crude drawing.

"Do you know what it is or what it does?" I asked.

"Oh, bother!" Lily exclaimed. "It will drive me crazy until I know. Follow me."

We followed her into the section of the castle where the royal quarters were. She took us to a rather impressive study with half as many books as the castle's library. Lily gestured for us to sit, then began looking at the spines of books.

"This one," she said after seeming to decide between three.

It was very thick and looked heavy. I offered to lift it down. She allowed me. I set it on a reading table and Lily found a particular section, then began leafing through the pages.

"Here it is!" she said. "A dodecahedron. It is thought to amplify the strength and reach of a mage of the Dark Arts. The last one spotted was hundreds of years ago and destroyed. That's all the information I have, but I knew I saw it before."

We shared with Lily the additional information Leora had provided—in particular, that the device might have given the Dark Lord access to our plane of existence, and dark mages might appear more frequently for a generation. Lily frowned at this and looked at Lucy pointedly. Fenwick cleared his throat to get their attention.

"Leora believes that the heads of the Temples of the Minor Gods on the southern continent have a greater wealth of historical information about both the Minor Gods and outbreaks of the Dark Arts," he said. "I don't know nearly as much as either of you, but I am inclined to give some weight to her words. One thing she freely admitted they lack almost entirely is knowledge of, as she calls her, 'the White Witch'—Ceridwen Sospita."

"We shared with her that you plan to seek out someone with affinity for Ceridwen Sospita," I said. "She will suggest that the head priest of the Temple of Freyja begin a search as well—if he survived the rule of the dark mage in Combrial. If they do find someone, Leora believes you would be the best person to train him or her."

"As it turns out, Caz," Lily said after sharing a smug smile with Lucy, "Mark has an assignment for you that will take you quite near the Temple of Freyja. If what this Leora says is even possible, it makes it enough of a priority that Freyja's priests would feel obligated to assist us in our search. I think Lucy should join you on this journey."

"And Miss Katherine," Lucy said. "She and I may decide to stay for a time to receive additional training."

"That's right! You have not visited the Temple of Freyja before," I remembered out loud. "Oh, my! This should be interesting. Why does Mark want to send me up there?"

"That is for him to say," Lily answered. "He has good reason. Now, I was sorry to hear about Shasha. I've lost a familiar, so I know the hole it leaves in your heart."

15

From the meeting with Lily, I proceeded to have lunch with the king. Fenwick was also included. We provided Mark with a high-level summary of our adventures on the southern continent.

"Order is restored?" he asked.

We assured him it was, for the time being. Naturally, he wanted to know what we meant by that. We explained that there would probably be greater incidence of dark mages appearing throughout the world. Fenwick also explained to Mark about Leora's suspicion that the monotheistic religion the Rhetians practiced was the creation of a powerful dark mage.

"That makes a great deal of sense," Mark said. "Interesting… I will be chewing on that one for quite some time, I think."

"Lily mentioned you have a task for me," I said.

"I do," Mark replied. "Fenwick, you are not needed on this assignment. I think you should return to the March. Duncan has pledged to teach you what you need to know about governing it. We have been neglecting your education in that for our other needs. You will need to return to the city in a month, though."

"I will take that as my cue to leave," Fenwick said.

"As well you should," Mark said with a smile.

"A property dispute has arisen between the Duke of Namie and Baron Westhaver," Mark said after Fenwick closed the door behind him. "I want you to go to adjudicate it."

"Mark, both of those men look down their noses at me, and always have—before you named me your successor *and* after," I protested.

"I know," Mark said with a sly grin. "That's why I want you to go. I want you to get to know them better, and for them to learn more about you."

"Mark, if you are thinking we will end up as friends as a result—"

"Oh, I think nothing of the sort," he snorted. "I count on them being as mad as wet hens that I sent you to rule on their squabble. They will be insulting and condescending—at least, at first."

"Then why—?"

"Those two are the focal points of a group of thirteen nobles who share their views," Mark said. "They are geographically contiguous in a swath of the north that begins above the Eastern March and stretches west about halfway across Aquileia. With the Braintree faction gone, they are the only threat that might ever develop into an armed uprising, though I doubt they have the courage. Neither do they have the resources. None of their holdings is significant. They just like to whine that their social inferiors are more successful than they will ever be. I want you to get to know them so that when the time comes you know how to pull their teeth before they bite. Perhaps you might pull their teeth now."

"What is the subject of their dispute?" I asked.

"There is a spur of the mountains that serves as part of the border between them," Mark explained, "No one ever cared about who really owned it because the only value in the land was whatever fur trappers could harvest—which wasn't much. Just before the winter solstice, one of the fur trappers came back with a report that there was gold in one of the streams. He had a small pouch of gold dust and tiny nuggets to prove it. The two of them are now fighting over where the boundary line is and to whom the gold belongs."

"This no longer sounds like a simple boundary dispute," I stated.

"But it is," Mark said with a grin. "Both of them are conveniently forgetting the law."

"What law?"

"All gold and silver mines in Aquileia are property of the crown, regardless of where they are located. The crown grants the nobles in whose territory they are located a tiny percentage of the value of the material extracted in compensation. There is a sound reason behind it that has nothing to do with whether the king is a greedy miser. Can you figure out what it is?"

"Control of the currency," I answered once I thought about it for a few minutes. "If a new supply of gold entered the market too quickly, the value of our existing coins would drop. This would cause economic chaos."

"Precisely," Mark said, "Well-reasoned, Caz. That is the reason why the crown controls gold and silver production. This is an aspect of governance that we have not talked about yet, but it is critically important. We have an army of scribes who work for the Chancellor of the Exchequer. Their sole purpose is to track tax receipts. From those numbers, we can gauge the growth of the economy. As the economy grows, we mint more ducats and florins and all the other coins to keep pace."

"In order for the value to stay the same over time," I said. "Meaning a ducat today is worth the same as a ducat five years ago—it still buys the same amount of whatever as it did. Since there is more being produced in Aquileia, we need more coins to keep things even."

"Very good, Caz," the king remarked. "Now, back to these two. It will be unpleasant enough when you arrive as the arbiter of their dispute. I hope you toy with them for a bit. Try to give them both the impression that you find merit in their arguments. Make them play up to you. They will both find that extremely galling and you should find it humorous. Then, when you announce that the point is moot, that the gold belongs to the crown—"

"I'll anger them so much they will both try to kill me," I interrupted.

"Perhaps," Mark smiled. "I think it is more probable that you will show them you are not to be trifled with, and you possess the authority to represent the crown in this and any other matters. You are also to rule that because control of the territory is in dispute, neither of them will be entitled to any compensation. There is sound legal precedent for that as well. I will make sure you have all the necessary documents to prove it, and one of our advocates will accompany you. There is one in particular who I think they will find particularly annoying."

"And you're not worried that I might provoke an uprising?"

"Neither of them has the balls," Mark said. "That is what will make it so satisfying for you—and me. And if they somehow find the courage to threaten us, we will crush them."

"When would you like me to leave?" I asked.

"I can only imagine how weary you are of travel," Mark said. "It is still Porri, and the north is still firmly in winter's grip. If you leave in the middle of Goa, that will be just about right. The two of them requested an audience. I have yet to respond. Instead, I will inform them that the crown is coming to render judgment. Because they both have highly inflated views of their own importance, they will assume that means I am coming. It will make it more satisfying for all of us when you arrive as the crown's representative."

"You do not care for these men at all, do you?" I asked.

"Can't stand them," Mark said. "When we issued the call to arms to meet the Rhetians in battle, they responded with the barest minimum of soldiers. The men they provided were poorly equipped and completely unprepared. Neither the duke nor the baron joined us in the field."

"Were their men the confused ragamuffin bunch who looked like they'd just left their plows?"

"Yes. We couldn't use them as soldiers. They were with the baggage train the whole time," Mark said. "Even Houlsin and Chafter's people were more trained and better outfitted than they were."

When I returned to our quarters, Mr. Gilbert was waiting for me. You recall that he was my valet and my secretary. He held a sheaf of letters in his hand.

"Now, Your Highness," he said in a calming tone, "most of these are quite pleasant and do not require a response."

"That's a relief," I said.

The first batch were letters from men who wished to join the men-at-arms currently aboard the caravels. The ships were fully manned, but six more were currently under construction. They would be completed in roughly two months.

"Please respond telling them to report by the middle of Einmann," I instructed Mr. Gilbert.

Then, he handed over a letter from a woman named Abigail Bresh. She wrote on behalf of what she said was the largest orphanage in the city, asking for money. An orphanage would be something I would always want to support, but something about the letter did not ring true. If this were the largest orphanage in the city, I was certain the queen would already be contributing to it.

"Please check with Her Majesty's secretary," I asked. "If this is a legitimate operation, the queen no doubt is aware of it."

"I have already checked, Your Highness, and the queen knows nothing of this particular organization."

"Please write this Madam Bresh and state that you need to inspect the facilities. See how she responds—if she does."

Following this were a number of requests for money. Those from individuals, I asked Mr. Gilbert to investigate. The requests from established entities, such as the primary Temple of the Three Major Gods, I asked him to research what Prince Albert had done in the past. In addition, I suggested we support all four of the Temples in the city.

The last group was made up of letters from friends. More than just an exchange of gossip, I also expected these to contain useful information. Freddy, Quint, Ratty Hawkins, young Lords Houlsin and Chafter, along with my father, all sent lengthy epistles.

Houlsin and Chafter were effusive in their thanks for being included in the solstice celebration. My father provided an update on construction in Port Charles and on the jute plantation. Freddy and Quint told me what was transpiring in their fathers' holdings, along with some interesting gossip. Ratty's letter was the least informative, though he did share that he and Inger Fairchild would be getting married on the summer solstice, and he hoped Lucy and I would be able to attend.

Lucy was due to deliver our baby then, so our attendance was questionable, to say the least. I dictated to Mr. Gilbert a quick response, telling Ratty that Lucy and I would do our best to attend. Lucy most likely already knew that they'd set a date. I would need to speak with her about the possibility of doing something for the couple in advance, such as hosting a party in their honor.

With that, Mr. Gilbert let me know we were all caught up on incoming correspondence, though he suggested I should also write the others in the next day or two. I promised I would but just then I found my mind a bit weary. Leaving the study, I stretched out on the sofa in our living room in front of a fire. Lucy found me there and curled up in my embrace.

"Busy day, love?"

"I find it difficult to understand why I feel so tired when I didn't *do* anything today," I commented.

"That's because you needed to shift your focus to more mundane things," Lucy said. "What did Mark have to say?"

"That I need to go north to put Duke Swietlik and Baron Westhaver in their places. Mark seems to think it's a lark. I'm afraid they'll try to poison me or murder me in my sleep."

"It would definitely be poison," Lucy said. "From what Lily tells me, neither of them would have the courage to attack you physically—even if you were asleep."

"That's not very comforting, dear," I complained.

"Caz, you have nothing to fear from poison," Lucy said, smacking me gently on the chest. "Simply open your connection to Eir before eating or drinking anything."

"That won't drain me?" I asked. "Before the lance, whenever I used Eir's power, it did not take long before I drained all my asomatous energy."

"That was because you were healing physical wounds—some of them quite serious, in case you've forgotten. A bit of poison will require very little energy to neutralize—if they try, which I doubt."

"But if they do, what then?" I asked. "They would be guilty of attempting to kill the successor to the throne. That's a capital offense."

"That you should discuss with Mark," Lucy said. "The duchy of Namie and Westhaver's holding are not significant territories—nowhere near the size of the Braintree estates or even what was left of Morningstar's land. Mark should not find it too difficult to replace either or both. It may provide him with an opportunity to reward someone with a patent of nobility. Mark also sends a message to the rest of their little clique that he will not tolerate their useless scheming."

"Are they really that dangerous?"

"Majors and Minors, no!" Lucy laughed. "They like to think they are, though. The reason why Mark is so giddy about sending you there is because he thinks you will serve as a lightning rod, enticing them to attempt something stupid which, because you are who you are, will be no real threat. Then, he will have the opportunity to pluck two bad apples from the barrel which should keep the other bad apples from rotting further."

"And you and Miss Katherine will be at the Temple of Freyja? Is it close by?"

"Two days ride short of either holding," Lucy said.

"And the midwife is not bothered by you traveling?"

"I'm not allowed to ride Bella, but the carriage will be perfectly comfortable. You probably didn't notice on the way up from the harbor, but the coachwright put new springs on it this winter. Lily ordered it to be done, knowing I would not be allowed to ride. Katie and I will enjoy a peaceful journey. Oo!" Lucy said suddenly. "Here!"

She clasped my hand and held it to her belly. It was the strangest sensation. I could feel the baby moving around.

"He gets restless sometimes," she explained. "Usually when I'm being still. He makes it hard to fall asleep sometimes."

"That is amazing," I said. "Is this normal?"

"Perfectly normal, my love."

"Are we any closer to deciding on a name?"

"Of those we discussed, the one I keep coming back to is Robert," she said.

"Hmm. Robert Gau was the first of Mark's family to sit the throne. I'll go along with that as long as we agree we call him Rob—not Bob, Robby, or Bobby."

"What about using his name—Robert?"

"It's natural for people to want to shorten that name," I said. "Insisting that everyone use 'Robert' makes us seem—"

"Like prigs?" Lucy said with a smile.

"Exactly," I replied. "Prince Rob sounds more approachable."

"Like Prince Wim?" Lucy teased.

That struck a sour note. Prince Wim, whose given name was William, had indeed seemed approachable and unpretentious, especially when compared to how his brother Albert used to behave. Lucy and I both learned that Wim's seeming affability was just an act. Underneath that façade was a cold-hearted, ruthless man intensely jealous of his older brother and determined to usurp Albert's place in the succession.

"Perhaps not Robert, then," I said.

"Dear, Prince Rob will be nothing like Wim," Lucy reassured me. "We won't allow it."

"I'm sure Lily and Mark—"

"Mark was young and a bit overwhelmed by taking the throne when his father died," Lucy explained. "He was unprepared to assume all the responsibilities. That is why he is taking pains to educate you on all the different aspects of the job. Lily did her best to help him and did not pay as much attention to the boys as she could have. She was also stubborn, and refused to accept the help that her parents offered."

"She's told you this?"

"Yes. We had many conversations while you were away," Lucy said. "I shared with her my fears that our son would grow up an insufferable snob like Albert was before he snapped out of it, or a devious schemer like Wim. She and Mark will help us raise our children, as will my mother and father—your father and Ariana will, too. I would like to think that I'm smart enough to accept their help."

"I know nothing about how to be a father," I admitted, "and I'm scared. My own upbringing was not something I would use as a model."

"Which is exactly why you will be a good father," Lucy said. "If nothing else, you will be determined not to repeat the mistakes of the past. And I believe your father, Mark, and Lily are all hoping this will be an opportunity for them to employ the difficult lessons they've learned to ensure that any child of ours will have the best upbringing possible."

16

The next four weeks saw me consumed by the minutiae of governance. My nose was buried in account ledgers and, as the day of departure for the north drew near, law books. Declan Loud was the barrister who would be coming with me to meet Swietlik and Westhaver. I could tell right away why Mark felt he would annoy the two nobles.

Loud's surname was apt, as he spoke in pronouncements, and at greater volume than was necessary. Coupled with that, his voice was grating. Listening to him for any length of time hurt my ears. The man did know the law, though—forward, backward, upside-down and sideways.

A full squadron of the Castle Shield would accompany us on our journey. Mr. Gilbert made arrangements for us in advance, having mapped out our itinerary. He wrote ahead to the inns where we would be staying, warning them of our arrival. In addition, he contacted the head priest at the Temple of Freyja, alerting him to Lucy and Miss Katherine's visit.

"How would I have ever managed without him?" I asked Lucy one night.

"With difficulty—great difficulty," she smirked.

We set out on the sixteenth of Goa, one of those early spring days that brings the promise of what is to come. That, unfortunately, was the last day of fine weather we enjoyed until it was time for Lucy and Katie to veer off to the Temple of Freyja. Two dozen of the Castle Shield would go with them. The rest continued with Mr. Loud, Mr. Gilbert, and me to the town of Brego, where Duke Swietlik's manor was located.

We arrived at the duke's manor near midday, two days later, on the last of the month. It was the first we'd seen of the sun since we set out. The men of the Castle Shield looked magnificent. They polished their armor the night before, and it gleamed. I contrived to position myself behind their banners to delay the moment when Swietlik would see me. It would amuse me to see his face when he realized that it was I who was coming and not King Mark.

The two Royal Surveyors did not join us. They split off and continued on their way into the mountains beyond. It would be two months or more before they returned to the capital.

I was not disappointed in the duke's reaction to my arrival. The duke failed to disguise his unhappiness. I could see his face turn red when I was still a furlong away. As I approached, the duchess turned and went back inside. Swietlik started to follow. He stopped, obviously having a second thought, and turned back to face us.

"The king has gone to Westhaver first, has he?" Swietlik sneered. "That's a breach of protocol. I outrank the baron."

"The king is in Aquileia, Swietlik," I responded coolly.

"But the letter said—" he began to splutter.

"The letter said that the crown would be visiting to judge your dispute, Duke. We are the crown," I snapped, using the royal *we* to drive home the point. "If you find this unsatisfactory, we will see if the baron is prepared to give us a more fitting welcome."

"He won't give you any warmer a welcome—Wait!" he cried as I began to wheel Andy around.

I caught Major Grunevald's eye and winked so Swietlik could not see. After nodding to him, the major waved his arm in a circle in the air to tell the men to turn around and depart. I gave Andy a squeeze with my knees and he took a step forward.

'Your Highness!" Swietlik called, from a throat that must have been choked with gall. "I apologize. I was expecting His Majesty, and—"

"And you thought you could treat us with the same contempt and disdain you've always shown us?" I barked, still using the majestic plural, as Andy responded to gentle pressure from my knee and hand to dance around to face

Swietlik. "Is that why your wife turned away in disgust when she saw us approach?"

"Yes—I mean, no, Your Highness," he stammered.

"Make up your mind, Duke," I snapped. "His Majesty has given us the distasteful task of adjudicating this spat between you and the baron. You seem intent on making our decision an easy one."

'Your Highness, please," Swietlik begged. "Allow me to welcome you into my home."

"From the reaction of the duchess to our arrival, we envision the hospitality you have to offer will be sorely lacking," I sneered. "We are inclined to think a bed of nails with snakes intertwined would be more comfortable."

'Your Highness, if I could beg just a moment's delay," Swietlik pleaded. "The duchess only went inside to make sure all was in readiness for your arrival."

"You are a poor liar, duke," I said, "but we will give you a moment."

"Thank you, Your Highness," Swietlik said.

He scurried into the house. When he found his wife, the men near me and I could not make out his words, but his pleading tone came through clearly. The sharp tongue of the duchess, however, carried to our ears quite clearly.

"No! I will not kowtow to a jumped-up bastard," she said in a querulous tone. "Go ahead and lick his boots if you must, but don't expect me to do the same!"

"This promises to be an extremely interesting visit," Major Grunevald whispered to me as we listened to the duke pleading and his wife spitting venom with every word.

"We haven't come close to the interesting part yet, Major," I said. "Wait until I rub both their noses in it."

"It doesn't sound like the duchess will give in," Grunevald said.

"There's money involved, Major—a great deal of it," I said. "Something Swietlik and his shrew of a wife want desperately. She will come around—if not today, then tomorrow."

"What do you mean, tomorrow?"

"If he doesn't appear in another minute, we leave."

The intensity of the discussion inside increased, while the volume dropped. There was quite a bitter argument taking place. While it amused me in a dark way, I also had no more patience for it. The duke would need to ride after us and beg me to return.

"Let's go," I said. "Have one of the men look back occasionally to see how Swietlik reacts when he sees us leaving."

"Where are we heading, Your Highness?" Grunevald asked.

"To Etiam, between here and Westhaver's town," I replied. "We should reach it before nightfall. They have an inn and are expecting me."

"How did you know you would not be staying with the duke?" Grunevald asked.

"The duke and duchess, and the baron and his wife, are among a group who have always scorned me," I said. "I've been dealing with people like this since I was a boy. The accident of my birth is far more important to them than my character or accomplishments.

"Thank all the heavenly beings the king doesn't think that way," Grunevald muttered.

"Why, thank you, Major."

"And if the king doesn't, why do they?" he asked. "It doesn't seem very smart if you ask me, Your Highness. I mean, if you're good enough for the king, shouldn't that shut their mouths?"

"These are unhappy people, Major, small-minded and bitter," I said. "Their families are older than most, and they think that this makes them better than everyone. The territories they hold are unimportant, and they were just as insignificant when King Robert, the first of the Gau line of kings, assigned these lands to their ancestors when he rewarded his supporters with territories. Their ancestors lacked influence back then, and merely hanging onto the land for a couple of hundred years doesn't make you remarkable for anything other than avoiding having the king take it away from you because you mismanaged it so horribly. They are not wealthy and have no power outside of their holdings, and they resent that terribly."

The innkeeper was expecting us. Mr. Gilbert and Mr. Loud were staying in the inn with me. The men of the Castle Shield encamped outside the village.

An hour later, I was in the dining room with Major Grunevald, Mr. Loud, and Mr. Gilbert, enjoying a mug of ale. Dinner would be served soon. We heard

Duke Swietlik burst into the inn. Breathlessly he asked the innkeeper where I was.

"Your Highness, please. I beg your pardon for the misunderstanding this afternoon. The duchess and I would be delighted if you would please honor us with your presence."

"Delighted, eh?" I toyed with him. "I distinctly recall hearing, 'I will not kowtow to a jumped-up bastard,' and, 'Go ahead and lick his boots if you must, but don't expect me to do the same!' Has the duchess had that much of a change of heart? We have no wish at all to spend a moment with people who do not wish to share our company."

"The duchess was disappointed," Swietlik lied. "She was very much looking forward to seeing His Majesty. It has been years since we've spoken to him, and—"

"And she, like you, thinks of us as a 'jumped-up bastard.' Let's not pretend, Swietlik. You've never made any secret of your scorn for us. You've known us for at least ten years, and the warmest greeting we ever received from you was an extremely reluctant and limp handshake when Lord Rawlinsford attempted to introduce us at the Earl of Dorch's gala several years ago. You both much prefer to sneer and snipe."

"Your Highness, I apologize for how we have reacted to you in the past," he stammered. "I swear we have changed."

"What has changed, my dear duke, is that you now realize that we have the authority to decide to whom the land in dispute belongs," I replied. "We presume you managed to communicate that to your wife, and though she still despises us, she is greedy and grasping, desperately hoping that we will rule in your favor."

"Your Highness, surely you know how flighty women can be," Swietlik said.

"No," I responded, "we do not. The women in our life are well-mannered and well-reasoned. None of them fall into the category of flighty."

"Well, I am not so blessed in my partner as you are, Your Highness."

"The first completely true thing you have said today, Swietlik."

"Will you please come back?"

"Not tonight. Our dinner is coming shortly. Perhaps we will consider it in the morning. Now be off with you."

The duke slunk from the room. There were only a handful of other guests, but I could tell from their faces that they enjoyed seeing Swietlik get a bit of comeuppance. They also realized that they were dining in the presence of royalty, which was something none of them expected.

"You seem to be enjoying this quite a bit, Your Highness," Major Grunevald commented.

"Oh, some," I said, "but not as much as you may think. It merely makes me tired. And there is much more I will add to this situation before we are through. Then, there is the baron. Baron Westhaver is similar to the duke in every respect, though very conscious that the duke outranks him slightly. Both of them are among the most worthless examples of the nobility in the kingdom."

"If you say so, Your Highness."

"Major, do you remember the men who arrived at the muster at Reedsford who looked like lost sheep?" I asked. "The ones who needed clothing, blankets, tents, and every other bit of equipment? For whom the only job we found that they could do was to distribute supplies from the baggage train?"

"Yes."

"They were Swietlik and Westhaver's contribution to the war," I said.

We took our time the next day before arriving at the duke's manor. He and his wife, who had one of the pointiest chins I've ever seen on a woman, were waiting for us. His wife, introduced to me as Eudora, wore a flagrantly insincere smile.

"Welcome to our home, Your Highness," she said unctuously.

"It's nice that you have changed your mind since yesterday, Eudora," I replied, avoiding using the honorific "milady."

Mr. Gilbert, accompanied by two members of the Castle Shield carrying my luggage, entered the manor immediately after I did. He went upstairs before anyone thought to stop him. Over dinner the night before, we discussed that he would move my things into the largest bedroom since we expected whatever guest rooms the building possessed to be rather shabby. Mr. Gilbert pointed out that the king would expect to be given the best room in the house.

The largest bedroom undoubtedly belonged to the duke and duchess. They would have moved their things out, expecting the king to come. When they learned it was me, they undoubtedly shifted everything back in.

Mr. Gilbert would state that my royal personage would only stay in the most well-appointed bedroom during my stay. He would phrase it in such a way that they could not argue, though I knew they would. I expected Eudora to lose her temper.

"Excuse me, Your Highness," Eudora said after hearing the thumps of my luggage hitting the floor in what could only have been her bedroom. "I must go check to make sure everything is in order."

"What are you doing in here?" she screeched after she went up the stairs like an arrow.

"Unpacking His Highness's bags," came Mr. Gilbert's calm voice in response.

"But he can't stay here!" Eudora squawked. "See here, you. We have prepared a guest room for His Highness. This is *our* bedroom."

"Very well, milady, show me the room," Mr. Gilbert said in an exasperated tone.

"Completely unacceptable," Mr. Gilbert stated flatly a few moments later. "This room is tiny. There is no attached lavatory. His Royal Highness cannot stay there."

"Daniel!" Eudora commanded in an unpleasant whine, accompanied by a stomp of her foot, "Come here at once!"

The duke, who froze in place when his wife raced up the stairs, excused himself nervously. He hurried as much as he could without making it look obvious that he was hopping at his wife's command. As soon as she saw him, the fun began anew. Mr. Loud looked at me with an evil grin. I returned it.

"Daniel, this man is demanding that we surrender our room to that low-born pretender!" she snapped. "I will not stand for such an indignity. You begged me to allow him in the house, and to be pleasant. I did as you asked, and now this *servant* claims the presumptuous bastard won't sleep in any other room. If it were the king, I would do it. Not for *him*!"

"Eudora, you know he can hear you," the duke cautioned.

"I don't give a rat's whisker whether he hears me or not!" she yelled angrily. "This is intolerable."

"Eudora, you know what is at stake," the duke hissed. "He'll grant the whole thing to Westhaver. Is that really what you want?"

"But, Daniel," she whined in a most unpleasant voice.

"We already planned to give our room to King Mark," the duke stated.

"The king isn't here," she sniffed.

"No, but the prince is," the duke whispered sharply. "I told you not to move our things back, but you wouldn't listen to me. Whether we like it or not—and I don't, not for a minute—this *creature* is the king's chosen successor. He is here on the king's authority and wields the king's sovereignty regarding our dispute."

"He's not the king. He's not fit to be king of anything more than a pigsty!"

"Your Highness, I'm afraid we will not be staying here after all," Mr. Gilbert called down.

"Now, wait just a minute, you!" the duke barked at Mr. Gilbert. "Stop that."

"I'm sorry, milord," Mr. Gilbert said. "It is quite clear that we are not welcome. His Highness thought it was foolish to return, but I did my best to convince him. I am disappointed to find out he was quite correct. If you will please get out of my way, I won't be a minute in packing everything up again, and we will depart."

'Quite right, Mr. Gilbert," I called up. "We don't take well to being called a 'creature,' let alone a 'presumptuous bastard.' We're sorry to have put you to all this trouble, Swietlik. It's clear now why His Majesty sent us on this unpleasant task. You and your lady-wife clearly have no respect for the crown."

By the time Swietlik made it downstairs, I was already in the saddle. Mr. Gilbert and the two soldiers exited immediately behind the duke. Before the duke said a word, I held up my hand, instructing him to remain mute.

"Don't bother, Swietlik," I said. "Anything you could possibly say now would only further damage the already low opinion I have of you."

17

We headed back to the inn. The innkeeper welcomed us back—unsurprising since we paid for our rooms for the whole week. What would have been a surprise is if we failed to provoke a reaction from the duchess. The men of the Castle Shield returned to their encampment, which they did not break down when we departed earlier.

The duke's point that they would have offered their bedroom to King Mark if he had visited was a good one. Mr. Gilbert told me they had moved all their belongings back into their room. They knew Mark would not have stayed in one of their shabby little guest rooms.

We would call upon Baron Westhaver the next day. I expected a similar reception to what we received from the duke and duchess. We would enact the same charade with, presumably, the same result. Then, I would summon the duke and the baron to the inn, where Mr. Loud would inform them of the law, and I would deny both of them any form of compensation.

Lest you think poorly of me, dear reader, be assured I was not enjoying this—much. I will admit it was amusing in spots, but on the whole, these people made my head hurt. The ability to suffer fools gladly was not something the Gods granted me.

We set off for Baron Westhaver's estate the next morning. As I did with the duke, I made it difficult for him to see me. As we rode up, the baron was quickly assembling his household out front, preparing to greet his sovereign. Just as with the duke, when he and his wife saw that I was coming with no sign of the king, the two of them began exchanging words.

"Where is the king?" Westhaver demanded of me, barking at me in the way a short-tempered master would speak to an incompetent servant. "Has he gone to Swietlik first?"

I did not dignify Westhaver's rudeness with a reply. Instead, I merely gazed at him as coolly as I could manage. My lack of response provoked him further.

"Well? Out with it, man!" he snapped.

"Baron, consider carefully the next words from your mouth," Major Grunevald warned after drawing his sword and nudging his horse closer to the baron. "One does not address His *Royal* Highness in this manner."

"How dare you draw on me! I'll address the bastard any way I please," the baron retorted.

"Baron Westhaver, you are guilty of insulting the dignity of His Royal Highness, the crown prince, in the presence of dozens of witnesses," Mr. Loud pronounced in his unpleasant-sounding voice. "If you do not retract your remark and beg immediate forgiveness, Major Grunevald is within his rights as an officer of the court to run you through. You will be dead, and your family dispossessed."

"Don't throw us to the wolves, you fool," the baroness hissed, seizing Westhaver's arm as he moved to draw his sword.

The baron yanked his arm free, then spat on the ground in my direction. Before Westhaver could pull his blade from the scabbard, Major Grunevald acted. He whipped the flat of his sword backhanded, catching Westhaver on the cheek.

The baroness screamed, "No!" as she tried to grab her husband's arm again.

His eyes spitting fire at me, Westhaver shook her off again. A red welt was already blossoming where the major struck. Before the baron freed his sword, the tip of Grunevald's weapon was touching his breastbone, the blade bending slightly from the pressure being applied. Westhaver froze.

"Beg forgiveness," Grunevald growled menacingly. *"On … your … knees."*

Other than a lone bird song, there was complete silence. Westhaver was considering what to do. He looked at his wife and frowned before turning back to me. With particular deliberation, he lowered first to one knee, then the other.

"Your Highness," he said, every word seeming to pain him, "Please forgive my poor behavior."

That was it. As far as apologies go, I've heard more sincere ones from people who accidentally brushed against me in the street. It was enough to satisfy me, and I did not want Major Grunevald to run the man through, which the major seemed all too eager to do.

"Get up, Westhaver," I barked. "Stop this foolishness. It benefits no one. If you think you wound us with your words and behavior, you overestimate yourself and gravely underestimate us. Our entire life, we've fended off more serious insults from better men than you. You're clearly no gentleman, however many years your family has clung desperately to the title you now bear."

As with Swietlik earlier, I made sure to use the royal *we*. Petty, I know, but I was making a point. I comforted myself that I had not sunk to his level and spared his ungrateful self.

The baron rose just as slowly and carefully as he lowered himself. The major had withdrawn his sword but had not yet sheathed it. Westhaver's attention flitted between my eyes and the sword.

"Put it away, Major," I ordered. "We're not going to kill the baron for being an imbecile and an ass."

Major Grunevald looked at me questioningly. It was clear he was more bothered by Westhaver's insults than I was. I waved my hand at him to reinforce my request. Grunevald sheathed his blade with obvious reluctance.

We waited in pregnant silence. His wife came and took his arm. I could tell she was squeezing it tightly with her hand. That reminded the baron of his responsibility to offer the barest minimum of civility.

"May I present my wife, the baroness?"

"We've met," I said.

A look of faint surprise crossed both their faces. It was clear they did not remember the incident. I did, though.

"At the Earl of Dorch's gala several years ago, Lord Rawlinsford attempted to introduce us to you. You turned your backs and walked away rather than acknowledge us," I reminded them. "Hello, Louella," I added, twitting them both by using her first name.

Louella, stunned, froze. After a moment, she remembered herself. She bobbed an awkward curtsy—first intending only a quick bob, then deepening it as she should have for the crown prince.

"Where are your children?" I asked.

This was another breach of protocol. The children should certainly have been present to be introduced to me. I suspected the baron sent them inside once he realized it was me approaching and not the king.

"I'll fetch them," Louella said and scurried into the house.

"It would have been a terrible thing for them to watch you die, Westhaver," I commented idly. "Especially over a fit of pique."

The baron glared at me. Major Grunevald's hand dropped to the hilt of his sword again. Westhaver caught the motion with his eyes.

"Yes, Your Highness," Westhaver choked out, still consumed with barely suppressed rage.

"May I present James and Edwina," the baroness said after she bustled the children up.

James was a boy of around eight years old. His sister looked to be a couple of years younger. The girl dropped a graceful curtsy, unlike her mother. The boy stood gawping until his mother cuffed him lightly on the back of his head. He remembered to bow then.

"Hello, James. Hello, Edwina," I said.

"Pleased to meet you, Your Majesty," Edwina replied, just as she had been taught—not understanding that she'd been prepared to meet the king, not the prince.

With easy grace, I dismounted. I approached her and squatted down to her level. I took her hand and looked her in the eye.

"Thank you, Edwina," I said, "but I am only the prince. The king is 'Your Majesty.' For me, 'Your Highness' is all I am entitled to, and some think not even that."

"Are you the one they sing the song about?" James asked, butting in. "The one where the Rhetians poop their pants?"

"Yes, that would be me, James," I said, shifting my gaze to him.

"That is so great!" he said excitedly. "Tommy and Alex will be so jealous that I got to meet you!"

"Tommy and Alex are your friends?"

"I go to school with them. Mother and Father won't let me play with them, though," he said, trailing off, looking over his shoulder nervously.

"That's too bad," I said. "I had the same problem when I was your age."

"Won't you please come in, Your Highness?" the baroness asked. "We would offer you some refreshment."

"Perhaps another time, Louella," I replied. "We prefer to keep those who despise us in the open, where we can see them. Your husband would be too tempted to do us harm inside. If you would like to call upon us, we are staying at the inn in Etiam until we reach a decision."

We departed and returned to the inn. Sadly, we arrived too late for lunch. So be it. My stomach was full of bile, and I was not hungry. I was chewing on my frustration and anger instead. It exasperated me that Westhaver was such a conceited fool. Insulting me in front of an officer in the Castle Shield—a man who accompanied me through the most perilous conditions imaginable for the last two years—was stupid. Testing Major Grunevald's resolve was imbecility of the highest order.

Part of me wondered if the king had foreseen something like this occurring. I hoped not. Though dealing with Swietlik had its amusing moments, this episode was entirely cheerless. More than anything, I wished Lucy were here with me. Her touch restored me, and it was when I felt like this that I wanted it most.

"Aren't either of you bothered by what happened earlier today?" I asked Mr. Loud and Major Grunevald over dinner later.

"It would have made our job easier if Westhaver had not backed down," Mr. Loud said. "The major would have run him through and the barony would revert to the crown. We would then declare that the area in dispute was considered within the barony's boundaries. Then, when the king assigned the territory to someone else, if he did, he could include the usual compensation as a reward to that person for loyal service, or deny it as a condition of assuming the holding."

"I'm glad it did not come to that," I said. "Still, why push things to the brink like that?"

"You said it yourself the other night, Your Highness," Loud said. "The family was never that important, and the territory is insignificant and always has been. In the last two years Westhaver saw the Braintree properties—any one of which is a jewel compared to his—given to others whose families were more recently ennobled. Then, you were named the successor. Westhaver saw all of this as an insult."

"But to die for it? It's such a waste!" I complained.

"A waste?" the major questioned. "Westhaver was of no importance and was never going to amount to anything more than an annoyance, which he was already. He shirked his duty to the realm when we went to war with the Rhetian Empire. He and his little group of friends here in the north were notable by their absence. Other lords with territories poorer than his joined us. In most cases, they served with distinction. I can think of a handful of examples easily. And of the others, none of them did anything to dishonor themselves."

"Fine," I sighed. "What do we do next?"

"You could simply announce your decision tomorrow and leave," Mr. Loud said. "I get the feeling you are not enjoying this."

"I'm not. It would be different if there was the slightest possibility of winning either of them over, but that is clearly not going to happen. Rubbing their noses in it gives me no satisfaction," I said.

Perhaps that is the lesson Mark wanted me to learn from this, I thought to myself.

"If I announce the decision tomorrow, they will know my mind was made up before I arrived," I said. "We should wait two or three days."

"It will be interesting to see if either of them comes to present his case to you," Loud said.

"And debase themselves further?" I remarked. "They probably will. I suppose I should give them the opportunity."

Before it was time for dinner, our two surveyors arrived looking much worse than when they split off. I noticed some of their equipment was missing. On closer inspection, almost all of their things were missing—their equipment, their supplies, and everything else.

"What happened?" I asked

"Your Highness, we encountered a fairly large group of people after our second day in the mountains," the one surveyor named Scott explained. "They were quite hostile. When they asked us why we were there, we lied and told them we were looking for gold, the same as they were. They accepted that answer, though it did not improve their attitude. Two days later, someone from another group saw us taking measurements and deduced that we were surveyors. The next thing we knew, we were surrounded by an angry mob. This bunch had more people than the first group we ran into. They attacked us and broke all of our equipment, then stole all of our belongings. We had no choice except to return."

"Major Grunevald, you'll need to take most of your men up there and roust those people out," I instructed. "Scott, did it look like any of these people were having success in finding gold?"

"No. That is one reason Chet and I think they were so angry," Scott replied. "We don't think either group was looking in the right place."

"Here's what we are going to do," I announced. "One of you will return to guide the men of the Shield to where the treasure hunters are. With any luck, you'll recover some of your belongings. The other of you will search Etiam, Brego, and the other nearby towns and find the trapper who found the gold in the first place and bring him back to me."

"I doubt he'll come willingly, Your Highness," Chet said.

"Then we'll have some men accompany you—but at a discreet distance," I said. "We don't want the man to run and hide."

"What will you do when we bring him back?" Scott asked.

"Pay him handsomely to help you make a map," I said. "I doubt the man came back with more than a couple of ducats worth of gold. If we offer him a couple of hundred, I think he will be very happy."

"May I tell him that?"

"If you think it will help, certainly," I said. "It has to be easier than scratching it out of the ground."

"Actually, Your Highness, I believe he sluiced it from a creek," Chet said.

"He what?"

"In the case of this trapper, he probably used a dish or a pan to scoop up gravel from the bottom of a creek and then allowed the flow of the water to wash away the lighter materials until only the gold was left," Chet explained. "The gold is heavier, so it doesn't wash away as easily."

"Huh!" I grunted. "That shows my ignorance. I thought gold came from underground, and you needed to dig for it."

"That's not wrong, Your Highness," Chet replied. "That is how most gold is obtained. But often, when a vein of gold is near the surface, some of it gets carried away by rain and weather and makes its way into the soil nearby. That's when you use the sluicing method. And when you find gold by sluicing, chances are there is a larger deposit nearby—one that you can dig up and where you would find much more than by sluicing."

"Ah! Now it all makes sense," I said. "Well, if this trapper can give us an idea of where he was, it will be a big help."

"How many men should we send into the mountains, Your Highness?" Major Grunevald asked.

"All but the two or three who will accompany Chet as he tries to find this trapper," I said. "Unfortunately, I think you will need to keep them there to prevent other treasure hunters from moving in. We will probably need to order others from Aquileia in order to do a thorough job of it."

"Your Highness, I cannot leave you unguarded," Grunevald said.

"I appreciate your sense of duty, Major," I said, "but if the agent of the Dark Lord himself wasn't able to kill me, do you really think I need to worry about Swietlik and Westhaver?"

"Your Highness, I will not leave you unguarded," Grunevald said firmly.

"Fine," I sighed, admitting defeat. "Leave two or three men behind with Mr. Loud and me. Send someone to fetch a dozen of the men we left with Her Highness and Miss Katherine. Is that acceptable?"

"I'll stay here with you and a dozen men, Your Highness. We'll fetch a dozen from the men waiting outside the Temple of Freyja," Grunevald countered. "Even so, I will be very uncomfortable. The duke and the baron *hate* you, Your Highness. I saw it in their eyes. You think they are just ridiculous snobs—which they are—but it's deeper than that if you ask me."

18

The soldiers left the next morning. Most of them went with the surveyors. Three went with Chet in search of the trapper. One rode to summon a dozen of the men waiting outside the Temple of Freyja. Major Grunevald and two troopers stayed with Mr. Loud and me.

Neither Swietlik nor Westhaver showed up to beg forgiveness. I expected it would be two or three more days before greed and curiosity compelled them to seek me out. For me, it was a rare day with nothing much to do.

That night, the smell of smoke woke me. I lit a candle using the tip of my finger and then could see the smoke. As quick as I could, I donned my clothes and buckled my sword, then went to open the door.

Before I did, I put my hand near the latch. I could tell before I touched it that the metal was already hot enough to burn my flesh. Wrapping my hand in one of my other shirts to protect it from the heat, I opened the door and then quickly shut it. The hallway was filled with flame.

I went to the window and threw it open. Another blast of heat greeted me. I guessed the entire first floor was on fire.

With the window open, smoke from below began filling my room. It was clear to me that I would need to jump. I picked up a chair and used it to bash the sashes out of the way. Satisfied that I could now jump through and not need to contort myself and crawl out, I opened my link to Bellona fully.

When I did, my body gave the illusion of appearing much larger. In addition to that, I also sensed that there was danger outside. My mind immediately reckoned that either Swietlik or Westhaver, or both, set the fire and would try to kill me.

Good luck with that, I thought with grim humor. I drew my blade and prepared to leap out. With Bellona's power fizzing in my veins, I did not worry about the drop from the second floor of the inn.

I took three running steps and jumped. For an instant, I felt the searing heat from the fire below. Then my feet hit the ground, and I tumbled forward over them, tucking my shoulder and executing a somersault.

When I reached my feet again, I could tell that my sudden arrival was unexpected by the mounted men waiting outside. There were nearly two dozen of them. In that group, I quickly spotted the duke and the baron. I decided I would save them for last. They set this fire in an attempt to kill me.

Their men were only now beginning to draw their blades. In the light of the fire reflected in their eyes, I could see their fear. I considered that they were only following orders.

"Drop your weapons or die!" I commanded.

A handful of them did just that. Several others froze, their swords still half in the scabbard. Two, braver or more foolish, tried to attack me. Even though they were mounted and had the advantage, their skill was no match for mine. I danced from one to the other and skewered them both. Their horses continued to move forward as the lifeless bodies of their riders started to slump and fall from the saddle.

"Get him!" Westhaver screamed as this was happening.

The men, seeing how easily I dispatched the two who came at me, did not follow his order. I crossed quickly to Swietlik and yanked him from the saddle. He screeched as I did so. On his way to the ground, I punched him in the head with the swept hilt of my sword.

Westhaver wanted to run away, but the men on either side of him, paralyzed by fear, prevented him from turning his horse. I shouldered my way between him and the man to his left. The baron had drawn his blade and took a swipe at me. I parried in quarte and then aggressively bound his blade with a counterclockwise twist. He dropped his blade before I broke his wrist. I then tugged him down, knocking him unconscious as I did Swietlik.

"You men," I said, breathing only slightly more heavily than normal, "return home. Tell the baroness and the duchess that their husbands are being taken to the capital for treason, where they will be hanged. You may inform them that they have two days to vacate the manors. After that time, I will have them arrested as squatters and imprisoned. Go!"

The men rode off like scared rabbits. After I watched them depart, I turned my attention to the inn. The entire building was now engulfed in flame.

Using the reins from their horses, I bound the duke and the baron securely. I then went to see if there were other survivors beside me. There were none. Mr. Gilbert, Major Grunevald, and Mr. Loud were dead, along with the two members of the Castle Shield and anyone else trapped in the building. I hoped they died in their sleep. Burning to death seemed to me to be a horrible way to leave this existence.

Murder would be added to the charges against Swietlik and Westhaver. I almost wished they could be hung more than once. It also complicated things for me greatly. As soon as one of the men of the Castle Shield returned, I needed to send him to the capital as quickly as he could ride with orders for reinforcements to come. Until more men arrived, I was stuck here with my two prisoners.

"Keep your mouth shut," I informed Westhaver when he began to stir. "I have no desire to hear anything you might have to say. If you disobey me, I will gag you."

When Swietlik returned to consciousness, I gave him the same instructions. Both men regarded me with hopeless fear. It was clear they did not imagine their plan would fail.

When the day dawned, people from the village smelled the odor of the smoke from the embers of the now-destroyed inn. They came to investigate. Seeing the baron and duke tied up puzzled them until one of the people who was present at the dinner a few nights before recognized me as the prince.

"Cor!" he breathed. "Yer Highness! Wha' happened?"

The onlookers gathered round me in a small crowd as I explained. Hearing that the baron and duke tried to kill me made their eyes grow wide as saucers. It also caused many of them to regard the trussed-up nobles with angry looks.

"Lemme git ya summat t' eat, Yer Highness," one of them offered.

"Wut else kin we do?" asked another.

"I sent some men looking for the fur trapper who came down from the hills with gold," I said. "If you could find those men and tell them to come back, it would be most helpful."

"They won't find him no how," one of them laughed. "If ole John don' wanna be found, ain't nobody gonna tell 'em where."

"That's good to know," I said. "Any chance you'll share his whereabouts with me? Not now—in a couple of days."

"Sure."

For some reason, that answer made me smile. These folks stuck up for one another. I respected that.

Blessedly, the weather stayed fair that day. The men who I sent in search of "Old John," as the trapper was known, returned that afternoon. I sent one of them to the town of Brego to inquire of the innkeeper there if he could house me for a few nights.

We spent the night in the open, borrowing some blankets from the stable for me and our prisoners. Some of the townspeople brought us food. We did not share with the baron and duke. I did give them water, but that was the extent of my largess. Our man returned from Brego to tell me that the innkeeper would be delighted to host me for as long as I wished.

In the morning, we headed there. The soldiers held the reins of Swietlik and Westhaver's mounts. We'd loosened their bonds every so often to allow circulation to return to their hands and feet, holding them at sword point the entire time.

On the ride to Brego, it started to rain—hard. The men and I had oilskins. Our noble prisoners did not. That pleased me.

At the inn, I explained that we had two prisoners who would be staying in the stable under guard. The innkeeper agreed and then asked who they were and why they were in custody. When I explained, he tried unsuccessfully to keep a smile from his face. Clearly, the duke was not beloved by the people in the area.

"What about the wife?" he asked with a false innocence.

"She must be out of the manor tomorrow," I said. "Or we will remove her by force and everything in the house then belongs to the crown. Same with the baroness. I feel bad for her children, though They seem nice enough. They didn't do anything to deserve misfortune."

"Eh, her family has money," he said. "Or so I'm led to believe. The moppets won't suffer."

"We need to feed the prisoners," I said. "I don't want them to starve before they face justice back in the capital."

"I'm sure I can prepare suitable meals for them, Your Highness," the innkeeper said.

From his smirk, I guessed the duke and the baron would be given the burnt part of any roast, yesterday's bread, and any other food the innkeeper would not normally serve to paying guests. My snort of amusement escaped before I could stop it. I wondered how quickly the word would spread and how soon locals would come to gawk at their duke.

I sent one of my men to watch the road. I expected the group we summoned from the Temple of Freyja to come today, heading to Etiam, since they did not know we'd needed to move. The other two would guard the prisoners in the stable.

That afternoon, the thirteen men riding from the south arrived. When I saw Sergeant Hewko among them, I breathed a sigh of relief. I called the men over and explained what happened. After I finished, I pulled the sergeant aside.

"Sar'nt, I need a lot more men than we have, but we'll make do for now." I said. "We sent a couple of men with Chet to find the trapper. Most of the men went with Captain Garnet and Captain Sample to get the people searching for gold to leave and go home. They attacked the surveyors. We need to send two men to go find them and bring at least a dozen back, along whichever of the surveyors is better at drawing maps."

"Aye, Your Highness."

"We also need a couple to help with guarding the prisoners. Then, we must send at least four men to each of the duke's and the baron's manors," I said. "They need to inform the wives that they had until tomorrow to vacate the premises. If history is any guide, they will have ignored my order. Your men are to remove them by force, then stay on the property until relieved. I'll go with them for the initial encounter.

"Westhaver has young children. We don't want to distress them any more than necessary, but they and their mother must leave. The duke and the baron are guilty of treason and murder. There will be no mercy, especially since I believe the wives goaded them into taking their ill-advised action."

"What about the servants, Your Highness?" Hewko asked.

"I would like them to stay—if they're willing," I said. "I will talk to them while I am at each location. If possible, I would like to keep them on until the king decides who the duke and baron will be. First thing tomorrow, you and I need to go to the inn in Etiam and look for Major Grunevald's remains. He carried the traveling funds with him. I hope some other scavengers haven't already found that. Whatever we find of the major, Mr. Gilbert, and Mr. Loud, we need to make sure someone says the proper rites."

"We need a priest, then, Your Highness," Hewko observed

"After we go through the ruins, we can find one," I said. "After that, I will ride with the men to the residences. Finally, we need to send a man back to the capital in the morning. He needs to travel as quickly as possible and summon at least one more squadron to join us here. I'll also give him a dispatch for the king."

"That means we're stuck here until at least Harpa," Hewko commented. "The princess and Miss Katherine will be finished at the Temple of Freyja soon. Do you want them coming here?"

"Much as I miss my wife, I think it would be better for her to return to the capital," I said.

"You should give the man we're sending to the capital a letter for Princess Lucy with your request," Hewko suggested. "Be prepared for her to ignore you."

"I am, Sar'nt," I said with a laugh. "My only hope is that she will keep her stay here short if I tell her not to come at all."

I obtained pen and paper from the innkeeper. My note to Lucy was brief. I shared only the bare details of what took place. When I finished, I ate dinner. After the meal, the letter I wrote to the king was much longer.

In the morning, Sergeant Hewko sent some of the men on their different assignments. He and I then rode back to Etiam. There was no more smoke wafting from what was left of the inn. We poked through the rubble for hours. Sergeant Hewko found Major Grunevald. He also located the remains of the chest in which the major was carrying the travel funds. Hewko scooped the contents into one of his saddlebags. There were nearly two thousand ducats.

The two soldiers were also easy to find due to their armor. As far as Mr. Gilbert and Mr. Loud were concerned, I thought I located what was left of them, but I could not be sure. After we retrieved the money, we went into Etiam to the Temple of the Three Major Gods. We found a priest, and I asked if he would conduct the proper ritual to ensure those who died in the fire would find their way to the afterlife.

He accompanied us back to the site. We pointed out the bodies we found. He led us in prayers for those who died. I thanked him when he finished.

"How did the fire start, Your Highness?" he asked as I escorted him back to the Temple.

"Baron Westhaver and the Duke of Namie started it," I said. "They hoped to kill me, but they only ended the lives of these unfortunate souls. I will be taking both of them to the capital, where they will be tried for treason and murder."

The priest hissed and made a warding gesture with his hands. What I noticed is that he did not appear surprised. Nor did he seem unhappy. I commented on his reaction, or lack thereof.

"Neither of them supported the Major Gods as members of the nobility should," he said. "Nor did they exhibit any sort of compassion for the residents of their holdings. They were small minded, selfish men, married to women who were even worse. I dislike wishing ill of anyone, but … good riddance!"

"When I return to the capital, I will urge His Majesty to select good people for Namie and the barony," I promised.

"He did well in choosing you as his successor, Your Highness," the priest said, "so I have hope he will choose wisely."

Sergeant Hewko and I returned to Brego. The remaining eight men rode with me to the duke's manor. As I expected, Eudora had made no effort to vacate the premises. I sent the men in to forcibly remove her. Her indignant screeching was easily heard. They dragged her out the front door. She was literally kicking and screaming.

"You!" she shouted at me. "You can't do this!"

"We already have, Eudora," I said calmly, using the majestic plural because I knew it would infuriate her further. "Your husband is under arrest for treason and murder. We are taking him to the capital. Although he will have a trial, I am an eyewitness, and my testimony is unimpeachable. The court will find him guilty, and he will be hanged. He is no longer the Duke of Namie. You are no longer the duchess of anything. This building belongs to the person who holds this territory in fief from King Mark. That is no longer your husband. You have no right to be in this house. We gave you two days' warning to pack and leave, Eudora. You now have thirty minutes. After such time, these soldiers will put you out of the manor, never to return for any reason. Do you understand?"

She shook her head violently.

"Your thirty minutes will pass quickly, Eudora," I said. "You should begin collecting such belongings as you can."

She stared at me malevolently. I returned her gaze with calm indifference, my arms folded across my chest. This "contest of wills" continued for several minutes. She finally realized she would not win.

"Mercy?" she pleaded, though her eyes still shone with anger.

"Our mercy was strained by your husband's attempt to burn us alive, Eudora," I said calmly. "It extended only so far as to give you two days to leave. You disregarded the warning you were given. You now have just over twenty minutes to gather what you plan to take with you. Do you own a horse?"

"Yes."

"You may take that as well," I said. "Our benevolence will allow you to take a wagon, even though you have no right to do so. Better hurry, Eudora."

She whirled around and broke free from the grasp the two soldiers had on her upper arms. Immediately, she began to bark orders at the household staff. I put a stop to that.

"Have every member of the household gather here," I ordered the men. "They no longer work for Madam Swietlik and have no obligation to assist her."

"You can't do that!" Eudora squawked.

"We just did," I snapped.

"Keep an eye on her," I ordered one of the men. "Make sure she does no damage."

Eudora stomped upstairs. The staff gathered outside the front door. There were two women and one man.

"I'm sure you heard what is happening," I said. "The duke has been deposed, and Madam Swietlik is no longer allowed to live here. Four of these soldiers will occupy the residence until the king assigns this territory to a new vassal. I would be grateful if you would stay and continue to keep the place in order. The crown will pay your wages."

All three of them smiled and nodded. Clearly, they did not feel much of a bond with Eudora. That surprised me not at all.

I asked one of the soldiers to take the manservant, identify which horse in the stable belonged to Eudora, and hitch it to a wagon. He drove it around to the front of the house. This might seem like an act of generosity, but it was only to get rid of the loathsome woman more quickly.

When I judged thirty minutes was up, I sent the soldiers up to retrieve Eudora. I could tell when they reached her by the howling and cursing. It took another fifteen minutes for her to carry what she wished to take and heap it in the wagon.

She sat on the bench and started to shriek at me again. One of the soldiers had heard enough of her. He withdrew his sword and smacked the horse on its rear. The animal jolted into motion.

19

When we arrived at Baron Westhaver's, the scene was slightly different. At first glance, it did not appear as though Louella was any more prepared to depart than Eudora Swietlik. She came outside upon our arrival.

"You were told to be gone, Louella," I said sternly.

"You cannot be serious," she scoffed.

"Deadly serious," I replied. "When people burn down an inn with the intent to kill everyone inside, we take that seriously indeed. Your husband is dispossessed. You are no longer a baroness, and this is no longer your house. We will be taking your husband to the capital for his trial, where he will surely be found guilty of treason and murder, and then sentenced to hang. Did you heed the warning you were given?"

"I did. Though I hoped you would relent, for the sake of my children, I prepared for the worst," she said.

"Your husband clearly did not take the consequences to his children into account," I said. "Blame him."

"Very well," she sighed. "Come, James, Edwina! Time to go!"

The boy and girl came out a moment later. Oddly enough, they looked happy. Louella saw the surprised expression on the face of one of the soldiers.

"They think we are going to visit their grandparents," she said quietly.

She took the children by the hand and led them around to the rear of the house. There, I spied a wagon loaded with trunks. The children clambered up. Louella climbed up after them and took the reins. She set the horse in motion and left without looking back.

It was four days after that when a dozen men returned from the hills. A few hours later, Chet returned with his men. They had no luck finding the trapper. The next day we rode into Etiam as a group and I began asking where we might find Old John. Recognizing me as the prince, we received a much different response than Chet had on his inquiries. The first person we asked started to give us detailed instructions, then stopped.

"Too much bother to explain," he said. "Let me take you there."

We found the fur trapper in a shanty buried deep in the woods. I explained who I was and why I was calling upon him. At first, he refused to share the location of where he found the gold.

"John, would it make a difference if I could offer you five hundred ducats, and in return, you help my surveyor with his map?"

"Yer jokin'," he scoffed.

"No," I said sincerely. "Come to the inn in Brego. We'll get you a room while you're helping with the map and feed you. When the map is finished, I'll pay you five hundred ducats."

"I guess I'm yer man, Yer Highness," he said.

Eight days later, Captain Garnet arrived, returning from the hills with three dozen men. This entire time, I'd kept Swietlik and Westhaver in the stable. Both were filthy and furious. Even though, at first, I possessed only the clothes I put on the night of the fire, at least I was able to bathe and visit a seamstress who was thrilled to make clothes for the crown prince.

I ordered Garnet to take two dozen men and escort the prisoners to the capital. He left the next morning. Swietlik and Westhaver were mounted, their hands bound and their horses led by two of the Castle Shield.

That afternoon, Lucy arrived. It never ceased to amaze me how comforted I was by Lucy's embrace. All the tension I'd been bearing seemed to melt away as soon as she enfolded me in her arms.

"How was the visit to the Temple of Freyja?" I asked. "What did you learn?"

"There was not much they could teach me," Lucy said with a sigh. "For Katie, though, it was eye-opening and life-changing. She will stay there for several more weeks. Let me warn you now, that when you next see her, there will be little that reminds you of the girl, Katie. You will see a poised, confident, and talented adult."

"I'll look forward to it. Will the Temple of Freyja help us find people with affinity for Ceridwen Sospita?"

"Yes," Lucy said. "They immediately saw the wisdom of the idea and are sending a group of eight acolytes to Aquileia to meet Lily. They need to observe her aura so that they know what to look for. After that, they will fan out through the kingdom. I also spoke to them about forging closer ties to the Temple on the Southern Continent. The records here are nowhere as extensive as what Leora told you exists on the southern continent. They had no idea about any link between the dodecahedron and greater incidences of dark mages appearing. The head priestess will make a journey there herself to invite some of their acolytes to come meet Lily. How are you bearing up?"

"Much better now that you are here," I said, embracing her again. "I am upset that things turned out so awfully. Mark will be disappointed in me."

"Don't be so sure," Lucy said.

"What do you mean?" I asked. "He sent me here to adjudicate a dispute. Granted, the outcome was determined before we left the city, but still, to have matters escalate to where they tried to kill me—"

"Mark will not be disappointed in you," Lucy said calmly. "I know from talking with Lily before we left that he suspected things might turn out badly, and perhaps even hoped that they would."

"What?"

"Not everything is easy or pleasant for the king," she said. "Consider the situation during the war, when Mark needed to deal with Houlsin and Chafter. Compare that to what you just experienced."

"Houlsin and Chafter did not try to burn Mark alive," I said.

"True," Lucy conceded. "Do you feel you goaded the duke and the baron into action they might not have taken otherwise?"

"I think that is what troubles me," I admitted.

I explained in detail the interactions when I arrived at each man's manor. Lucy laughed in a couple of spots. When I finished, she laid her hand on my arm.

"You are the crown prince, Caz," she said. "Regardless of their feelings toward you, they must respect your position. They did not. You had every right—no, you had a duty—to insist that they do so. Mark would have been disappointed in you if you did not."

"I pushed them."

"No, you held your ground," Lucy said. "They demonstrated disrespect for you and, more importantly, your title. Nothing you did merited their attempt to kill you. If you are looking for where to place blame, I think Eudora Swietlik is the likely instigator. In the trial, I suspect we will learn that the idea of torching the inn came from her. Westhaver, as you saw firsthand, has always been a hothead. Majors and Minors! He nearly forced Major Grunevald to run him through."

"It angers me greatly that the major, Mr. Gilbert, and even Mr. Loud died in the fire," I said. "Especially Mr. Gilbert."

"That is a loss. Mr. Gilbert became like family. Mr. Williston will need to find you a replacement," Lucy said.

"I will struggle without him."

Lucy and I stayed at the inn until another squadron of the Castle Shield arrived two days after the start of the month of Harpa. They brought with them letters from Mark and Fenwick. Most of the men of the Shield would remain in the area. Lucy and I were invited to return to the capital.

The king did not mention his plans to replace Swietlik or Westhaver. He did express concern over the danger to my person and lamented the loss of Major Grunevald and Mr. Gilbert. His most pressing issue was the imminent completion of the six newest caravels.

They were named *King Mark*, *Prince Albert*, *Ceridwen Sospita*, *Sparrowhawk*, *Griffin*, and *Njörun*. Before Lucy and I returned, the ships would have set sail to join the others off the Rhetian coast. Fortunately, Fenwick was present and was overseeing the assignment of the commanders and crews and the fitting out of the vessels. I was sure Fenwick would attempt to make me feel guilty for not being there to handle it myself.

Indeed, when I opened his letter, he immediately chided me in a good-natured way for shirking my naval duties. The existing ships were meeting with success. Captured prizes arrived regularly.

He expressed concern and bafflement regarding the attempt on my life. Then, he urged me to return promptly. Lucy and Julienne were both due to deliver near the summer solstice.

His last bit of news was to inform me that Julienne had hired someone to replace her at Traval & Company. Pierre Luin, my financier, recommended a bright and eager young man named Caleb Knowlton. Fenwick had met Knowlton and approved of him. While Fenwick freely admitted he knew little about Julienne's business, Knowlton impressed him.

In closing, Fenwick informed me that Julienne wished to deliver at Easton Manor. Julienne stated that she was now Lady Easton, and it was only proper for their daughter to be born and raised in the Eastern March. I immediately worried that we would see them only rarely in the city, but Fenwick's next line assured me that there would be regular visits back, and extended an open invitation to us to visit the March whenever we wished.

The journey back to the capital was difficult for Lucy. Jouncing along in the carriage over the ruts made earlier in the spring would have made it unpleasant for anyone. For a pregnant woman nearing her term…

It was with profound relief that we arrived at the castle. Mark and Lily were almost as happy as we were. Lucy vowed that she would never take such a long journey while pregnant ever again.

Mr. Williston arranged a replacement for Mr. Gilbert before I returned. Mr. Fields was cut from the same piece of cloth as his predecessor. With his help, we made short work of the correspondence that was waiting for me.

The highlight of these letters was news from Freddy and Greta, Linc and Nellie Ellsworth, and Quint and Siobhan that all three couples were expecting children in the fall. Our son and Fenwick's daughter would have contemporaries whose parents were already friends. Though their homes were geographically separated, I hoped there would be frequent enough visits to the capital that Rob would come to know them well.

As it turned out, Lucy and I were unable to attend Ratty and Inger's wedding on the summer solstice. At about the same time that they were exchanging their vows, Lucy was straining to push Robert FitzDuncan Barry Austermain Gau into the world. The midwives said it was an easy birth. If that was easy, I hope I never see one that is difficult!

My entire world changed the first time I held that red-faced, bald-headed, squalling boy in my arms. I had never seen anything more beautiful than Lucy cradling him to her breast. It felt as though my soul more than doubled in size.

20

I suppose it falls upon me to bring this series of anecdotes to a logical conclusion. Apologies for the lengthy delay. The last collection of tales my father wrote previous to this stated that the story would continue in his next batch of scribbles to be published.

Instead, my father grew too busy living his life to document it. I suppose I'm as much to blame as any other reason. Newborns are pretty demanding, I'm told, though they say I was no more or less demanding of attention than any other infant. Mr. Fields, new to his position, did not push my father to continue writing as Mr. Gilbert did before. The incomplete manuscript you've read to reach this point lay forgotten in the bottom of a drawer.

In speaking with my mother after I found this, she told me how much of a role Mr. Gilbert played in the publication of my father's earlier adventures. According to her, though written in the first person, it was Mr. Gilbert who took my father's journals and diaries and prepared them for publication. He believed my father's stories were inspirational and that sharing them with the public would prove to be both popular and beneficial.

By now, you're probably wondering who I am. I'm Rob—Prince Rob—son of King Casimir and Queen Lucille, older brother of Princess Miriam. After seven years on the western border with the Rangers (like my father before me), I returned home to the castle two years ago. In that time, I've had adventures of my own, but we will get to those.

Like you, I've read the earlier stories of my father's life. It's easy to say that my youth was nowhere near as difficult as his—he and mother made sure of that.

I grew up surrounded by love. At the same time, both my parents, and all three sets of grandparents, presented me with plenty of challenges. They taught me the value of hard work and a job done well and never allowed me to wallow in luxury.

My sister and I have also had the benefit of lifelong friends. Diana Fenwick—Lady Oritur—was my primary partner in mischief when we were younger, and we are still as close as two friends can be. Second only to her by the thinness of a hair, is Artie Austermain, Lord Rawlinsford. Martin Cullen, now Lord Tulley, is another member of our group, along with Bruce Hawkins, and Joanna Ellsworth. Only Diana and I have links to the supernatural, but it plays no part in our friendships with others, as is the case with our parents.

We grew up calling each other's parents "Aunt" and "Uncle," even though I'm only related to the Austermains by blood. Diana is a cousin by virtue of Uncle Fenwick being adopted by my grandfather Duncan Barry. Miss Katherine, now Lady Chafter, was Aunt Katie. My Uncle Jerry is in charge of the royal stables and taught me and my sister to ride. There's also Aunt Amanda, but I'll get to her.

I look like my father, though with my mother's wheat-colored hair and blue eyes. Perhaps an inch taller (when I stand up straight) compared to him, and a bit broader in the shoulders. Miriam has our father's dark hair, but otherwise takes after our mother in nearly every respect, including her supernatural abilities.

One thing that frustrates my father greatly, and that he cannot understand, is why Theo likes me. Theo still manages Easton Manor for Uncle Fenwick and Aunt Julienne. From the first time he saw me as an infant, Theo decided I was worthy of his affection. When I first visited, he eagerly took me from my mother's arms and held me, looking down on me with utter adoration. Theo is old now but still huge and imposing. He treats my father like dirt. The fact that my father is the king doesn't matter at all to Theo.

As I said, my father is now the king, and has been for the last three years. His elevation to the throne set my departure from the Rangers in motion. Though I will share some of what he and Uncle Fenwick did after I was born, what follows will be more about me—and my friends—as the tale unfolds.

My birth was the beginning of a hectic period in my mother and father's life. Before I was weaned, Aunt Katie brought a woman back to the castle. She had a striking appearance, like a hawk, and would, in time, become Aunt Amanda.

By now you understand about supernatural affinities and abilities. Amanda possessed affinity with Ceridwen Sospita. That is her primary. She has minor links to Sadu (the Goddess of art, literature, and music) and Andvar (the God of crafts and smiths).

A few years later, another woman, Celia, came from Scaramouche on the southern continent. She also possesses a primary affinity with Ceridwen Sospita. Celia stayed with us for a few years while she learned what my grandmother Lily needed to teach her, then returned to Scaramouche.

Amanda continued to live with us until King Mark died. She then started living with my grandmother. The two of them still have quarters in the castle. They are now teaching two new students, Byron, from Dunland, and Castor, from Vanda on the southern continent.

Every so often, Aunt Amanda disappears. Acolytes from the Temple of Freyja are still roaming the country. They have the ability to see the auras people have and identify their supernatural affinities. In addition to looking for anyone with a link to Ceridwen Sospita, they also search for affinities to the Dark Arts. When they find someone with that affinity, they send a message to Aunt Amanda. She rides out and removes the person's affinity to the Dark Lord before it awakens. Grandmother Lily calls it "preventative medicine."

Until assuming the throne, my father was away for several months every year. Uncle Fenwick accompanied him some of the time. Later, Amanda often joined them. I learned later that when the three of them went somewhere, it involved the appearance of dark mages. When my father traveled by himself, he was calling on vassals. My grandfather tasked him with visiting each one on a regular schedule until he assumed the throne.

My father's absences often provided an occasion where Aunt Julienne and Diana, or Aunt Greta and Artie would come visit, or we would leave the castle and stay with them. On a few occasions, all of us would gather, and those are some of my fondest childhood memories. Oh, the trouble we got into—but only when Uncle Fenwick was away with my father.

When I was three, Uncle Fenwick bonded with a charmingly scruffy dog named Ralph. At least, that was the human equivalent of how he referred to himself. A mixed breed, Ralph was Uncle Fenwick's familiar until he passed just after Diana and I went away to school. Diana was heartbroken, thinking her departure broke the dog's heart, but her father traveled to school to reassure her that Ralph died of old age. Chauncey, the owl who is my mother's familiar, is still alive.

We quickly learned that Ralph spied on us. Whenever we got into mischief, Uncle Fenwick would suddenly appear. We were never able to shake Ralph. He followed us everywhere. Despite not allowing us to misbehave, Ralph was the greatest dog I think I will ever meet.

When King Mark died, the nation mourned. The last twenty-five years of his reign were a time of unbroken peace and prosperity. Every ruler from the southern continent came to his funeral, and even the Rhetian ambassador attended.

Yes, the Rhetians. The navy my father commanded forced the Rhetians to beg for peace. Mark placed my father in charge of negotiations. He made only one demand—that the Rhetians separate their government from their strange church. They refused initially.

Two years later, envoys reappeared and said they represented a new, secular government. During these negotiations, my father shared with them his belief that the Rhetian church was created by the Dark Lord to enslave the Rhetians. They denied it, of course. In the peace treaty, one of the stipulations was for a theological exchange, sending leading religious scholars from each country to study the ways of the other. My father hopes that they will eventually realize that the Dark Lord led them astray. No one held his breath, waiting for that to happen.

The Rhetians still don't like us much. We distrust them. But we can usually talk now—the occasional border skirmish aside.

Though saddened by Mark's passing, Aquileia was happy that my father was taking the throne. They still sang the song about his exploits, which always irritated Uncle Fenwick since he was barely mentioned—in only two verses. And, happy as they were about "King Casimir," they were overjoyed that my mother was now "Queen Lucy."

Miriam and I grew up with any number of advantages besides being a prince and princess. For one, we had three sets of grandparents—all of whom loved us, none of whom indulged us. We also, from the moment of our birth, possessed not just affinities with the supernatural, but fully awakened abilities.

The same was true for Diana Fenwick and her younger brother, Charles. We were educated in the supernatural just as much as in regular school subjects. It's also one of the reasons Diana spent so much time at the castle growing up. When school was not in session, she and Charles, and Miriam and I, were being taught by Grandmother Lily, my mother and father, and Uncle Fenwick.

When we reached our teens, during school breaks we also made pilgrimages to the Temples of Bellona, Freyja, Njörun, and Mielvanir. Miriam and I have no connection with Mielvanir, but Diana and Charlie do. The priests there could not help Miriam and me in the supernatural sense, but they did teach us some great sleight-of-hand tricks.

We were also well-traveled in addition to that. With my father and mother, we visited every fief in the kingdom, though some of those visits came when I was too young to remember much. Twice we visited the southern continent.

At the age of ten, Uncle Fenwick and my father allowed me to spar with Diana for the first time. Both of us had been training in fencing, wrestling, and fisticuffs since shortly after we were able to walk. All that time, Diana and I were prohibited from using our skills against each other.

We quickly learned why. Within minutes of starting our first bout, both of us were a bloody mess, even though we were only using wooden practice swords. Both of us cheated, accessing our links to Bellona when our fathers explicitly told us not to.

In all my practice, I never met anyone as fast or who hit as hard as Diana. She said the same of me later. In less than five minutes, we struck each other with a number of glancing blows—bruising, breaking skin, and, in my case, nearly having my ear torn off. Neither of us was able to land what would have been a killing blow, but if we had fought with real blades, we would have been severely injured. Our stores of asomatous energy were exhausted at almost the same moment, and both of us collapsed on the practice floor.

When we regained consciousness the next day, both of us had the same thought. As soon as I was allowed out of bed, I ran to see her to apologize. Diana was my best friend, and I had no desire to hurt her. By the same token, I could hardly wait until the next time we fought.

On our fifteenth birthdays, our fathers gave us the tan-zyan rings they took from a pair of assassins who kidnapped Grandfather Duncan and who tried to kill them. On our sixteenth birthdays, while our parents were busy, Diana and I made an important discovery. Her father still carried the sword of Bellona. His sword belt was hung in the vestibule.

Not far away was the lance, which my father still possessed. The lance was of little interest to me and never had been. Uncle Fenwick's sword, however, had always pulled at me like a magnet.

Diana followed me as I tiptoed into the vestibule. As I went for her father's sword, I half expected her to stop me. When my fingers touched the grip, I was unprepared for the immense surge of Bellona's energy. I yanked my hand back as though I'd been bitten. Out of the corner of my eye, I saw Diana staggering backward, away from the lance.

"Did you—?" I asked.

"Mhm," she said, nodding her head, then, "Hey! I've got an idea."

Needless to say, three of our parents did not appreciate it when the two of us appeared in the dining room, holding the weapons and fully manifesting the Goddess Bellona. We presented the illusion that we were both roughly twelve feet tall. Aunt Julienne nearly fainted. Our fathers were instantly angry. My mother, oddly enough, laughed and clapped her hands in delight.

My mother's reaction saved us from what I'm sure would have been drastic punishments. It was only later that our fathers realized that I held Uncle Fenwick's weapon, and Diana held the lance. They made us do it again, then took the weapons away and held a private discussion. The result of that discussion was that we were not to touch them again without permission.

They also taught us how we could spar with one another, without actually fighting. Using the immense power of the sword and the lance, we could have Bellona conjure simulacrums and spar against these supernatural duplicates. We also used this method to spar with phantoms of our fathers. As far as we knew, these specters were just as skilled. Diana and I can hold our own, I'm proud to say.

My sister Miriam and Diana's brother Charlie were often our companions in our naughty escapades. Miriam's abilities were the same as my mother, with Freyja dominant and Njörun and Eir as her lessers. Charlie's primary was Mielvanir, with Sadu and Njörun his lessers.

Charlie was the originator of many bad ideas whenever we all got together. His dominant, Mielvanir, is the God of travel and commerce. He is also known for charm and a strong sense of mischief. Charlie talked the rest of us into doing the most outlandish things.

We quickly learned that when we were caught, as inevitably happened, our only chance of avoiding punishment was to send Charlie out to deal with whichever grown-up apprehended us. Even Grandfather Mark and Grandmother Lily were not immune to his ability to persuade. And, as you might expect, he had both Jenny, our cook, and Laurie, the cook at Easton Manor, completely bamboozled.

Cousin Artie, Uncle Freddy and Aunt Greta's son, often joined us. He could imitate the speech and mannerisms of all of our families, and when we were shunted aside after meals so the grown-ups could talk, Artie was often our entertainment. He would make up the conversations from which we were being excluded, although his imagination had them covering ridiculous topics.

I learned from my mother later that Uncle Freddy possessed the same skill. During the midwinter holidays, the two of them showcased their talent for the rest of us by spending an entire dinner acting as Lord Compote and his equally dim-witted and lecherous son, Lord Arbuthnot. The entire extended group was present, including the Ellsworths, Cullens, and Hawkinses. I was just old enough to understand how bawdy and inappropriate "Lord Compote" was.

Up to that point, I never saw anyone laugh so hard that they cried. That night, all the grown-ups reached that state. It was an evening I will never forget.

So, what was my father doing after the incident with the Duke of Namie and Baron Westhaver? For most of the next year, he said that he did nothing exciting except watch me being born. Grandfather Mark buried him in the account books. He oversaw the naval efforts against the Rhetians, and he helped my mother with me.

After reading the stories of his adventures, you would think he would be bored. He denies that. When I asked him recently, he told me that was the start of some of the happiest years of his life.

Just before my second birthday, news reached the castle of the appearance of a dark mage in a town named Carmarthen. My father and Uncle Fenwick rode out and dealt with the problem. I later figured out that they "dealt with the problem" by killing the mage.

On future trips in Aquileia, Aunt Amanda accompanied them. If the dark mage they found was not too deeply in the clutches of the Dark Lord, she was able to remove his or her affinity for the Dark Arts without killing them. Later, Celia was able to do the same on the southern continent.

Every two or three years, my father would learn of another appearance of a dark mage, and he, Aunt Amanda, and Uncle Fenwick would travel to neutralize the threat. When I was not quite eight, and then again when I was ten, these appearances were on the southern continent. Mother and Aunt Julienne decided we would travel there. While my father and Uncle Fenwick rode off to confront the dark mage, the rest of us visited the countries on the northern shore, along with Nagah and Combrial, and the different Temples of the Minor Gods I mentioned earlier.

It was on these journeys that I first experienced what "being spoiled" meant. Everywhere we went, we were treated like royalty—which we were, I know, but that's not the way things were in Aquileia. This also applied to Miriam, Diana, and Charlie.

As young as we were, it went to our heads, and we began acting high-handedly. That lasted until we were aboard the ship sailing for home. The four of us spent the entire return voyage sanding the decks and mucking the horses' stalls.

You would think we would be older and wiser on the second visit, but having people eagerly catering to our every whim was too seductive for us to resist. I remember being so tired on the voyage home that even Charlie had no desire for mischief.

At the age of thirteen, my parents sent me away to school. Martin Cullen, Bruce Hawkins, and Artie joined me there. Diana went to our "sister school" across the lake. She had Joanna Ellsworth for company.

School was the first time in my daily experience where people treated me differently because I was the son of Prince Casimir. Many of the older boys attempted to bully me. None of them had much luck. Almost from the time I could walk, I trained with the Castle Shield. I'd faced off against much tougher opponents.

The bullying stopped after an incident in the second month. Three older boys had somehow separated me from the group and cornered me. Without even accessing my link to Bellona (something I refused to do), I thumped all three. When it was over, we became friends of a sort. Word spread immediately that you trifled with me at your own peril.

More annoying to me were those who tried to ingratiate themselves with me. My father and King Mark spoke to me about this in detail before I left for school. I found it difficult to get my point across that currying favor was not the way to gain my friendship. When Charlie came to school in my third year, I leaned on him to explain it to people. He was much more successful than I ever was. Some still tried to cozy up to me. I trusted none of them.

21

Immediately after I graduated from school, I went to the western frontier and joined the Rangers. Diana went home to the Eastern March and joined her father's armsmen, acting as a sheriff. I climbed through the ranks, first earning a commission as a lieutenant, and then as a captain.

Two years and four months after receiving my promotion to captain, King Mark died. Before we conducted services for him, the horse nomads on the distant side of the mountains far to the east of the kingdom sent word that a dark mage had appeared in a rival tribe of horsemen. My father, now the king, was unable to go to help them.

He and Uncle Fenwick instead decided that Diana and I would accompany Aunt Amanda over the mountains. Before that, we needed to attend to the king's funeral rites. Instead of requesting leave to attend the services, my father instructed me to resign my commission. I returned home for Grandfather Mark's memorial ceremony. Once those were finished, Uncle Fenwick gave me the sword of Bellona. My father gave Bellona's lance to Diana. With Aunt Amanda, we left for Easton, with a hundred and twenty of the Castle Shield.

Over the years, my father and Uncle Fenwick tasked Lily and then Amanda with creating enough wards to protect the soldiers who accompanied us. All of them wore a chain around their necks with a small piece of topaz to which Lily or Amanda added the warding spell. As a result, they would be immune to the power of a dark mage.

Relations with the horse nomads on the other side of the eastern mountains had been cordial since my father's first visit to them. Every year since, just after the summer solstice, a group would arrive at Oritur at the head of a herd of cattle. They would trade the animals for weapons mostly.

There were now a number of people in Oritur who spoke their language, and as the years passed, more of the nomads picked up some Aquileian. The people of Oritur were under the strictest orders from Uncle Fenwick to treat the nomads fairly. The last thing he or my father wanted was for them to grow angry and resume their annual raids on the Eastern March.

Along with Aunt Amanda, we started off from the capital on the first day of Heyannir. My horse is a handsome gray gelding. Uncle Carl found him, and Uncle Jerry trained him and decided he wanted to be called Casey. Diana rides a bay mare named Millie. Like Casey, Uncle Carl and Uncle Jerry were involved in her purchase and training.

We reached Easton three days later, and Oritur two days after that, after stopping to look at the old camp at Bannock Hill that served as the main base for the armsmen when the nomads used to conduct their annual attacks. Continuing east, we came to the location of the funeral pyre where my father and Prince Albert burned the bodies of the nomads they massacred. It was now the site of a huge rock barrow. Every year as they passed, the nomads collected stones from nearby and heaped them up over the bones. The landscape around was now denuded of rocks.

From there, it took us three days to reach the river that marked the end of the desert. The river ran north to south at the foot of the eastern mountains. We camped on the far bank. Before we started up to the pass, we left most of our wagons behind. They held the water barrels that enabled us to cross the desert, and food to last us until we reached Oritur on our return. We brought with us just enough provisions for the four-day journey over the pass. Water was not an issue—we would come across many streams on both sides of the mountains.

On the fourth day, we reached the lower slopes on the other side and could see a party waiting for us. They saw us and began approaching. We met where the trail began to level out. A man with long gray hair in a braid rode forward. Diana rode out to meet him. Like Uncle Fenwick, she was fluent in the nomad tongue.

It was easy to see the meeting was off to a positive start. Diana and the old man embraced, leaning from their saddles. She beckoned me forward.

"Rob, this is Polim," she said.

I knew exactly who he was. He and his cousin Bynar were the first emissaries the nomads sent to negotiate with Aquileia. Diana explained who I was. Upon hearing it, he wanted to greet me warmly. Like Diana, I met him with an awkward embrace, both of us still in the saddle.

We spent the night nearby. Diana and Polim conversed for hours. She was kind enough to translate for me every so often. The gist of the conversation was that Kushedt was still the chief of their tribe, and Polim and his cousin Bynar also enjoyed positions of influence. The tribe had achieved a position of regional dominance as a result of the armor and lances King Mark gave them decades earlier when he sent Uncle Fenwick, Prince Albert, and my father back to meet with the nomads. No one had dared to make war upon them for nearly three decades until recently.

Polim was delighted to learn who our parents were. We told him that my father recently assumed the throne. While Polim was pleased to hear about that, he was distressed to learn that King Mark had died and that his people missed the opportunity to pay their respects.

"We owe him and your father a great debt," Polim said. "Looking back, I cannot believe how foolishly arrogant Bynar and I were when we rode west to complain about how your father dealt with us. Your father had defeated us utterly, and we had the audacity to criticize his actions. Your king could have ordered your father to put his boot on our throats. Instead, he showed us a different path, and both our peoples have benefited."

The conversation turned to their more recent problems. A tribe on the southeastern fringe of their territory had gained strength recently. Polim and his tribe had been yielding ground slowly. He described how the majority of the enemy horsemen seemed to lack all emotion. They attacked until either their force was utterly spent or they drove the men of Polim's tribe from the field.

Polim's people crossed the mountains to trade in Oritur earlier than usual that year. One of their people described what was happening, and someone in Oritur sent word back to Aquileia, suspecting a dark mage was at work. From what Polim described, it seemed pretty clear.

Aunt Amanda had many questions for Polim. In particular, she wanted to know how well-trained their priests of the Three Major Gods were. The nomads worshipped the same Gods and Goddesses as we did, though they called them by different names. Polim promised he would introduce Amanda to the head priest of the tribe.

"The problem we have will be freeing the thralls after we neutralize the mage," Amanda explained to us later. "The incantations are language-specific. I'm worried that these people don't have the written lore to know the cantos."

"Doesn't that present a problem for you, Aunt Amanda?" I asked. "You don't know the nomad tongue, or whatever variant this other tribe uses."

"That's another of the unique qualities of Ceridwen Sospita," Amanda said. "She was from Aquileia. As a result, Aquileian—although in an archaic form— works for her incantations. Even Celia on the southern continent must summon Ceridwen Sospita's power using old Aquileian."

"That seems odd," Diana said.

"It is what it is," Amanda said. "I don't pretend to understand the Gods, I just know what works. Getting back to our problem with the thralls—to free them, we need priests of the Three Major Gods who know the proper invocation, or the men of the Castle Shield will need to spread out quickly and use their wards. The issue is that these tribes are spread out over large areas. From the time we counteract and banish the Dark Arts, the enthralled will be frozen in place. If we don't reach everyone by the end of the third day, we will start to lose people who will die of thirst."

"You can't get the mage to un-thrall them?" Diana asked.

"None of us have ever been able to," Amanda said. "Even Lily."

We broke camp in the morning. As we rode to the village where Kushedt was waiting for us, Amanda explained the problem to Major Entenman of the Castle Shield. He nodded gravely.

"We'll need guides and many of them," he said. "People who know the area and, preferably, can speak a smattering of Aquileian."

"I'll inform Kushedt," Diana said.

The greeting we received from Kushedt and then Bynar was every bit as warm as the way Polim met us. Kushedt admitted he had been looking forward to seeing my father and Uncle Fenwick again and was slightly disappointed to hear they were not coming. He told us that when he learned that Diana and I were their offspring, his curiosity rose, and he was delighted to meet us.

We spent little time discussing the current problem. When Diana explained that she and Amanda needed to meet with the head priest of the Three Major Gods, Kushedt summoned a young man who spoke passable Aquileian to translate for me so we could continue our conversation. Kushedt was full of questions about my father and Uncle Fenwick.

I fielded his inquiries as best I could. In return, Kushedt explained that he and his tribe had been successful in subduing the five neighboring tribes one by one. These tribes were now vassals to Kushedt, though he placed only the lightest burden upon them.

Each year, they were expected to deliver a single heifer to Kushedt. The animal was then sacrificed to the Three Major Gods. A feast followed, attended by the leaders of both tribes.

"You used to blood your young men by sending them over the mountains and the desert to attack us. Do you still test your youth?" I inquired.

"The five subject tribes have unfriendly neighbors," Kushedt explained. "We send our young men to help patrol the borders. It is better training for us than our attacks on the Eastern March were. We fight in the open, on horseback. When we came to attack you, we needed to assault walled villages. There are no walls here on the plains."

Diana and Amanda returned a couple of hours later. As Amanda feared, the head priest of the Three Major Gods knew only the most basic incantations. They had no written lore. The tribe's priests would be of no assistance in freeing those enthralled by the dark mage.

We explained the situation to Kushedt, and how our soldiers would need to spread out to free those whom the dark mage bound to him. Kushedt grasped the problem quickly. He pledged that he would have guides ready for our men once we neutralized the mage.

"When this is over, would you like to send some of your priests to learn from ours?" I asked. "We can help educate them and translate some of our books into your language."

"I can see how that would be helpful," Kushedt said. "There is only one problem. We have no written language."

Hearing that astounded me at first. Then, as I considered it, I realized why this might be the case. Kushedt's people were nomads. Even their largest villages, like the one where we were, tended to be semi-permanent at best. There was no place in their culture for books, which they would need to haul around, and they managed to do just fine without the written word.

"I would offer to have our scholars help you create a written language," I said, "but I fear it would only be of use to the priests. The rest of your people would be uninterested."

"Perhaps things will change in the future," Kushedt said. "Who can say?"

We left the next day. Bynar led us to where the tribe's forces were. It took three days to reach them. The group enthralled by the dark mage had been advancing from their former territory a league or two at a time. Kushedt's people had not taken many casualties up to this point. They yielded territory because their enemies simply would not stop.

"The dark mages I have encountered with His Majesty and Lord Easton have been unskilled," Amanda told us that evening. "None of them have any training in how to use their ability. As a result, they have a limited span of control—typically line-of-sight. I will remain with the main body of soldiers to prevent any of them from being enthralled by the mage."

"We will advance with the Castle Shield and try to touch him or her with our ward," I said. "Lord Easton and my father went over this with us before we left. Once we succeed, you come forward to see if the person can be saved."

"Just remember," Amanda said, "an arrow, even inexpertly fired, can still kill you. Be careful. I do not want to return to Aquileia without both of you."

"Don't worry, Aunt Amanda," Diana said.

"Major Entenman, we will advance in a wedge formation," I instructed. "We'll be in the center. The mage who is our goal will be where he or she can see the entire field. That will make him easy to spot. Lady Oritur and I will move directly toward the mage. When we reach him, we'll disable him by touching him with one of our wards. You'll know that happens when—"

"Your Highness, I've ridden with your father and Lord Easton in these situations before," the major said. "The only significant difference is this is a cavalry fight, and not on foot. When the enemy freezes up, the men know not to kill them."

"Right. Sorry, major," I said. "This is all new to me. I forget that most of your men have already experienced it."

"That's fine, Your Highness," he said with a smile. "You're just being thorough. Nothing wrong with that."

Diana checked with the leaders of our nomad allies. They would ride on our flanks until it was time to engage. At that point, Diana and I would lead our wedge straight for the mage.

As we approached the enemy, we saw them mustering for battle. I wondered, not for the first time, how the people took care of themselves while under thrall. The mage would need to relax his grip on them to allow them to cook, eat, and manage various bodily functions. Perhaps there were different degrees of control the mage exercised.

The enemy horsemen mounted and began to assemble, facing us. We continued to approach at a walk. A common misconception people have about cavalry battles is that the horses gallop all the time. Galloping for a horse is like sprinting for a human. There's a limit to how long you can maintain the pace.

In cavalry encounters, a rider wants to conserve his mount's energy and stamina. When two forces come together, chances are that it will be at a gallop, but the approach will be at a much slower pace. Only when you come within bowshot will you urge your horse to gallop.

I tried to look beyond the enemy line to see where the dark mage was. Then I cursed myself for being an idiot. I accessed my link with Bellona and tugged out a tendril of her power. After I did that, I could sense exactly where the mage was. I also knew the mage was a woman. Just to check, I also opened my connection to Freyja. Using it, I was able to see the woman's aura. The aura of the Dark Arts is repulsive to those with a link to Freyja who can perceive auras. I quickly shut down my connection to Freyja.

"See her?" I asked Diana.

"I don't have eyes on her yet, but I know where she is," Diana answered.

We were nearing the range that an enemy archer could be expected to reach. I unsheathed the sword of Bellona. As soon as my fingers touched the grip, I felt a massive surge of power and energy infuse my entire body.

Within myself, I threw my connection with Bellona open without limit. The blood in my veins seemed to fizz. Immediately, I manifested the Goddess. Casey and I appeared larger than life. I heard the men near me gasp at my sudden transformation. Most of them had seen my father or Uncle Fenwick do this before, so it was no surprise. Nevertheless, it was, as one told me later, awe-inducing.

Diana did the same thing as she rode next to me. She unlimbered the lance from under the fender of her saddle. She and Millie suddenly seemed monstrously huge. I'd seen it many times before, but it was still impressive.

I flashed a hand signal to Major Entenman. He nodded to the bugler riding next to him. The bugler raised the horn to his lips and sounded the staccato signal for the Castle Shield to charge.

Casey responded to the call without even a nudge from me. I swear that he could read my mind. Diana had told me she felt the same about Millie. My father claimed that every horse Carl Stensland bought and that Uncle Jerry trained had the same uncanny ability. My mother said neither Carl nor Jerry possessed any supernatural connections, but she acknowledged that they had a special way with horses.

If we were facing normal soldiers, I would imagine they would quail at the sight of Diana and me manifesting the Goddess. Instead, we were facing emotionless thralls. They displayed no reaction to us at all. Their mounts did, though, and were not too keen on meeting our approach. Quite a few of them veered away.

We thundered toward them. Diana and I led the charge. In less than a minute, Diana and I met the enemy line. Up to now, I had never wielded Bellona's sword in battle. I'd used my abilities in fights against Rhetians, but what I experienced now was on a much higher plane.

My father once described fighting using Bellona's abilities as moving as quick as thought. With her sword in my hand, I swear I was even faster. My quicksilver movements were more akin to reflex reactions. On our charge, I batted away three arrows in midflight, inches before they would have struck me. I'd never done anything like that before. A part of my mind marveled at it.

Diana and I sliced through the thralls. Ahead of us, we spotted the mage. The mage had surrounded herself with more thralls, but they slowed us only briefly. Diana was able to reach down from her saddle and touch the mage with her ward.

As soon as the topaz touched the mage, she slumped to the ground as every muscle in her body relaxed. When that happened, the thralls froze in whatever posture they happened to be in. The tumult of the battle ceased, replaced with an eerie quiet.

Aunt Amanda rode up. On her way to us, she summoned Ceridwen Sospita. She drew a square in the dirt surrounding the fallen mage. When the square was complete, she began reciting a chant. I could not see any physical evidence of what she did.

"The mage's influence is trapped in the square I created," Amanda said. You can have your people begin freeing the thralls. They are safe now."

22

"Once you free some of this tribe," Amanda asked, "find out what her name is. It will speed things up."

Diana took charge of this. Those recently freed from the thrall of the mage were disoriented. It took Diana a few minutes to learn the mage's name: Fatima.

It took about four hours, as near as I could tell, before the mage regained consciousness. When she did, she was clearly furious. She hissed and snarled.

"She is threatening to kill us," Diana reported.

"Your powers are confined to this square," Amanda said, and Diana translated. "In addition, the three of us are protected by wards, and you cannot influence us. Test what I say. You have no power outside of the square in which I have confined you."

"What's to prevent her from walking out of the square you drew?" I asked Amanda while Diana translated for the mage.

"Something Lily and I learned," Amanda answered. "Trying to cross the boundary will cause her unspeakable agony."

The mage muttered in a harsh-sounding tongue. Even though we stood in the bright midday light, the world seemed dimmed. When Fatima ceased speaking, the midsummer light returned.

Fatima snarled something else and reached her hand to the invisible barrier Amanda had created. When her hand reached it, Fatima screamed in pain. Her eyes glowed red. Looking directly at Amanda, she tried another incantation that had no effect. Fatima stopped and composed herself.

"If you plan to kill me," she said, "you should hurry up and do it."

"That may not be necessary," Amanda replied. "If the Dark Lord has poisoned your soul, death will be the only answer. Your soul will become the possession of the Lord of the Seven Hells, and you will face eternal torment. The Dark Lord reserves special punishments for those who fail him."

The fire in the mage's eyes flared, and she snarled like an animal. Amanda hardly reacted except to begin chanting in archaic Aquileian. I could barely understand what she said. As Amanda went on, Fatima appeared to relax. The red glow faded from her eyes.

"Ask to speak with Fatima," Amanda asked Diana.

A succession of different reactions flew across Fatima's face. Eventually, they stopped, and her eyes glowed red again. She glared at Amanda.

Amanda recited the same incantations as before. When Fatima's normal appearance returned, Diana asked to speak with Fatima again. It took four more attempts before she received a response.

"I am Fatima," Diana reported. "Who are you? What do you want?"

"Are you aware that you have been under the control of the Dark Lord?" Amanda asked.

When Diana mentioned the Dark Lord in the nomad's tongue, Fatima's eyes glowed red again. Fatima snarled, then laughed in a particularly chilling way. Amanda turned to Diana and me with a glum expression.

"This one is irredeemable," she said in a sad tone. "The Dark Lord's hold is too deep and too strong. Lily and I have learned from experience that when we see that sort of response, there is no point in continuing to try to reach the person she was."

"Diana, I suggest you ask the nomads to execute her," I said. "None of us should have any part of that."

Diana rode off briefly. When she returned, Polim was with her. Four archers trailed behind them.

As the archers dismounted and took position, Fatima started to shriek curses at them. Diana reassured the men that the mage had no power outside the lines scratched in the dirt. The men nocked their arrows and bent their bows. On a signal from Polim, they let fly.

All four arrows pierced the center of Fatima's chest. As my father and Uncle Fenwick warned us, a black whirlpool opened up underneath her. As we watched, her body was captured by it and dragged down and out of sight. With a whoosh, the hole disappeared, and Fatima's body was gone. The nomads standing nearby who observed this were visibly upset.

Again, Diana reassured them that they had nothing to fear. Polim apparently echoed this, and they nodded and mounted their horses. Diana then spoke to Polim and gestured for me to signal Major Entenman. Within minutes, the men of the Castle Shield set off to free the thralls.

Eight days later, the last of the Castle Shield returned. Major Entenman reported that they continued freeing thralls until they encountered people free from the mage's influence. A few of the men found some thralls who died from exposure before they reached them, but thankfully, there were few of those.

Kushedt hosted a grand feast to fare us well the night before we departed. He tried to give us cattle as a gift, but I refused them as gently and politely as possible. Eventually, he understood we were not prepared to conduct a cattle drive on our return, and I think I managed to avoid a diplomatic incident. At least, Diana said I did. I took her word for it.

On our way back over the pass, Major Entenman pointed out to me the place where the trail collapsed out from under Prince Albert. It was a sobering moment. That was an event that changed the course of my father and Uncle Fenwick's lives. I paused to consider everything that happened as a result.

We reached the other side of the mountain and rejoined the teamsters and wagons we left at the river. As we crossed the desert, Diana asked us to gather rocks along the way and load them in the empty carts. When we reached the huge cairn after three days, we added those stones to the ones already heaped up.

"Kushedt asked if we would consider helping them in this way," Diana explained.

Only a few of the men, like Major Entenman, were left in the Castle Shield who had been present when my father massacred the nomads. They attended to adding to the barrow reverently. The newer men treated it like a chore until the major and a couple of others barked at them. That night, around the fire, Major Entenman and the other older veterans told the story of the battle.

"The nomads, the same people we just met and who were so friendly, came over the mountains for hundreds of years," Entenman explained. "They used to attack the Eastern March every summer, using it as a way of blooding their young men and teaching them how to be warriors. Our kings did not realize how much of a drain it was on the Eastern March. The earls did the best they could, which was only to hold the nomads at bay and prevent them from sacking any of the towns. Every year, it sapped the resources of the March. The earls were usually successful in this, but there were occasional failures. The worst of these, a summer when three towns were pillaged, brought the matter to King Mark's attention.

"From this, King Mark learned how hard-pressed the March was and had been. He declared that King Casimir, who was just a commoner at the time and the bastard son of the Earl, would now be the legitimate heir and named him Lord Oritur. As Lord Oritur, he took the fight to the nomads in his first year and inflicted huge losses upon them.

"The next year, the king sent Prince Albert and some of us to the March. Lord Oritur planned to ambush the nomads when they arrived, just between those two crags over there. The nomads were completely unprepared. We slaughtered them. There were three hundred dead. It took us three days to gather enough wood from the forest to the south to create a pyre to burn the bodies. We couldn't bury them—the soil is too shallow.

"When the fires died away, there was a huge pile of bones left. The nomads sent emissaries to complain about the massacre if you can believe it. I won't get into how peace was achieved, but it was. The nomads continue to come over the mountains every year, but to trade, not to make war. On every trip, they add stones to cover the pile of bones. Their chief, Kushedt, asked Lady Oritur if we would add some more on our journey past.

"Our two peoples are friends now," Entenman said. "Our trip just now is proof of that. Why would we not help them honor their dead? That battle, if you could even call it that, was the last bit of enmity between us. The cairn over there marks a significant turning point in the history of Aquileia."

When we reached Easton, we sent the bulk of the Castle Shield with Aunt Amanda back to the capital. Twelve remained with me. I decided to take advantage of the opportunity to go south to see Port Charles and visit my grandfather Duncan and grandmother Ariana. Diana remained in Easton since her mother and father were away, and she wanted to make sure all was well. She would return to the capital with me when I returned from my visit.

Port Charles was quite different from the last description my father wrote. It was now a port that was active year-round, equal in size to Aurora. Of all the towns I've visited, Port Charles was one of the most affluent. Perhaps as a result, everyone there always seemed to be in a good mood.

We rode through the center of town and to the bridge. A couple of the men dismounted and lowered the bridge so we could ride across to the jute farmstead my grandfather managed. This was another success. Enough jute was grown, processed, woven into rough cloth, then sewn into bags that the kingdom had no need to import from Mooresa.

Grandfather Duncan lived in a magnificent house on the farmstead. Unlike Easton Manor, this building was constructed entirely from wood. I always enjoyed my visits.

My grandfather, now in his eighties, was still spry and sharp. As my father wrote in earlier books, it was as though Duncan had shed about two decades of age when Ariana came into his life. The two of them were sitting on the veranda in front of the house when we rode up.

Grandfather wanted to know all about my journey over the mountains and my visit to the nomads. He himself had never visited them. Although he accepted that our two peoples were now friends, he claimed that he spent too many years fighting against them to be able to set his old feelings aside.

The thing is, I imagined that if he and Kushedt ever met, they probably would have ended up as friends. It was easy to picture the two of them swapping stories and getting drunk together. That would be a sight! I made a mental note to mention it to my father when I returned to the capital.

The men and I left in the morning and returned to Easton. We collected Diana and returned to Aquileia. When I returned to the castle, after greeting my mother and father, I learned that Artie Austermain was planning a party for the next evening, on Njordday. I was very happy not to have missed it.

When I told my mother about it the next morning over breakfast, she went through my wardrobe and pulled out a specific set of clothes. When I returned from my stint in the Rangers, the only civilian clothes I had no longer fit. Before

Diana and I headed east, mother commissioned the tailor to make me a number of outfits.

She made me try them on to make sure they fit and to see how they looked. I squirmed and protested the way I did when I was younger, but secretly I was enjoying it. Mother knew somehow that it was just an act. She just laughed at me.

"This is an important night, Rob," she said.

"Why?" I asked, wondering if she knew something about the future.

"You haven't seen most of your friends for seven years," she said, sidestepping my inquiry neatly by presenting an entirely sensible reason. "Don't you want to look your best? I'm pretty sure all the young ladies present will be dressed in their summer finery. You're the crown prince. There are certain standards, you know."

"Fine," I sighed heavily, pretending to be exasperated.

"Keep up that act, and you'll be able to compete with cousin Artie," she cracked.

"Oh, I do hope 'Lord Arbuthnot' makes an appearance tonight," I said, chuckling. "I haven't seen him in years."

"He and 'Lord Compote' put on quite a show at the winter solstice," she said. "You did know that Artie has been seeing Joanna Ellsworth, didn't you?"

"He wrote me and told me back when it started," I said.

"Well, Artie as 'Lord Arbuthnot' was just as lewd toward her as 'Lord Compote' is with your Aunt Greta. Artie definitely takes after his father," she said. "This is what you should wear."

"Blue and buff," I commented. "Like father's wedding clothes."

"Not quite," my mother said with a wistful smile, "but the colors suit you just as well as they do him. And the fabric is lightweight, so it will be comfortable here in the summer heat. Don't forget to bathe and shave later. Miriam has been invited as well. The two of you will take the carriage."

"Aw," I groaned.

"You may both spend the night at Artie's if things run late," she said. "I won't force either one of you to be dragged home by the other. If one of you wants to leave and the other stay, we'll send the carriage back in the morning at a reasonable hour."

Late in the afternoon, after cleaning up and dressing, I was waiting for Miriam in the sitting room. My mother and father still occupied the same quarters as when they first moved into the castle. When King Mark died, they could have moved into the more traditional royal chambers, but those were in an older part of the castle. They preferred the sense of light and space where they were, so they decided to stay put.

Miriam found me sitting there. She is two years younger than I am and we have always gotten along well. I can say, with a brother's pride, that she is a beautiful young lady.

"Ready to go, Robby?" she asked.

"Whenever you are, li'l sis," I replied.

Miriam was one of the few people in the world who could get away with calling me "Robby." I hated the diminutive, but it had become a running joke between us. I got her back by calling her "li'l sis," which she disliked in equal measure. In this exchange, however, it made both of us smile. I offered her my elbow, and she took my arm.

"Are we spending the night at Artie's?" I asked.

"I plan to," she said.

Miriam and Martin Cullen—Lord Tully—had been seeing one another for more than a year. I figured their relationship was far enough advanced that this would not be the first time they spent the night together. As for me, I'd been away.

I spent seven years in the Rangers and never came home during that time (though my mother and father visited once a year). Before that, I was in boarding school for four years and only home during breaks. As a result, I had no young lady of interest in my life.

When my father was my same age, he told me he had no experience with women at all—none. The only female influence in his life was his stepmother, Victoria. If you've read any of my father's chronicles, you know she was hardly a good example.

I, on the other hand, grew up surrounded by beautiful and intelligent women. My best friend was Diana. Back in our school days, she and I had practiced kissing, so I had that going for me. Sadly, that was the extent of my intimate experience. And, lest you think something might happen along those lines, allow me to disappoint you now—it won't.

The carriage was waiting for us outside the castle. A dozen of the Castle Shield were formed up behind. I helped Miriam into the carriage and then went to speak with the sergeant.

"Sar'nt, my sister and I will be spending the night at Lord Austermain's house," I said. "Once you see us safely in the door, you may leave."

"Appreciate it, Your Highness," he said with a grin. "Hope you have a good time."

Lionel, Artie's manservant, greeted us at the door. He took the light shawl Miriam wore, and then my sword. My father still wore the blade his grandfather left to him. The emir of Garo sent mine to me as a present when I was born.

It's funny how things turn out. Of the rulers on the southern continent, the one my father and Uncle Fenwick trusted the least upon first meeting was the emir. Yet, in the years after they freed Combrial from the dark mage, the emir turned out to be Aquileia's most staunch and trustworthy ally.

Made by the finest swordsmith on the southern continent, it must have cost a fortune. It is a swept hilt rapier, like my father's, and simple in design. The blade is, as close as we can tell, the equal of my father's in quality.

Miriam and I proceeded to the sitting room to find the gathering in full swing. She left my side when she saw Martin. I cast my gaze over the room. My visual survey stopped when my eyes encountered a young woman chatting with Artie.

23

She was tall and slender. Her hair was auburn, tied back in a complicated plait. In the late afternoon light, it seemed almost purple. Bright blue eyes above freckled cheeks, with skin not the pale hue redheads often have but lightly tanned, and a mouth slightly opened in a broad smile, struck me dumb. I don't know how long I stood there gawping, but it was enough time for Charlie Fenwick to notice.

"Rob?" he asked, appearing next to me. "Have you turned stupid?"

"Huh? What?" I answered intelligently.

"I asked if you've gone simple in the head," he reiterated. "You're standing there with your mouth open."

"Charlie," I said, grabbing his arm—a bit more fiercely than I intended, judging by the way he winced. "Who is that goddess talking to Artie?"

"Goddess? You're kidding, right?" he responded after looking at who I referenced.

"Just tell me who she is!" I demanded in a whisper.

"You *have* gone simple in the head," Charlie said, shaking his head. "Don't you recognize her? That's Patricia Ellsworth, Joanna's younger sister."

'It can't be. Patsy's hair is carrot-colored, and she's all gawky and awkward and pale, and…" I trailed off as I realized that the last time I had seen Patsy Ellsworth might have been seven years earlier, when she was fourteen or so. "Majors and Minors!" I breathed as I realized it was indeed her.

Charlie's response was to laugh at me. Looking at the young woman more closely, I could now see the family resemblance to her sister Joanna. There was only tenuous similarity to the girl of fourteen or so that I remembered, but enough that I could see she was the same person. I heard Miriam chuckle behind me.

"Charlie, is there a reason my brother is standing there like a fopdoodle?" she asked.

"Yes," he replied over his shoulder. "He's drooling over Patsy."

"Are you, Robby?" she asked, sidling up next to me.

"Um … she changed," I muttered lamely. "The last time I saw—"

"Mhm. Not only is she a rare beauty, Robby," Miriam whispered in my ear, teasing me, "she is intelligent and fun, *and* she has ability like us. She is the first person on either side of her families who has possessed any connection to the supernatural in generations. Her abilities are the exact same as mine and mother's and, as a result, are extremely compatible with yours, in case you're curious."

"Wha—?" I started to say, but then Patsy looked directly at me from across the room, and I lost the power of speech.

She turned and said something to Artie. As I watched, she started to cross the room toward me. She seemed to float, she was so graceful. I was frozen in place—I'm pretty sure I stopped breathing.

"Good luck, Robby," Miriam teased me with a giggle as Patsy approached.

"Your Highness," Patsy said when she reached me, dipping gracefully into a curtsy and holding it.

"Puh-please," I stammered, reaching to draw her upward by her hand, "call me Rob. You—you're Patsy?"

When my hand touched hers, I felt something. It was as though a gentle charge passed between us. Embarrassed, I pulled my hand away quickly. As soon as I did, I wished I hadn't.

"Most people call me Patricia these days, Rob," she replied with a glint in her eye.

"Oh. I—I'm sorry, Patricia," I mumbled.

"*You* can call me Patsy," she said with a smile. "I kind of like it coming from you."

"I—I didn't recognize you," I said, trying to fumble for the right thing to say, hoping to explain my staring at her. "Charlie needed to tell me who you were. I apologize if I made you uncomfortable."

"I wouldn't say you made me uncomfortable," she replied, "but I could definitely feel the weight of your stare."

"I, uh, well, it's been a long time since I last saw you," I said lamely. "You've… Uh, you've grown up."

"The last time was at the party that my parents always throw just before the winter solstice," she said. "Seven and a half years ago. I was fourteen."

"How do you remember that?" I blurted.

"It is easy to remember. I had a massive crush on you," she admitted. "You were one of the few older children who paid any attention to me that night—or ever, for that matter, at least, in those days."

"You looked very different then," I said, struggling to keep the conversation flowing and kicking myself mentally for such a stupid remark.

"I know," she said and laughed.

At that point in my life, I know I never heard a more pleasing sound than her laughter. Her eyes seemed to sparkle with delight and mischief. I was wishing, hoping, that I could touch her again. She put her hand on my arm. Without skin-to-skin contact, I didn't feel anything. It disappointed me subconsciously.

"Oh, it wasn't long after that when everything changed," she said, a pleasant lilt in her voice. "I grew several inches in the new year. My hair darkened and wasn't pumpkin-colored anymore. My body filled out and I was no longer stick-thin."

"You're still quite slender," I commented, and immediately regretted saying something so dull and obvious, and perhaps unseemly.

"Why, thank you, Rob," she said and laughed again. "I was all knees and elbows before. Surely you remember."

"I do," I said.

"Do you remember dancing with me that night?" she asked.

I cast my mind back. Yes, I thought I could recall dancing with her. I remember thinking she seemed to be so much younger than my sister and her friends, even though there was only a year difference. There didn't seem to be anyone her age at the party.

"I do," I said.

"I do, too," she said. "In fact, I've never forgotten it."

"Oh, my," I said, then suddenly thought of a clever remark—unusual, since all too often in these circumstances, my wit deserts me. "I hope I didn't step on your toes too hard. I probably mashed them pretty good if you still remember it."

"No, you goof," she said. "You made me feel graceful, perhaps for the first time in my life."

Her laughter delighted my very soul once again. She took her hand from where she was resting it on my arm and smacked the back of my hand gently when she called me a goof. Again, I felt some sort of current pass between us. Experiencing it the second time, the nearest thing I could associate with it was the way I felt when I opened my connection with Bellona completely and felt her energy surge through me.

This was softer, and more subtle. It had a sensuous feel to it. Then I remembered what my sister told me. Patsy had supernatural ability. If she matched my sister and my mother, her dominant was Freyja. That was one of my lessers. I wondered if her connection to the Goddess of love was the reason for the sensation.

"Um, did you feel that?" I asked awkwardly, worried that she would deny it.

"Of course," she replied. "How could I not?"

"Miriam told me you have ability," I said quietly. "Please excuse my lack of tact, but did you *try* to make that happen, or is it just—?"

"I did not do anything," she said. "My dominant is Freyja, and my lessers are Njörun and Eir, just like your mother and sister. Judging from that, our abilities are probably very harmonious."

"That's what Miriam said," I mumbled.

"Rob," she whispered seductively in my ear, having stood on her tiptoes and put her hands on my shoulders to lean extremely close to me, "if I decided to make something happen, you'd be powerless to resist me."

As she backed away to where she previously stood, I realized I was as physically aroused as I had ever been. That discomfort and realization made my cheeks flame red with mortification. At the same time, it was all I could do to resist the temptation to grab Patsy and enfold her in my arms. She laughed and patted my hand again.

"Poor Rob," she said, laughing lightly at my discomfort. "Let's get you a glass of wine so you can calm down."

"Majors and Minors!" I hissed when I regained the ability to form words. "You certainly did something that time!"

Patsy merely gave me a sly smile, then took me by the hand to the sideboard where Artie had put out decanters of wine and glasses. With a slightly shaky hand, I poured a glass for each of us. Patsy guided us to a settee. She sat and patted the cushion next to her. When I sat down, she took my hand in hers.

This time I felt a subtle undercurrent in the feeling that flowed from where we touched. My father had written many times how my mother's touch brought with it a feeling of calm comfort and quiet confidence, and I had experienced the same feelings from her. This was like that, but there was a difference to what I felt from my mother's touch. I resolved to ask her about it when I saw her tomorrow.

"After I finished school, I spent the next two years learning from your mother and the queen," Patsy said. "They taught me all sorts of wonderful things, then sent me off to the Temple of Freyja and the Temple of Njörun."

"Is that what you've been doing since school?" I asked.

"Not entirely," she said. "For the last year and a half, I've been in Bergin mostly."

Linc Ellsworth, Patsy's father, is one of my father's oldest and dearest friends. He is now Count Bergin. As holdings go, Bergin was one of the smallest. Within its borders, however, was the richest copper mine in the kingdom. The Ellsworths were among the best examples of our nobility. They managed their holding for the benefit of their residents.

Joanna Ellsworth, Patsy's older sister, was my age and part of the group of friends I grew up with. Patsy was a year younger than my sister Miriam and her group. As a result, I did not see as much of Patsy growing up as I did of other younger siblings who were Miriam's age.

While I always thought Joanna was pretty—at least, once I became aware of the difference between boys and girls—Patsy was, as she put it, 'all knees and elbows.' Patsy was now tall—only an inch or so shorter than me, though I noticed she was wearing shoes with a low heel that added another inch or two.

And whatever physical awkwardness might have plagued her in her youth was long gone, based on what I saw so far this evening.

"What have you been doing back home?" I asked.

"We have a healer in Bergin," she said. "I've been helping her. She's getting older and doesn't get around very well these days."

"Oh," I said. "Will you stay on and take her place eventually?"

"It wouldn't be a bad life," Patsy said, "but I found a girl in the county for whom Eir is her dominant. Gladys—that's the healer's name—and I started to teach her. When her affinities blossomed, I convinced my father to send her to the Temple of Eir for training. She just arrived back in Bergin."

"Wow!" I exclaimed softly, "the Temple of Eir. I've never met anyone who actually visited it. What did she say it is like?"

"Well, first of all, it's difficult to reach," Patsy said. "It's far to the north and requires seven days of walking through the perpetual snow, even in midsummer."

"I knew that," I said. "I hear that the Temple of Eir on the southern continent is just as difficult to reach."

"I heard that, too," Patsy said. "Anyway, Amelia—that's the girl—reached the Temple. She says that she was amazed to find that the land around the Temple had no snow and was full of growing crops. It's in a valley that seems untouched by winter. Amelia explained that for a portion of the summer, the sun does not set. As a result, the crops grow quickly."

"What about during the winter?" I asked.

"In the middle of winter, the sun does not rise for days on end, according to Amelia."

"That would be unpleasant, I think," I said.

"I agree," Patsy replied, delighting me again with her laugh.

"Why does Eir want her Temples to be so difficult to reach?" I asked.

"Amelia told us that she learned there is a reason for it. The head priest explained to her that the Goddess wants only those who are committed to the life of a healer to share in her wisdom. The difficulty of the journey is a proof of commitment."

"None of the other Gods and Goddesses—" I started to say.

"Eir does not want people to use her gift to make money," Patsy said.

"Huh," I grunted. "I wonder why the others don't feel the same."

"Well, if you think about it, the ones who come readily to my mind have the opposite view," Patsy said. "Andvar expects his students to be successful and to support the Temple with some of their earnings. Mielvanir is the same way."

"What about Freyja?" I asked.

"Freyja wants us to spread love and joy throughout the world," Patsy said. "Think about your mother."

Patsy's comment was like the missing piece of a puzzle. In considering my mother and how she behaved at home and in public, spreading joy and love was exactly what she did. I think I always knew that but was not able to articulate it so neatly before. I told Patsy that.

"Why didn't I learn that when I went to her Temple?" I asked.

"How long did you stay?"

"Only a week," I replied. "They didn't really teach me anything about how to use my connection to Freyja, now that I recall. A lot of it was about ethics and morality."

"That's because Freyja is one of your lessers, and your mother probably told them to limit your instruction," Patsy said. "All you would be able to do is use her gift to manipulate others and cause trouble. For those of us for whom Freyja is our primary, we get an even heavier dose of morality and ethics."

"Mother has never taught me anything about how to use my connection to Freyja either, except how to read auras," I said. "Now I understand why."

"You didn't miss much at the Temple," Patsy said. "They didn't have much to teach me because your mother told them she had already trained me on how to make use of my ability. I'm very lucky that way. Your mother and Queen Lily are wonderful teachers."

"She never told me that you were studying with her," I said. "But I'm sure she had her reasons."

"What does that mean?" Patsy asked.

"Father told me a long time ago that my mother is clairvoyant," I explained. "She gets glimpses of the future from time to time. Unfortunately, she cannot talk about them. He told me never to press my mother—simply to trust that she would tell me what was appropriate for me to know and that she wasn't keeping secrets from me from any sort of ill intent."

"It's good that you understand that," Patsy said. "Your mother is a remarkable woman. Da was telling me—"

"Da?" I asked.

"My father," Patsy said.

"I'm sorry," I said quickly, feeling like a boor.

"My father was telling me how much attitudes regarding the supernatural have changed in the cities since your father was named as King Mark's successor. People in the country have always believed in the supernatural, and any little town without a hedgewitch considered itself unfortunate. Folks in the cities liked to pretend that magic did not exist. Your father made no secret of his ability—they still sing that song about him and Lord Easton and how they saved King Mark—but it was your mother and how she lived her life that provided an almost daily example of the benefits of magic. Of course, all the people she and Queen Lily taught have helped spread that as well."

"So, is your time in Bergin—?" I started to ask.

"Bergin is home," she said, "so I'll always spend some time there. "For now, though, Da wants Joanna and me to live in the city and, well, have fun. His father allowed him the same freedom before getting married, and he feels we will be better prepared for the life of duty we will lead if we get our fill of freedom when we are young enough to enjoy it."

"Fun—that's an interesting concept," I joked. "It's been unending duty for the last seven years. I just resigned from the Rangers you know. And then father sent Diana and me over the mountains far to the east of the March."

"I know," Patsy said.

"Oh," I sighed. "Sorry."

"No, I want to hear all about the horse nomads," Patsy said, "and what you and Diana did. Charlie told me a little, but it sounds exciting."

The two of us spent the rest of the evening on that settee. It was only when her sister Joanna came to collect Patsy to take her home that I realized I had monopolized Patsy's time and attention, and hadn't mingled at all with the other guests. The Ellsworth sisters were the last remaining guests I could see. I walked Patsy to the door and helped her put on a thin wrap that Lionel produced.

On the threshold, Patsy turned to me quickly. She kissed me quickly and lightly on the lips. I stood there, stunned for a moment, then dashed down to assist her and Joanna to climb into the carriage. When they drove off, I watched them go. I heard Patsy's laugh.

24

"You look like someone smacked you in the back of the head with a heavy stick," Artie commented when I returned to the sitting room.

It was just the two of us. Artie was sprawled on the couch as though his long limbs were made of jelly. From reading my father's chronicles, I understood this posture was a trait he shared with his father.

"I do feel a bit addle-pated," I admitted, "even though I drank only the one glass of wine all night and I didn't even finish it."

"Then pour us another, Rob, and tell me what ails you," Artie said.

"I think everyone here tonight knows what ails me," I said as I followed his order and poured us each a glass of wine. "My apologies, Artie. It was rude of me to take up all of her time and not to circulate. This was the first chance I've had to see many of the old crowd in seven years, and—"

"Don't worry about it," Artie said. "You provided a great deal of entertainment."

"Oh, Seven Hells!" I muttered. "Was everyone talking about us?"

"Everyone but Lionel," Artie said.

I put my head in my hands and groaned. This was not good. People would talk. I felt awful that I would cause people to gossip about Patsy. Whatever chance I might have had to get to know her better, poisonous gossiping would probably scare her away.

"Why so glum, chum?" Artie asked.

I explained. He listened intently. When I finished, he shook his head.

"You have little to worry about, Rob," he said. "There is no one who was here tonight who is not a friend of yours or of Patsy's. If there is any talk at all, it will be only that of delight."

"What do you mean, delight?"

"Well, Charlie and Miriam told me that they had never seen you react to a woman's presence the way you did when you saw Patricia," Artie said. "I mean, we grew up in the company of some very pretty women. Of all of us, you're the only one who never 'experimented' at all."

"I don't understand," I said.

"Tut, tut, Prince Rob," he said, using his Lord Arbuthnot voice. "Do you mean to tell me that the king and queen never bothered to explain certain things to you? Facts of life and all that? Damme, I suppose I shall need to do it. You see, my prince, there comes a time when boys grow into men and girls grow into women. Their bodies change, as I hope you've noticed. For most young men, including your very own Lord Arbuthnot, the change in the female form is most appealing and the subject of intense curiosity. I myself have endeavored to indulge that curiosity as many times as possible."

"Do tell, Lord Arbuthnot," I encouraged him.

"Well, whilst you have been away, playing at soldiers, the rest of us have been engaging in maneuvers of a more *intimate* nature, shall we say," he continued, stressing the word "intimate" in a way to make it sound especially obscene. "Different members of our group of friends have formed temporary liaisons for the purpose of *experimentation*, shall we say, satisfying our *curiosity*, if you will."

"I see. Tell me, Lord Arbuthnot, are some of these experiments of a *horizontal* nature?" I asked, trying to match the tone of his lewd innuendo.

"Oh! Your parents *did* explain some things to you. Excellent!" he exclaimed, rubbing his hands together. "There are only two people in this broader group whom no one has observed in *experimentation*, so to speak—you, since you were away, and the delectable Patricia, with whom you renewed your acquaintance this evening."

"Even my sister?" I asked incredulously.

"I would never say a word against dear, sweet Princess Miriam," he protested.

At that moment, as though on cue, we both heard a feminine moan from upstairs. It came from my sister, who was spending the night with Martin Cullen upstairs. Although we both tried to pretend for a moment that neither of us heard it, we couldn't help but begin to laugh. It took us a couple of minutes to recover. When we stopped chuckling, Artie laid his finger aside his nose and gave me a lascivious wink. That started the hilarity anew.

"If I may be so bold as to inquire, Lord Arbuthnot, why did Miss Joanna depart this evening? Is she not your favorite?"

"Well, you see, my prince, while various of us have been trying others on for size, in a manner of speaking, the scrumptious Patricia has not indulged her curiosity—not once! Oh, she flirted, she teased, she used all the weapons the Gods gave to women to enslave us poor men, but she never took the next step. Anyway, Joanna, my poppet, being the kind sister that she is, felt it would make Patricia uncomfortable if she were to spend the night and make Patricia depart by herself. Although, my prince, methinks you would not have been averse to spending more time with the lovely Patricia."

"That is true, Lord Arbuthnot, but we would not have engaged in horizontal experimentation," I said.

"Ah, but I predict you will, my prince. Lord Arbuthnot has an eye for these things, you know!"

"Artie—seriously, now," I said in a somber tone. "Don't be making a match right away. Tonight was the first I've seen her in over seven years."

"Rob, let me just say this—the way you looked at her, it was as though a blind man was suddenly gifted with sight and saw a flower for the first time. She looked at you the way hounds look at hares," Artie said. "All of us in the room could feel the attraction you have for one another. And all this time, she never encouraged any man to get close to her. Perhaps she has been waiting for you."

"That's nonsense!" I sputtered.

"It probably is," Artie admitted. "You both seem intrigued by one another. Play the hand out and see what happens."

"Um, Lord Arbuthnot, I do have a problem," I said, thinking that appealing to his comic persona would be less embarrassing for me. "While you and the rest of the group have been *experimenting*, I have not had the opportunity. The women my comrades in arms would visit in the towns near where we were positioned were not—"

"Not of suitable quality for Prince Rob, eh?" Artie replied. "Who would have thought? Our handsome prince, completely innocent in the amorous arts."

"Not completely," I said. "Back when we were all still in school, Diana and I practiced kissing one another. But that was the full extent of any *experimentation* that I did."

"You and Diana?" Artie said in his normal tone. "Most of us suspected that—"

"Once we figured we grasped the concepts, we stopped," I said. "It felt … wrong."

"I can understand why," Artie said. "Judging by how close the two of you have always been, it would have felt akin to incest."

"Ugh," I grunted in revulsion. "I was trying to avoid that word, but you're right."

"It doesn't matter anyway," Artie said. "She and Bruce Hawkins—"

"So, it is Bruce!" I exclaimed quietly. "I suspected she was involved with someone, but she would not share any secrets. For how long? How serious are they?"

"Long enough and serious enough to cause a problem," Artie said.

"A problem?"

"Lady Easton still controls Traval & Company, though Caleb Knowlton handles the day-to-day work," Artie said. "Bruce's father—"

"Majors and Minors!" I gasped. "I never thought about that. Let me guess… Bruce is being groomed to take over Hawkins Trading."

"Not so much lately," Artie said. "His younger brother Scott now seems to be the heir apparent. Diana's brother is going to take over Traval."

"That's why she wouldn't talk to me about it. Do Diana and Bruce have a chance? Will the two families be able to work through this?" I asked.

"There has never been enmity between the two sides, just a fierce competition," Artie said. "I think it will work out. Bruce and Diana will probably need to renounce any claims to the companies. That will leave Charlie and Scott as fierce rivals who are also brothers-in-law—hardly ideal."

"What do their grandfathers think?" I asked, referring to Ben Hawkins and Herbert Traval.

"I believe they're actually rather amused," Artie said.

"Returning to the subject of your inexperience," he continued, switching back to his Lord Arbuthnot persona, "part of the fun is *exploring* together, don't you know?"

"Artie, don't tease me," I protested.

"Fine," Artie sighed disappointedly. "Look, Rob, I think you and Patricia are on equal footing. She's always been different from the rest of the group. Everyone else is either older or younger, which I'm sure made it difficult when we were all younger since she didn't quite fit. Plus, she has a link with the supernatural. Charlie and Miriam do as well, but they were always thick as thieves, the way you and Diana are. I don't think they *meant* to exclude Patricia, but they were so wrapped up in what they were learning that they didn't think to include her."

"Will that be a problem?" I asked. "Does Patricia have hard feelings—?"

"I don't think so," Artie said. "Patricia is very self-confident and self-reliant. And, as we've all grown older, she's been brought into the greater group. That she is a year younger than Charlie and Miriam no longer matters."

"She told me that she spent two years learning from my mother while I was away," I said. "I never knew."

"Your mother, Queen Lily, and your Aunt Katie," Artie corrected. "As far as why you didn't know—ask your mother or your sister."

"They won't tell me anything," I complained.

"Why not?"

"My mother won't tell me because it's probably related to… Oh, never mind," I said.

"Rob, we all know Queen Lucy can see the future sometimes," Artie said. "And we know she cannot talk about it. Is that why you think she won't tell you anything?"

"Yes."

"That's probably a good thing, then," Artie said. "Why won't Miriam talk to you about it?"

"Because she's my younger sister and believes her mission in life is to torment me as much as possible."

"True," Artie admitted. "Is Miriam able to see the future like your mother?"

"Not as far as I know," I said. "That would be something she could not use to torment me, so—"

"I wonder if Patricia can," Artie mused. "I'm told her abilities are the same as your mother and your sister. Anyway, back to your situation—my advice is to simply let events unfold as they will."

"Would it be unseemly if I called on her tomorrow?" I asked.

"See what tomorrow brings, Rob," Artie suggested.

In the morning, we started our day in a leisurely fashion. I was the only one who woke early. Lionel made me some qava (a taste I acquired from my father), and I kept him company while he began preparing breakfast.

Artie was the first to appear. Martin Cullen and my sister came downstairs a little later. When Miriam saw me, she turned beet red. I gave her a nasty smile. Oh, yes—I would tease her relentlessly.

At ten o'clock, our carriage arrived, accompanied by a dozen of the Castle Shield. Martin helped my sister climb in, and I followed. I waited until we began moving before launching my attack on my sister.

I did my best to imitate the moan that Artie and I heard the night before. Her cheeks turned crimson, and she buried her face in her hands. Just for good measure, I moaned again.

"Unfair," she protested. "You should be careful, Robby. The day will come when I will be able to return the favor."

"Fine. I'll ease off for now," I said. "Tell me about Patsy."

"You spent the entire evening with her," Miriam countered, "to the exclusion of everyone else. Didn't you learn everything there is to know?"

"Actually, she didn't share much," I said after I mentally reviewed my interaction with Patsy the night before. "She kept asking me about the nomads and what Diana and I did while we were there."

"Surely you got more from her than that," Miriam scoffed.

"Let's see … she had a crush on me when she was a girl—"

"Still does," Miriam quipped.

"No," I said with some disbelief.

"Mhm. Go on."

"She studied with mother and grandmother for two years after she finished school—"

"And Aunt Katie."

"Artie mentioned that," I said. "I didn't know Aunt Katie came back to the city."

"She was back and forth for a few years while you were away," Miriam explained. "Lord Chafter came for council meetings, and they often stayed for a few weeks at a time."

"And she has been in Bergin the last year or so but just returned to the city to 'have fun,' as she put it," I said.

"That's all?" Miriam asked.

"That's all I'll tell you," I said.

"Hmm," was Miriam's response.

"Would it be too forward of me to call on her today?" I asked.

"See what the day brings," she said.

"That's uncanny!" I exclaimed quietly.

"What is?"

"Artie used almost the exact same words."

"It must be good advice, then," Miriam said smugly.

When we returned to our residence in the castle, I found my mother in the sitting room. From the way she reacted to my entrance, I suspected she was waiting for me. She gave me a smile and nodded to a seat at right angles to where she was on the sofa.

"How was the party?" she asked with an innocence I suddenly suspected was contrived.

"It was very interesting," I said, "but I think you already know that."

She pursed her lips. Then she tilted her head to the side, looking at me with a thoughtful expression as she tapped her chin with her finger. Finally, she sighed.

"Rob, you know—"

"Father has warned me many times not to interrogate you about certain things," I said. "And I don't mean to now. I'm not upset. But I do ask you to consider things from my point of view. I feel as though I am in a play, and you and Miriam know all the lines before I even say them."

"Has Miriam been teasing you?"

"A little, but don't worry mother," I said. "After last night, I have ammunition of my own."

"Nevertheless, she should stop. I will speak to her."

"Mother, I'm not upset," I repeated. "I just think that I'm the only one who isn't in on the joke."

"That's a harsh way of putting it," she commented.

"You knew I would run into Patsy last night," I said, ticking items off my fingers. "I was dressed in a specific set of clothes you picked for me to wear. You knew Patsy and I would hit it off. That's all I can state with confidence, but I'm sure there is more. I don't want to ask any questions because, well, father told me never to do that, and he told me why. There are some questions I do want to ask, ones that I don't think will cause any issues."

"I will admit to what you have already figured out," my mother said with a smile. "Yes, I knew Patsy would be there and that you two would get along. She's absolutely lovely, both inside and out, and your supernatural abilities are well-matched—possibly even better than your father's are with mine. Patricia is very bright, has a strong sense of humor, and is intelligent and independent. It's no wonder you meshed well. I also dressed you in those clothes for a reason. Beyond that, I don't plan on saying much."

"Mother, I'm not angry," I said. "I know you have your reasons, and perhaps I will understand later. Is there a reason you did not tell me that Patsy was a student of yours?"

"I have lots of students," she replied. "How many of their names—?"

"Oh," I said. "Good point. My next question is about what I felt. When Patsy touched me, something passed between us. I've often received a similar sensation from you and Miriam, but this was different. There was a subtle undertone that was new. Does that mean anything?"

"I don't know," my mother replied.

I was looking at my mother intently as she answered. She gave nothing away. I could not tell whether she was telling the truth. Then I realized I should not have asked that question.

"I'm sorry," I said. "That's the second time I've shoved my foot in my mouth on the same subject."

"Oh? What was the first?"

"I asked Patsy last night if she was doing it on purpose," I said. "She told me she was not, but then she did do something that ... well ... let's just say that she demonstrated what she could do to me if she wanted."

"Good girl!" my mother said with a laugh as she clapped her hands happily.

"I was embarrassed," I admitted.

My mother said nothing but gave me her slyest smile.

"She did tell me something interesting," I commented. "Patsy said that you believe your purpose is to spread joy and love in the world. I think I always understood that, but I could never put it into words."

"She's very intelligent," my mother said with a proud grin.

"My last question for now, mother, is whether it would be too forward for me to call on Patsy today."

"I don't think you'll have the opportunity," she said.

"Why not? What will I be doing?"

"Moving out."

25

"Moving out? What?"

"Your father and I feel that it is in your best interest to live elsewhere for a couple of years," she said. "You just spent seven years in the Rangers and had no freedom to do whatever you wanted to do. We believe it will be better for you to be on your own and pursue your own interests and desires. After all, your father and I had that same opportunity, and we believe we are the better for it."

"Does this have anything to do with Patsy?" I asked.

"It has more to do with me and your sister," she said. "No matter what happens in your life in the next couple of years, I worry that you will be tempted to ask us questions we should not answer."

"Is Miriam able to see the future, too?" I asked.

"Yes."

"This happened while I was away," I stated.

"It did. Now, regarding moving you out—you were careful today regarding what you asked me, but I sense your frustration. By moving you to Uncle Fenwick's, we will avoid that tension."

"Am I being punished?" I asked. "Are you casting me out of the family?"

"By all the heavenly beings!" she breathed exasperatedly. "No! Absolutely not!"

"Will the Castle Shield be camped out at Uncle Fenwick's now?"

"That might be the best part, Rob," she said with a smile. "They won't. I believe I can share this safely—as long as you don't behave recklessly or irresponsibly, you won't encounter any danger you can't handle."

"Really? I can be like everyone else?"

"Rob, you'll never be like everyone else," she said with a smile. "But you'll be able to live like Charlie or Artie or any of your other friends. You'll be sharing the house with Charlie. Miriam told him not to say anything last night because I had not explained it to you yet."

"So, it will be just Charlie and me?" I asked.

"And Roberta and Johnny," she said, referring to the housekeeper and her husband. "Otherwise, just the two of you, except when Diana is in the city, as she is now, or when Fenwick and Julienne come."

"And Charlie and Diana don't mind?"

"What do you think?" my mother replied, rolling her eyes.

"This doesn't sound so bad," I admitted. "Thank you."

"Go thank your father as well," she said. "Then help Mr. Fields organize your things and cart them over to Uncle Fenwick's place."

I went to my father's office and thanked him for the opportunity to live on my own. He repeated the things my mother said. As he did, I sensed a certain wistfulness.

"Do you miss those days when you lived above the bookshop?" I asked.

"Sometimes," he admitted. "I would be lying if I said I didn't. You deserve the same opportunity to be on your own. Your mother assures me that you won't be in any great danger, so have fun. Don't get too comfortable right away. I may need you to do another errand for me in the near future."

"Where should I keep Casey?" I asked.

"You'll need to board him at the Foaming Boar, I suppose," my father said. "Tommy will take good care of him. After all, Uncle Jerry taught him."

For the first time since I left to go away to school, I gave my father a hug. It surprised both of us, I think. We thumped each other on the back a few times before we broke apart. I could tell his eyes were a bit watery.

Before I started with Mr. Fields to gather my belongings, I found pen and paper and wrote a quick note to Patsy. In the midst of all this, I came to the conclusion that it would have been too forward to try to see her today, but a brief note expressing my pleasure at having renewed our acquaintance was appropriate and, I hoped, seemed intelligent and respectful. Time would tell.

We loaded up four chests of clothing and my other belongings, almost all of which my mother had just purchased for me. I didn't even know what I now owned. Mr. Fields told me he would arrange for a wagon to deliver them to the house along with some furniture I would need. I went to the stable and collected Casey. Uncle Jerry was not there. One of his assistants told me that he was on the exercise grounds.

We saddled Casey, and I rode to the Foaming Boar. I went around behind and whistled for Tommy, the groom. He was a boy of twelve or thirteen years old. No one knew exactly, as he, like Jerry before him, was an orphan.

My father told me that Jerry, not long after being placed in charge of the royal stables, had noticed Tommy skulking about the kitchen that fed the men of the Castle Shield. Tommy was begging for scraps from the cooks. Instead, the cooks brought him into the kitchen and fed him. Jerry came in to speak with the lad, then sent him to the Foaming Boar.

On Jerry's recommendation, Uncle Carl hired Tommy on the same basis as Jerry started years before. Tommy lived in Jerry's old room above the stable. Carl insisted he go to school. As Jerry did before him, Tommy was making the most of his opportunity. He also solved a big problem for Uncle Carl, who was having great difficulty in replacing Jerry after he left.

Tommy slid down the ladder from the loft. When he saw me standing there, he bobbed his head. He did not know me.

"Hello, Tommy," I said. "My name is Rob. This fine gentleman here is Casey. If Carl agrees, I'll be boarding Casey with you."

"Nice to meet you, Mr. Rob," he said, "and you, too, Casey. My, aren't you a handsome gentleman."

He was addressing my horse, not me. When Tommy said that, Casey put his head alongside Tommy's. Tommy's face broke into a huge grin. It was as though Casey understood what Tommy said.

"I'll go talk to Carl," I said. "I think Casey is in excellent hands."

"Majors and Minors!" Uncle Carl exclaimed when he saw me. "Your Highness! What brings you here? Did you resign your commission?"

"Hello, Uncle Carl," I said as I crossed to him and embraced him.

He hugged me back just as tightly. The last time he saw me was just before I rode west seven years before. He poured me a mug of cider and I spent the next couple of hours getting him caught up on my life.

"I just left Casey in Tommy's hands," I said. "My mother and father are allowing me to live in Uncle Fenwick's house for now. I hope you'll allow me to board Casey here. My father asked if you would offer me the same terms as you did for him."

"Well, I don't know, Rob," Carl said, scratching his now-bald head. "Your pa and I served together, so I gave him a friendly rate."

He was pretending to be serious, but I knew better. I just started to laugh. He looked disappointed that he wasn't able to pull my leg a little.

"Your money's no good here, Rob," he said.

"I insist, Uncle Carl. If you won't accept it, pass it along to Tommy."

"I'll do that," he said. "Does this mean we might see you dining with us every so often?"

"On Roberta's nights off," I said.

I left not much later and walked to Uncle Fenwick's house. To my surprise, the wagon with my baggage was not there. When I went inside, Roberta met me with a curtsy.

"Roberta, thank you, but please let that be the last time you do that," I said. "If I'm going to be living here, please just consider me simply as Rob."

"Very well," she said. "I must say, Mr. Rob, your timing is impeccable."

"Why?"

"They just left," she said. "They took up two wardrobes, an armoire, two chests of drawers, and four trunks. The gentleman unpacked everything and put it away. All the work is done."

I ran upstairs. It didn't take long for me to figure out which room was mine. The master bedroom was obviously for Aunt Julienne and Uncle Fenwick when they came to the city. There were two rooms that showed signs of habitation. One was clearly Charlie's and the other, Diana's. The fourth room on the second floor was to be mine.

As Roberta said, everything was neat and tidy. Even the bed was made. I looked through the wardrobes and the chests of drawers. Everything was there. I sent a silent thanks to Mr. Fields.

"Now, I need to warn you, Rob, that every day is not a holiday, and there won't be a party every night," Charlie said as we sat down to dinner. "Some of us need to work for a living."

"Charlie, if I misbehaved that way, I'm pretty sure my father would post me to the Persimmon Islands," I said.

"We haven't had a garrison there for twenty years or so," Diana said.

"Exactly. That's why he'd put me there."

"So," Diana said. "Patricia."

"By the way, you left marks on my arm where you seized it last night," Charlie snarked.

"What?" Diana asked.

"He was standing there like the village idiot, with his mouth hanging open, trying to catch flies," Charlie explained.

"I saw that," Diana said.

"When he saw Patricia across the room, he dug his claw into me and demanded, 'Who is that goddess talking to Artie!' When I asked if he was joking since it was just Patricia, he went sort of mental."

"Patricia *is* beautiful, Charlie," Diana said. "Just because you didn't get anywhere with her—"

"No one ever got anywhere with her!" Charlie nearly shouted. "Then Rob shows up for the first time in years, and—boom! It's all over!"

"What do you mean, 'It's all over'? All we did is talk," I objected.

"I'm going to tell Saoirse you said that, Charlie," Diana teased.

"Don't you dare!" Charlie shouted. "I got over Patricia a long time ago."

"Saoirse Cullen, Charlie?" I asked.

He nodded.

"Wow!" I breathed. "All these relationships between the group of us who grew up together. It's almost like—"

"Don't say it, Rob," Diana cautioned. "You would be the nine-hundredth person to make the same comment."

"Tell me, Rob," Charlie asked, "am I the only person other than Patricia that you spoke with last night?"

"Well, I said hello to Lionel when Miriam and I came in," I said.

"As I said," Charlie said to Diana, "Boom!"

"I had a rather lengthy conversation with Lord Arbuthnot later," I said defensively.

"That was probably amusing," Diana remarked. "What did His Grace have to say?"

"He was his usual lewd self," I said. "His Grace told me that while I was protecting the realm, the rest of you have been engaging in *experimentation* with one another of a *horizontal* nature."

"Seven Hells!" Diana muttered. "I hope he didn't name names."

"He did not. Why? Are there some liaisons that embarrass you, Diana, dear?"

"I think every one of us, except for you and Patricia, has an evening or two which they wish never happened," Charlie said.

"Even Miriam?" I asked with disbelief.

"No, Miriam never fooled around," Diana pointed out. "Once Miriam set her hooks into Martin, that was it."

"But he—"

"Shush, Charlie. That was before Miriam."

"True."

"Lord Arbuthnot and I did have the misfortune to overhear my sister late last night," I said, then imitated the moan we heard.

"Thank all the heavenly beings that the walls are thick in this house," Charlie said, making a warding gesture. "Diana, I hope I never have to experience what Rob endured."

"So," Diana said, ignoring Charlie, "Patricia."

"Didn't you just ask me that a minute ago?" I complained.

"I did, and Charlie interrupted to whine about something," she said. "Let's hear it, Robby."

"Ask nicely, Dinah," I replied, using the nickname she hated as much as I detested being called Robby.

"Oh, Rob, please tell us about your conversation with Patricia," Diana said with exaggerated sweetness, placing her chin on top of her entwined fingers and batting her eyelashes at me.

I did. Then I told them of my fruitless conversation with my mother. Charlie and Diana both started shaking their heads as I recounted how my mother deflected my inquiries.

"Robby, Robby, Robby," Diana chastised me quietly. "Your mother is the *last* person we go to when we want information about anything. Haven't you figured that out?"

"And Miriam is second-to-last," Charlie added.

"Your mother is an expert at the non-answer answer, or deflecting by inquiring why we want to know what we asked, or simply changing the subject and pretending not to have heard our question," Diana said.

"Or all of those," Charlie added.

"Your turn," I said. "Tell me what I should know about Patsy."

"Well, first of all, she made us quit calling her Patsy years ago," Charlie said.

"She told me she liked me using it," I said.

"What do you think?" Charlie asked Diana. "A year?"

"Less. Nine months—tops."

"What are you talking about?" I asked.

"How long it will take before you propose," Diana said.

"Propose?" Charlie interjected. "Marry."

"You're on," Diana said. "A florin?"

"You think I'll be married in a year?" I asked Charlie.

"Or less," he replied.

"And you think it will take longer?" I asked Diana.

"Hmm," she mused. "On second thought, Charlie, no bet."

"You both think I'll marry Patsy in less than a year?"

"From what we saw last night and from what we think we know about Patricia? Yes," Diana said.

"What is it that I need to know about Patsy?" I demanded.

"Nothing bad," Diana said. "You can trust me on that."

"She's as pretty on the inside as she is on the outside," Charlie added. "Yes, I tried to get her interested in me. So did Artie and Bruce, and a couple of other lads. She was polite and friendly and let us know in a kindly and gentle way that she was not interested. Then, last night, she was hanging on your every word."

"Is this because my father is—?" I started to ask, warning bells ringing in my head.

"No," Diana said with a laugh. "Obviously, she knows you're the crown prince, but I don't think she cares."

"What is it that you're not telling me?" I demanded.

"Think about it, Rob," Charlie said.

"Well," I ventured after replaying the conversation from last night in my brain, "she did mention that she had a crush on me when she was younger."

"So did Joanna, and Saoirse, at different times," Diana said. "I would have, too, if I hadn't grown up with you so closely. That's not it, Rob."

"Then what is it?"

"You need to figure it out," Diana said.

"You're not going to tell me?"

"No," Charlie said. "It will be much more fun for you and for us to let you figure it out by yourself. I promise—you'll thank us later."

"If you say so," I said uncertainly. "Isn't there anything you can tell me?"

"Unrelated to what you're digging for, did you happen to read her aura?" Diana asked.

"No," I said scornfully. "I feel like that's rude. It's *snooping*."

Charlie and Diana both shrugged, clearly not agreeing with me but not willing to argue the point. "You should," Diana said.

"What would I see?" I asked.

"Did you learn how to judge the strength of a person's connection with the Gods from his auras?" Diana asked.

"Yes."

"What have you seen?"

"Well, my mother is stronger than my father by enough that I can tell the difference," I said. "My father and yours are about the same. Both of you are not quite as powerful as your father, but that might be a function of age. Miriam is nearly as strong as my mother. Queen Lily is about even with Miriam, if I remember correctly. Aunt Amanda is the weakest of those I can think of, but not *weak*, if that makes sense. Why?"

"Just checking to see if we agree," Diana said. "We do. Now, if you 'snooped' and checked Patricia's aura, you would have been stunned. She's crazy powerful. I don't know if you can quantify these things exactly, but the difference between her aura and your mother's is like the difference between your mother's and your father's."

"Really?" I said, feeling rather pleased to learn this. "That must explain it."

"Explain what?"

"You know that feeling you get when you access Bellona, or Mielvanir in your case, Charlie? I'm not talking about just a wisp, but a fairly open connection. How you can feel the energy flow through you?"

"Yes," they answered almost in unison.

"When Patsy touched me, skin-to-skin, I felt something like it, only gentler," I said.

"Like when your mother gives us a hug?" Charlie asked.

"Yes," I agreed, "but it was stronger. When I asked her if she was doing it on purpose, she showed me what she *could* do if she wanted."

"I think I saw that," Charlie said. "Was that when she whispered in your ear, and then you turned all red?"

"That would have been it," I admitted bashfully.

26

Since I couldn't figure out what it was about Patsy that Diana, Charlie, and my mother wouldn't tell me, I decided to quit worrying about it. They all indicated it was obvious. In the past, when I had difficulty and was overlooking something I should have seen, turning my attention elsewhere usually brought the answer to my mind.

When I woke in the morning, I remembered it was Njordday, one of Roberta's days off. That meant I would need to cook breakfast for myself. I was capable of handling the basics. Jenny, our cook in the castle, taught me the rudiments when I was a boy.

After I rekindled the stove, I found eggs, bread, and sausages. I searched for qava and did not find anything. That would be something I needed to get and then teach Roberta to make

Diana and Charlie wandered downstairs while I was still cooking. It was easy to cook for them while I was still in the midst of preparations. Diana helped, and sliced and toasted some bread. She then handed it off to Charlie and he spread butter on all the slices. Everything was ready at nearly the same time.

"I cooked," I said as I finished eating. "One of you gets to clean."

"Odd or even?" Diana asked Charlie.

"Fine," he replied with a shrug. "You call it."

"1-2-3, even!" Diana said.

This was a game I first played with Diana when we were only single digits in age. On "even" (or "odd" as the case might be), each person flashed either one or two fingers. One person called either odd or even, and the total of the fingers determined whether he won or lost.

In this case, both of them showed only one finger. Diana won. Charlie lost. Without a grumble, he started clearing the plates from the table.

There was a knock at the front door. As the newcomer in the house, I didn't feel comfortable answering, so gestured for Diana to go. I did look over her shoulder.

"Milady," a member of the Castle Shield said as he knuckled his forelock. "Is His Highness here?"

"Right here, Teddy," I said, recognizing the trooper.

"This is for you," he said and waved a letter at me.

"Thanks, Teddy," I said as I took the paper from his hand.

Teddy knuckled his forelock again and stepped away. While Diana shut the door, I examined the letter. It was addressed to me, and the handwriting was my father's.

Rob,

Just after you left, I received some information I have been waiting for. As a result, I have an important errand for you and Diana to complete. Both of you will come to the castle for lunch at noon.

C.

Without a word, I handed the letter to Diana. She read it quickly. When she finished, she handed it back. Before either of us could comment, there was another knock on the door. When Diana opened it, Joanna Ellsworth was there. I could see her horse on the street behind her.

"What are you doing here?" she asked with some surprise when she saw me.

"With my parents' permission and encouragement, I will be living here with Charlie for a while," I said. "It just happened yesterday."

"Oh! That sounds fun. Anyway, the reason I'm here is that Patricia and I decided to host a gathering tonight," she said. "The main reason is that last night at Artie's, no one had the chance to speak to Patricia or to you, Rob. Both of you have been away, so we all want to catch up. And, Rob, you are invited for dinner. It's cook's night off, so we will eat early. Come at six. Diana, you and Charlie should come at eight."

"Thank you, Joanna," I said. "Is there anything I can bring to help?"

"We have it well in hand, Rob, but it's nice of you to offer. See you at six?"

"Of course," I said.

"And you and Charlie at eight?" she asked Diana.

"We'll be there."

"Terrific. Ta!"

"Well, well, well," Diana teased after she shut the door. "Invited for dinner! You should start praying now that your father's errand doesn't require us to leave right away. I wonder if you'll be invited to spend the night."

"Diana!"

"You wouldn't know what to do anyway," she joked.

"Diana!"

She laughed at me and headed for the stairs. As she was departing, with a sinking heart, I knew her comment was all too accurate. I decided to take a chance.

"Um, Diana?" I called up.

"Yes?"

"Can we talk?" I said as I started to follow her up the steps.

"About?"

"About what you just said," I said quietly as I reached her. "You're right. I wouldn't know what to do."

"What do you mean?"

"I've never been with a woman," I whispered desperately, hoping Charlie didn't suddenly appear. "Other than vulgar conversations I overheard while I was at school or in the Rangers, most of which I think I can safely ignore, and the kissing we did so long ago, I don't know a damned thing about how to please a woman."

"You're not joking, are you?"

I shook my head solemnly. Diana frowned in thought. Suddenly, she brightened and smiled.

"What?" I asked.

"I just realized that Patricia doesn't know a damned thing either," Diana said with a broad grin. "She might not even know how to kiss properly, so you would be ahead of her there. Her lack of experience is a blessing, otherwise I would need to try to explain things to you that I would greatly prefer never to discuss—especially with you. Let me just give you this advice—if your relationship progresses on the physical plane, let her set the pace at first. Be patient. Be gentle. Enjoy each step along the way. Don't be in a hurry to move on to whatever is next. Pay close attention to her. She, or her body, will let you know what she likes, so do that until she indicates it's time to move on. Keep things slow and easy. Later on, she may not want that, but that will be later on. Above all, communicate—don't assume. You're a good man, Robert FitzDuncan Barry Austermain Gau. You'll do fine."

As I thought about what Diana said, I gained confidence. If Patricia was just as innocent as I was… Then I remembered how she enflamed me the night before. I dashed to Diana's door and knocked vigorously.

"What?"

"Diana, I have another question."

"Fine," she replied with a sigh so filled with exasperation I could hear it through the door.

"What, Robby?"

"Diana, remember I told you about that thing Patsy did to me last night?"

"I remember you mentioning it, but I didn't see it."

"She leaned up against me and whispered in my ear," I said. "When she did that, I was, uh, I became, uh—"

"As randy as Lord Arbuthnot?" Diana said, imitating Artie's Lord Arbuthnot voice.

"Yes, exactly," I replied, slightly flustered. "Maybe even more so. And I just wondered … if she knows how to do that…?"

"Knowing how to do it and actually using it are two different things, Rob," Diana said. "I'll bet you a florin that you are the first person she has ever tried that with."

"A whole florin?" I joked, suddenly relieved. "How about a demiflorin? I don't think I can afford to lose a whole florin at once."

"Fine. A demiflorin. Now get out of here. Go annoy some random people in the street. I'll see you at the castle at noon."

I went to my room and dressed, then decided to do as Diana suggested. This was a new experience for me. Everywhere I went, I was usually accompanied by at least a dozen of the Castle Shield. I remembered what my father wrote about Prince Albert and how he never was able to experience things my father took for granted, like buying food from a street vendor with a cart. Though I had done that, I reckoned it's a different experience if you're not surrounded by soldiers whose presence advertises the fact that you're the crown prince.

For the next couple of hours, I just wandered through the streets. Though I was dressed well, no one recognized me. I felt a sense of freedom, and I had an inkling that this was one of the reasons my parents wanted me to live at Uncle Fenwick's.

Just after half past eleven, I reached the Foaming Boar. Tommy and I saddled Casey, and I flipped the boy a florin when we were finished. He tried to protest that it was not necessary, but I just winked and smiled, then turned Casey around.

I encountered Diana when we were a block short of the guardhouse at the bridge to the castle. We rode up together and handed our horses to two of the soldiers. After checking at the guard post, we crossed the bridge.

"What do you think it is?" I asked.

"Well, going to visit the nomads is probably out," Diana joked. "He's going to send us to the southern continent."

"Nah," I said with a frown. "It's something in Aquileia."

The seneschal saw us approaching and met us when we reached the far side of the bridge. He took us inside to one of the small dining rooms. We were slightly surprised to see Uncle Fenwick, my mother, Queen Lily, and Aunt Amanda all there, in addition to my father.

"This is serious," I whispered to Diana. "Have you done something wrong?"

"This is serious, Rob," Queen Lily said, "and neither of you has misbehaved that we know of."

We exchanged greetings and sat down at the table. Servers came and brought a first course of cold soup. That wasn't my favorite, but I forced myself to eat enough of it so as not to appear finicky and rude.

"I'm surprised to see you, father," Diana commented. "When did you arrive?"

"Last night, on the tide," he said. "I sailed from Port Charles to save a day of travel and stayed here."

He offered nothing more, but it was unusual for him to sail from Port Charles. From Easton, it would be no quicker than riding overland. That meant Uncle Fenwick had been in Port Charles for some reason. It was not until the second course was laid before us and the servers disappeared that we learned more.

"One of my agents just returned from Rhetia," Uncle Fenwick explained. "He brought disturbing news."

"For many years, Fenwick and I have held the suspicion that the origin of the Rhetian's strange religion was actually the doing of the Dark Lord," my father said. "What this agent told us indicates that we might be correct. As you know, we insisted on theological exchanges in the treaty we signed with the Rhetians. We hoped they would lead to some sort of common understanding. Unfortunately, whenever we feel we are beginning to make progress, the head of the Rhetian church, the patriarch, summons his people for a meeting. When they return, they are no longer willing to discuss anything. This has happened several times."

"In the most recent exchange," Fenwick said, "I included one of my agents. He posed as a servant to one of our priests. It took some time, but he managed to slip away and gain access to the patriarch's residence."

"From the agent's written description," Queen Lily said, "we believe there is a grimoire."

"If that's true, it validates your theory completely," I said to my father.

"It does," he said. "But it creates a new set of problems. If it is a grimoire, we must destroy it. Fenwick, Queen Lily, and your mother and I are burning to go to Rhetia for this purpose, but we cannot. We must allow you, Diana, and Amanda to go in our place."

"There will be another member of your party," my mother added. "You will learn about her later. Nine priests of the Three Major Gods will also accompany you."

"This will be a state visit of sorts," my father said. "The Rhetians know Fenwick and me because we negotiated the treaty with them. We would have no freedom of action. You will go in our place as our official representatives."

"Will they know we are coming?" Diana asked.

"Only a few days before," Fenwick replied. "Though this will be a state visit, it will not be one of the boring, pleasant ones where nothing important happens. You are traveling there to complain that they have not attended to the theological exchanges in good faith and to demand that they change their ways, upon threat of resuming conflict."

"Uncle Fenwick, having just returned from the western border, I can tell you that there has never been a cessation of hostilities," I said.

"We're all aware, Rob," he said. "We're speaking of a resumption of the naval blockade."

"So, by the nature of our complaint," Diana said, "that should bring us close to the patriarch. Is that the plan?"

"Yes," my father said. "We have a map of his residence and where we think the grimoire is located within it. Diana, Amanda, and you will gain possession of it by whatever means necessary. Amanda, with the help of the priests, will destroy it."

"Sounds simple," Diana said with a mischievous tone. "Should be easy as pie."

"It's my job to make the sarcastic remarks, young lady," Fenwick chided her with mock sternness, wagging his finger. "I'm not dead yet. You'll need to wait before you inherit the privilege."

'Yes, father," Diana said glumly, pretending to be chastised.

That exchange lightened the mood at the table as we all laughed. It also ended the discussion for a time, and we began to eat. We did not return to the subject until the servers removed our plates.

"When do we leave?" I asked.

"Maniday," my mother said. "Amanda, the queen, and I need to prepare a few things for you to take with you."

That is one of the quirks of the castle. When anyone refers to "the" queen, they mean my grandmother Lily. They call my mother, Queen Lucy. When I was very young, I asked her about it once, wondering if she felt it was disrespectful.

"No!" she said with a bright laugh. "Those are my orders!"

"Rob, Diana, please come to my office," my father requested after my mother spoke.

We followed him. Uncle Fenwick joined us and shut the door behind us. My father gestured for us to sit.

"You'll take the lance and the sword, of course," he said. "If you are unable to bring the grimoire to Amanda and the priests, or if what they do is ineffective, we believe there is a good chance you could destroy it with either weapon—though the sword would probably be easier."

"Diana, on this journey, we think it will be to your benefit to pretend to be a noblewoman who is, quite frankly, a domineering biddy," Uncle Fenwick said.

I groaned out loud upon hearing this. Diana stuck her tongue out at me. Uncle Fenwick and my father both grinned.

"Women have little to no independence in the Rhetian culture," my father said. "They expect women to be subservient. If you appear to be in charge of this undertaking, it will make the Rhetians uncomfortable. We suspect it will not be difficult for you to play this part,"

"What part?" I cracked. "Diana is the youngest old biddy I know,"

"That's enough, Rob," my father said, though he was smiling in agreement. "Your personality might make it more difficult for you to get close enough to the grimoire, but it might make it easier for Rob."

"One of the reasons you are not departing immediately is that new clothes are being made for you right now," Uncle Fenwick explained. "It's safe to say they are unlike anything you currently wear."

"As for you, Rob," my father said, "you need to be as much like Lord Compote as possible—or, if you prefer, Lord Arbuthnot. The more dimwitted, lewd, and inappropriate you act, the more you play into Rhetian conceptions that Aquileians are decadent and stupid. This may allow you to get closer to the grimoire because they will not see you as a threat."

"I have a question," Diana said. "If I am to be a fussbudget noblewoman, how do I bring the lance?"

"We think we have the answer, but you need to confirm it," Uncle Fenwick said.

"We are fairly sure the two of you have been chosen by Bellona to wield her weapons," my father explained. "If you are chosen, you can ask the Goddess to alter the lance to your own use."

"Or purpose," Uncle Fenwick said.

"How?"

"Open your link to the Goddess, grasp the lance, and pray to her, asking for the lance to be whatever you need it to be. It's that simple. I would suggest you try to change it to a parasol. That would allow you to carry it with you everywhere."

Uncle Fenwick handed Diana the lance. She grasped it with her hand. When she blinked, I knew she connected with Bellona. As we watched, the weapon changed shape.

"Majors and Minors!" Diana gasped as she dropped it in surprise since the lance of Bellona was now a dainty beige parasol.

"Pick it up and change it again, asking the Goddess to make it the ideal size and weight for you," Uncle Fenwick asked.

When Diana did so, the lance returned to nearly the same state as before. It was difficult to tell, but I thought it was a smidgeon thinner. Diana's eyes were as big as saucers as it transformed again.

"Did you ever do anything like this?" I asked.

"I did," Uncle Fenwick said. "One time I changed the sword into a knife so I could conceal it in my boot. That was the only instance after your father and I altered them to suit us in Nagah."

"I never needed to," my father said.

27

"Before we let you go, we have one word of caution," my father said. "Use the sword or the lance to destroy the grimoire only as a last resort."

"Why?" Diana and I asked, almost in unison.

"We don't know for sure, but there is a possibility that it might result in a kind of cataclysmic event," Uncle Fenwick said. "One that would almost certainly be fatal. Our only source for this information was a conversation we had years ago with the head priestess of the Temple of Bellona in Nagah."

"Uh, that's good to know," Diana said.

"Diana, you need to go see your Aunt Lucy before you leave," my father said. "You can go, Rob."

"Don't you even think about teasing me!" Diana hissed after the door shut behind us.

"Fine, fine," I said, holding my hands up defensively. "I happen to like women who are strong and independent, in case you didn't know. That said, I can't promise the occasional snarky comment won't escape my lips. I will try to keep it to a minimum."

"I suppose that's an honest answer," she said. "At least I don't have to be Lord Arbuthnot."

"I might need to hit myself in the head with a hammer a few times to make me stupid enough," I agreed.

We reached an intersection in the corridor. Diana went to find my mother. I headed outside. As I was walking from the Foaming Boar after dropping Casey off with Tommy, I heard the clock chime three.

I decided I would prepare a bath, wanting to be as clean as possible for dinner with Joanna and Patsy. After finding the huge pot we used to heat the water for this purpose, I stoked the fire in the stove. Then I began hauling buckets of water from the well. Four went into the pot to warm up. The last two I put on the hoist, then went to the second floor and pulled them up and dumped them in the tub. Diana returned while I was waiting for the water to heat.

"Thanks for pulling a bath for me, Robby," she said.

"It isn't for you," I said.

"Please?" she whined coquettishly, fluttering her eyebrows.

"Sure," I replied graciously.

Then the thought hit me that I agreed even though I did not want to do it. Yes, Diana was a woman, and it is always polite to defer, blah, blah, blah, but that was not the kind of relationship Diana and I had. I started to tell her to fend for herself, but I couldn't. The words would not form on my tongue. She'd done something to me. I didn't know whether she accessed her link with Mielvanir or Freyja, but she manipulated me with her ability.

"Why did you do that?" I hollered up the stairs at her.

"Do what?" she answered innocently.

"What are you doing in my room? I demanded.

"Laying out the clothes that your mother wants you to wear tonight," she said.

"What? Never mind. Why did you just trick me into agreeing to let you have this bath?"

"Because I could," she stated. "Your mother told me to begin using my womanly wiles. I want a bath, so it seemed like a good place to start."

I tested the temperature of the water on the stove. It was warm enough to begin. After all, it was a fairly warm summer day, so a tepid bath would be more refreshing than a hot one. I pulled two buckets of water from the large vessel on the stove and loaded them onto the hoist.

As I trudged up the stairs to haul them up, I wanted to be cranky about it, but it was as though the emotion was blocked. Pulling the buckets up to the second floor made me feel almost happy. I knew Diana worked something on me.

"It was Freyja, wasn't it?" I asked looking in the door of my room to see what she was doing.

"What was Freyja?" she responded innocently.

"Seven Hells, Diana!" I shouted. "Cut it out! You just did it again?"

"Did what?" she said as she strutted past me.

"Diana, stop it this instant!" I demanded. "Or by all the heavenly beings, I swear Lord Arbuthnot will subject you to every possible humiliation I can think of."

"Fine," she sighed. "Get the last two buckets and I'll quit. And, no, not Freyja. Mielvanir. Freyja would have had a different effect that I would have found undesirable."

"What do you mean?"

"You would have wanted to share the bath with me. Ew!"

After I brought the last two buckets of warm water up, I went to see what clothes Diana laid out for me. This was a tan ensemble with a purple-ish trim. Looking at it, I realized the hue of the trim was similar to the color of Patsy's hair in the late afternoon sunlight.

That made me stop and think. *My mother is the one who chose the fabrics with the tailor after Diana and I left to help the nomads.* That notion pushed over the first tile in the row arranged in my mind. They quickly began to topple and click into one another in my mind. *Mother is clairvoyant. She knew I would encounter Patsy. Mother chose the clothes I wore to Artie's, and again tonight. She was arranging things to agree with what she has seen. Whatever this is, she wants to encourage it.*

Then I started thinking about the conversations I had with my mother and then with Charlie and Diana. Both Charlie and Diana stressed that Patsy did not engage in any romantic relationships even though she had eager suitors. *Just like my mother before she met my father!* I suddenly remembered.

"Oh, Dinah!" I called out, using the childhood nickname she despised.

"Yes, Robby, you pest?" she responded.

"Patsy is clairvoyant, isn't she?"

"Yay!" she shouted. "You just won me a florin!"

"What?"

"I bet Charlie that you would figure it out before the end of today. He thought you weren't smart enough to solve it so soon. I win."

"So, she is?"

"Yes, sir! Now clear out. Go draw the water for your bath."

"Sure," I said.

Halfway down the stairs, I shouted, "Damnit, Dinah! Quit that!"

I heard her laughing as she ran to her room while I went to draw more water. While I was pulling buckets from the well, I thought about Patsy, and what her clairvoyant ability meant against what happened at Artie's. I also measured it against what I knew of my mother and father's courtship period.

While I worked, I tried to remember what my father wrote about it. I was pretty sure that my mother admitted she was clairvoyant not long after they began seeing one another. From what I recalled, she told him directly and early on in their courtship that she had avoided other relationships because she knew they wouldn't lead to anything. My father had little knowledge of the supernatural when they met. After all, it was spending time with my mother that woke his affinities. It did not take him long to realize that his union with my mother was inevitable. He certainly never resisted. Of course, by that time, he was hopelessly in love with her. He was besotted from the moment he met her.

Was I besotted with Patsy? Considering that every moment my mind wasn't occupied, it turned toward thoughts of her, I'd say I was pretty well smitten. My only hesitancy was that I barely knew her. On the other hand, those who did thought highly of her. Charlie said she was as pretty on the inside as on the outside. Miriam probably knew what was happening and seemed happy about it. And my mother…

I realized the water on the stove would get too hot if I dawdled much longer. After dampening the fire, I finished preparing my bath. As I was pouring the last bucket of almost hot water into the tub, Diana appeared.

"Use this," she said, handing me a cake of soap.

"Why?

"Because it has a nice smell—not overpowering, but pleasant."

"Are you being nice to me again?" I asked.

"When have I ever not been nice to you?"

"Just now, when you stole my bath."

"I was just helping you out, Robby," she said innocently. "If I let you have it, you would have had too much time to mope around. Instead, you've been busy. Much healthier for your poor, addled brain. Plus, you helped me out, which I know makes you happy."

"Grrrr," I snarled.

Diana skipped away. I thought about slamming the door but merely shut it firmly. Sniffing the soap, I had to agree it had a pleasant scent. I stripped quickly and slid into the water.

If my relationship with Patsy is inevitable, why fight it? I thought. *What was it Diana said? Something like enjoying it as it unfolded and not to be in a hurry. Oh, and pay attention to her. I can certainly do that—Patsy is fascinating.*

By the time I finished washing and then getting dressed, it was time to leave. Perhaps Diana did do me a favor. As I was leaving, Charlie was returning from the office of Traval & Company.

"You owe your sister a florin," I said as we passed one another.

"Figured it out, did you? Good for you."

It did not take me long to walk to the Ellsworth's city residence. I was pleased I still remembered how to get there. After all, it had been more than seven years since my last visit.

Before I had the chance to knock, the door opened. Patsy was standing there. She leaned forward and touched her lips to mine. As my body was still registering the thrill that produced within me, she took my hand and pulled me inside.

"Come in, come in," she said happily. "Thank you for your lovely note. I was so happy to receive it."

She pulled me into the nearest sitting room. I was barely able to take my sword belt off and hang it up on the way. There were already two glasses of white wine sitting on a low table in front of a sofa. She flounced over and planted herself, then patted the cushion next to her.

"Patsy, you seem almost giddy," I remarked. "Is everything alright?"

"I'm sorry, Rob. Yes. Everything is fine. Better than fine. Things are *wonderful.* Oh, Seven Hells! I'm babbling, aren't I?"

I took her hand in mine, and patted it gently with the other. Her face was flushed with embarrassment. I tried to convey calm reassurance with my expression.

While trying to calm Patsy down, I took the opportunity to open my connection with Freyja and observe her aura. Up to this point, of the auras I perceived, my mother's had the most vibrant hues. The colors of Patsy's were not only vibrant, they had a deep richness to them. Diana had said Patsy was 'crazy powerful.' I now saw for myself what she meant.

"My father wrote about times my mother behaved somewhat like this," I said. "It occurred when something my mother called a 'hinge point' passed. Do you know what my mother meant by a hinge point, and did we just pass one?"

"Oh! Thank all the heavenly beings!" she breathed, then reached up, pulled my head to hers, and kissed me firmly on the lips.

"I take it that means yes," I said. "Now, I just figured you that you are clairvoyant an hour or so ago. From that, I know better than to ask you about what you saw. Clearly, it's something good—certainly for you, probably for both of us. Did the hinge point have something to do with what I am wearing?"

"It did! How did you know?"

"I didn't know," I admitted. "I guessed. My mother gave Diana specific instructions on what clothes to lay out for me tonight. Mother also chose the outfit I wore to Artie's. Her visions and yours are probably in agreement."

"They always are," Patsy said. "Oops! I didn't just say that!"

"It doesn't trouble me at all, Patsy," I said.

"I've always watched my tongue about such things," she explained. "At least, once I figured out what I was perceiving, I stopped talking about them. Except with your mother and Miriam—I could talk with them."

"I just learned that Miriam is clairvoyant as well," I said. "I guess it blossomed after I joined the Rangers."

"Actually, it was during your last year at school," Patsy said. "It happened to both of us. That's when Miriam brought me to your mother's attention, and she started teaching me."

"I don't remember seeing you at the castle," I said.

"How many times did you encounter your mother with her students?"

"Almost never," I confessed.

"I wasn't a regular fixture until you left for the Rangers," Patsy explained. "Once you were gone, I spent my school breaks mostly in your mother's workshop or study."

"You were much closer to my mother than I ever knew or suspected," I said.

As these words came out, I understood why no one told me. If my mother foresaw a future where Patsy and I ended up together, she would have kept her mouth firmly shut. She would have warned everyone else to stay quiet as well.

"There's probably a reason for that," I said quickly with a smile.

"Probably," she agreed, matching my pleased expression. "Rob, I'm really happy right now, in case you couldn't tell."

"It trickled out a little bit," I teased.

"May I ask you a big favor?"

"If it's in my power to grant it, ask away," I said magnanimously.

"Will you kiss me? Like lovers? Long and slow and sweet?"

"Your wish is my command," I said.

Trite and hackneyed, I know, but it seemed to please her. I leaned toward her, and she tilted her head up to meet mine. Our lips touched gently, and after some time, our mouths opened. We both squirmed around until we found the most comfortable posture, with our arms wrapped around one another and Patsy lying back on the sofa. I was just thinking of sending my tongue on an exploratory mission when—

"Ahem," came Joanna's voice.

"Oh, my!" Patsy squeaked from underneath me.

We quickly sat up, both red in the face. Joanna's look was one of great amusement. Patsy and I realized at nearly the same time that our clothing was in slight disarray.

"Dinner is ready," Joanna said.

I stood and helped Patsy up. She strode quickly to her sister. I picked up our two wine glasses, which we never touched.

"How long were you watching us?" Patsy hissed.

"Long enough," Joanna teased. "Don't worry about it. You two make an attractive couple."

As we entered the dining room, I heard a clock far away chime the half-hour. Patsy pointed me to a seat. As I moved to take my place behind it. Artie strolled into the room.

"Oh, good! I'm not late," he said, giving Joanna a kiss on the cheek.

Artie looked around and realized that, while Patsy and I had glasses of wine, there weren't any poured for Joanna or him. He took care of that, then claimed the seat at the head of the table. Joanna and Patsy disappeared through a rear door and reemerged a moment later with shallow bowls of cut fruit. After they placed them at each setting, Artie and I assisted the women with their chairs.

"It's a cold dinner tonight, I'm afraid," Joanna said. "As I said, it's cook's night off."

"Fresh fruit on a warm summer night is a great way to start," I said.

"Oh, peaches!" Artie exclaimed in his Lord Arbuthnot voice. "You know how we love peaches, poppet!"

Artie stabbed a slice of peach with his fork. He then proceeded to lick it in a licentious way. Adding to the scene, he was making guttural groans of pleasure as he did so.

"Lord Arbuthnot!" I said cheerily. "I'm very happy you are here tonight. You see, my father gave me an assignment today. He suggested that, while on this errand, I should endeavor to act as much like Lord Arbuthnot as possible."

"Well, damme, I'm flattered the king thinks so highly of me, what?"

"Actually, his first suggestion was to model myself on Lord Compote," I teased.

"Compote? Compote? The man's an idiot; trust me on that, Rob, my boy. No, no—stick with the one you know and love best—me. Who is joining you on this errand?"

"Diana and Aunt Amanda," I said. "And someone else, but they didn't say who it was."

"Is Diana going to play the part of your saucy maid?" Artie asked in his normal voice.

"I think she would be furious if they expected her to do that," I said.

"No," Patsy said quietly. "Diana is to play the part of Lady Frothingham. I will be the saucy maid."

28

"What? No!" I exclaimed.

"It's your mother's idea," Patsy said.

"She's lost her mind, then," I said.

"Rob, according to your mother, I am at least as well-prepared to handle this as she was when she and your father went to Eatonford with the queen," Patsy said firmly. "She would not have suggested it if she felt it was beyond my ability or if she believed I would be anything less than an asset."

"Or she's lost her mind," I said. "Patsy, can we please talk about this separately?"

"What do you have to say that you wouldn't want my sister or Artie to hear?' she demanded.

"Nothing," I admitted after I considered her question. "It's just … I need a minute to think. Please excuse me. I'll be back in a few minutes."

I stood hastily and bolted from the dining room. There was a chair in the hall outside. I plunked myself down and tried to clear my mind the way my mother and father taught me long ago.

"Don't, Patricia!" I heard Artie say. "He's feeling overwhelmed. That was quite a surprise that you just dropped in his lap. Our Rob is as steady as they come. He'll sort it out."

I appreciated Artie's comment and then tried to relax and think. Part of the problem was that so much had happened in the last couple of days. I seemed to be the last to know everything. I felt like I was riding a wagon going downhill, and I couldn't find the brake lever. Going to Rhetia—to the very heart of a hostile country—in search of a grimoire seemed to be the most dangerous task my father could have given me. It was inconceivable to me that my mother would send Patsy along, especially since it seemed as though Patsy was meant to be my life partner.

Wait! What? My mind juddered to a stop. *If Patsy is meant to be my life partner, and my mother and Patsy both believe that, then they both must have seen that we would emerge safely on the other side. Yes, it will be dangerous, and yes, I will need—both of us will need—to be careful, clever, and alert. Yet, the fact that I am figuring this out could alter the future they foresaw. Argh! My only choice was to act as though I did not know—except for right now. I need to go reassure Patsy.*

But what about Patsy as a life partner? I thought. *Majors and Minors! You hardly know her—at least not as the woman she has become. But—mother and Miriam both seem smug about it. That means they approve. Otherwise, they wouldn't tease me in this subtle way. Mother knew before she met father that he was the one. Argh! Too much! Too much! One thing at a time. Go reassure Patsy that you welcome her coming on this assignment.*

I stood and took a deep breath. When I felt composed, I opened the door. They were waiting silently. I noticed the fruit plates were cleared from the table.

"Relax, everyone," I said. "Patsy, I will be happy to have you join us. I have no doubts at all about your ability or your courage. Please accept my apology for my negative reaction to your announcement. Though we have only recently begun to renew and deepen our acquaintance, I find that I care deeply about your safety."

"There is nothing to apologize for," Patsy said, "but if you want to atone, you can help me serve the next course."

I helped her with her chair and followed her to the door, opening it for her. After we stepped through, I closed it. When I turned around, Patsy was right there. She threw her arms around my neck and kissed me as passionately as when Joanna interrupted us on the sofa.

"Thank you," she breathed when we broke apart for air.

"For what?"

"For understanding," she said. "I know you must feel as though you are caught in a whirlwind lately, and I'm not making things any easier. Going to Rhetia will be dangerous. Destroying the grimoire will be dangerous. I know that just because I have seen things, it doesn't guarantee they will happen. We might stray from that path. Other hinge points could occur. But your mother has confidence in me. I have confidence in you, and in Diana and Amanda. And I'm really looking forward to being your saucy maid!"

With that, she turned away and almost pranced to where a platter was. She picked up four plates and left the platter for me. It was covered with cold fried chicken, with green beans to one side. I followed her back into the dining room.

"Your Grace," I said as I placed the platter in front of Artie, then backed away like a well-trained servant.

When Patsy finished distributing the plates, I helped her with her chair again. After I sat down, we passed our plates to Artie, who served us. I liked cold fried chicken. As a meal for cook's night off, I thought it was a great idea—especially since the cook did all the work the day before. Plus, I liked fried chicken, hot or cold.

"Now, Rob, what would Lord Arbuthnot say in this situation?" Artie asked.

"Oh, we love fried chicken, don't we, muffin? Gets our fingers all greasy and slick, eh?" I said to Patsy with a leer, after I thought of the most obscene thing I could.

Patsy gasped and blushed deeply. Joanna looked shocked. Artie leaned back and laughed.

"Marvelous!" he exclaimed. "I could hardly have done better myself. Just remember, though, you can almost always make it worse."

With that, Artie took Joanna's hand. He removed the piece of chicken she held and then proceeded to lick her fingers sloppily. She batted him in the face with her napkin as she yanked her hand back.

"Artie!" she exclaimed as she vigorously wiped her fingers.

Patsy and I couldn't help but laugh. After a moment, Joanna joined in, shaking her head. Artie merely looked smug.

"Jealous, muffin?" I asked Patsy. "I can do that for you if you'd like."

I reached for her hand. She quickly withdrew it. Picking up her fork with her free hand, she threatened to stab me if my hand came any closer.

"Oh, muffin," I said sadly. "That's not very nice. I shall need to punish you later, hmm? A bit of a spanking from Lord Arbuthnot? Except you'll enjoy it all too much. Won't be much of a punishment, will it, muffin?"

Joanna couldn't suppress her snicker. Patsy's face turned bright red, but then she started to laugh. Artie looked pleased.

"It's so gratifying that you paid attention," he said, pretending to wipe a tear from his eye. "Some of us suffer for our art. To see someone inspired by our example…"

"I think we've seen enough of Lord Arbuthnot tonight," Joanna said. "You've proved you can do it, Rob. No need to practice more."

"What sort of person is Lady Frothingham? Artie asked. "A female Arbuthnot?"

"Not at all," Patsy replied. "Lady Frothingham is a cantankerous cow—a nasty old woman trapped in a young body. She is furious about needing to be in Rhetia to translate for Lord Arbuthnot because she knows he is a complete moron. Unfortunately, she's his sister, and the king demands that she must go to assist with the mission."

"That reminds me, Rob," Artie said. "If you don't have Diana to translate, Lord Arbuthnot would try to make himself understood by speaking loudly in Aquileian, enunciating clearly, and saying one word at a time. Do. You. Under. Stand?"

"Oh! Treat them like idiots since they don't speak our language?" I asked.

"Exactly," Artie confirmed.

"Are you sure you want to go?" Joanna asked Patsy. "It sounds more horrendous the more we learn."

"I want to go," Patsy said quietly but firmly. "I think it will be both fun and terrifying. Queen Lucy wants to go, but she cannot. I am going in her place. It's a way of repaying her for everything she has done for me."

"I'm going to pray for you every day," Joanna said.

"I would appreciate it if you would pray for all of us," I said. "This is no trip to the market."

The rest of dinner was filled with idle chat. I observed how Patsy interacted with Artie and her sister. What were my impressions? She was sweet, intelligent, and able to hold her own in the crackling banter that Artie initiated.

I learned that I could not look into her eyes for more than a moment, or I would become absolutely lost. They were a shade darker than mine and my mother's and seemed to have a tinge of violet to them. Was I falling in love? I had no idea and no basis for comparison. Whatever it was, it felt good—pleasant, not frantic.

I remembered some of my schoolmates telling me about their infatuations with different girls back in those days. This did not resemble their descriptions. Yes, the swarm of recent developments in my life made it seem out of control, but Patsy could calm me with a look and a smile.

My father had written about how my mother was able to affect him. I now understood what he was trying to convey. Yes, I might be seated on a wagon rolling downhill at a breakneck pace, but I was beginning to enjoy the thrill and set aside my worries about the lack of control.

The other guests started to arrive not long after we cleared the table. I made sure to spread myself around and catch up with everyone. One of the more interesting conversations I had was with Bruce Hawkins about the complications his relationship with Diana brought about.

He had no qualms about leaving the family business to his younger brother. That did not mean he was abandoning the world of commerce and trade. Instead of representing Hawkins Trading, he planned to put his skills to work for the people of the Eastern March if he and Diana married, as seemed increasingly likely. I decided that he and Diana would be a formidable couple.

Diana teased me that I needed to be on my best behavior, or Lady Frothingham would need to chastise me. Bruce Hawkins overheard and asked what she meant by that. I left while she was explaining.

At one point, I tracked my sister down. She smirked at me when I informed her that I had figured out what she and our mother would not tell me about Patsy. I admitted that I had been feeling a bit overwhelmed by everything.

"I was a bit upset to learn that Patsy was coming on the assignment Father gave us," I said.

"Mother and I knew you would be," Miriam replied. "You seem to have accepted it, though."

"I am choosing to trust that the Gods have a plan," I said. "I do not know what it is, but if I continue to move forward and do my best at every turn, everything will unfold the way it is meant to. It seems to me that this is the way father approached things, and it worked out well for him."

"I believe that you are more of a thinker than father was at the same age," Miriam said. "Just don't think too much, or you'll make yourself crazy."

I found Charlie Fenwick and Scott Hawkins in a genial argument. They grew up together and would soon be fierce rivals in the trading world if they weren't already. We had an interesting discussion about it.

"It's no different from our grandfathers," Scott said. "They beat each other's brains out all week long, then play cards together at the Metropolitan club every Njordday afternoon."

"Are you also friends with William Albrecht?" I asked.

"We're friendly," Charlie said, "but not friends. Will was a couple of years behind us and just started with his father's company."

"You know, Rob, that's a good thought," Scott Hawkins said. "We should reach out to him."

"He's a solid guy," Charlie agreed, "at least as far as we've seen."

It was a pleasure to see Saoirse Cullen for the first time in years. Like Patsy, she was a girl then. Now she was a pretty young woman.

I learned from Martin Cullen that Lord Chafter and Houlsin were due to visit the capital in a week. That was a small disappointment. It meant that I would miss seeing Aunt Katie. I had not seen her in more than a decade. She was part of our household when I was a young boy. Now I was an adult myself, and I wondered what she would think of me.

As the hour approached midnight, the guests started leaving, mostly two-by-two. I was waiting, hoping to spend some private time with Patsy. Yet, when Joanna and Artie said goodnight and left (with Artie giving me a lascivious wink), I was a bit surprised. I was also suddenly apprehensive that the two of us were alone in the house.

"Rob, you look like a poor little bunny rabbit who has suddenly seen a wolf," Patsy said with a laugh. "Don't be afraid. I'll shove you out the door soon enough. Now, come sit."

I joined her on the sofa. She reached over and took my hand. When she did, I felt the sensation of tranquility and assurance flow into me that Patsy's touch gave me at Artie's party and every time we touched afterward. I let out a breath that I didn't know I'd been holding in. Patsy giggled at this.

My fear that the night would progress in further physical exploration was unfounded. Instead, we talked. We talked about everything and nothing.

Patsy told me things I never noticed. She talked about how my mother spotted her aura and helped counsel her parents. Patsy told me how my grandmother guided her development.

"Why the queen and not my mother?" I asked.

"At the time, I thought it was because your mother was busy with you and Miriam, as well as her other students," Patsy said.

"You say, 'at the time.' Do you think differently now?" I asked.

"I wonder if the reason the queen was my first tutor in the supernatural was because they wanted to keep us apart until the time was right," Patsy said. "In the last few months, I've meant to ask your mother and the queen about it, but when I'm with them, the thought disappears. It's only later, after I've left, when I remember and kick myself for not mentioning it."

"Mother is masterful at deflecting," I said.

"It's one of Freyja's gifts," Patsy said.

"How come I was never taught these things?" I complained. "Freyja is one of my lessers. I don't know how to use that connection at all! The only thing they taught me was a load of ethics and morality. Oh, and how to perceive auras."

"There's probably a reason. You should ask your mother," Patsy said.

When I gave her a stern look of reproach, Patsy burst into laughter. Majors and Minors, did that sound make my soul sing! She was laughing so hard she was rocking back and forth.

"Careful, muffin," I said, wagging my finger at her, using my Lord Arbuthnot voice.

Patsy stuck her tongue out at me. I gave her a look of mock disapproval. Then, I reached over and wiggled my fingers along her ribs to see if she was ticklish.

"Stop! Stop!" Patsy shrieked as she convulsed with uncontrollable laughter. "I'll be good. I promise!"

"Give us a kiss, then, muffin," I said, "so we know your promise is true."

"Never, you brute!" she cried.

So, I tickled her some more.

"Please! Mercy! Mercy!" she begged through her laughter.

"Will you be a good girl, muffin?" I asked.

"I don't think you want me to be a good girl, Lord Arbuthnot," she teased once she recovered her breath. "I think you want me to be very, very naughty."

Now, in our playful wrestling, I ended up slightly on top of Patsy. When she said this, she looked directly into my eyes. For a moment, I felt the flare of intense arousal she infused me with at Artie's party. Thank all the heavenly beings, she only let me feel it for a brief instant, or the night would have ended up much differently.

Immediately, I sat bolt upright. I was panting as though I had just run a race, and my cheeks were flaming with embarrassment. Patsy sat up slowly next to me.

"Sorry," she said, patting my hand. "I shouldn't do that. Not yet, anyway."

"I'm not angry, Patsy," I said. "If anything, I'm scared."

"Scared of what?" she asked.

"I'm scared I won't be the man you need me to be," I said quietly.

"Scared that I'll disappoint you. And not just in *that* way—like what you just did. I mean in everything—anything."

"Rob, that you can even think that, let alone say it, shows me that you will try never to disappoint me," Patsy said gently. "And, as far as the trick I just pulled, I know you have no more experience than I do. We will figure it out together, a little bit at a time. Now, I don't want you to leave on such a sour note, so will you kiss me a little more? Just kissing."

We started off gently, as we did earlier, before dinner. Things progressed in much the same way. When I found myself mostly on top of Patsy, and we broke for air, I pushed myself up to a sitting position.

"I think that's enough for tonight," I said in a trembling voice.

"I agree," Patsy answered, the timbre of her speech sounding just as shaky as mine felt.

I stood and helped her up from the sofa. She entwined her fingers with mine as we walked to the door. When we reached it, we exchanged a much more chaste smooch than a few moments before.

After we exchanged goodnights, I walked backward until she shut the door. I turned around and suddenly felt like jumping up and clicking my heels. There was no one around to see me, so I did. I felt *marvelous*!

29

Morning came early, as I ended my night late. As I was undressing after I returned to Uncle Fenwick's, I heard a clock chime three. A knock on my bedroom door woke me.

"Who is it?" I called.

"Fenwick," he said as he entered. "It's nine, and time you were out of bed. Mr. Crenshaw will be here at ten."

"Who is Mr. Crenshaw?" I asked.

"He is an assistant of Mr. Fields," Uncle Fenwick said. "He is coming to help you pack. Come downstairs and eat breakfast, or you will need to fend for yourself."

I groaned but dragged my weary body from bed and dressed quickly. When I reached the dining room, only Uncle Fenwick was there. I smelled qava and saw that he had a mug in front of him.

"Qava?" I asked in a hopeful whine.

"Yes."

"I didn't think there was any in the house," I said.

"You didn't look in the right place. Roberta keeps it in the pantry," he said. "Sit. I'll get you something to eat and a cup of qava. Do you take anything in it?"

"No, sir."

"Good lad," he said. "And I'm not 'sir' to you, Rob, unless you want me to start calling you 'Your Highness' all the time. And if you insist on that when it's just the two of us, I'm not so old that I can't give you a sound thrashing."

"Yes, Uncle Fenwick."

"You can still call me 'Uncle' when we're in private, Rob," he said when he returned and put a plate of eggs and sausage in front of me, and handed me a mug of qava. "When you return from Rhetia, and we're in meetings with others, it will be just 'Fenwick.' Then, I'll have to call you 'Your Highness.' Sound fair?"

"I understand," I said quickly before shoveling some food into my mouth.

"Are you nervous about the errand we've asked you to do?" he inquired.

"Nervous would be an understatement, Uncle Fenwick," I said. "I have so many worries—I don't even know where to start."

"Let's begin with the one that bothers you the most," he said.

"That's easy. Patsy."

"Your mother has complete confidence in her," Uncle Fenwick said.

"I reckon."

"Therefore, your concern is due to your budding romance."

"You know about that?"

"Of course. Your mother and your sister are so relieved that things have finally begun."

"What do you mean?" I asked.

"I'm not privy to all the details," he said, "but from what I've overheard, it seems as though they have known for years that you and Miss Patricia would eventually connect and have needed to keep their mouths shut."

"I would be more upset if I didn't grow up with mother's reticence," I said.

"How does this make you feel?" he asked. "Do you feel trapped at all?"

"Huh!" I grunted. "No. That's an interesting question. I have not felt that a bit. That idea never occurred to me. Yes, things have moved quickly. And although there is a certain sense of inevitability to it, I feel, well, good, I suppose. She's the most beautiful woman I've ever seen, other than my mother and sister—but they're different."

"I would hope so."

I winced at his remark.

"Everyone who knows her says she is just as nice on the inside as she is pretty on the outside," I said. "In the limited time we've shared, that certainly seems to be true. When she touches me, she transmits the same sense of calm and assurance that mother does, but there is a subtle undertone of something that is… I don't know the right word. A sense of deeper connection, perhaps? It's hard to describe. As far as what the future holds, I think my only option is to relax and let it unfold as it will. I can say that I find her fascinating."

"You don't feel overwhelmed? When you're apart from her, do you crave her company?" he asked.

"Crave? That's much too strong a word, Uncle Fenwick," I said. "I look forward to when I will see her next, but it doesn't dominate my every breath. It's hard to explain, Uncle Fenwick. My feelings toward Patsy are very 'comfortable.' I don't know if that's the right word, but it's close. 'Pleasant' is also how I feel when I think about her. It's as though it's an old feeling, even though I know it's not."

"Good. So, your concern about Patricia being with you on this errand is…?"

"I don't want her to be in danger or hurt in any way," I said. "And I don't want Diana or Aunt Amanda to get hurt either."

"Well, you're going to their capital, Tarentia, and will be searching for a grimoire," Uncle Fenwick said. "You'll be surrounded by danger. You're not worried for yourself?"

"I know it will be difficult and dangerous," I said. "After reading my father's account of what happened to you both in Beata, I have a pretty good idea of the challenge that might be waiting for us."

"How did you read that?" Uncle Fenwick asked. "That's never been published."

"I found it in a drawer, along with some other stuff," I said.

"Interesting," he said. "Well, if you've read that, I suppose you're as mentally and emotionally prepared as you can be."

"I'm going to be careful, Uncle Fenwick," I said. "You know I love Diana and Aunt Amanda. I think what I feel for Patsy is love, but it's different from anything I've ever felt before."

"Rob, I just wanted to make sure you are heading into this with your eyes wide open and your head firmly attached to your shoulders," Uncle Fenwick said. "It seems that way."

"Thank you, Uncle Fenwick," I said. "Just talking about it has helped me sort things out a little."

"Do you understand the parts you all need to perform?" he asked.

"Yes. As Lord Arbuthnot, I reinforce the view that the Rhetians have of us—that we're stupid and decadent. Patsy, being my scantily dressed maid, adds to that picture. I assume her appearance will be scandalous?"

"Yes," Uncle Fenwick said with a smile. "I have no doubt she will look just as delectable as your Aunt Julienne, Aunt Greta, or your mother were when they played the part."

"Diana will throw them off because they are not accustomed to strong-minded, capable women. Aunt Amanda is to be Diana's servant?" I asked.

"Yes. It sounds as though you have a good idea of how to play this."

Mr. Crenshaw appeared not long after I finished eating. He arrived with a wagon loaded with two trunks and a valise. Together, we packed the two trunks. He advised me on what to include in the valise, which is what I would use on the journey to Rhetia.

After Mr. Crenshaw left with the two trunks, Charlie reappeared. I reckoned he spent the night with Saoirse. It seemed rude to ask, so I didn't.

I did convince him to join me when I became hungry for lunch. We headed out and walked to the market square which was not far away. It was a pleasant Soliday, and there were plenty of people out enjoying it. Best of all, we found a variety of food vendors and wandered from one to another until our hunger was pleasantly sated.

Diana did not reappear until late in the afternoon. She was not in a good mood. I was happy to leave her be, but Charlie wanted to poke the bear.

"Long day, sis?"

"Don't even start with me, pipsqueak," she snapped.

"I thought you would have had a pleasant enough night," he said.

"Oh, that part of it was fine," she admitted. "This afternoon was torture."

"You don't like your new clothes?" I guessed.

"They're hideous," she snarled. "After we leave Rhetia, I will happily burn them."

"What's wrong with them?" I asked.

"They are as plain and dull as an overcast day," Diana said. "I look like an old lady in them."

"Well, Lady Frothingham is supposed to be a biddy, isn't she?" I inquired. "Wearing these dresses will surely bring it out of me."

"What time do we need to leave tomorrow?" I asked.

"A carriage will come for us at nine," Diana said. "The turn of the tide is just before eleven."

The caravel *Griffin* was waiting for us when we arrived at the harbor. *Griffin* was one of the ships that wreaked havoc on the Rhetians and forced them to the negotiating table. After the treaty was signed, the crown maintained twelve of the ships. They scoured the shipping lanes, keeping the seas between Aquileia and the southern continent free from pirates.

Patsy and Aunt Amanda were already aboard, as were the nine priests. The women would be sharing a cabin. I would sleep in a serpentin with the priests and the rest of the crew.

After we stowed our belongings, we headed up to the quarterdeck and stood by the rail as the crew untied *Griffin* from the bollards on the pier. There was just enough of a breeze to push us away. The further into the harbor we went, the stronger the wind—though it was still quite gentle.

Patsy came over to me. She tugged me by my elbow so I faced her. Then she put her hands over my ears for a moment, closing her eyes while she did.

"What was that?" I asked.

"Preventing you from getting seasick," she said.

"I don't get seasick," I said.

"Because every other time you sailed, your mother prevented it from happening, as I just did," she said.

"She did not," I said uncertainly.

Patsy just shook her head at me.

"She did?"

"She called upon Eir," Patsy said. "According to her, you are just as susceptible as your father."

"Oh. Then, thank you."

"You're welcome."

As *Griffin* neared the mouth of the harbor, we could tell when the tide started to pull us out. We picked up speed. When we cleared the headland, the sails filled with a snap. *Griffin* heeled over in the wind, and we started to race along.

It took us only six days to reach Sagun, the nearest Rhetian port. Patsy and I spent a great deal of time with one another. It was on the second day that I realized I felt as comfortable with Patsy as I did with Diana. As I mentioned, I grew up with Diana. But, unlike Diana, I could feel physical yearnings for Patsy. We had no opportunity to explore that aspect of our relationship further while we were aboard but were able to admit to one another that we were both looking forward to it in the future.

Along the way, we passed *Sparrowhawk*, the caravel that delivered the news to the Rhetians of our impending arrival only a couple of days before we would appear. We hove to late the next day. The captain informed us that we would reach Sagun the next day. He did not want to overshoot it in the dark.

We arrived outside of Sagun near midday. Then we needed to wait until the late afternoon to take advantage of the incoming tide. Shortly before we headed in, we changed into the proper clothes to play our parts.

The only change to my attire was that the cravats were lacier than I usually wore. Mr. Crenshaw supplied them. When I saw Diana, I learned why she complained about her clothes.

Her dress was a drab shade of dark greenish brown. It did not flatter her figure. Instead, it made her look dumpy. Aunt Amanda's dress was a dull black.

Patsy was the last to appear. When she did, I lost my ability to breathe or speak. Her dress was black, but of a shiny fabric. The top of it was cut low, and she must have been wearing some sort of undergarment that forced her bosom up into a dramatic décolletage.

I noticed she was wearing two necklaces. One, simple and plain, had a single topaz. I knew that was a ward against the Dark Arts, like the one I was wearing. The other necklace was similar to one my mother wore, and contained a ruby, a sapphire, and an emerald, arranged in a triangle around a central diamond, and set in platinum. The different gems aligned with Freyja, Eir, and Njörun, and the diamond stored numinous energy.

The front of the skirt reached only the middle of her thighs, though the back swept down to behind her knees. On her legs, she wore sheer black stockings, and dainty black shoes adorned with bows on her feet. The final touches were a small, frilly white apron tied around her waist, and an equally frilly cap perched on her head.

"Majors and Minors!" I whispered when I recovered the power of speech.

Patsy approached me with a confident stride—almost a strut. She batted her eyes at me, then dipped down in a curtsy. Her cleavage was on display for the delight of my eyes. She never broke eye contact with me.

"Do you find this pleasing, Your Grace?" she said in a flirtatious tone, then licked her lip with the tip of her tongue.

"You are quite the delectable muffin, aren't you, you naughty girl?" I remarked in my Lord Arbuthnot voice.

"Oh, milord!" she protested coyly as she stood.

Diana and Aunt Amanda laughed at this exchange. I looked around and noticed every sailor had stopped what he was doing and was staring at Patsy goggle-eyed. Fortunately, the captain noticed, too, and hollered at them to get back to work.

When we tied up, I marched down the gangplank, expecting someone else to gather my luggage. There was some local functionary waiting for us with a carriage behind him. I strode over to him with Patsy on my heels.

"HELLO. I. AM. LORD. AR-BUTH-NOT," I announced.

The man did not understand a word I said. He bowed slightly with an awkward look on his face. Diana, her parasol tucked under her arm, brushed past me and spoke to him in Rhetian. Her tone was imperious. He responded, clearly apologizing for something.

"Is the man simpleminded?" I asked Diana, playing my role.

"He doesn't speak Aquileian, you fool," she snapped. "He also has no one to take our luggage."

Diana spun on her heel. She shouldered Patsy out of the way and marched back to the gangway. The disembarking priests quickly got out of her way. I could hear her yelling at the captain to have some of his men bring our things. The priests traveled more lightly and were carrying their own belongings.

This was more playacting. We saw from the ship as we approached that there was only the one person on the pier. The sailors planned to offload our trunks all along. Bearing them on their shoulders, they delivered them to the carriage. They heaved them onto the roof, where the driver arranged them to ride securely.

Diana returned and berated the Rhetian functionary some more. He again replied hesitantly and apologetically. Diana's tone conveyed outrage and disbelief. I heard "Arbuthnot" and "Frothingham" in what she said. When she finished the conversation, she was angry. I hoped she was acting.

"In the carriage," she snapped. "The only preparations the idiot made for our arrival was to have two rooms set aside at an inn."

"How is that a problem, Lady Frothingham?" I inquired innocently. "Muffin will, of course, stay with me."

"I know that, you degenerate," she snarled. "It means I will need to share my room with *her*."

Diana was referring to Aunt Amanda. In real life, she would have no problem sharing a room. As Lady Frothingham, having a servant share your space was unacceptable.

"And they have no rooms for the priests," Diana added. "Nor do they have transportation for them.

"Oh, well, surely they have a stable where the priests—"

"Lord Arbuthnot!" Diana screeched at me. "These are priests of the Three Major Gods! You will sleep in the stable before I ask them to do so!"

Diana explained to the priests that we would send the carriage back for them. We climbed into the cab. I handed all three of the women up before climbing in myself. I raised my eyebrows at Diana, but she shook her head, indicating that we should stay in character.

The next hiccup occurred at the inn. After a lengthy argument, I think Diana managed to secure three more rooms for the priests to share. After that, the Rhetians were very troubled that Patsy would share my room. It was clear to them that we were not married, and they were scandalized. I added fuel to the fire by demanding they prepare a bath for me. It was obvious from Diana's tone that Lady Frothingham did not approve of my behavior but made them fulfill my request.

The innkeeper showed us to our rooms. There was a chair in the room Patsy and I would share. I sat down and gestured for her to sit on my lap. She smirked but came over and sat, draping her arm around my neck in a familiar way. We began kissing lightly. The people who delivered our trunks saw us sitting like that. A few minutes later, a man delivered a metal tub and he saw us as well. The servants bringing the buckets of water looked with wide eyes.

When the tub was filled, Patsy stood up. She walked a few feet away and started to undress. I started to turn around to preserve her modesty but she tsk'd me.

"I want you to see," she said, "just as I will want to see you in a little while. We do not need to be modest. I am taking the first bath, though. You would dirty the water, and I need to shave you. That will leave a mess."

I watched as Patsy disrobed. Clothed, she was beautiful. Naked, she looked like a goddess. She twisted her hair up and secured it with a pin, then stepped into the tub and sat down.

"Scrub my back, Lord Arbuthnot," she teased over her shoulder.

I scurried over and got on my knees next to the tub. Taking the small cloth and cake of soap they delivered, I worked up a bit of lather. Patsy leaned forward slightly, and I began running the soapy cloth over her back gently. Even her back was beautiful. She sighed with pleasure. I was pretty darned happy myself.

"Soon, Rob, we will enjoy one another the way the Gods intended for men and women to take pleasure in each other," she whispered.

"Soon, but not tonight," I whispered back.

"Not tonight," she agreed. "We will take our time. But you will hold me, and I will sleep in your arms for the first time."

30

It took us four days to reach the capital, Tarentia. Fortunately, carriages were obtained for the priests. I learned on the second day that all the priests spoke Rhetian. Then I realized that they would be useless in a theological exchange if they didn't.

Someone must have ridden ahead, and rooms were waiting for us at every inn. That Patsy and I shared a room continued to scandalize them. At every meal, I demonstrated how lewd Lord Arbuthnot was. There were also many opportunities to show his lack of intelligence. Both Patsy and I were enjoying our roles. Diana, however, was not.

Patsy and I continued to sleep together. And though we kissed and slowly began to take advantage of the opportunity to explore each other physically, we were both content to enjoy the journey. She would cuddle up to me and pull my arm around her, and then we would drift off to slumber.

When we arrived in Tarentia, our driver took us to the ruler's residence. It resembled Grandfather Duncan's manse at the jute farmstead. In other words, it was a nice place but not as grand as you would expect for the ruler of the Rhetian Empire.

As we rode into the city, we saw a much more palatial edifice. It sat atop a hill, overlooking everything. Clearly, this was the seat of power. It had to be the residence of the empire's religious leader, the patriarch.

We exchanged formal greetings with the ruler. Diana later tried to explain what his title was. It didn't translate well. In our initial meeting, Lord Arbuthnot made an ass of himself, speaking loudly and slowly in Aquileian to the ruler as though he were stupid.

He invited us to a formal dinner that evening. We went to the inn where they arranged for us to stay. After bathing and changing clothes, we returned to the residence.

Immediately, there were problems. They objected to the priests being included. Diana, as Lady Frothingham, clearly put her foot down. Then, they did not want Patsy and Amanda present at the meal since they were servants. This argument escalated to the point where Lady Frothingham grabbed me by the elbow, and we started for the door. The last squabble was when Lady Frothingham learned that the patriarch would not be attending.

"You ineffectual fool!" Lady Frothingham shouted at the ruler (I am reporting what Diana later told me she said). "Your patriarch is the person we came to see! In the treaty we signed, where we agreed to drop our blockade and stop seizing your ships, the most important provision for King Casimir was the theological exchange. Your patriarch has sabotaged this effort time and time again. King Casimir wants to resume naval operations against you. It is only because Lord Arbuthnot pleaded with him to give Rhetia another chance that we came on this fool's errand. If the patriarch will not be at the dinner, neither will we. We will depart in the morning and return to Aquileia."

"Lord Arbuthnot?" the ruler replied. "You cannot be serious! The man is a blockhead and entirely ruled by his unbridled appetites!"

"You are not wrong," Lady Frothingham said. "Nevertheless, he pleaded with the king and interceded on your behalf. It's becoming quite clear to me that only an imbecile like him would think that the Rhetian Empire would ever abide by our treaty."

"Lord Arbuthnot," she said, "the patriarch will not be present at the dinner. I told him that is unacceptable."

"Quite right, Lady Frothingham," I said pompously. "I don't care who this flunky is. We meet with the patriarch, or return home and allow the king to do as he wishes. It pains me to admit that you were correct, Lady Frothingham. These Rhetians are untrustworthy, and the patriarch the worst serpent of them all. Go on—tell him."

The ruler blanched when Lady Frothingham translated my serpent remark. After that, with Lady Frothingham in the lead, we did march out. We returned to the inn. As we were finishing a rather poor meal, the ruler appeared.

"I have met with the patriarch," he said. "He will meet with you tomorrow morning, but only you, Lady Frothingham, and Lord Arbuthnot. The priests and your servants, especially the harlot, are offensive to the patriarch and may not come."

"I will not leave my little muffin, the very flower of Aquileian femininity, behind," I thundered when Lady Frothingham translated for me. "She would not be safe. These Rhetians, scum that they are, would take her and harm her. Even Lady Frothingham's maid would not be safe. And the priests must be present. They are the entire point of the whole exercise. Lady Frothingham, we depart for Sagun in the morning. The king was right, I am sad to admit. There is no reasoning with these people. They understand only the iron fist and do not deserve the velvet glove."

After Lady Frothingham translated, the ruler's face fell. He left without another word. I was bluffing, of course, and I opened my connection with Njörun, the Goddess of good fortune (one of my lessers), and prayed silently that they would call my bluff. That night, Diana came to my room and chastised me thoroughly.

"Rob," she whispered, "I threw my connection to Mielvanir wide open when I translated what you said to the ruler. Every trick I know, I used to convince him to get us that meeting. If it's not enough, what in the Seven Hells are we going to do?"

"I hope it doesn't come to that," I whispered back. "If it does, we will figure it out. I didn't know what else to do. If we leave Patsy and Amanda behind when we meet with the patriarch, I fear they might use them as hostages. Besides, we need them there."

I did not sleep well, despite Patsy's presence in my arms. In the morning, we delayed a fair amount of time, but eventually needed to begin loading our luggage onto the waiting carriage. There was only a single trunk remaining to be hoisted up when the ruler's carriage came clattering down the street.

"The patriarch will allow the priests and the servants to come to the palace, but they must stay where his people instruct," he said. "They are offensive to the patriarch, and he does not wish to see them. Nor does he wish for them to desecrate any of the holy spaces."

We agreed to these terms. After loading the last trunk, we climbed into the carriages and followed the ruler to the palace. Gray-cloaked priests, their heads covered by hoods, met us in front. It was clear that they were not happy to see our priests. It was even more apparent that Patsy's appearance shocked them. One of the gray-cloaked men approached us. Lady Frothingham, with her ever-present parasol, stepped forward to meet him.

"The priests and the servants may not enter," he said. "They must stay here.

"Our priests will stay," Lady Frothingham told him. "But our servants accompany us."

Diana later told me she used her link with Mielvanir when she said this. I suspected as much when the priest indicated we should follow him without argument. As Lady Frothingham, she instructed our priests to stay where they were.

Our gray-cloaked guide led us through the massive doors facing us. When we passed through them, I nearly gasped out loud. We were in what was clearly a Temple of the Three Major Gods at one time. The design and floorplan were very similar, perhaps even identical, to the largest Temple in Aquileia. What was missing were the statues of the Three Majors. The walls and the altar were marked with the symbols of the Rhetian church. Seeing that made me angry.

We followed our guide through the sanctuary into a corridor. This part of the building was not of the same construction. It was clear we were entering a residence—a magnificent one at that.

"We're getting close," I heard Amanda whisper very softly. "Be prepared."

Putting my hand on the hilt of the Sword of Bellona, I accessed my connection to her and opened it. I restrained it just enough that I would not manifest Bellona with the accompanying illusion of huge size. The others were probably doing something similar.

As we proceeded, even I could sense we were approaching something malevolent. I wondered if the patriarch could sense us. My question was answered a moment later when the cloaked priest suddenly whirled toward Diana with a knife in his hand.

Having the lance in the form of a parasol, she was unarmed. She did the best thing she could and jumped back out of the way. That was all the opening I needed as I unsheathed and, in one continuous motion, severed the priest's head from his shoulders. Patsy and Amanda both flinched, but neither cried out.

"We need to hurry," I said. "More will come."

"The next door," Amanda said.

We strode to it quickly. By the time we reached it, Diana was once again holding the lance and not a parasol. Of course, we could not open the door. I opened my link to Bellona completely. From the corner of my eye, I saw Diana do the same. I could feel the numinous power bubbling in my veins and knew I appeared to be immense in size.

I drove my shoulder against the door. It did not move at all—not even the slightest quiver. I was preparing to do so again, but Diana laid her hand on my arm to stop me. Her eyes were closed. I wondered what she was doing.

"Now!" she said.

I threw myself at the door again and this time it burst open, but not where the latch was. Instead, it flew open on the hinged side. There was an old man standing there, in the same gray cloak as we saw the other Rhetian priests wearing.

The sense of evil in the room was profound. Every step I took toward him was more difficult than the last. My father had written about this feeling. I darted my eyes to my right. Diana was experiencing the same difficulty. It was as though the air was as thick as mud.

Then, I sensed something that I did not expect in this room in these circumstances. I turned to my left from where the feeling was radiating. Patsy was there, equal in immense size to Diana and me.

Praise all the heavenly beings—I never saw anyone so beautiful, and fierce, and passionate. Her hair was flowing back as though she stood in a strong breeze. Though she did not give off light, there was a feeling that she was glowing. I felt as though the Goddess Freyja herself stood by my side. Patsy smiled at me, and my entire being was filled with joyous love—love that came from Patsy, focused on me.

Whatever was impeding me evaporated. I crossed the remaining few steps easily and pierced the dark mage through the heart. The instant I did, a cold shock ran through Bellona's sword and into my arm. I nearly let go of the blade as my hand and arm went numb. A black abyss opened beneath the dead man and began dragging him down.

My numinous strength failed me, even though I still held Bellona's sword. The greater size and strength I possessed when manifesting the Goddess was no more. I felt myself being pulled into the swirling depths. It was as though my body was no longer of corporeal substance. My physical form was dissolving and flowing away into the darkness.

"No!" I heard Patsy shout.

Her tone was an irresistible command. I fell backward, released from the pull of the gaping blackness. When my butt hit the floor, my asomatous energy flowed back into me, though I was not able to manifest Bellona. My right arm was still numb, limp, and unresponsive. The last of the dark mage disappeared into the void, and it closed with a thundercrack.

As I turned to look at Patsy, she returned to normal size. She was looking at me, and I felt the care, concern, and love in her gaze. I struggled to my feet, still trying to make sense of what just happened.

"You saved me," I said wonderingly.

My words sounded strange, as though I was underwater. The closing of the passage to the Seven Hells had deafened me. Patsy smiled at me, then saw my dangling arm. Her eyes opened wide in worry. She reached over and took the sword from my right hand, and put it in my left.

"You mustn't drop it," she said, though I could hardly hear her. "There is still grave danger."

I saw Amanda enter the room. She went immediately to the table behind where the mage had been standing. There was a thick book there, lying open. It had not been visible before the mage disappeared. Amanda quickly shut the thick tome.

"Can you carry it?" she asked me.

"No," I said regretfully. "Something is wrong with my arm. It feels … numb."

"Can you—?" Amanda asked, turning to Patsy.

"I am nearly drained completely," Patsy replied. "It will take an immense amount of energy to restore his arm's strength."

"Right," Amanda said. "Diana, you will need to carry the grimoire to the Temple. It will fight you and grow heavier with every step."

"I'll do my best," Diana said. "I haven't contributed much at all yet."

"You got us in the room," Patsy said.

"Mielvanir did," Diana replied.

"Rob, go summon the priests," Amanda ordered. "Have them come into the Temple and do what they can to remove the desecrations."

"I'm going with him," Patsy said.

I sheathed the sword awkwardly with my left hand, though I rested my hand on it and maintained contact. Then, I tamped down my link with Bellona, keeping it open only a small bit. We left the room and walked quickly back the way we came. At the first corner, we encountered a gray-cloaked priest, seemingly cemented in place. He had been enthralled by the patriarch and was now frozen.

"That's creepy," Patsy commented. "He's enthralled, isn't he?"

"Yes," I said. "We'll need to free them. Majors and Minors! Who knows how many there are in the city? In the country?"

"Rob, we can only do what we can do," Patsy said. "You did not create this evil."

We saw six more thralls before we reached what used to be a Temple. There were more immobile thralls inside, all of them arrested as they were heading in the direction from which we came. Clearly, the patriarch had been summoning reinforcements.

Our nine priests were waiting outside where we left them. We waved at them and beckoned them to come. When they stepped inside, all of them gasped. In other circumstances, I would have found it humorous, but the urgency I felt shoved that aside.

"Amanda asks you to remove as much of the desecration as possible," Patsy said. "She and Lady Oritur are bringing the grimoire."

The priests set about the task with zeal. They began pulling down any of the physical symbols that they could lay hands on. Gathering the wall hangings, they threw them outside. They smashed the wooden and stone emblems. There were still some figures painted on different surfaces, but they could not do anything about those.

After about ten minutes, Diana staggered into the Temple. She was still manifesting Bellona and appeared to be twelve feet tall. From what I saw, she had placed the lance under her dress and along her back so she would retain physical contact with it but have her hands free. She was carrying the grimoire, but even with her enhanced size and strength, she still appeared to be struggling, as though it was incredibly heavy. When she reached the altar, she dropped the grimoire on top of it.

"It's time," Amanda announced to the priests.

The nine priests made a circle around the altar. Amanda began a chant in archaic Aquileian. She recited the chant by herself the first time. On the second rendition, the priests joined in. They clearly had memorized it in preparation for this.

Even though I didn't know exactly what I was saying, I joined in on the fourth time through. I noticed that Patsy and Diana were also reciting.

The chant had an almost hypnotic effect. Our voices rose and fell together, and I felt the rhythm of the chant deep inside myself. All at once, Aunt Amanda manifested Ceridwen Sospita. She appeared to be twice her usual height, and, unlike when Diana or I, or even Patsy, transformed, she seemed to be suffused with a clear, white light. Though the brightness was such that it hurt my eyes, it was such a captivating sight that I could not look away.

Aunt Amanda stretched her hands out over the grimoire. The book floated into the air slowly. Suddenly, she made the warding gesture that every child in Aquileia knows. With a flash like a bolt of lightning, unaccompanied by any sound, the book vanished. A cyclone of wind blew through the Temple. I was forced to crouch down and cover my face with my elbow from the force of it and from the flying remnants of the things the priests smashed. When it stopped, I stood and saw that all the remaining marks of the Rhetian religion had disappeared from the entire space, even those that were painted on different surfaces.

Amanda returned to her usual appearance, slumped with exhaustion. Diana quickly crossed to her and supported her with an arm around her shoulders. Both of them looked exhausted. The priests fell to their knees and began praying.

That seemed like an excellent idea. Kneeling down, I did the same. I thanked the Gods for my many blessings, for the abilities They granted me, for the opportunity to participate in this great deed, and for Patsy, who saved my life. To that, I added my gratitude for my family and friends, and asked for the guidance of the Gods in the future. I finished by asking for their blessings upon Aquileia, and for Rhetia. I finished and was standing up when the first gray-cloaked Rhetian walked in.

He was dazed. From this, I suspected that the destruction of the grimoire freed the thralls. I hoped that was the case.

One of our priests began to speak with the Rhetian. After a few minutes, he disappeared. I learned later that our priest sent him to collect as many of his colleagues as he could.

I turned my attention back to Patsy and crossed the short distance to her. Her smile as she watched me approach filled me with happiness. I gave her a brief kiss.

"Thank you for saving my life," I said. "And thank you for your love."

That was the last thing I remembered until I woke in a bed in a strange place that I did not recognize. An older woman with plump, rosy cheeks was sitting by the side of the bed. She smiled as she saw my eyes open.

"Miss Patricia!" she called excitedly as she rose from her seat and left the room.

31

"Just when you kissed me, you collapsed, Rob," Patsy explained a short time later. "You stopped breathing. It was not until I put your hand on the hilt of the sword that you drew another breath. Thank all the heavenly beings your connection to Bellona was still open. Then I noticed the condition of your right hand. It was like a deep purple bruise—almost black. I tore open your sleeve and the darkness was creeping up your arm.

"I opened my connection with Eir to see if I could heal you, or arrest the spread of the darkness, but I used almost all of my numinous energy to counter the mage when he was holding you back," Patsy said. "And whatever was happening to your arm was like nothing I ever encountered or heard of. That was the arm you used when you killed the mage so I figured the spreading blackness was probably dark magic. I screamed for Amanda and begged her to do something.

"She came over and saw your arm turning black. It was clear from her expression that she didn't know what to do either. We were both scared. Diana came over and then yelled for the priests. She begged, 'Do something, Aunt Amanda!' Amanda asked the priests to begin repeating a chant. She started it, and then the priests took over. It was different from the one they recited earlier. Then, she did something—I didn't know what—and then she collapsed. Whatever she did, it stopped the darkness from spreading further, but your right arm, almost up to your shoulder, was now an ugly deep purple."

I lifted my right arm to look at it. It felt very weak. That weakness corresponded to the general exhaustion I felt, even though I was lying in bed and clearly had been sleeping. Raising my arm was more difficult that I thought it would be. Happily, there was no evidence of any blackness or bruising.

"Yes, it should be fine now, Rob," Patsy said when she saw what I was doing. "But for two weeks, we thought we might need to cut it off in order to save your life."

"I'm glad you didn't," I mumbled. "Thank you."

"Oh, Rob, I've been so scared," Patsy said.

A sob bubbled up from her chest. Tears welled up in her eyes. I wished I could comfort her. All I could do was pat her arm with my left hand.

"All of us were frightened," Patsy continued with a sniff as she regained control of her emotions. "We left the priests behind to help sort things out in Tarentia, and we climbed into the carriage. If your left hand fell off the hilt of the sword, you stopped breathing. Bellona's power was the only thing keeping you alive. We rode like mad men. Diana abused the Rhetians in every town we passed to get fresh horses so we could keep moving. We stopped only to eat and change the teams. *Griffin* was waiting for us in Sagun when we arrived just over two days later.

"We set sail as soon as we could. The journey back to Aquileia was agony. It took almost ten days since the winds were against us. As soon as we tied up, Diana commandeered a Traval wagon. We drove to the castle with you lying in the back and took you to the queen. She examined your arm, then retreated to her study with your mother and Amanda.

"When they emerged the next day, the queen felt she understood what to do. The queen and Amanda determined how far the corruption spread within your body. Although we could not see it, the degradation passed above the shoulder and into your chest. That was the reason your breathing would stop. Together, Amanda and the queen worked to remove the supernatural infection from your chest. The effort exhausted them both so much that they slept around the clock for two days. Your father used his link with Eir to repair any physical damage. Even though Eir is only one of his lessers, with the power of the lance, he was able to accomplish a great deal.

"I know," I said quietly. "He wrote about it."

"No, he didn't," Patsy said. "I grew up reading all his stories."

"Yes, he did. I found one that no one has read," I said tiredly. "It wasn't finished. I was going to complete it."

"When you're feeling better, I want to read it," Patsy said. "Anyway, once Amanda and the queen recovered, they added the queen's students, Byron and Castor, to help them. They kept working to remove the contamination from your arm. It has been a slow process. They were only able to clear a few inches at a time, then needed to take several days to restore their supply of asomatous energy."

"How long?" I asked.

"Tomorrow, it will be six weeks since we destroyed the grimoire."

"Don't joke," I said.

"I'm not," Patsy protested. "You have been unconscious for almost six weeks."

"Why am I so tired?"

"Let's see," Patsy said. "You almost died and were in a sort of near-death state for most of the time. Some sort of dark magic infected your body. You haven't had anything to eat or drink this whole time."

"I'm not complaining," I protested weakly. "Just asking."

Patsy burst into tears. Her upper body was wracked with deep sobs. I patted her with my left hand again, but it didn't seem to help.

"I'm sorry," she said when she recovered control of herself. "Your mother calls it, 'the curse of clairvoyance.' None of what I saw before showed this. And since the episode with the mage, all my visions have been horrible."

"They haven't come true," I said.

"Thank all the heavenly beings," Patsy whispered fervently. "None of them have come to pass. The hinge points did not occur."

"Are there any still—?"

"No," she said. "All praise to the Gods, Major and Minor."

"That's good."

"Oh, Rob," she cried softly.

She laid her head on my chest. I could not determine whether she was laughing or crying. It was probably both.

"Miss Patricia?" I heard from across the room. "I brought the soup you asked for."

"Thank you, Maggie," Patsy said.

Patsy sat up. The plump-cheeked woman who was by my bedside when I woke appeared, holding a tray with short legs underneath. On the tray, I could see a bowl, and I smelled what I thought was chicken soup.

"You'll need to sit up, Yer Highness," the woman said.

I began to try to scooch backward so I could sit and lean back against the headboard. It was much more of a struggle than I anticipated. The two women saw my difficulty, and both tried to help lift me. They did more than I was able to, but I finally ended up in a sitting position.

Maggie put the tray over my lap. The short legs allowed it to rest securely and level on the mattress. I reached for the spoon with my right hand. As I lifted it, I could see it trembling.

"I'd better do that," Patsy said. "You need to eat it, not wear it."

"Where am I?" I asked.

"In our house," Patsy said, "in one of the guest rooms. We moved you here after the queen was confident that your body was free of supernatural taint. I've been sleeping next to you every night, though I'm sure you had no idea."

For the next three days, I ate and slept. They started me with soup and then fruit. On the third day, I demanded something more substantial. They gave me meat—chicken—and I felt more satisfied.

"Today, you get a bath," Patsy announced the following morning. "You'll be getting visitors later."

"I will admit I'm a bit ripe," I said. "Do I need to shave?"

"Desperately," Patsy said. "Your whiskers never stopped growing. You look like a hermit."

By now, I was able to get out of bed—as long as I moved slowly and carefully. When the bath was prepared, Patsy guided me to the lavatory and helped me ease into the water. She then proceeded to strip off her clothes.

"Why are you getting undressed?" I asked. "Not that I mind, muffin," I added, in my Lord Arbuthnot imitation.

"Because I'm going to wash you, then shave you," she said. "I would get my dress soaking wet, so it's easier this way."

I must admit, it was an extremely pleasant half-hour. Patsy scrubbed me gently everywhere and finished by scraping my beard from my face. When she pronounced me suitably clean, she dried me off and helped me dress.

Artie was my first visitor from outside of the house—Joanna did not count since she lived there. He did not stay long. Patsy invited him over for the sole purpose of helping me down the stairs and establishing me in the sitting room.

Shortly after he departed, Uncle Fenwick, Aunt Julienne, and my mother and father arrived. We shared tear-filled embraces. When everyone sat down, Patsy positioned herself on the arm of my chair with her hand on my shoulder.

"We are extremely proud of you, Rob," Uncle Fenwick said.

"I'm sorry it was so dangerous. We did not think it would be," my mother said, glancing at Patsy as she did.

"From what I understand," Aunt Julienne added, "you may have brought about a huge change in our part of the world—one that will benefit thousands and thousands of people."

My father said nothing, even though it seemed to be his turn to speak. I looked at him and raised my eyebrow. He shrugged.

"I don't know what you're all gushing about," he said, though I could see a mischievous glint in his eye. "Did you expect any less of Rob?"

My mother smacked him in the chest with the back of her hand. Fenwick began laughing. Even I started to snicker.

They wanted to hear all about what happened from my viewpoint. Patsy, Diana, and Amanda had related their versions of what took place, but they wanted my impressions. They listened attentively while I told the story.

"Do you understand now why I wanted Patsy to accompany you?" my mother asked. "And, in case you have the absolutely wrong idea, it was not for your titillation."

"Well, the outfits you created for her to wear—"

"We didn't create them," my mother interrupted.

"No. They came from my closet," Aunt Julienne said. "Patricia and I are the same size."

Now, I read the story of Aunt Julienne traveling to Mooresa with Lord Compote and playing the part of his naughty maid. Somehow, I never really imagined her in the sort of risqué costume Patsy wore. I was slightly boggled by the realization. Aunt Julienne laughed at my reaction.

"Mother, Patsy saved us all," I said. "When the mage was preventing Diana and me from reaching him, Patsy dispelled whatever it was he was doing. And I know full well that I would not be here if it were not for her."

When they noticed I was getting tired, they made excuses and departed. I did not feel like climbing the stairs, so Patsy helped me to the sofa. When I stretched out, she tucked herself next to me and drew my arm over her.

As my consciousness faded away, I realized I felt truly and deeply content. Yes, Patsy had the ability to make my heart beat faster—like no one else I ever encountered—but at other times, her presence comforted me and strengthened me on an emotional and, dare I say, spiritual level. *Is this what love is?* I wondered.

Patsy squirmed slightly, and moved a little closer. Without thinking, I tightened my embrace of her just a bit. She gave a happy sigh. The sound touched my heart.

Thinking she was already asleep, I whispered as quietly as I could, "I love you, Patsy."

"Good," she murmured back, surprising me. "I'm glad you finally realize that."

ABOUT THE AUTHOR

John Spearman has been a Fortune 500 sales and marketing executive, a Latin teacher and coach at a prestigious New England boarding school, and is now an author. He lives in coastal Maine with his wife and their dogs. He began writing because his wife challenged him. He was lucky enough to find an audience and has not looked back (except to fix the mistakes he made in the early days!).

This book is the ninth of the FitzDuncan series. Spearman has four other book series, all in the category of military science fiction. The first was the Jonah Halberd series of four books. The Sandy Pike series is set in a different universe from the Halberd books. The next series is of three novels featuring a female hero named Perseverance Andrews which is related to his first four books, the Jonah Halberd series. The Andrews books take place in the same universe as the Halberd series, though over three hundred years earlier.

Spearman's latest series is published by AethonBooks. Set in a new universe, it features a main character named Cliff Rawlins. Mr. Rawlins' story has a rocky beginning.

If you enjoyed reading this book, please consider leaving a positive review on amazon.com or goodreads.com. It will help other readers like you find books they might enjoy. To learn more about the author's different works, please visit www.johnjspearmanauthor.com

www.ingramcontent.com/pod-product-compliance
Lightning Source LLC
Chambersburg PA
CBHW070451300726
48975CB00007B/2119